KERRY BARRETT is the author of many novels, including the *Strictly Come Dancing* themed *A Step in Time,* and *The Girl in the Picture*, about a crime novelist who solves a 160-year-old mystery.

Born in Edinburgh, Kerry moved to London as a child, where she now lives with her husband and two sons. A massive book-worm growing up, she used to save up her pocket money for weeks to buy the latest Sweet Valley High book, then read the whole story on the bus home and have to wait two months for the next one. Eventually she realised it would be easier to write her own stories. . .

Kerry's years as a television journalist, reporting on *EastEnders* and *Corrie*, have inspired her novels where popular culture collides with a historical mystery. But there is no truth in the rumours that she only wrote a novel based on *Strictly Come Dancing* so she would be invited on to *It Takes Two*.

When she's not practising her foxtrot (because you never know. . .), Kerry is watching Netflix, reading Jilly Cooper, and researching her latest historical story.

Also by Kerry Barrett

The Smuggler's Daughter

KERRY BARRETT

ONE PLACE. MANY STORIES

HQ
An imprint of HarperCollins*Publishers* Ltd
1 London Bridge Street
London SE1 9GF

This edition 2021

21 22 LSC 10 9 8 7 6 5 4 3 2 1
First published in Great Britain by
HQ, an imprint of HarperCollins*Publishers* Ltd 2020

ISBN: 9780008430160

Printed and bound in the United States of America
by LSC Communications

I wrote most of this book in lockdown, so it is dedicated to my children's teachers, with massive respect and gratitude.

Chapter 1

Emily

Cornwall, Spring 1799

I put my hands over my ears and pushed my palms hard into my scalp, trying to block out the sound of the argument. I hated shouting at the best of times, but tonight my parents were louder than ever. They were making no attempt to keep it quiet – normally I heard whispered barbs and hissed insults but tonight it was full-blown screaming. From my mother, at least.

'He will starve us out,' she was shouting. 'He's warned us, and I don't doubt he means it. We'll go hungry, Amos.'

'It won't come to that,' my father said. He was a calm man most of the time but his temper had been short lately, and tonight I heard a tremor in his voice that I'd never heard before. 'He'll get bored and go away.'

'He'll only go away when we give him what he wants,' my mother screeched. 'And if we don't give it to him, he'll take it.'

Something smashed and I cowered under the blanket. I didn't understand what they were arguing about. I only knew they'd been fighting like this for days and days. Weeks, even. I didn't know who they were talking about, nor why my mother sounded so frightened. It wasn't like her at all. She was always smiling, my mam. Or at least she had been until recently. Da always said that most of the drinkers at The Ship came to see Mam, serving drinks and keeping the customers happy, not to drink his ale.

'Your father had this inn, Amos Moon, and his father before him,' my mother said, sounding defeated. 'I don't understand why you want to give it away.'

'I don't,' Da said. 'I want it to be a home for you and Emily.'

'Then let him use it.' Mam was hissing now, her voice sounding urgent and high-pitched. 'It's just once. No one will know.'

'It won't be just once,' Da said. 'If we let him in, he'll keep coming. He'll take more and more liberties, and it'll be me who hangs for it.'

I huddled in my bed. What did Da mean? Why would he hang? I wished I could run to him and ask him what was going on. Da was the only person who took time to explain things to me properly. Mam did her best, but she was always busy, laughing and chatting with the drinkers in the bar. It was Da who spared the time to talk. He knew that I didn't always understand the world. That I couldn't always follow a conversation, that I misunderstood some phrases or took things too literally. I sometimes wondered if he felt the same way – not as strongly as me, but enough that he understood the troubles I had – and that was why he preferred to spend time in the cellar, or with his kegs of ale, while Mam dealt with the drinkers and the entertainers.

'It's not right,' Da was saying. 'How can we be a part of that?'

'God's teeth,' my mother shrieked. 'You and your principles, Amos Moon. Those morals of yours will see us starve to death, you'll see.'

'Janey, calm yourself.'

'Calm myself?'

I heard the clink of a bottle as my mother poured herself a drink. She'd never been bothered by the riches on offer at the inn before. Da said she was as full of fun without the grog inside her, as any man who'd taken a drink. But lately, she'd been helping herself more and more. Her face was more frowns than smiles recently, but when she knocked back a measure of rum or brandy, her lips turned upwards again.

Da said something I didn't hear, and Mam roared. 'Get out!' she screamed. 'I'm sick of the sight of you. Get out.'

'This isn't finished,' Da warned.

'Yes it is,' Mam shrieked.

The whole inn shook as Da slammed out into the yard, whistling softly for his dog, Tully, as he went. I scrambled up on to the window seat, peering out into the darkness to see where he was.

Da was sitting on a barrel, Tully by his side and a flickering lantern at his feet. I wanted to go down to him, but I could hear Mam clattering about in the inn, pouring herself more drinks, and I didn't want to see her. Instead, I reached under my bed, and pulled out my sketchbook and my charcoal.

I loved to draw. I'd done it since I was tiny, and Da – and Mam – had supported me. As I got older, and my difficulties had become clearer, Da had encouraged me to draw people's faces. I found sketching their expressions helped me understand their emotions. Copying the tilt of a lip, or the creases around someone's eyes taught me what sadness, happiness, or anger looked like.

Now I watched my father, his brow furrowed. My charcoal rasped across the page as I captured his eyes narrowed in thought, and his tight lips. Determined, I said softly to myself. He looked determined.

A quiet knock at the courtyard gate made me and Da both jump. Who was coming to The Ship at this late hour? Surely everyone in Kirrinporth was in bed?

Da turned his head. He could see who was out there, though I couldn't. He sat on his barrel for a moment, then he stood up and opened the gate, standing aside to let the visitor in.

An older man came through into the courtyard, crouching down and rubbing Tully's ears in greeting.

'Some guard dog you are,' I muttered with fondness.

The man was my father's friend, Petroc, I realised now, recognising his wide shoulders and his love of animals. But whatever was he doing here so late? The inn was long closed and Da was only awake because he and Mam had been arguing.

'Take that mutt and tie it up by the stables.' Another man came into sight below my window. I didn't recognise him. He was tall and his face was hidden by the three-cornered hat he wore. He waited for Petroc to take Tully across the courtyard and out of sight. I narrowed my eyes, peering down into the darkness to see better.

'So, do we have an agreement?' the man said. He took his hat off and rubbed his forehead. He had dark hair with one white streak that seemed to glow in the moonlight and a handsome, though rugged, face. On the same page as my sketch of Da, I began drawing the man's expression. He was smiling, but as I drew, I saw that his eyes were angry. That was something I'd not seen before. 'I'll be very disappointed if we don't,' he added.

'No, we do not have a deal,' said Da. He was whispering but it was so quiet that his voice carried clearly across the cobbled courtyard. 'It's too risky.'

'You never used to be frightened of a bit of risk,' the man said. His voice sounded amused, as though Da had made a joke. But I didn't think he had said anything funny. 'Never used to worry when you were younger.'

'Well we all did stupid things when we were young,' Da said. He turned away from the man and lifted the lantern up so it illuminated the courtyard better.

'Stupid?'

My father sighed. 'This is different. The risks are too great; the benefits are too small.' He looked at the man, his chin lifted slightly. 'Except for the benefits to you.'

'Come on, Amos, you're not being fair,' the bigger man said. He reached out and, quick as a flash, pulled my father's arm and twisted him round so they were facing each other again. From my viewing point at the window, I gasped.

'No. You're not being fair, Morgan,' my father said. He sounded angry. 'Things are different now. I've got a wife and a daughter.' He nodded up towards where I sat watching and I shrank back against the wall so I wouldn't be seen, wondering if he knew I was spying on him.

'Reckon your woman will be easier to persuade than you are,' Morgan said. 'Or that pretty daughter of yours.'

My father snorted. 'Janey knows her own mind. You're no match for her.' I smiled to myself; he was right about that. 'Now you need to leave, before I throw you out.' He turned his back and went to walk away, but the other man was getting angry. I flinched, trying to capture the glower on his face on my paper and then watched in helpless horror as the man yanked Da's arm again. There was a flash of metal and my father slumped on to the cobbles.

For a moment, I didn't understand what I'd just seen. What had happened? How did a conversation between two men suddenly end like this? My head was reeling with the horror of it all.

Sobbing, I pressed myself up against the window, watching the blood trickle from my father's stomach. Morgan pulled his knife from the wound, wiped it on his britches and turned to where Petroc had just emerged from the stables without Tully.

'What have you done?' he said, his mouth open in shock. 'What have you done to Amos?'

Morgan shrugged. 'Made things easier for myself.'

Almost without thinking I found a new sheet of paper and started drawing the faces down below. I drew my father's dull eyes, blood pooling around him, Morgan's white streak in his hair and his calm expression, and Petroc's horrified wide eyes. As I drew, tears ran down my cheeks and splattered on to the paper.

'But . . .' Petroc began.

Morgan prodded my father with his foot. 'We'll throw him

down one of the mineshafts over Barnmouth way,' he said. 'No one will find him there.'

'No we will not,' said Petroc. 'We need to get help for Amos.'

He went to crouch down to my father, just as he'd crouched next to Tully, but Morgan grabbed him by his collar and threw him against the wall. There was another flash of metal and I saw the knife at Petroc's throat.

'We will throw him down one of the mineshafts,' said Morgan. 'Or you'll be joining him.'

I was frozen with shock and fear. I wanted to scream and bang on the window, but I was scared of what the big man would do to me if he knew I was watching.

Shoulders slumped, Petroc tramped across the courtyard to where my father lay. As he approached, my father's eyes flickered open and he looked up at me. Still crying, I pushed my hand against the window in a sad goodbye and my father, slowly, painfully, put his finger to his lips. Stay quiet, he was telling me. Stay silent.

Tears ran down my cheeks as the men hoisted my father up on to their shoulders and carried him out of the inn's courtyard. Morgan picked up a rain bucket we left for the horses and emptied it over the cobbles, where the blood was staining the stone. He watched as the water washed away any evidence of what he'd done, then he paused for a minute looking at the inn.

Suddenly, I leapt into action. I had to stop them. Da was still alive; I had to tell my mother. I had to save him.

I jumped off the windowsill and raced into my parents' bedroom. Mam was lying face down on the bed, fully clothed.

I shook her roughly by the shoulders, hoping she would open her eyes. Her lids flickered but I couldn't rouse her. She'd had too much to drink and she was out cold.

Crying so hard I could barely catch my breath, I left her lying there, and ran downstairs through the courtyard and out into the night. But the men were nowhere to be seen. It was quiet and still.

All I could hear were the waves breaking on the beach far below. They'd gone. But – I thought, with icy cold fear trickling down my spine – what if they came back? Morgan had mentioned my mother, and me. What if he came for us too?

Trembling with fright, I crept to the stables and untied Tully. He licked my face, drawn to the salty tears on my cheeks, and I rubbed his head. 'Come on, boy,' I whispered. Obediently, he followed me back into the inn. I drew the bolt across the door, checking and double-checking it was firmly closed, and then, with Tully at my heels, I climbed the stairs to my parents' room. Tully jumped up on to the bed, and I lay down too, clinging to my mother's back. I'd stay here all night, I thought, in case they came back, and then in the morning, I'd raise the alarm. Tell everyone what I'd seen.

But it didn't happen that way, despite my intentions. Instead, when my mother woke, ill-tempered and sweating from all the drink, she glared at me.

'Why are you here?' she said, heaving herself off the bed. 'Where's your da? He stormed off in a state last night. Is he back?'

I was not much of a talker. Never had been. I couldn't talk to strangers, never passed the time of day with the drinkers in the inn. And even with Mam, I'd only ever said what was needed. I was better with Da, and my friend Arthur. They never rushed me, never tutted when I couldn't find the right word, or finished my sentence for me, too impatient to wait. When I was nervous or upset, or even sometimes if I was excited or happy, it was worse. It was like my throat clenched and my voice just wouldn't work.

Now, I sat up in bed, ready to tell her what had happened, how I'd seen Da's blood spill on the cobbles and watch Morgan drag him away.

'Mam,' I began. 'Mam . . .'

And then. Nothing. The words wouldn't come. Mam stared at me for a moment and then, frustrated, she rolled her eyes. 'He'll be back when he wants food,' she said.

At the mention of food, Tully got to his feet, shaking his fur out and giving a soft bark in my mother's direction. She looked at the dog. 'He left you behind, did he?' she said. 'Then he'll be back even sooner.'

She turned to me. 'Floors need sweeping.' And off she went, downstairs, unaware of what had happened to my da, because I'd not been able to tell her.

Three days went by. Three awful days. The inn was quiet. Mam was silent. Tully sat by the window, his front paws on the sill, watching for Da. And try as I might – and believe me, I tried – I couldn't get the words out to tell Mam what had happened. I tried to mime it, clutching my stomach and falling to the floor. Pointing at the spot in the courtyard where the blood had splattered. I tried to show her the drawings of Petroc and Morgan, but she pushed me away. I wanted to scream in frustration and fear and grief. But I couldn't do that, either.

On the morning of the fourth day, I was awakened by my mother's wails. I was on my feet and downstairs before I'd even properly realised what I was doing, so scared was I that Morgan had returned. But Mam was in the inn, sitting at a table with the parish constable, Mr Trewin. His three-cornered hat was on the table, making me shudder as I remembered Morgan wearing a similar one. I flew to my mother's side and she gathered me into her arms – an unfamiliar state of affairs as usually I shunned physical contact. Her face was blotchy with tears. Had they found Da? I wondered. Was this it?

'Emily,' Mam said softly. 'Your father is gone.'

Mr Trewin nodded. 'Your mother is afraid he has fallen from the cliff.'

I shook my head. That wasn't what had happened. Again, I opened my mouth to speak, to tell them about the man with the white streak in his hair, and the blood on the cobbles, but again I couldn't make a sound.

'Emily,' Mr Trewin said. He was using the tone people often

used when they spoke to me. Many of the people from Kirrinporth believed me to be simple because I didn't talk much and because I was much happier observing from the edge of life than being in it. 'Emily,' he said again. 'Your mother says your father has been gone these last three nights. But the tide has turned so if he had fallen he would have washed up at Barnmouth.'

Desperately, Mam reached across the table and clutched the front of Mr Trewin's coat.

'We argued,' she said. 'We argued and he went off in anger. He wasn't thinking straight. He could have fallen.'

Mr Trewin gave a small shake of his head. 'But there is no sign of him,' he said. 'And if you argued, then perhaps he has just gone for some peace.'

Mam pulled Mr Trewin closer to her. He pulled back but her grip was strong. 'You want to speak to Cal Morgan,' she hissed. I stiffened at the mention of the name. 'Because it was him we argued about.'

Mr Trewin stood up, forcing Mam to release his coat. 'I'd be very careful what you say, Janey Moon,' he said. 'Spreading rumours like that.'

I stood in between Mam and Mr Trewin, looking at the man and trying my hardest to speak. But the only sound that came from my treacherous mouth was a kind of desperate croak.

Mr Trewin looked at me in sympathy. 'Your da is alive,' he said, speaking slowly and carefully as though it was my ears that didn't work, not my mouth. 'He has gone off somewhere.' He gave my mother a sideways glance. 'With another woman, no doubt. Who doesn't argue.'

My mother began to wail again and Mr Trewin patted her kindly on the hand. 'Janey, we men are simple folk,' he said. 'We are often not worthy of the love our women give us. Your Amos has let everyone down.'

There was a scratching at the inn door and with a disgusted glance at Mr Trewin, I went to let Tully in. He bounded inside, his claws clattering on the stone floor, and nosed his way around the inn.

'He's looking for Amos,' my mother said, watching him through swollen eyes. 'Amos would never have left without Tully.'

'I'm sorry,' said Mr Trewin, picking up his hat and putting it on his head. 'But it seems he has.'

As though he'd understood every word, Tully sat back on his haunches, lifted his head up and howled mournfully. My mother followed, her sobs echoing round the empty inn. I tugged desperately at Mr Trewin's sleeve, trying to get him to wait so I could get the pictures I'd drawn and perhaps make him understand what had happened. But he picked my fingers off one by one, as though I was dirty, and then brushed some invisible muck from his coat where I'd been clutching him.

'I have to go,' he said in that tone again. 'Good day.'

Chapter 2

Phoebe

London, February 2019

I yawned and stretched at my desk, glad to be clocking off and not working the night shift. Saturdays were always challenging and I was pleased I wasn't back in the police station until Monday morning now.

'I'm heading off,' I said to no one in particular, just as my colleague and friend Stacey – DC Maxwell – who sat next to me in the CID office, put the phone down and made a face.

'Do you have to go now?'

'What have you got?'

'Missing teenage girl. Probably nothing, but uniform are all tied up with that brawl after the football.'

'Where?'

'Hanson Grove.'

I pulled my coat from the rack and put it on. 'I'll go on my way home,' I said. 'Who called it in?'

'Her mum. But according to PC Malone, she sounded a bit funny.'

'Funny how?'

Stacey shrugged and I groaned. 'Give me all the details, and I'll check it out.'

'Will you be all right on your own?'

'I'll be fine.'

As I walked to my car, I read the paperwork Stacey had given me. The missing girl was called Ciara James, and she was sixteen years old. I frowned. She'd probably just gone off with her boyfriend somewhere. This was a job for the neighbourhood PCSO, not CID. Still, it was on my way and it would only take five minutes.

My car was iced up when I got to it. I had no scraper, obviously, so I had to improvise with my Tesco Clubcard and when I finally got inside, I had to peel off my wet gloves, and use them to demist the windscreen so all in all it took me ages to get to Ciara James's house. It was gone 10 p.m. when I finally pulled up outside. There was a light on in the front room, though, so I knocked on the door.

A man looked out of the window, frowning. He was wearing a thick jumper and he had reading glasses on his nose.

'Mr James?' I said through the glass, showing him my warrant card. 'DS Bellingham.'

He looked worried as he dropped the curtain and a few seconds later, the front door opened.

'Is everything okay?' he said. 'What's wrong?'

That was strange. 'We had a call from your wife? She said your daughter Ciara is missing.'

A shadow crossed his face, but then his expression changed to look more confused than annoyed. 'Ciara's not missing,' he said.

'Where is she?'

'Cinema, I believe.' He looked at his watch. 'Her friend's dad is dropping her home. I don't like her getting the bus this late. I worry about her being out on her own. There are some dodgy people around. I'd have picked her up myself but I don't like staying up late on Saturday because I have to be at church early in the morning.'

'But your wife said . . .'

'She gets muddled,' he said quietly. 'She takes pills to help her sleep and sometimes they make her misunderstand things.'

I looked at him. He seemed totally genuine. And yet, there was something niggling at me. 'Have you seen Ciara this evening yourself?'

'No, I'm afraid not. I've been at my choir practice.'

'At church? Which one?'

'St John's.'

I nodded. 'And your wife was here?'

'I assume so. When I got home she was in bed. Perhaps she took a pill and couldn't remember where Ciara had gone.'

'Can I speak to her?'

He made a face. 'If she's taken a sleeping tablet, I won't be able to wake her.'

'Could you try?' I smiled at him. 'I really should speak to her, or my boss will give me grief.'

I was still standing on the doorstep, and the evening was bitterly cold. I didn't wait to be asked, but just stepped inside. He looked like he was going to say something and then changed his mind.

'Wait here.'

I had a good nose round the hall while I waited. It was very ordinary. Dull, in fact. Neat and tidy. Ciara's school photo on the wall, showing her to be a pretty but unremarkable teenager. Boots stacked neatly in a rack and three coats hanging from pegs. Three coats. I frowned.

'Does Ciara have another coat,' I asked as Mr James came downstairs again.

'Pardon?'

'Does Ciara have another coat?' I gestured to the coat rail. 'I presume that's hers? But it's very cold outside.'

He screwed his nose up. 'No idea, sorry. I don't pay much attention to what she wears.'

'Right. Is your wife awake?'

A noise upstairs made me look up. A middle-aged woman was coming downstairs, wearing pyjamas and looking pale and sleepy.

'So sorry to disturb you, Mrs James,' I said. 'We had a call that Ciara was missing.'

She rubbed her eyes like a toddler. 'Ciara is at the cinema.'

'That's right,' her husband said. He looked at me and I saw a flash of something in his eyes – triumph? 'You get back to bed.'

Obediently, Mrs James turned and went back upstairs before I could stop her.

'Terribly sorry to waste your time,' Mr James said with a smile. 'I trust my wife isn't in trouble.'

'Not at all.'

We stood in the hall for a second. I looked at him and he looked back at me. All my instincts were telling me that something was off, but I had nothing. I wished Stacey had come with me. Another pair of eyes on this outwardly normal family would be useful.

'If Ciara doesn't come home, please call the station,' I said.

'Of course, thank you so much, Constable.'

I forced myself to smile instead of correcting him about my rank. 'Call us if you need to,' I said again, more sternly this time.

My car was already icing up again, so I blasted the heater and drove a little way down the road, before I parked up and called the station.

As I waited for someone to answer, I thought about calling uniform out. Being a bit forceful with Mr James. Pressing him. Checking Ciara did come home later. But then I shook my head.

'Have a word with yourself, Phoebe,' I said out loud. He was a boring bloke wearing slippers and corduroy trousers, who went to bed early on a Saturday night so he wasn't tired at church. Uniform would probably laugh at me if I asked them to come round.

And so when my call was answered, I asked to speak to Stacey. 'She's not missing,' I said when she answered. 'She's at the cinema.'

'Okaaaay.'

'The mum got confused, apparently.'

'Fine,' Stacey said. 'Good.'

'Can you flag the name?' I asked. 'And ring me if anything else comes in.'

'I thought she was at the cinema.'

'Just in case.'

'All right,' said Stacey amiably. 'See you Monday.'

It was Monday morning when I got the call to say that Ciara James was gone. I felt my stomach plummet into my shoes, leaving me with a sick feeling that stayed with me for days and days as we searched fruitlessly for the missing teenager.

'There's definitely nothing on the parents?' my boss, DI Blair, said on the Friday evening, fixing me with his steely glare across the room.

I shook my head. 'I've been over it and over it,' I said. 'They're just . . . normal.'

I twisted my hair into a ponytail in my hand and pulled it over my shoulder, the way I always did when I was thinking. 'But it was all just misunderstandings. The mother – Molly – she can't even remember phoning us last weekend. She's in a state. Blaming herself. And the father – Steve – he's the same. They were up early for church and it wasn't until the evening that they realised Ciara was gone.'

DI Blair nodded.

'I should have searched her bedroom,' I said. 'I should have pushed the mother more.'

'You had no cause to search the house, and the mother sounds like she didn't know whether she was coming or going,' DI Blair pointed out.

I said nothing. I knew he was right, but I felt completely awful.

'Do you think it's the parents?' DI Blair asked, looking at me intently. 'What's your instinct telling you?'

I shifted in my chair, feeling uncomfortable under his glare.

'I just don't know,' I admitted. 'My heart said they were to blame, but my head says no. They're so . . .'

'So?'

'Nice.'

He sighed. 'You know as well as I do that bad things happen in nice families, too.'

I bit my lip. He was right. Of course he was.

'We should speak to them again,' I said, firmly.

'Sure?'

I shrugged. I really was at a loss. I'd spoken to everyone in Ciara's life. She was a happy sixteen-year-old girl growing up in the suburbs of south London. Her teachers had no concerns. Her parents were normal. Her friends were sweet. There was nothing suspicious about the family whatsoever. Her mother didn't sleep well but apart from that she was ordinary and her father – well, stepfather actually though he'd brought her up since she'd been tiny – was an all-round nice chap. But her parents being to blame was the only thing that made sense. Wasn't it? I had no idea any more.

'Focus,' DI Blair said. 'And let me know when you're ready to decide on a next step. I might even come with you.'

He marched off towards his office and I sighed. He'd never been this bolshie or unpleasant to work with before, but I understood the strain he was under. Ciara's picture had been on the front of every newspaper today. She smiled out at me on every news website, her drab school uniform unable to dull her youthful prettiness.

The rest of the team were looking at me, waiting for a decision, so I forced myself to focus.

'Right,' I said to two uniformed PCs who were helping with the door-to-door inquiries. 'Benny and Joe, can you go through the information from the neighbours and friends?' They nodded and I turned to another colleague. 'Stacey, you double-check the reports from her school, and I'll reread the parents' statements. We must be missing something.'

There was a bustle of activity. Stacey – DC Maxwell – squeezed my arm as she walked past me to her desk, letting me know she had my back. I gave her a grateful smile. Eventually everyone settled down and silence fell as we all read through every bit of information we had about the girl's disappearance.

Ciara's mother, Molly, was a nursery school teacher, and the stepdad, Steve, had his own business doing accounts. He rented a desk in an office near the station and everyone there said he was always pleasant. As I already knew, they were both fairly religious – regular churchgoers. Upright. Moral, even. Steve, I'd heard, had turned down the contract to do the accounts for a local betting shop because he didn't approve of gambling. Molly was sweet-natured and kind. No criminal records. Not so much as a speeding ticket. Nothing.

Ciara had been messaging a boy online – someone from a nearby school – and we'd originally thought she might have gone to meet him. But he'd been playing football the evening she disappeared, and he admitted – slightly sheepishly – that he'd never met her.

I put aside the statements from Ciara's parents. This was getting me nowhere.

'Phoebe, I spoke to the dad's mates at his golf club,' Benny said, appearing at the side of my desk. 'I just uploaded the statements.'

'Anything worthwhile?'

He shrugged. 'Just what a nice bloke he is.'

'I'll have a look,' I said half-heartedly.

I scanned the statements. This was so hard. There was just nothing to go on at all. Gut instinct went a long way in police investigations, even though lots of my fellow officers would deny it and claim it was all legwork and asking the right questions. But just now, my gut instinct was switched right off. I had unfounded doubts about the dad and that was it. All I could see was that Ciara was a nice, normal sixteen-year-old. In fact, I thought, she was even nicer than her parents made her sound – but that wasn't unusual. I had friends who claimed their babies were absolute nightmares while smothering them with kisses. Maybe parents of teens did the same?

I sighed, looking at the statement from Steve's friend. 'Steve's one of the nicest blokes I know,' he'd said. 'We all thought he was really good to take on Ciara as his own.' Yawn. I rested my head on my hand, and scrolled on. 'Considering,' the friend had added. I sat up straighter. 'Considering,' I murmured to myself. What did that mean?

I pulled my phone to me and dialled the number on the bottom of the statement. The friend answered straightaway.

'Sorry to bother you,' I said. 'This is DS Bellingham from Lewisham police station. I just wanted to double-check something in your statement.'

'Right,' the man said, sounding nervous.

'When you said Steve was good to take Ciara on as his own child, considering . . . What did you mean? Considering what?'

The man laughed. 'Well,' he said. 'You probably know more than me. But she sounds like a right handful. Always in trouble. Last I heard, she was messaging some lad. Steve was worried about it. Sounded like she was sending him all sorts, if you know what I mean?'

I had no idea. We'd found Ciara's phone in her very tidy room – another odd thing about her disappearance. What teenager went anywhere without their phone? There had been the messages to the football-playing boy, and to her friends, and that was it. Nothing dodgy. No sexting, or inappropriate photos. Just a few sweet words saying how much she wanted to see the lad she'd been getting to know.

'Is Steve a strict father?' I asked.

'He has to be, by the sound of it,' the friend said. 'That girl would be on the streets if it wasn't for him.'

I thanked him for his time, and hung up the phone, shouting for Stacey as I pulled on my coat. We had to go and see the parents again.

From there on, it all unravelled. It turned out, Steve was more than just strict. He regularly punished poor Ciara for any perceived misdemeanour, from not stacking the dishwasher properly, to a poor mark on a test. And the messages from her new friend had tipped him over into disgust.

'She was messaging some filthy little turd,' he hissed at Stacey and me, his lip curled. 'I check her phone, of course, and she didn't even try to hide it.'

I thought about how innocent the messages were, and how I'd been mildly surprised by their chaste tone, and winced. 'What did you do then?'

He lifted his chin up, looking pleased with himself. 'I said to Molly that she needed to be punished and Molly agreed.'

Molly, sitting next to him, looked alarmed. 'We hadn't agreed on that,' she said. 'I felt a bit of a hypocrite. I had boyfriends at her age.'

'And look where you ended up,' Steve spat at her. 'Pregnant.'

Molly stayed quiet after that, as Steve explained how he wanted to teach Ciara a lesson, so he'd taken her to his allotment on Saturday afternoon and left her in the shed.

'It's freezing,' Stacey said. 'And her coat is still here. She must have been so cold.'

The thought of poor Ciara in the icy shed made me shiver. I shook my head. 'But we searched the shed,' I said. 'And the allotments. She's not there.'

'I just wanted to give her a scare,' Steve said. 'But when I got back to the allotment after church, she wasn't there.' He shrugged, not looking remotely worried. 'She'll be with that lad,' he said. 'Getting up to all sorts.'

'She's not with him.' My voice was cold. 'They never met up.'

Molly gave a little gasp and he patted her hand. 'She'll be fine,' he said. 'They'll find her.'

We did find her. In the woods, behind the patch of allotments, that skirted the railway line. She'd obviously found her way out of the shed, but in confusion from the cold, she'd curled herself into the roots of a tree, gone to sleep and never woken up. The freezing February weather, and the vest top and thin leggings she'd been wearing made sure of that.

'She wouldn't have suffered,' the pathologist reassured me.

But I kept thinking about how scared she must have been, and how cold, and how if I'd followed my instincts right at the start, we might have found her sooner.

'It's not your fault,' DI Blair said over and over, as we watched Steve being put into a police car and Ciara's mother wailing from inside the house. 'The only person to blame, is that bugger. This is not your fault.'

But somehow I felt that it was.

Chapter 3

Phoebe

Three months later

'I'm popping to the shops,' Mum said, poking her head round the living room door. 'Why don't you come with me?'

'I don't think so.'

'Phoebe . . .' Her voice went from being overly perky to concerned. 'Sweetheart.'

'I'm fine.' I dragged my eyes away from *Homes Under the Hammer*. 'I just want to watch this.'

Mum raised an eyebrow but she didn't push me further. 'I'll put the kettle on,' she said.

'I thought you were going out.' I knew she hadn't been going anywhere really. She just wanted to get me off the sofa and out into the world. But I didn't want to go out because I didn't want to risk bumping into Ciara's mother. She was thinking of selling up, I'd heard. Moving on. I couldn't blame her. But for now, I worried I'd see her in the Post Office queue, or at the self-checkout in Sainsbury's. And I couldn't deal with her sorrow and her guilt on top of my own, selfish as that sounded.

Mum gave me a look that suggested this wasn't over and went off to make tea. I pulled my knees up to my chest and watched the bouncy blonde woman over-enthuse about a chimney breast. I watched a lot of daytime television these days because I had nothing else to do. I'd been signed off from work after it became apparent I wasn't coping with what had happened. I'd become frozen with indecision at work, incapable of choosing tea or coffee from the canteen, let alone making choices that affected people's lives. I felt like I couldn't trust myself. I'd ignored my instincts and Ciara had died. So now I suspected everyone of having some ulterior motive, or of hiding some awful secret, even when they weren't doing anything wrong. I couldn't function at work so I had some counselling and the counsellor, Sandra, gently told me I needed some time away to heal. And I was now on sick leave, and I had no idea when I'd go back.

I couldn't afford my flat-share on my reduced pay, so I'd slunk home to my parents' house to hide. It wasn't the best place for me. My parents lived just a stone's throw from the allotments where Ciara had died. Where she'd have lived, if I'd been more thorough. If I'd asked the right questions. It had been a miserable few months, no question. Though, I told myself whenever I felt myself descending into self-pity, not as miserable as it must have been for Ciara's poor mother.

The doorbell rang, jolting me from my thoughts. I listened to make sure Mum had gone to answer, and turned the volume up on *Homes Under the Hammer* when I heard voices in the hall.

'What's this bollocks?' said a voice. I raised my head to see my oldest friend Liv standing in the doorway.

'This couple think they can do up a house and sell it in six weeks,' I told her, turning my gaze back to the screen. 'But Dion Dublin thinks they're putting too much pressure on themselves.'

'I agree with Dion,' Liv said. She sat down next to me and finally I looked up at her. 'You look like shit, Phoebe.'

'I know.' I shrugged. 'So?'

'So, it's my job as your best friend to help you.'

I rolled my eyes. 'I've got a counsellor.'

'What I can offer you is better than any counsellor.'

'What?' I sighed. 'What can you offer me?'

Liv grinned at me. 'First, tell me how great I am.'

'No.' She was great, of course, but I really wasn't in the mood for Liv's games.

She frowned, and then her expression softened. 'Look, Phoebe, I know how hard it is when things go wrong.'

I felt guilty. She wasn't exactly having an easy time of it right now herself. She was still recovering after breaking up with her long-term boyfriend, Niall. What a pair of losers we were.

'But you're wallowing.'

'I'm not.' I looked at her. 'Honestly, Liv, I'm not. I'm just not ready to get back to work.'

'I don't want you to go back to work.'

I blinked at her. 'Really?'

'Really.'

'So what do you want?'

'I want to take you away from all this.'

She picked up the remote control and turned off the TV. I tried to grab it back but she held it out of my reach.

'I was watching that,' I complained. Liv ignored me.

'I've got a proposition for you,' she said.

I sighed. Liv and I had been mates since primary school and I'd had a lifetime experiencing her propositions.

'No,' I said.

'Hear me out.' She waved the remote control at me. 'And then I'll put your house programme back on.'

'Fine.'

'I've been offered a job for the rest of the year,' she said. I managed to raise a smile. That was good news. Liv was the quintessential rolling stone. She worked for a pub chain, para-chuted in to take over. She'd done new openings, brand launches, big events like running the pub in the Olympic Park in 2012. She'd worked in Glasgow and Manchester and all over Wales, and down in Brighton for a while. I always joked she was institutionalised – she never had to find a flat or pay rent or even go to the supermarket. She just lived on site in each pub, ate pub food, drank pub drinks. She'd had a brief stint in head office when she'd moved in with Niall, but I'd never thought she'd been very happy staying in one place.

Since they'd broken up she'd been back at her mum's too. She'd not had a proper job for a while and I knew she was beginning to worry about it. I'd enjoyed having her nearby though. It was reassuring to know that while I may have been in my early thirties, single, jobless and living with my mum, I wasn't the only one.

'Where is it this time?' I asked.

'Cornwall.'

'Nice,' I said.

'Bit remote.' Liv screwed her nose up. 'But beautiful location. Right by the beach. Amazing views.'

I nodded, wisely. 'A good view can add as much as £10,000 on to the value of a property.'

'No more house shows for you,' Liv said. She threw the remote control across the room on to the battered old armchair my dad sat in to watch the football. 'It's just a temporary manager job. Nothing fancy. So I'll be bored to tears.' She paused. 'Come with me.'

'Where?'

'Cornwall.'

'I can't go to Cornwall for the rest of the year.'

'You don't have to stay the whole time. Just come for the summer.'

'No.'

'Why not?'

I thought about it, but actually I couldn't think of a reason why not. I opened my mouth and then closed it again without speaking and Liv gave me her best gimlet stare.

'It'll be good for you to get away,' she said.

That was true. But I didn't feel strong enough to start again in a new place, with people I didn't know. I liked being at home with my mum and Liv round the corner.

'It won't be like starting again in a new place,' Liv said, reading my mind. 'Because I'll be there the whole time.'

'You'll be busy,' I said. I could well imagine how frantic a beachside pub could be at the height of summer.

'I'll need help.'

'I'm not a barmaid.'

'So you can collect glasses. Or if you don't want to work, you can sunbathe. Or learn to surf.'

It was beginning to sound more appealing. Liv sensed weakness. 'You might meet a new man,' she said. 'A posh boy in chino shorts and deck shoes.'

I wrinkled my nose up.

'Fine, a surfer dude with long hair and a great tan.'

'Better.'

Liv bounced on her seat. 'Or that Poldark bloke. With the hair. You could meet someone like him.'

I smiled despite myself. 'That would be worth the trip,' I said. 'But I don't know, Liv. I'm not in a good place.'

'That's why you should come. You can be in your bad place in a great place.'

Mum came into the lounge carrying two mugs of tea. She gave one to Liv and put the other on the table next to where I sat. 'Where's a great place?' she asked.

'Georgie, tell Phoebe she needs to come to Cornwall with me,' Liv said. Mum looked at her adoringly. She thought Liv was marvellous and the feeling was mutual. But I didn't mind, because I thought the same about Liv's mum, Patsy, and her gran, Jada. Liv had adored my noisy chaotic house growing up, bickering with my two older brothers as though they were her own. And I'd spent hours in the peaceful house Liv called home, helping Jada cook the Jamaican dishes Liv had no interest in, and watching Patsy studying for her degree at the kitchen table.

Mum sat down on the sofa next to me and beamed at Liv. 'A holiday in Cornwall is a wonderful idea.'

'It would be for the whole summer,' Liv said. 'I've got a job down there.'

Mum looked thrilled and, I thought, a bit relieved. 'Even better.'

I made a face. 'I'm not sure, Mum,' I said. 'It just seems a bit much.'

'Rubbish,' said Mum briskly. 'It'll do you the world of good. Get some sun on your skin. Really relax and put all your troubles behind you.'

'And you'll be doing me a favour,' Liv said. 'You know what these remote places are like for people like me.'

'Cornwall's not remote,' I pointed out. 'It's a couple of hours down the motorway and full of stockbrokers from Surrey.'

'When I took that job at that country inn, someone asked me every single day where I was from,' Liv said, scowling. 'And believe me, they didn't look satisfied when I said Lewisham.'

'That was shit, but I'm sure Cornwall's not like that,' I said, not unsympathetic because I'd seen first-hand the casual racism Liv had put up with over the years, but not convinced she really needed me as much as she said she did. Liv was more than capable of standing up for herself.

'Please come,' Liv pleaded. 'Please, Phoebe. You can collect glasses and flirt with the Poldarks and arrest all the racists.'

'I can't arrest anyone in Cornwall,' I lied, but my arguments were getting weaker.

'I think it's just what you need,' said Mum. 'And in Cornwall you know you won't have to run the risk of bumping into Ciara's mother.'

I shrugged. 'I think she'll be moving soon anyway.'

Mum reached out and took my hand. 'I wanted to talk to you about that. I walked past the house the other day and saw the for-sale sign had gone so I spoke to Mrs Morrison at the Post Office – you know what she's like for knowing everything. And it seems the mother has decided to stay.'

I felt sick. 'She's staying?'

'For now. She doesn't want to leave all her memories behind.'

'Doesn't want to leave her husband behind, more like,' I said in disgust. Ciara's stepfather had pleaded guilty to manslaughter and was serving his sentence at Belmarsh prison – not far from where we lived. Her mother had stood by him, convinced he'd just made a terrible mistake.

'Come with me, Moon Girl,' Liv said, using the nickname she'd given me when we were kids and we'd found out that Phoebe meant "moon".

I thought about spending the summer trapped inside the home where I'd grown up, not venturing out for fear of seeing the woman whose daughter I could have saved. And then I thought about spending the next few months in a seaside town. All the space and the fresh air. I'd be able to breathe properly for the first time in months. I could go running on the beach, I thought. Get my fitness back.

'Fine,' I said to Liv. 'I'll come.'

She clapped her hands and exchanged a look with Mum that told me her visit and her invitation had been planned, and that today was definitely not the first time Mum had heard about Liv's new job. Somehow, though, I didn't mind them colluding behind my back. I quite liked someone else taking responsibility for my life. It stopped me having to make decisions.

I gave Liv a weak smile. 'When do you have to be there?'

'Friday.'

Two days away. I was glad I didn't have too much time to think about it. With a fair amount of effort, I dragged myself to my feet.

'I suppose I should go and pack,' I said.

Chapter 4

Emily

Cornwall, Autumn 1799

The walk into Kirrinporth had never felt longer than it did that day. My legs were weak and my stomach empty, and each step was an effort.

'Keep going,' Mam said, each time I stumbled. 'Nearly there.'

Two seasons had passed since Da was killed, and now autumn was here and the weather was colder, and we were hungry. No one came to the inn now. Mam still got ready each evening, putting on a clean dress, pinching her cheeks to make them pink, and tying her hair up. But she sat there alone every night, drinking until she took herself off to bed.

I wanted to help. I wanted to comfort her. And most of all, I wanted to tell her what had happened to Da. But each time I tried to speak, I couldn't get the words out. My throat clenched and I couldn't talk. I could write a few words – Da had taught me – but Mam couldn't read well so even if I could have written down what happened, she wouldn't have been able to make sense of the words. She wouldn't look at my pictures, and they were just the men's faces anyway, and the awful sketch of Da's lifeless eyes with the blood spilled around his head. And always, in my head, was the memory of Da putting his finger to his lips and telling me to stay quiet, and the fear that Morgan might come back for Mam. It was frustrating not to be able to tell Mam the truth, but it was safer.

So time went on, and Mam still thought Da had left because of their argument, and every day I saw the hope she carried that he might come home again die a little bit more.

I spent my days cleaning or sketching because it was all I could do. I drew Mam's face over and over, then gazed at my pictures of her drooping mouth and sad eyes.

The only person I could speak to now was my friend Arthur. But it had taken me a long time after Da's death to even manage that. To begin with, all I could say was 'Da's gone' before my throat tightened and the words stopped coming.

Arthur never rushed me, and eventually, I managed to talk more with him. But only when it was just the two of us, and only if we talked of things that didn't matter – the weather, or Arthur's cat. I never told him what had really happened to Da, and I never told him how bad things were at the inn.

Because bad they were. Mam and I had been all right at first. But the drinkers soon stopped coming. There were a few travellers who wandered in but not enough to stop Mam worrying over the books or crying as she counted the coins each evening. And eventually they stopped too. I didn't know if the customers had stopped coming because they didn't approve of a woman running a pub by herself, or because they thought we were unlucky, or cursed even. I'd heard mutters when I was in Kirrinporth. People shrinking away from me as I walked by.

'That's the Moon girl,' they would say. 'She's a strange one.' I'd heard talk of ghosts and spirits. Stories that I'd never heard before Da died. And I remembered Mam warning Da that we would be starved out, and I wondered if her strange prediction had come true.

Now we were down to our last few coins and our bellies were aching with hunger, and Mam had looked at me that morning, hollow-eyed and so thin that she had to tie a ribbon round her waist to stop her dress trailing on the floor.

'We need help,' she said. 'We will go into Kirrinporth and ask Mr Trewin to help us in whatever way he can.'

I widened my eyes. Did she mean a workhouse? I felt a fluttery, panicky feeling in my chest. The inn was all I'd ever known. What about my drawing? And my bedroom? Would we have to sleep with other people? I didn't like to be around others.

As we left the inn, it felt like a goodbye. I wasn't sure we'd ever come back again. My insides felt hollow and I thought it wasn't just hunger making me feel that way. Mam shut the door, and I tried not to look at the empty space on the hearth where Tully had slept before Da went. He'd just faded away after Da had gone. He died of a broken heart, Mam said. Sometimes I wished I could do the same.

Mam hooked her arm through mine and, half carrying each other, we stumbled along the road to Kirrinporth. The village was busy, and I tried to keep close to the buildings, hiding in the shadows so no one saw me. Mam did the same, which wasn't like her. Before things changed, she would always stride down the middle of a group of people, calling greetings to friends and making jokes. Now she turned her face away from the crowds.

Mr Trewin's office was off the main street, in a building with leaded windows and three steps to the door. Mam almost pulled herself up the stairs, holding on to the iron bannister. I followed.

Inside, Mr Trewin's assistant – a small, mousy man – offered us both a chair. His eyebrows were so far up his forehead that they almost disappeared into his thin hair and I wished I could draw him.

We heard muffled voices as he went to fetch Mr Trewin and I closed my eyes, tired from the long walk.

'Janey Moon,' Mr Trewin said, his booming voice startling

me. I opened my eyes again. He was wearing his coat and hat. 'I can't stop long, I'm afraid. What can I do for you? Is there news of Amos?'

Mam shook her head. 'Amos is long gone,' she said. She took a breath and then launched into her plea for help. She'd been muttering it under her breath as we'd walked, going over and over it. Now the words spilled out of her, falling over each other as she stared at Mr Trewin with her hands clasped together.

'I've done all I can to make our money stretch but there's nothing left, and we are starving. I have nowhere else to go now, Mr Trewin, nowhere to turn. What choices are there for a woman on her own with her daughter? We both work hard, we can clean and we can cook and sew, and we are not afraid to get our hands dirty.'

She stopped. 'Can you help us?'

Mr Trewin rubbed his nose. 'I'm afraid not.'

'But the workhouse . . .'

'Is for the elderly and infirm.' He looked us up and down, his lip curling.

'I thought we could . . .'

Mr Trewin shook his head. 'Twenty years ago, perhaps. But not now. Poor relief is really only for those who can't help themselves. And you, Janey Moon, are able-bodied. You yourself have told me how capable you are. You could get a position as a scullery maid, no doubt, though you are rather old for such a job.'

Mam glanced at me, and then she lowered her voice. 'What of Emily?' she said. 'She is not right in her head. She can't take a job like that. Can you find space for her in your workhouse?'

'She is simple, but not incapable,' Mr Trewin said. I kept my gaze fixed firmly on my boots, which were falling apart. Just like my dress and my cape. 'If I helped her, I would be breaking the rules.'

I knew Mam didn't mean to be nasty. She was well aware I was different, and really she was right, I thought. I wasn't sure

31

I would cope with a job in a big house. Like Mr Kirrin's home on the hill outside the village. I wasn't even sure Mam would cope. How could she go from running her own inn, entertaining the drinkers and telling stories, to sharing an attic bedroom with girls young enough to be her daughter and taking orders from a belligerent cook?

'I could sell the inn,' Mam said desperately. 'Can you find someone to buy it?'

'My dear Janey, it's not yours to sell.'

Mam stared at him and he gave her a small smile. 'It belongs to Amos.'

'Amos isn't here.'

'The law is the law.'

To my horror, Mam fell to her knees. 'We have nothing, Mr Trewin. No money for food.'

'But enough drink, I am certain,' Mr Trewin said. He tipped his hat to her and, leaving her on the floor, went out of the office and shut the door behind him. Mam struggled to her feet. Her cheeks were damp with tears.

'Come,' she said to me.

I followed her as she marched to the bakery and stayed outside as she bartered with the shopkeeper, handing over a bottle she'd brought in her bag in exchange for a loaf of bread. It didn't seem a fair swap to me, but what choice was there? She did the same for some cheese and then wearily, she turned to me. 'Let's go home,' she said. I looked at her, questions in my eyes, and she nodded. 'Back to the inn.'

If it had been a long journey to Kirrinporth, it felt longer on the way back. Though as soon as we were out of the village, Mam sat on a rock and took the bread and cheese from her bag. She tore off some bread and handed it to me and I ate it greedily, and the cheese she gave me. I even took some of the ale she offered to wash it down.

With our energy boosted by the food, we walked back to the

inn. Mam was talking the whole way. 'We could offer rooms, perhaps,' she said. 'Lodgings.'

I nodded, but I knew that would come to nothing. No one would stay in The Ship Inn, because if I'd heard the rumours of ghosts and bad luck, they would have too.

'Or I could take in mending,' Mam said. But who would bring their mending all the way out here, when there were seamstresses in Kirrinporth?

As we reached the inn, Mam's chatter ceased. She paused by the door, looking out across the sea. Her face wore an odd expression. 'He'll be here soon,' she said. 'This is what he was waiting for.'

I wanted to ask who she meant, but of course, I couldn't. Mam unlocked the door and put her hand to my cheek suddenly. I flinched at the unexpected touch, but then relaxed as she stroked my skin gently. 'I won't see you starve, Emily Moon,' she said.

Chapter 5

Phoebe

2019

It was a glorious day when Liv and I set off on the long drive to Cornwall. The sun was beating down, we had some of our favourite music for the car, and I felt my spirits lift – just a bit. Liv had been right. Getting away was the best thing to do. A summer down in Cornwall would reset me ready for coming back to work in the autumn.

'So tell me about the pub,' I said, as we left London behind and headed out on to the motorway. 'I'm imagining bleached wooden floorboards, and signs on the door saying "no beach wear". Am I right?'

Liv shrugged. 'No idea,' she said. 'Honestly, it's been so last-minute I've basically got the address and nothing else. Apparently the family who were there before had to leave in a hurry.'

'Why?'

'I don't know,' she said, indicating to overtake a lorry. She flashed me a dazzling smile. 'I do know the name though.'

'Of the family?'

She tutted. 'Of the pub.' She let out a little giggle, like she knew an amazing secret. 'It's brilliant. It's a sign that you coming with me was the right decision.'

I was intrigued. 'What is it?'

'You're not going to believe it.'

'Tell me,' I groaned in frustration.

'It's called The Moon Girl.'

I stared at the side of her head in astonishment. 'It never bloody is?'

'No lie,' she said, triumphant. 'Isn't it perfect?'

'Completely perfect.'

I put my hand up to the necklace I always wore, with a little silver crescent moon dangling from the chain. Liv had bought me it for my twenty-first birthday. I'd bought her a bracelet with a dove on it for her twenty-first – just ten days after mine – and we wore them all the time, even more than a decade on. It all went back to our last year in primary school, when we'd been set the task of finding out what our names meant. We'd discovered that Olivia meant peace, and Phoebe meant moon. Since then I'd called Liv, Peace Girl, and she'd called me Moon Girl – hence our jewellery. And why we were so delighted to be heading to a pub named after me. Well, not after me exactly, but it felt like I already had a connection.

'Do you know where the name comes from?' I asked, curious to know why it had such an unusual moniker. 'It's a bit different from the normal Red Lions or Queen's Heads.'

'No idea,' Liv said. 'But we can find out, I reckon.'

I nodded. 'I'll google when we get there. What sort of pub do you want it to be?'

Liv thought for a second, looking at the road ahead. 'I'm hoping for a beachfront gastro pub,' she said. 'Lots of fancy fish and chips on the menu, jugs of Pimm's and big balloon glasses of gin. All the posh holidaymakers flooding in, making the profits boom and giving me a big fat bonus. It's going to be great.'

I settled back in my seat, gazing up at the bright blue sky through the sunroof of the car. 'It really is,' I said. 'Thanks, Liv. This is just what I needed.'

'It wasn't your fault you know, what happened,' she said.

'I do know.' I nodded. 'But that doesn't stop me feeling guilty.'

'Three months in sunny Cornwall will put that right, Moon Girl,' Liv said. She gave me a sudden grin. 'Trust me.'

It was a long drive to the south west. We stopped a couple of times to swap over the driving, and to get coffees and stretch our legs, and we listened to a lot of Steps and S Club 7 – the music of our schooldays. And we tried not to be disappointed when, as we got nearer to Cornwall, the sky clouded over and the first splatters of rain hit the windscreen.

'There's a little seaside town but the pub's actually just outside it,' Liv said, peering at her phone screen where she had the map, its glow illuminating her face in the gloomy evening dim light. 'The town should be off there, to the right . . .' She flung her arm out across my face as I drove and I shrieked at her to move.

'Liv,' I said. 'You're the worst sat nav ever.'

A sign gleamed in the headlights showing a turn-off marked Kirrinporth and Liv said a triumphant "ha". 'That's the town! I'm actually the best sat nav.'

I chuckled. 'So the pub should be coming up then?'

'I hope so,' Liv said, because otherwise we're going to end up in the sea.

She was right: the ocean spread out in front of us, flat and grey. But thankfully the road bent round and . . .

'Slow down,' Liv cried. 'There should be a turning any second . . . here.'

Just in time, I saw the entrance and pulled the car into it. It was a steeply sloping track that led to a large car park. I pulled into one of the many, many empty spaces and stopped the engine, and Liv and I clambered out, taking our jackets from the back seat because the rain was still falling lightly. We blinked as our eyes adjusted to the twilight.

The pub wasn't obvious at first, because we were right on the edge of a cliff and the only light came from a streetlamp in the far corner of the car park behind us.

'There,' Liv said, nudging me and pointing. The pub was lower down than we were. We could only see the roof and the first-floor windows, which were level with the tarmacked area where we stood. Beyond the pub the ground fell away sharply so it looked as though The Moon Girl was balanced on the edge of the world. A flight of concrete steps led down from the car park to the pub's door. Liv scanned the area for another way down, then rolled her eyes. 'Disability access nightmare,' she said. 'I can't believe they don't have a ramp.'

I thought that there would probably be a ramp by the end of next week, now Liv was in charge. She was a doer, my friend. She tugged my sleeve. 'Let's get the bags out of the car and go in.'

The rain was getting heavier, so we did everything twice as fast as we would normally, dragging our bags from the boot and dashing across the car park, down the steps, and into the pub. The heavy door slammed behind us, and as though we were in one of the horror films my oldest brother liked, the few people who were inside all stopped talking and looked up at us.

There was a group of three men sitting at a table by the window on the far side of the pub, looking out over the darkening sea, and a young woman behind the bar.

'Fuck,' Liv breathed, looking uncharacteristically rattled. 'We're not in Lewisham now, Toto.'

'Hello,' said the young woman. She was drying an old-fashioned pint glass with dimples. I'd not seen one of those for years. She did at least sound fairly cheerful. 'Can I help you?'

I waited for Liv to speak, but she was still gazing round in, I thought, despair. So I took charge – or at least I tried to.

'Hello. This is Olivia Palmer. She's the new stand-in manager.'

The barmaid grinned so broadly, it looked like her face might split. 'Brilliant,' she said. 'That's brilliant.'

Boosted by the warm welcome from one person – the pub's three customers were all still looking at us curiously – Liv recovered herself. 'Liv,' she said, hurrying forwards and shaking the barmaid's hand vigorously. 'And this is Phoebe. She's helping me out for the summer.'

'Kayla,' said the barmaid. 'I don't work here.'

Liv blinked. 'You don't?'

'Nope,' Kayla said. She put down the glass and turned round, taking a raincoat from the peg behind her. 'I was just helping out. But now you're here, I'll go.'

'Already?' Liv sounded alarmed and Kayla shrugged.

'You're here,' she said again.

One of the men who'd been sitting by the window appeared at my elbow.

'I'll give you a lift, Kayla,' he said. He had a strong Cornish accent and was quite handsome in a rugged, weather-beaten way. Like how George Clooney would look if he spent his days outdoors.

Kayla grinned at him. 'Thanks, Ewan,' she said.

He nodded to me and Liv and we both nodded back. Kayla came out from behind the bar and threw a bunch of keys in Liv's direction. Liv didn't move; she just watched as they landed on the floor in front of her.

'You'll want to lock up when we're gone,' Kayla said. She looked serious, but the man – Ewan – laughed.

'Welcome to The Moon Girl,' he said.

He pushed open the door and a gust of wind blew in, making Liv and me shiver. Kayla and the other two men followed him out into the night and the door banged shut again.

'What on earth was that?' I said. Liv looked at me, her eyes wide, and then she burst out laughing. I did the same.

'I don't work here,' I said, in a very bad approximation of Kayla's west country drawl. 'I just chuck the keys about.'

'Welcome to The Moon Girl,' Liv said, deepening her voice so much that she sounded like a Cornish Batman. She bent down and scooped up the keys.

'Are you going to lock the door?' I asked, feeling weirdly nervous. This was a strange place, with the rain beating against the windows and no customers even though it was only seven o'clock in the evening. If the weather was better, it would still be light. That picture I'd had in my mind of the beachside bar with brightly coloured umbrellas on the terrace and bleached wooden floors was fading fast.

Liv didn't answer; she just walked to the door, checked it was properly closed, and then locked it.

'No one else will come this evening,' she said. 'The rain's obviously making everyone stay away.'

'Shall we have a look round?' I tried to sound enthusiastic but it wasn't easy.

Liv gave me a bright, very fake, smile. 'Let's go.'

We both picked up our bags.

'Not much to see here,' Liv said. She was right. The pub was small. I imagined that in winter, with a fire in the empty fireplace and fairy lights round the bar, it could be cosy, but now it just seemed a bit bleak. It had dark wooden floorboards with flaking varnish, and equally dark tables with red velour stools and chairs. It smelled faintly of old smoke – even though no one had smoked inside a pub for more than a decade – and stale beer. The building was fairly wide and as you came through the door, the bar was in front of you and slightly to the left. A door at the back to that side had a gold sticker, half peeling off, reading "ladies" and another underneath showing it as a fire exit. To the right of the bar, there were more tables and chairs, a large television, a dartboard, and a door with no sign. Instead, someone had scrawled "men" on the wood in black marker pen.

The one saving grace of the whole place was the view from the dirty windows at the back. It was stunning. We could see for miles across the bay, from where the pub perched on top of the cliff. Way out to sea we could see bobbing lights – presumably from fishing boats or buoys – and off to the left was a lighthouse. It wasn't lit yet, though with the gloom drawing in, I thought it wouldn't be long.

'Ohhh, Liv,' I said. 'This is beautiful.'

'It feels like we're on a ship.' She knelt on one of the stools next to the window and gazed out. 'There's virtually nothing between us and the water.'

I joined her on the stool and she shoved me off. 'Get your own,' she said.

'Selfish.' I tutted as I pulled another chair closer and knelt on that instead. 'Is there a beach?'

Liv tried to see but she banged her head on the glass. 'Ouch. Can't tell.'

'We can look tomorrow when it's lighter,' I said. 'I bet there's a little path down the cliff. I might go for a swim every morning. It's an amazing location.'

Bored with the view, Liv slid off the stool and picked up the three empty pint glasses the men had left on the table – once a barmaid, always a barmaid, I thought. She put them on the bar and wandered round to the fire exit door. 'Come on, let's look upstairs,' she said.

I followed her, reluctant to drag myself away from watching the swell of the sea but not wanting to be left alone. Through the door was a corridor, leading to the ladies' loo, a fire exit straight ahead, and a flight of stairs with balding carpet.

Liv set off, taking two stairs at a time.

'So, all I know is there was some sort of family emergency or something,' she called over her shoulder. 'And the people who had been managing this place had to leave in a hurry.'

'Are they coming back?'

'Not as far as I know,' she said. 'The company's recruiting for someone to take over permanently. Shit.'

She'd gone into the first room at the top and stopped dead, and I bumped into her as I followed.

'What?'

'Look.'

Liv stood to one side to let me see. We were in the living room of the flat. It was a nice room with a big squishy sofa and the same amazing view out across the sea. What had stopped Liv short, though, were the pictures on the walls, the television in the corner, and a book face down on the coffee table.

'What. The. Fuck?' I gazed round. There was a sideboard at one end of the room, with school photos on it. A small boy with sticking-up hair grinned out at us. 'They really did leave in a hurry.'

'This is creepy as,' Liv said. I nodded, taking in all the personal belongings that had been left behind.

Liv looked upset. She picked up the book, folded down the corner of the page and put it back down again, closed. 'What on earth could have happened to make a whole family leave their home so fast?'

'No idea. Must have been a pretty bad emergency.'

'I can't believe they've left all this stuff here.' Liv stood in the middle of the room glancing from side to side, taking it all in. 'I suppose we can box it up and send it on. I'll call head office tomorrow and get a forwarding address.'

Feeling just as unsettled as Liv clearly was, I wandered into the bedrooms. The master bedroom was much the same, though the wardrobes were open and empty. The bed had linen on it and the television on the wall was on standby. A clean patch in the dust on one bedside table, though, told me the family had taken some belongings. Maybe a precious photograph or a jewellery box?

Silently, Liv and I checked out the rest of the living quarters. There were two more bedrooms. One, which had obviously been the boy's room, had toys on the floor and pictures of footballers on the walls. Again, though, the wardrobe was empty.

I shivered. This was so strange. It was like the *Marie Celeste*

41

or an episode of *Doctor Who*. I half expected David Tennant to leap out at us and make everything normal again. Or was that just wishful thinking?

The third bedroom was clearly a guest room. The linen on its twin beds was fresh and pristine, it had an en-suite bathroom, and there were no creepy abandoned personal belongings.

'Dibs this room,' Liv and I said in unison. We both looked at each other and then Liv laughed. 'Share?'

I nodded in relief. 'Share.'

We each dropped our bags on to a bed. I chose the one by the window so I could look out across the sea. Then Liv threw her arm round my shoulder. 'Welcome to The Moon Girl,' she said, using her Batman voice again. 'Fancy a drink?'

Chapter 6

Emily

1799

'Make sure you get right into the corners. That's where the dust gathers.' That evening, after our trip into Kirrinporth, Mam leaned over the bar and pointed to where I was sweeping. Deliberately, I angled the broom so it got into the little nooks and crannies she always worried about me neglecting, and made sure there was no dirt there. There wasn't. There never was. The pub was spotless.

'Good girl,' Mam said. I gave her a quick smile and carried on sweeping, though I couldn't see the point. But Mam was strange this evening. Skittish and nervy. Jumping at every sound.

A clink of glass made me look up and I saw her pouring herself a drink. Another one. She'd been drinking steadily since we'd got home, ignoring my worried glances.

I finished the sweeping and tidied away the broom, but Mam caught me by the arm as I was heading back upstairs to my room.

'Polish the brasses for me,' she said. I looked at her, wondering why she wanted me to stay. She was normally happy enough on her own. Her fingers dug into my arm. 'Won't take long, Em,' she said.

I nodded and she let me go.

'Polish is on the side.'

She handed me a cloth and with a sigh, she slumped down on to a chair, watching the door just as she had done all evening.

As I finished polishing the brass, the inn door opened, bringing the night air inside, and a man came in, stomping his feet on the doorstep and trailing mud over the freshly swept floor. I blinked in surprise at the unexpected guest. He was tall, with a travelling cape over his shoulders and a three-cornered hat pulled down low over his brow. I couldn't see his face.

'Janey Moon,' he said to Mam with a broad smile. 'It's been too long.'

Mam had stood when the door opened and now she stayed frozen on the spot, a fixed smile on her face.

'Evening,' she said. Was there a tremor in her voice? I thought so. 'I've been expecting you.'

'I didn't think you'd hold out so long,' he said. Under the shadow cast by his hat, I saw his lips twist into a smile. 'I must confess, I'm impressed.'

Mam said nothing and the man nodded. 'So, we have a deal?'

'I didn't say that.'

'You will,' he said. He pulled his hat from his head and with a terrifying start of recognition, I saw the white streak gleaming in his dark hair. This was Cal Morgan – the man who'd killed Da.

'Mam,' I squeaked, terror clenching my throat. My voice was tiny, and even in the quiet inn, it didn't carry far enough for Mam to hear. She didn't even glance in my direction; all her focus on Morgan.

'What if I don't?'

Morgan laughed. 'Why wouldn't you?' he said. 'I'm not asking you to do this for nothing, Janey. You'll be rewarded, of course. Handsomely.' He looked round. 'Seems you could do with getting some drinkers back here. I can help with that, too. When the time's right.'

Mam's head drooped, just for a second, then she pulled her shoulders back. 'Do I have a choice?'

Morgan laughed again, loudly, making me wince. 'There's always a choice, Janey.' He pulled up a chair and sat on it the wrong way round, resting his crossed arms on the back. 'But why would you say no? I'm offering you enough money that you never need to go hungry again. You and your brat of a daughter.'

For the first time, he looked round the inn and saw me standing there. His eyes rested on me for a second in a way that made me feel exposed and on display.

'Well I never,' he said. 'You're the Moon girl?'

I nodded and he smiled at me approvingly. 'All grown up, eh?'

He turned to Mam. 'I've got plenty of soldier friends who'd pay for a night with a pretty girl like that. If she was made available to them.'

Heat flooded my cheeks. I looked at Mam, but she kept her eyes fixed on Morgan.

'What are you saying?' she asked.

He stood up and took a step towards her. He towered over her as he looked down, running his eyes over her like she was a pig going to market. My mother had always been small and curvy, with wild dark hair and eyes that flashed with fun. Now she was thin and her eyes were sad, but it seemed Morgan liked what he saw.

'I'm saying you seem to have misunderstood what I'm offering,' he said. 'I'm doing you a favour, not the other way round. I'll pay you for the use of the inn, and you can make it your business to keep me happy when I'm here.'

'With drinks?' Mam said in a small voice.

'That too.' He gave her a broad smile. 'And if you won't cooperate, maybe I'll try your daughter instead.'

Mam swallowed. 'I'm sure we can come to an arrangement,' she said.

'Clever girl.'

'Should we discuss it in private?'

'I think that would be best,' Morgan said. He reached out a hand and with his thick fingers, traced a line down Mam's cheek. She stood there and let him touch her, but I knew she didn't like it. 'Just you and me,' he said. 'Come on.'

Silently, Mam turned and let him follow her out of the bar, through the door that led upstairs, and I heard the steps creaking as she took him into her room.

I stayed where I was, frozen with fear. He'd killed my father and now he was making my mother do his bidding. His nasty, twisted bidding. What I didn't understand was what he wanted the inn for. What did we have that was so precious to him that he'd kill Da and hurt Mam?

After what seemed like hours, Mam and Morgan came back downstairs. There was a red mark across Mam's cheek and her eyes were dull. She poured herself a drink and knocked it back in one gulp.

'Mr Morgan's going to be doing some business from the inn,' she said to me. Her voice was casual but she couldn't meet my gaze.

Morgan chuckled loudly.

'Business,' he said. 'That's right.' He took a pouch of money from his pocket and threw it on the bar where it landed with a loud jangle of coins. Mam's cheeks were flushed with drink or shame. I couldn't tell which. But she picked up the pouch and stuffed it in her skirt anyway.

Morgan laughed again and crossed the bar in just a couple of strides of his long legs. 'I'll be back,' he said, over his shoulder.

Mam didn't look at me. She just reached out her hand and I gave her the cloth I'd been using to polish the surfaces. 'You can go and hide in your room now,' she said. 'Do your drawing.'

I wanted to say something, but as usual, I didn't have the words. Instead I touched her lightly on the arm and then I turned and fled upstairs.

Chapter 7

Emily

1799

In my tiny room I slumped down on to the bed, thinking about what had happened. Then I pulled my box of drawings from my shelf and leafed through, looking for the pictures I'd sketched on that awful night when Da had been murdered. And there was Morgan, staring up at me from the paper, broad-shouldered and brutal, with his white stripe gleaming like a badger's fur in the moonlight. I remembered him saying that Da's missus would be easier to persuade and felt a wave of fear. Da had resisted Morgan so strongly that he'd died for his belief. He'd put up a fight and he'd lost his life. But now whatever it was had come to our doorstep anyway and Mam had to go along with it, to protect me.

I felt that fluttery panicky feeling in my chest again and pressed my hands against my sternum, trying to calm down. I breathed in deeply, in and out, in and out, as Da had taught me to do.

When I was small, Da had told me stories about a wonderful place – a new world with only a handful of people. Where there was so much space, you could travel for miles and never see another soul. Where you could load your belongings into a cart, and head off into the unknown, and build a new life for yourself, away from the bewildering rules and expectations that caused me so much worry.

Mam used to tut when he told me the stories and say: 'Stop filling the girl's head with dreams.' But I knew that Da understood how my brain worked and I thought he wouldn't have told me about this place if it wasn't real.

I'd been too big for bedtime stories for a long time, but I still thought about that place. I drew pictures of myself sitting on a cart, driving through the wilderness. And when I was scared, or overwhelmed, or things – life – just got to be too much, I would close my eyes and imagine what it would be like to live in such a quiet place, and soon I would find myself calming down.

Now, sitting in my room, breathing deeply, I thought about my place, seeing myself in my mind's eye, perched on top of my cart. Lately though, when I'd thought about it, I'd not been alone. My friend Arthur was in my dreams now too. Sitting next to me, as our horse took us to a new life far, far away from Kirrinporth.

Arthur.

He was the only person who understood me like Da had and the only person I would even think about sharing my place with. And, I thought, he could be the only person who would listen when I told him about Morgan.

I would go and see him in the morning, I decided. I'd go and tell him the truth about what had happened to Da, and see if there was any way we could bring Morgan to justice.

Feeling a tiny bit better, I crept downstairs to see what state Mam was in. She was slumped over a table, staring into the distance and she looked at me when I walked in.

'What time is it?' she mumbled.

'Time for bed.'

She didn't argue. She just let me take her by the hand and walk her upstairs to her room. Then, like an obedient little girl, she sat quietly as I helped her off with her dress and pulled her nightgown over her head.

'Emily Moon,' she said, as I pulled the blanket over her. 'You're a good girl, Emily Moon.'

A tear trickled from underneath her closed eyelids. I tried to say something back, to reassure her or comfort her, but I couldn't. So instead, I put my hand on her shoulder, very briefly, and then went to bed myself.

I was up early the next day. I laid out some bread for Mam to eat when she eventually woke, swept the floor of the mud left from Morgan's boots. Then I picked up the sketches I'd drawn on the night Da had been killed and shoved them into a bag that I slung over my shoulder. I pulled on a cloak as the weather was turning colder and then, filled with a new feeling of determination, I marched along the clifftop track towards the village. I needed help, I knew, if I was going to stop this man, this Cal Morgan, from taking more from my family. And I knew the only person who would be on my side.

I found Arthur in the churchyard, picking blackberries. His freckled face lit up when he saw me. 'Come and try these, Em,' he said. 'They're so good. I've been trying to make them sweeter for an age and I think I've done it this year.'

He held one out and I took it in my mouth, enjoying the sharpness on my tongue and then the rush of sweetness that followed. Arthur was so clever when it came to growing fruit. It was like he understood the land and how to make it produce the crispest apples and the juiciest berries.

'Delicious,' I said.

Arthur, my friend, grinned at me. 'Must be good if they're getting you talking,' he said, but he was teasing because I always talked when I was with him.

'Do you have chores? Or studying?' Arthur's father was the vicar and he was stern when it came to learning. But today was Friday and I hoped that meant Arthur didn't have to work.

Arthur shook his mop of red hair. 'Nothing. I'm free as a bird. Want to walk?'

We dropped the basket of blackberries off to the cook, Winnie, in the kitchen at the vicarage and then wandered through the village and out into the fields where we found our favourite spot under a tree and settled down.

'What's wrong?' Arthur said as soon as we were comfortable. I frowned at him. He knew me so well it was as though he could read my thoughts. 'You're jumpy and distracted and you look like you haven't slept. What's the matter?'

I bit my lip. 'Difficult.' My voice sounded croaky to my own ears.

'Take your time.'

I took a deep breath. 'Secret,' I said. 'Don't tell.'

'I promise,' Arthur said. 'You know you can trust me, Emily.'

I nodded, looking at his friendly, familiar face.

'Da was murdered,' I said, forcing the words out.

Arthur looked shocked. 'I thought he'd gone,' he said. 'That's what everyone said.'

I shook my head vigorously. 'I lied.'

'Why would you lie?'

'Scared,' I admitted. I felt the flutters in my chest again and breathed in and out, aware of Arthur's eyes on me.

I lay down the grass and stared up at the sky. Sometimes it helped me to talk if I didn't see the person who was listening.

'I saw it,' I began. I had to talk slowly, because each word was an effort. But I knew if I kept going, it would become easier. At least, that's what I hoped.

'You saw your father murdered?' Arthur said in horror. 'And you didn't say anything?'

'Da knew I was there. He told me to stay quiet; put his fingers to his lips.'

'You must have been so scared.'

'Very scared.'

There was a pause. 'Why are you telling me now?' asked Arthur.

'I know who did it.'

Arthur was quiet for so long that I turned my head to check he was still beside me.

'Who?'

'Cal Morgan,' I said.

'Who?'

I sat up suddenly. 'He came to the inn today,' I said.

'Are you sure?'

I sat up and pulled my sketchbook out of my bag. My words were coming easier now. I didn't understand why being with Arthur helped, but I was glad of it. 'I drew his face when he killed Da,' I said. 'I drew the man who killed him. And that's the man who came to the inn. He . . .' I trailed off. 'He hurt Mam.'

'You must tell someone? Mr Trewin? Or the magistrate? Get help.'

I shook my head. 'No.'

Arthur frowned. 'Why not?'

'You know.' I looked straight at him. 'You know why.'

'You don't think they'll believe you?' Arthur's kind face twisted in doubt.

'I don't,' I whispered.

'Why not?'

'Because . . .' I stopped talking, my throat tightening. I took some deep breaths. Arthur waited patiently. 'Because they think I'm simple.' I said, eventually. 'They'll say I can't talk and that I'm stupid.'

Arthur looked like he might cry. 'You can talk, though. I know that. You could talk to them and show them you're not simple.'

But I shook my head. 'I can't,' I said.

We sat there together, both deep in thought, for a while.

'Why did he come to the pub?' Arthur said.

I looked up at the sky. 'Business.'

'What kind of business?'

'Bad.'

'Criminal?'

'Maybe.'

Arthur had been lying on the grass next to me but now he sat up. 'Did he hurt you?' he said sharply.

I shook my head vigorously. 'Not me.'

'Just your mother?'

My eyes filled with tears and I nodded.

'And you have no idea what this business is?'

I shrugged. 'Bad,' I said again.

Arthur raised his eyebrows. 'Free trade?' he asked. 'Smuggling?'

I held my hands out, showing that I didn't know. I remembered the days when everyone in Kirrinporth had been involved in free trade some way or other, flocking to the beach when boats came into shore and swapping goods between each other. But times had changed and so had smuggling. It was a shady, dangerous business now, and I wasn't sure if that's what Morgan was doing.

'He'll be hanged,' said Arthur. I remembered Da worrying he'd end up on the gallows and widened my eyes. Perhaps Morgan was smuggling after all?

'I will find out,' I said quietly. 'I can watch him.'

'That's dangerous, Emily.'

I didn't answer. I knew Morgan was dangerous but I wanted to see him pay for what he'd done to my family.

'Justice,' I whispered.

'What can you do?' Arthur said. 'You're just a girl.'

I grasped his hand. 'Will you help me?'

Arthur looked at me in horror. 'Absolutely not.'

Chapter 8

Phoebe

2019

I woke up late the next day when the sun was high in the sky, fighting its way through the dirty windows of the guest bedroom where Liv and I had slept. With my eyes still half-closed, I yawned and stretched my toes, feeling well rested for the first time in months.

'Liv?' I whispered, turning over so I could see her bed. But she was up – her bed was neatly made and now I realised I could hear music coming from the kitchen. I bounced out of my own bed, leaving the duvet messily strewn across it, and went to find my friend. She was sitting at the kitchen table in her pyjamas, hunched over her laptop and frowning.

'Hello, sleepy,' she said. 'You were dead to the world when I got up.'

'Morning.' I leaned over her shoulder and peered at the screen. 'What are you doing?'

'Trying to get into my emails so I can find out more about this sodding pub,' she said. 'There's coffee in one of those jars on the side if you want some. But there's no milk.'

I flicked the kettle on and turned back to Liv. 'What do you need to know?'

'Some accounts would be handy,' she said. 'Staff records. Sales figures. I literally know nothing about the place.'

'A forwarding address for the family who lived here would be useful, too,' I said. The kettle boiled and I dumped a large spoonful of instant coffee into a mug and poured some water on top. 'Have you emailed your head office? Have they replied? What do they say?'

'They say nothing,' she said. 'Because there is apparently no Wi-Fi here, or it's been disconnected, and my phone's got no signal. And I've phoned on the landline but the temporary staff manager, Bobby, is in a meeting first thing. And the regional manager for Cornwall, whose name is Des, isn't answering his phone.'

I made a face. 'So we're in the dark?'

'Totally.' Liv sighed. 'I'm going to go into the village and see if I can get Wi-Fi somewhere. If I can log on then I can get sales information from the pub's tills, and staff records too. Do you want to come?'

I shook my head. 'I'm not properly awake yet. I'll stay here for now. Maybe I'll go and explore later.'

'Good stuff.' Liv closed her laptop and stood up. 'Listen, come downstairs with me, will you? And lock the door behind me with the bolt?'

'Really?'

She shrugged, looking a bit embarrassed. 'It's just weird here. I'll feel better knowing you're locked in.'

'Unless there's a fire,' I said. 'Then I'll be in trouble.'

Liv shuddered. 'Don't.'

I was surprised she was so spooked; it was very unlike her. 'I'll be fine,' I said, wanting to reassure her. 'I'm a police officer, Liv. Nothing's going to happen to me.'

'Sure you'll be okay?'

'I'm sure. I'll sort upstairs out a bit, and when you're back, I'll go and explore.'

'Right then, I'll get going.'

I followed Liv downstairs to the empty pub, let her out of the front door and then locked it behind her. I even checked I'd done it right. Her being rattled was rubbing off on me.

It was sunny outside, but in the pub it was cool and dim. It made me shiver. I never liked pubs when they were closed – I thought they needed people and laughter and chatter to bring them to life. Liv always said she liked the smell, which I thought was odd. Stale beer and cold chips didn't do it for me. But that was why I wasn't a pub manager and she was.

I looked round the large bar. It was clearly a very old building. I wondered what stories its walls could tell, and then rolled my eyes at my romantic notions and went back upstairs for a shower.

After I'd showered and dressed and unpacked a bit, I threw open all the windows upstairs. I could hear the waves crashing on the rocks below and smell the salt. From our bedroom I could see little boats bobbing about on the water and a larger ship moving slowly across the horizon. It was very pretty and summery and I sighed in satisfaction. Liv had been so right to persuade me to come here.

I pottered about happily for a while, arranging my clothes in the wardrobe, and then I went into the living room and felt my good mood dip. It was so creepy that everything had been left exactly as it had been. Who moves house and leaves virtually all their belongings behind? Someone in a hurry, I thought. Someone who thinks leaving is more important than any possessions. Maybe there was a proper reason. A fire or a gas leak or something. But nothing looked charred, and though I breathed in deeply through my nose, I couldn't smell anything toxic.

Perhaps it had been an emergency elsewhere. An elderly parent who'd had an accident or something similar. It didn't really matter,

I supposed, but we police officers were nothing if not nosy and I wanted to know what had gone on.

For now, though, I wanted to pack up all the things that belonged to the family who'd lived here before. I went downstairs to the bar, hoping there would be some boxes, and was relieved when I found a few flattened and stacked behind the crisps. I'd been worried I'd have to go into the cellar and I hadn't been thrilled at the thought.

It was gloomy in the pub and a glance out the window told me the sky was darkening again as rain clouds gathered over the sea.

'Great,' I said out loud. Still, at least I hadn't been planning to go anywhere. I took my boxes upstairs and as the raindrops began splattering against the window, I started carefully packing up all the possessions that had been left behind. I winced a little at the school photos, which reminded me of the picture we'd circulated of Ciara James when she went missing, so I laid them in the box face down because I couldn't bear to see them every time I put something else away.

I filled two boxes and was just starting on the third and wondering when Liv might be back, when I heard knocking at the pub door. Ah ha. There she was. I ran down the stairs and opened the door, cautiously in case it wasn't her.

It wasn't. Instead, Ewan – the man who'd been here yesterday – stood there, filling the doorframe. He gave me a broad smile.

'Olivia Palmer?'

Immediately I went on the alert, though I wasn't sure exactly why. It seemed I was as spooked as Liv was.

I matched his grin. 'Afraid not,' I said. 'She's popped out. Can I help?'

'Olivia's the temporary manager, right?'

'Right.' My smile didn't falter. My first ever sergeant always said the best weapon an officer had was their charm.

'I did a bit of business with Mike Watson,' Ewan said. 'The old landlord.'

'Right,' I said again. I didn't want to engage him in conversation because all my police officer senses were tingling and I had already decided I didn't trust this man. I knew this was part of my reaction to Ciara's death but I still didn't want to give him any more information than I had to. So instead I just kept quiet.

'I wanted a quick chat with Olivia about it.'

'Great,' I said. My smile was so wide it almost split my face in two. 'That sounds great. I'll let her know. Nice to meet you.'

I went to shut the door but Ewan moved his foot so I couldn't. Over his shoulder I could see his two henchmen, standing at the bottom of the stairs up to the car park like two bookends. One of them was about Ewan's age – late forties perhaps or even early fifties. He had broad shoulders and a bald head and was watching my conversation with Ewan with an air of amusement. The other man was younger – nearer to me in age. He had a beard and longish hair that was swept back. He looked more like he should be hanging out in hipster bars in south London than in this isolated Cornish clifftop and, I couldn't help but notice, he was very easy on the eye. He caught me looking and grinned at me, sending heat to my face immediately.

'Sorry,' Ewan said. He moved his foot a fraction. 'Didn't mean to get in your way.'

'No problem.'

'Will she be back soon?'

'Who?'

'Olivia.'

'No idea,' I said honestly, hoping Liv wouldn't choose that moment to come round the corner in her car. 'We'll be up and running in a few days. Why not come back then?'

'I'd rather wait and see her now.' He flashed me another smile. 'If that's okay?'

I felt a flicker of fear. I may have been fit but if these men decided they wanted to come inside then there was nothing I could do about it. I thought of my old sergeant again and decided to try to talk my way out of it.

'Of course,' I said. I made to open the door wider, and then stopped. 'Oh bum, I forgot I've got to Skype my boss. Sorry. Maybe another time?'

'You can make your call; we won't bother you,' Ewan said.

'I'm afraid I can't risk you overhearing,' I said. 'It's private.'

'It is?'

I nodded gravely. 'I shouldn't tell you this but I work in television and I'm on the lookout for a location to film a new show,' I said. 'I know I can trust you not to say anything because if the locals find out, they'll go crazy.' I tried to sound weary. 'This is the fourth location I've tried. If this one goes wrong, I might lose my job.'

'Television, eh?' Ewan said, looking impressed. 'Like *Poldark*?'

'We're hoping even bigger than that. Could be huge.' I lowered my voice. 'We've got American money.'

'Sounds interesting.'

'It could be.'

I waited expectantly and thank goodness, he took the hint.

'I'll let you get on.' He moved his foot and I took the chance to shut the door a bit more.

'Must go. I'll tell Liv you called.'

'Tell her Ewan wants to chat,' he said. He moved away from the door and I fixed the smile on my face, hoping I didn't appear too relieved. Ewan put a business card into my hand. 'Ewan Logan,' he said.

He strode off up the stairs, his boots splashing in the puddles, and the bald man followed, matching his stride. The younger one had been leaning against the metal bannister on the stone steps. Now he peeled himself off and smiled at me.

'I'm Jed,' he said.

The effect he had on me was immediate. Again. I felt all tingly and my stomach flipped over. Jed looked at me, slightly

58

quizzically, and I felt my face flame. 'I'm Phoebe,' I croaked. 'Nice to meet you.'

Jed gave me a wonky smile which, in my opinion, added to his good looks. 'Are you staying here too?'

'I'm a friend of Liv's,' I said, trying to be cool. 'Thought it would nice to hang with her for a while.'

'How long's a while?'

I swallowed. 'Most of the summer.'

He grinned again. 'Sounds good. I guess I'll see you around, then.'

He took the stairs two at a time, bounding up them with his long legs. I watched him go, noting how his skinny hipster jeans hugged his bum. At the top of the stairs the bald man nudged him, and gestured to me, obviously teasing Jed about hanging back to talk to me. I pretended I hadn't noticed as I shut the pub door, but I was secretly glad. Because that meant I hadn't imagined the spark that was between us.

I drew the bolt across the door, still smiling, and then shook myself. Jed may be really hot but there was something odd about the way these men were sniffing round the pub. It was entirely possible they were up to no good. What on earth was I doing lusting after one of them so brazenly? Still, I couldn't help hoping, as I heard their car engine start, that I'd see Jed again soon.

Chapter 9

Phoebe

2019

As soon as Liv came back I pounced on her. I was feeling on edge and nervy after the visitors that morning and I wanted to know what she'd found out.

'How was it?' I said, as I let her in and carefully locked the door behind her. 'What did head office say?'

Liv waved a carton of milk at me. 'Put the kettle on first, eh?'

She trailed upstairs, shoulders slouched, and I felt sorry for her. She'd been so excited about coming here, and totally convinced it would be the perfect place for both of us and it clearly wasn't working out the way she'd planned.

I made tea for us both and took the mugs into the lounge. Liv was lying on the sofa, playing with the little dove on her bracelet.

'You've done a good job packing away the stuff,' she said.

I nodded, putting her mug down on the table in front of her. 'I just wanted it gone. It was giving me the creeps. Did you get anywhere with a forwarding address? I've boxed most of it up so we can send it. Though it'll cost a fortune.'

Liv winced, and sat up, reaching for her mug. 'And a fortune is one thing we definitely don't have.'

'Meaning?'

'Meaning this pub is a money pit. I'd never have taken the position if I'd seen the accounts first – and head office know that. I'm sure that's why it was all so last-minute.' She frowned, looking round at the now bare lounge. 'The HR manager knows nothing about why it all happened so fast, but he's temporary so he didn't deal with the family that were here before.'

'Could they have been stealing?' I said, thinking of Ewan Logan and his friends. 'Could the old landlord have been taking cash out of the business and that's why it's in trouble?'

'The thought crossed my mind,' Liv said. 'But I spoke to the regional manager – Des – and he swears this Watson was a sound bloke. Honest as they come, he said.'

'Maybe they just ran out of cash.'

'More like it.' Liv groaned. 'It's really bad, Phoebe.'

'Don't worry, we can live on a budget for the summer. It might be quite fun.'

But Liv was shaking her head. 'Really bad,' she whispered.

I sat down next to her. 'Tell me.'

'Remember when Niall left, I was worried he'd been cheating?'

I nodded, not sure why we were talking about Liv's loser ex now. 'He was being so shifty but you said he was just worried about the break-up.'

'I lied,' Liv said. 'He wasn't cheating but he was keeping secrets. After he'd gone, I discovered he'd run up so much debt on credit cards that it was eye-watering.'

I shrugged. 'So? That's his problem.'

'Some of the cards were his own, but a lot of the debt is in my name,' Liv said. 'I was so stupid, Phoebe. I let him look after all the money, because I hate doing stuff like that and it was easier just to give him access to everything.'

'Oh, Liv,' I said.

She made a face. 'You always say I can't cope with real life. Guess you were right.'

'I was joking.' I felt bad that my off-hand quips had made her feel worse, but also that I had actually been right. Liv was bright and savvy and knew how to handle a balance sheet in the pub – how had she made such an error of judgement?

'Don't look at me like that,' she said.

'Like what?'

'Like you're disappointed in me.'

I forced my face into a more neutral expression. 'I'm not disappointed,' I lied. 'Just worried.'

Liv twirled some of her curls around her finger. 'The worst thing is, I knew,' she said, almost to herself. 'Deep down I knew that my salary and his wouldn't cover the lifestyle we had. But I never questioned anything.'

'Have you asked him to pay you back?'

'I don't even know where he is. I think he went to stay with his dad's family in Ireland, but he was always talking about moving to the States. Perhaps he's gone there. I was an idiot.'

'You trusted him.'

She nodded. 'I did, and now I owe thousands of pounds.'

'Why didn't you tell me, Liv? I could have done something. Spoken to the fraud team even. Surely it's illegal to open credit cards in someone else's name?'

'It probably is if you do it on the sly, but he told me what he was doing and I signed everything he asked me to.'

'Oh, Liv,' I said. 'How could you be so . . .' I stopped talking, but it was obvious what I'd been about to say.

'Stupid?' She looked at me, on the defensive suddenly. 'You're right. I was stupid. He made out like he was being really savvy – moving balances to cheaper cards and saving us loads. I didn't ask any questions. I just went along with it all. So there was nothing you could have done.'

'Still should have told me.'

'I was embarrassed,' she said, looking down at her knees. 'And you had a lot on your plate.'

'I never have so much on my plate that I don't have time for you, Liv. You know that.'

'I know.' She sighed. 'But we Palmer women are nothing if not hard workers, right? My mum and my grandma are proper grafters. So I thought, the best way to get myself out of this trouble would be to work through it and I thought a summer in a busy tourist pub would be enough to sort me out. I thought I'd make enough that I'd get a bonus and I could pay off a big chunk of the debt and get myself back on track.'

'It was a good idea.' I meant it. 'Working hard is always the best way.'

She snorted. 'I negotiated a share of any above-average profits,' she said. 'Told them I was dropping down a level to take this pub on and they had to make it worth my while. Bloody Des, the sodding regional manager, must have been rubbing his hands in glee.'

'And he never said how badly the pub was doing?'

'Not a thing.'

'That's really shonky.'

'The pub's doing so badly that I asked him why it wasn't marked for closure but he just said it would pick up and there were plans.'

'Maybe it will pick up,' I said. 'Maybe it's just the bad weather.'

'And whatever happened to send the Watson family packing.'

'That bloke was here earlier,' I said, wondering if Ewan Logan had anything to do with why the other landlord left. 'The one from yesterday. He knew your name and he said he'd had some business with the old landlord.'

'Oh okay,' said Liv. 'If he knew my name then maybe he's a local supplier or something.'

I made a face. 'He seems a bit off but he gave me his card.' I eased it out of my back pocket where I'd shoved it that morning and looked at it. It just said Ewan Logan with a mobile number underneath. I handed it to Liv and she took it, looking at both sides quizzically.

'I'll give him a ring,' she said.

'Just be a bit wary,' I warned and she grinned.

'If there's one thing this shit with Niall has taught me, it's not to trust anyone.'

I gave her a hug. 'You may be crap with money, Liv, but you're an excellent pub manager and I reckon it's going to be okay.'

'How would you know?' Liv said, but she was smiling.

'I know.' I hoped I was right, because I'd seen how debt could spiral and get people into more and more difficult situations. But Liv seemed on top of things, didn't she? I made a mental note to keep an eye on her, but I was sure she'd be fine. I got up. 'Right, if you're done with the car for now, I think I might go for a drive and see if I can find the nearest supermarket. I'll get some food for the week and perhaps something nice for dinner?'

Liv grinned at me. 'Sounds good,' she said.

It was the first time I'd stepped outside The Moon Girl in the daylight and I had to admit the location was astonishing. The pub was perched on a clifftop where a narrow piece of land jutted out into the dark grey sea. If you stood with your back to the pub and the ocean behind it, you would be facing the road into the small town called Kirrinporth that was the nearest bit of civilisation. The road bent round to the left, past the pub, and ran along parallel to the cliffs towards the larger market town I'd seen on the map last night. In between the road and the sheer drop to the sea, was a wide expanse of bright green grass, dotted with large rocky boulders. And behind the road were trees, which were now swaying as the wind got up.

Standing in the car park, I breathed in deeply, appreciating the fresh air after London. Yes, it was definitely strange here and it wasn't quite what we'd expected, but it wasn't all bad.

Google maps told me there was a supermarket not far along the main road to my left, so I headed there. The selection wasn't great, compared with the huge superstore at home, but it was good enough. I loaded up with basics – more teabags, coffee and milk, a loaf of bread, eggs, pasta, some fruit and veg – and chose a chicken to roast for dinner. Comfort food, I thought. Liv and I could both do with some of that.

I trundled the trolley across the car park and started unloading bags into Liv's small boot, shoving her gym bag and a pair of wellies which, I thought with a wry smile, she'd probably be glad she'd brought, to one side so I could fit it all in.

'Location scouting?' a voice said behind me. I jumped and turned to see the younger man from the pub – Jed – smiling at me. My stomach twisted as I took in his tight black T-shirt, which was hugging his broad chest in a most satisfactory fashion.

He was looking at me in a way that suggested he expected me to talk to him, rather than just gaze at his muscles, so I swallowed. 'Location scouting?' I said, quite breathlessly.

'To get your boss off your back?'

'My boss . . .' His good looks may have got me distracted but what on earth was he talking about? Did he mean DI Blair?

'You said you had to make a call,' Jed said. His expression had changed from mild interest to concern. 'Are you okay?'

'A call,' I said as my white lie came back to me. 'Of course.'

'So did you? Find a location?'

I shut the boot with a thud and leaned against the car. 'Noooo,' I said. 'No luck there. Nothing doing.'

'That's a shame – would be good to have some more interest in the area,' Jed said. 'We could do with some of that *Poldark* magic.'

I frowned. 'That was Cornwall wasn't it?'

'It was, but it was filmed up the road a bit. Not far but far enough that we've not really had any of the boost in tourism,' he said. 'More's the pity.'

'It does seem quiet.'

'It comes and goes,' he said. Then he looked at me, making my cheeks flush. 'So will you be moving on now you've not got a location?'

God, I knew nothing about TV. Why on earth had I said

that? Luckily I saw a get-out and took it. 'Actually, no,' I said. 'I've decided to take some time off and help Liv out at the pub.'

Jed looked pleased. 'Great,' he said. 'That's really great. I'm pleased about that.'

He made to walk off and suddenly desperate to keep talking to him, I said: 'You're a regular, then? At The Moon Girl?'

'A regular,' he said. He looked like he was amused by a joke that only he understood, which irritated me a bit. 'I guess you could call it that.'

'With Ewan Logan, and your other mate?' I stood up a bit straighter.

'Mark.'

'With Ewan Logan and Mark?'

'Why do you care?'

'I don't,' I said. He was properly starting to annoy me now. 'I'm just interested. Liv's worried the pub wasn't very busy when we arrived.'

Jed was looking at me curiously. 'Has she opened?'

'Not yet,' I admitted. 'I think Liv's planning to open tomorrow evening. There's a football match on so she thought people would come to watch.'

'She's right,' Jed said.

'Will you spread the word a bit? Tell people we're opening?'

'Well, I'm not sure what I can do . . .'

'Please, I'd really appreciate it.'

He shrugged. 'I'll mention it to some mates.'

'Thanks.'

We stood there for a second. I felt a bit awkward though I wasn't sure why. He was odd, this man. Friendly one minute, then prickly when I mentioned his friends.

'I'd better go,' I said. 'I've got ice cream. Don't want it to melt.'

Jed looked up at the darkening sky and then straight at me. 'Not much chance of that,' he said. 'Bye, Phoebe.'

As I got into the car, I was smiling. He'd remembered my name.

Chapter 10

Emily

1799

Mam was drunk. And for once, I didn't blame her because Morgan had been to the inn again. She had been skittish all afternoon before he arrived. Nervy. Snapping at me when I got under her feet so I retreated to my bedroom to brood. I'd tried to persuade Arthur to help me come up with a way to find out what Morgan wanted with the pub. Or to stop him hurting my mother, or even think of a way to prove he was the man who killed my father, but Arthur said gently that maybe it was too late for that. That I should have said something when Da was killed, because now no one would believe me. I had a horrible feeling that he was right, but how could I rest when my father's murderer was lurking round the inn, and doing goodness knows what with my mother?

I'd stayed in my room most of the day, wincing every time I heard the clinking as Mam poured herself another drink. I watched the sea and the birds, and sketched the boats that bobbed about on the waves. There were a lot of boats out there, I thought. And one or two seemed closer to shore than usual. Apart from the fishermen, most boats and ships just skirted the Lizard and sailed on by Kirrinporth on their way to Falmouth or up the river to Truro. Today, though, there were more, even though it was a gloomy day with the clouds gathering over the water and the waves swelling bigger and bigger. I looked out at the sea again and shivered. I loved living so close to the water but sometimes it scared me.

Downstairs, I could hear Mam banging about so I closed my sketchbook and went to find her. The inn was empty and she was draped across the bar, head resting on her outstretched arm, while the other hand held a glass of something. Rum? Brandy? It didn't matter to me – she'd clearly had a lot of it whatever it was, even though the sun was still in the sky.

She looked up at me through bleary eyes.

'Emily,' she said. 'Are you hungry?'

I nodded and tugged her sleeve gently to get her to move. Unsteadily, she stood up, and grasping my hand, followed me obediently to the kitchen at the back of the inn. I let her slump down at the table and set about trying to find some food. The shelves were mostly bare, but we still had some cheese and bread in the pantry so I cut chunks and put them on a plate then I sat down too and pushed the plate towards Mam.

'Is there anything to drink?' she asked.

Sighing, I got up again, filled a mug with water and put it down in front of her with a thud. Some of the water spilled on to the table and Mam traced the drops with her finger. I pushed the plate nearer again and she picked up a slice of bread and nibbled it. I took a piece of cheese.

Eventually, when all the food was eaten, Mam spoke. 'Morgan said he'd come today but he didn't.'

I nodded. I'd assumed that was why she'd been so jumpy. I was glad he'd not arrived. I didn't want him looking at Mam the way he did. Touching her with his big hands. Drooling over her like how Tully had drooled over the pig's ears my father gave him.

A tear rolled down Mam's cheek. 'I miss him, Emily.'

I took her hand and squeezed it. I knew where this was going; I'd heard her say the same words so many times since Da died.

'I loved him,' Mam said. 'And he loved me. He did. He loved me. "You're my girl, Janey," he would say to me.'

She grimaced. 'Was he lying?' she said, her voice harsh from the drink. 'Was he stringing me along? I know we rowed but I don't understand why he'd leave, if he loved me like he said.'

She looked at me, her face ugly and twisted suddenly. 'I don't understand why he'd leave me here with this inn a millstone round my neck.'

I winced at her sadness, wishing I could take it away. Make her feel better.

Mam pushed the cup of water away and more slopped on to the table.

'I can't drink this,' she said. She got up and wobbled out of the kitchen, hitting her hip on the chair as she went. I got up and followed her as she went back into the front of the inn, ricocheting off the wall on the way. She took a bottle of rum from the side and sloshed some into a glass. I put out my hand, trying to stop her.

'What?' she said. 'Want some?'

I shook my head.

'Nah. Course you don't.'

She swigged from the glass and I stared at her, wondering where the old Mam, the one who'd laughed and danced round the inn with Da, had gone.

'Don't look at me like that, Emily,' she said. 'I'm doing the best I can.'

Suddenly out of energy, she slumped down heavily on a chair and began to sob. 'I'm doing the best I can,' she said again, groggily this time. Her head nodded and jerked, and then dropped on to the table in front of her.

I knew that she'd fall asleep soon and that her head would

hurt when she woke up so I stroked her hair and nudged her to keep her awake. Then I pulled her arm and like a child she let me take her upstairs to her bedroom. I helped her take off her dress and when she lay down in bed I pulled the blanket over her. With her eyes drooping, she looked up at me.

'You're a good girl, Emily,' she said. 'What would I do without you?'

I smiled and gently brushed her cheek, which was wet with tears.

'I don't want you to worry,' Mam went on. 'Morgan will see us right. I know he will.'

I froze with my hand still on Mam's face and shook my head. He wouldn't see us right. How could he, when he was the reason we were struggling so much?

Mam snuggled down into the pillow. 'He's not a bad man, Emily. He's just trying to make a living. He'll take care of us.'

My throat felt tight and narrow. I gasped in air and tried to speak but nothing happened. I tried again. 'Mam . . .' The word was croaky and stilted but it made her eyes snap open. I took a deep breath. There was so much I wanted to say about Morgan, but all I could manage was: 'Bad.'

Mam's hand shot out from under the blankets and grabbed my hair, yanking my head painfully downwards.

'Stop it,' she said. 'You know how things were. You know how bad it had got and how no one would help us. Morgan is offering us a way out and he's the only chance I've got of putting food in your belly. I know he's not perfect but he's the only one round here bothering with us, and he's not going to up and leave like your da did.'

I wriggled around so she would let go of me and stood up out of her reach. It had gone so far now that I didn't know if telling her the truth would hurt her more. How would she feel if she knew she'd let the man who killed her husband into her bed? If she knew there was no chance of Da ever coming home. So I stood there and looked at her, taking in the bruises round her wrists and her dark eyes that were dull and hopeless. And then I turned and walked out of the room, leaving her on her own.

I stood at the top of the stairs for a minute, listening in case Mam called out for me. But she was quiet, so rubbing my hair where she'd pulled it, I went back down to the inn to lock up for the night. There were no customers. It was dark now and quiet on the clifftop. All I could hear was the waves crashing down below. And a shout. Then another. I opened the door and stepped outside into the night. The earlier rain had stopped but the clouds covered the moon and it was as black as the dead of night, though it wasn't late. I stood still listening. There was nothing.

Carefully, I walked round to the side of the inn and looked out over the dark sea. No. No sign of anyone or anything. But as I turned to go back inside, a light on the cliff to my right caught my eye, glowing red through the darkness. It wasn't a house – there was nothing there – but there was definitely a steady glow from somewhere. Was it a lantern? I wasn't sure. Squinting through the night I tried to see if there was someone there but it was impossible to make out any shapes in the gloom.

I felt the hairs on the back of my neck stand up. And then I heard a wail, like the yowl of a cat or a woman in pain. With a gasp, my heart thumping, I darted back inside the inn and slammed the door shut, sliding the locks across with trembling fingers. What was that noise? Was someone hurt? Should I help? Quickly, I ran up the stairs, looking in on Mam to check it hadn't been her crying out, but she slept peacefully.

In my bedroom, I went to the window and looked out. On the cliff I could see an ethereal glow – different from the glow earlier and sort of other-worldly. I'd seen it before, that phosphorescent glimmer, and it always made me shiver. Again I felt that prickle on the back of my neck. Something was very strange here, I thought as I picked up my sketch book and quickly sketched an outline of the cliffs, to remind me where the odd lights were; I wanted to tell Arthur all about them when I had a chance.

I put that paper aside, and hunching down in my blankets, I began to draw another picture of Arthur and me on top of our cart, heading out into the wild to build a new life together. We'd be safe there, I thought. Safer than we were here.

Chapter 11

Mam was like a bear with a sore head the next morning. I wasn't much better. I'd barely slept all night, watching the strange lights on the clifftop and trying to draw them so I could show Arthur.

While I was sweeping the floor, lulled half to sleep by the rhythmic swishing of the broom, Mam tutted at me.

'You're no use to me today,' she said, wrenching the brush from my hands. 'Go and fetch me some meat for dinner.'

I was surprised. We ate little meat, because it was so expensive. Mam saw my expression.

'You know I've got the money,' she said. Then as she saw understanding on my face, she added, almost smugly: 'Morgan isn't so bad when he puts food in our bellies, is he?'

She dropped some coins into my outstretched hand and I put them into my pocket.

'Don't hurry back,' she said.

I stared at her, searching for the right words and not finding them. Mam turned away from me, swirling her skirt, as though she was at a ball. But as I watched her go, her shoulders slumped. I knew she was trying to talk herself into feeling happy with this arrangement with Morgan. But she wasn't. How could she be?

For now, though, I wanted to see Arthur and tell him all about the lights I'd seen on the cliff. I gathered my sketch book and hurried off into the village to find him.

He was in the church with his father, stacking hymn books.

'Hello, Emily,' said Reverend Pascoe. I nodded to him, feeling my throat closing up. He smiled. He was a kind man, I always thought, though Arthur said he was weak. 'Was it me you wanted, or my son?' I gestured to Arthur and the vicar smiled again. 'Why don't you and Emily finish up here, Arthur?'

'Will do,' Arthur said. He handed me some books. 'Let's get started.'

His father said goodbye and I waited as his footsteps echoed through the empty church and out through the vestry, before I spoke.

'There were lights on the cliff last night.'

Arthur looked interested. 'Did you draw them?'

I pulled out my sketchbook and showed him. He looked carefully at my drawings, asking questions. 'Have you seen these lights before?'

I nodded. 'When I was a little girl.' I licked my lips, trying to stop my voice from drying out. 'The light was red this time. It was yellow light before, like from a candle.'

'It was a full moon last night,' Arthur said.

I nodded. 'But cloudy. It was really dark,' I told him. I waved my hand in front of my face, showing him how black the night had been.

Arthur nodded, understanding what I meant. He looked down at the picture again, pointing to the glow I'd captured. 'What's this?' he asked.

'A glow,' I said. 'Not the red light.' I thought for a moment. 'Other-worldly.'

'Other-worldly?' Arthur raised an eyebrow.

I tugged his sleeve and pointed to the stained-glass window that showed the Angel Gabriel appearing to Mary. 'Like an angel.'

'Do you think it was a spirit?' Arthur's eyes were wide.

I chuckled, knowing it sounded ridiculous, and shrugged. That was what it had looked like, but there had to be a more realistic explanation.

Arthur straightened the pile of hymnbooks. 'We should go,' he said. 'See what's up there.'

'To the clifftop?'

'Yes.'

I felt a shiver of fear. The cliffs were unstable and the sea below was rough. I shook my head.

'We won't go near the edge, Em.'

'It's not a spirit.'

'Then what is it?' Arthur's eyes gleamed with curiosity.

'Morgan,' I said.

Arthur sighed. 'Really? How could these lights have anything to do with him?'

I thought for a moment. 'Because,' I said, slowly. 'The lights were there when Da died.'

'Right . . .'

'And now. Again.' It seemed more than a coincidence to me, but Arthur didn't seem to be persuaded.

'You said it was a spirit from another world.'

I shook my head. I'd said it *looked* like a spirit, not that it *was* something unearthly.

Arthur grinned. 'So let's go up on the cliffs,' he said.

I nodded, as the banging of the church door made us both jump.

'Why would you want to go up on the cliffs?' a voice said.

Arthur made a face at me and then put on his best vicar's son smile. 'Hello there, Mr Trewin,' he said.

'Hello, young Arthur,' Mr Trewin said. He was a rotund man with a large moustache and ruddy cheeks. He looked healthy and well-fed, unlike me with my hollow cheeks and bony arms. I looked at Mr Trewin's round belly and remembered the shame my mother and I had felt when she'd asked for his help and he'd not given it. I didn't trust him one tiny bit, and I disliked him even more. 'I was looking for your father but I heard you talking.'

He looked at me through narrowed eyes. 'Cat got your tongue, Emily Moon?'

I dropped my gaze, feeling my throat clench. I couldn't speak to him now even if I wanted to.

Mr Trewin raised his bushy eyebrows and then turned his attention back to Arthur. 'Why would you be going up on the cliffs? They're not safe, you know.'

Arthur shrugged. 'Emily likes to draw. We wanted to look at the view. We're not going to go close to the edge.'

'That's what they all say,' Mr Trewin said. 'Before they fall.'

I felt a shiver down my spine. What did he mean? It sounded like a threat. But surely not?

Beside me, Arthur stood up straighter. 'It's nice of you to be concerned but we've grown up here. We know this area well and we won't take any risks.'

Mr Trewin nodded. 'Of course you do,' he said. Then he grinned. 'Do you know the stories?'

Arthur and I exchanged a look. 'Stories?' Arthur said.

'About the spirits that walk along the clifftop on dark nights?'

Again we looked at each other, but this time I saw a flash of fear in Arthur's eyes. He swallowed. 'There are no such thing as spirits,' he said. His voice had a quiver in it and I saw his glance dart to my sketchbook. 'That's a tall tale.'

Mr Trewin sat down in a pew. 'Ah but it's a good one. Want to hear it?'

I nodded enthusiastically, sitting down in the pew in front of him and turning round on the smooth wooden bench so I could look at him. Arthur followed me, more reluctantly.

'Years ago when my father was a boy, there was a beautiful young woman who lived in Kirrinporth,' Mr Trewin began. 'She was like you, Emily Moon, with blonde hair and pale eyes.'

I smiled, despite myself. I knew this story was silly but I liked hearing it.

'What was her name?' Arthur said.

'Her name was Theodora,' Mr Trewin said. 'And she had a sweetheart, did Theodora. A young man called Diggory.'

'Diggory and Theodora?' Arthur said, sounding sceptical. 'All right. So what happened to them?'

'They loved each other very much, but Theodora's father was strict and had promised her to another,' said Mr Trewin. 'The young lovers were forced to meet in secret, on the clifftop where Emily's inn now stands.'

He lowered his voice, forcing Arthur and I to lean in towards him so we could hear his story.

'One dark night, when the clouds covered the moon, Theodora and Diggory arranged to meet on the top of the cliff. But it was so dark, they couldn't find each other and they had no lamps.'

He paused and impatiently I tugged his sleeve to make him carry on.

'As they looked for each other on the dark, dark clifftop, first Theodora and then Diggory plummeted into the sea and died.'

I breathed out slowly. What a sad story. But Mr Trewin wasn't finished.

'Now, on dark nights, it's said the young lovers walk the clifftops, carrying ghostly lanterns to entice others up. But if anyone ventures on to the path, they're pushed to their deaths so they can suffer like Diggory and Theodora did. Sometimes you can even see the couple walking along the edge of cliff, their unworldly figures glowing in the night, and their spirits doomed to roam the earth forever.'

He raised his voice as he said 'forever' and the word bounced around the echoey church.

Wide-eyed with fear, I looked at Arthur. Had it been Theodora and Diggory's spirits I'd seen on the clifftop last night?

Arthur shivered dramatically. 'Poor Diggory,' he said. 'What a sad tale, Mr Trewin.'

Mr Trewin nodded. 'I'd stay away from the cliffs if I were you.'

'We will, sir,' Arthur said. 'Thank you.'

Mr Trewin edged his solid frame out of the pew. 'Where might I find your father?'

'He went home, I believe,' said Arthur politely. 'I'm sure he'll be glad to see you. Come, Emily, let's finish these hymn books.'

We both slid along the pew and went back to the books we'd already stacked once. I wasn't sure what Arthur was doing but I followed his lead as Mr Trewin said goodbye to us and left the church, letting the heavy door bang shut behind him.

As soon as he'd gone, I took a moment to gather myself, waiting for my throat to unclench. 'Arthur,' I said carefully. 'We can't go on the cliff. What about Theodora and Diggory?'

Arthur shook his head and frustrated I sighed. 'You heard the story Mr Trewin told.'

'He made it up,' said Arthur. 'He must have heard us talking about the lights and made it up.'

'Why would he do that?'

'I don't know. He clearly doesn't want us to go up on the cliffs for some reason. Maybe he's just protective, or maybe there's something else going on. But either way, he made it up.'

'How do you know?' I said. 'He sounded very convincing.'

Arthur took my hand and, enjoying the feeling of his fingers in mine, I let him lead me to the side of the church, close to where we'd been sitting.

'Look,' he said, pointing to a memorial stone in the wall. 'He was facing this as he was talking.'

I looked at the stone he was showing me. Along the top on the memorial it said DIGGORY and beneath were listed the names of the Diggory family who'd died several years before. The first name was the family's baby daughter, Theodora.

Astonished, I gasped.

'He read the names from the stone,' Arthur said. 'Diggory and Theodora are figments of his imagination.'

I nodded and squeezed Arthur's hand, which I was still holding. 'Let's go,' I said.

'Go where?'

'To the cliffs.'

Chapter 12

Phoebe

2019

Liv and I went into Kirrinporth on the morning of the pub opening. Like everything else so far, it was totally different to what I'd expected. Disappointing, in fact. I'd pictured a sweet seaside village winding up the hill from the sea, with quirky little shops, perhaps some cobbled streets. Maybe even some bunting. What I got was a small town that could have been anywhere in England – right down to the Co-op on the corner and the weather-beaten Costa on the seafront. If it hadn't been for the deserted beach, with one miserable-looking family perched under an umbrella while their kids dug in the sand, we could have been in any corner of South-East London.

'There's a fish and chip shop,' I said, trying to find something positive to say.

Liv had nodded. 'I went in there yesterday actually. Because I can't afford to do food at The Moon Girl right now, I thought we might be able to do a deal where I take orders from customers and they deliver fish and chips.'

'That's a great idea. What did they say?'

'They said no.' Liv shrugged. 'So I'm just going to buy a load of crisps from the Co-op and put them on the tables for tonight and worry about the food later.'

'We could do sandwiches, perhaps?' I suggested. 'Even I can manage to put together a ham sarnie.'

We'd wandered round the town for a while, bought the crisps and peanuts, and window-shopped our way along the road, though there wasn't much to see. There was a big church at one end of the main street, and a few shops selling tourist tat. We walked past a hardware store with brushes and buckets stacked outside and Liv stopped.

'Just going to get a new mop for the floor,' she said. 'Do you want to wait here?' She gave me all the bags of snacks and went inside.

I leaned against a lamp-post and contentedly watched the people going by, sizing them up, thinking about what they might be doing.

And then I saw her.

She was a little girl, maybe about four or five years old. She had a shock of messy hair that fell over her forehead and rainbow wellies. She was coming towards me, on the other side of the road, hopping from one puddle to another and, as far as I could see, she was completely on her own. I stood up straight, watching her, senses on alert. There was no one near her. No one who looked as though they were with her.

Splash! She landed in another puddle. Splash! And another. Then she stopped jumping and stared across the road at one of the shops near where I stood. It had a slushie machine outside and one of those cars that you put 50p in and they moved around and played an annoying tune. A small boy was riding in the car, waving a balloon and laughing madly and he'd obviously caught the little girl's eye. She took a step towards the edge of the pavement and, worried she was about to step out into the road, I dropped the shopping bags and ran across to where she stood.

In one quick movement, I grabbed her and picked her up, taking her away from the danger. The little girl stared at me, open-mouthed with surprise, and then she threw her head back and screamed so loudly I thought the windows on all the shops nearby would shatter.

'It's okay,' I said, putting her down on her rainbow wellies. 'It's fine. You just got a fright, that's all.'

'Get off her.' I turned to see a woman, red-faced and angry, coming towards me. 'Get off my daughter, you perv.'

'Oh no,' I said quickly. 'She was on her own and I thought she was going to step out . . .'

'I was right there,' the mother said. 'I was right there. I had my eye on her the whole time. You've got no right touching my daughter like that.'

Before I'd been worried and apologetic, but suddenly I was absolutely furious. 'You weren't right there, were you? I watched her for ages and she was on her own. You weren't looking after her and she almost walked out into the road.' I took a breath. 'She could have been killed and it would have been all your fault.' I felt very close to tears. 'She's only little,' I said. 'You need to take care of her.'

The girl was still sobbing, looking at me in confusion. The mother gathered her into her arms and glared at me.

'Who are you to tell me what to do?' she said. 'You're the one grabbing a child that doesn't belong to you. Perv.'

'Phoebe, what's going on?' Liv appeared next to me, looking worried. 'What's happening?'

'She tried to take my daughter,' the woman said.

'I've called the police,' a man said, emerging from the shop next to us with a phone in his hand. 'Let them deal with her.'

'I am the . . .' I began and then stopped as a large PC with a shiny bald head waddled up behind the mother and the sobbing child.

I looked from the police officer to the mother, to the man with the phone, and to Liv. They were all staring at me with expressions that ranged from confusion to anger.

'This woman left her child all alone,' I said.

'This woman tried to take my daughter.'

'I tried to stop her walking into the road and being run over.'

The PC walked in between us. 'Ladies,' he said. 'Seems to be a difference of opinion. Let's not get hysterical.'

'I was right behind her,' the mother said. 'I was watching her jumping from puddle to puddle.'

I blinked at her. Had she really been there? I shifted awkwardly on my feet. 'You were there?'

'I was just a few steps behind the whole time.'

I started to cry and Liv put her arm around me. 'It's fine, Phoebe,' she said. 'It's fine. You thought you were doing the right thing.'

The mother looked awkward. 'No harm done eh?' she said. 'We'll get off.'

The police officer nodded and the woman hurried away with the little girl, clearly desperate to be gone. Liv let go of me and went over to the policeman, drawing him a bit away from me.

'Listen,' she said to him in a low voice, obviously not wanting me to hear. 'She's had a few issues recently. Some personal stuff. She just misinterpreted the situation.'

The PC glanced over at me and I wiped away a tear, feeling foolish.

'Okay,' he said. 'But make sure she doesn't do anything like that again.'

I was quiet all the way back to the pub. I felt silly and also unsettled. How could I have been so wrong about what had happened? I hadn't listened to my gut on Ciara James and she'd died. But when I did, I made a huge mistake, like I'd done today. Clearly, I couldn't trust my instincts. I couldn't even trust my own eyes. What was wrong with me?

'Are you stewing about it?' Liv said, as she pulled the car up at the pub. 'Because you shouldn't.'

I bit my lip.

'Listen.' Liv sounded uncharacteristically stern. 'You are a very good police officer. You had a feeling about Ciara James's stepfather but you waited until you had all the evidence before you acted. That was the right thing to do.'

'I waited too long,' I muttered.

'You did the right thing,' she said firmly. 'And today was just a knee-jerk reaction. Imagine if that little girl had stepped out into the road?' Liv said. 'And you'd just stood there watching? You'd be feeling a lot worse than you are now.'

I nodded. 'Just be careful,' she said. She reached out over the gear stick and squeezed my hand. 'Not everyone is awful, like Ciara's father.'

'Stepfather.'

'Whatever.' She sighed. 'Don't jump in, all guns blazing is all I'm saying.'

'I know,' I said quietly. 'It's exhausting being suspicious of everyone all the time.'

'What does your counsellor say? That thing about taking a moment?'

I breathed in. 'She says that when I'm feeling like things are out of control, I need to anchor myself in the moment.'

Liv made a face. 'I'm not totally sure what that means but it sounds to me like she's saying just think before you speak. Or act. Or do anything.'

'I've been doing much better,' I said. 'At least I thought I had been. But maybe being here has unsettled me.'

'Completely understandable,' Liv said. She gave me a sudden, broad grin. 'It's weird as fuck here.'

I started to laugh, despite myself. 'It really is.'

'But just because it's weird, doesn't mean everyone's a baddie.'

I unfastened my seatbelt. 'I know.'

Chapter 13

I forced myself to keep busy, helping Liv get ready for opening night. I pushed my own worries aside because I felt really sorry for Liv. I understood her money concerns and though there was nothing I could do to make them better I wanted to help in any way I could.

As the pub began to fill up with drinkers, I felt a bit better. It wasn't busy, but there were enough customers that it didn't seem ridiculous to be open. Hopefully this was just the beginning. And if the pub got more popular, then I wouldn't have time to think about my own shortcomings.

'Can you collect some glasses?' Liv said to me as I loitered by the bar, feeling slightly like a spare part. 'I can serve everyone by myself but I could do with you clearing empties.'

'Course.'

Liv handed me a plastic basket to stack the glasses in and I got busy, picking up the empty pints, then stacking them in the glasswasher behind the bar.

'I'll top up the crisps,' I said. I grabbed a couple of bags and went round the tables again, filling the bowls and smiling at the customers. I was glad Liv wasn't here all alone because even though everyone seemed nice, I knew how the atmosphere in a pub could turn in a minute when you mixed men, beer and football. I eyed a group of lads with suspicion and then forced myself to stop. *Anchor yourself, Phoebe*, I said inwardly. *Think about where you are and what you're doing.* I took a few deep breaths, thinking about all my senses and what was happening around me. And sure enough, nothing was happening. Everyone was fine. There were no raised voices, no trouble brewing. I let myself relax a bit.

As I made my way round the pub, I saw Jed and I felt myself stand up a bit straighter, glad I'd put on a clean top and done my make-up for the evening. He was sitting with the bald man – Mark – at a table close to the door. I topped up their bowl of crisps, trying to ignore the way my stomach flipped when I saw him, and smiled at them both. But mostly at Jed.

'Thanks for coming,' I said.

'It's not a bad turnout,' Jed said.

'It's great,' I said. 'Better than Liv hoped, I think. Thank you for spreading the word.'

He shrugged. 'Wasn't all me.'

'We're grateful anyway.'

'She looks happier, your mate,' Mark said, nodding to where Liv was handing a pint to a customer and laughing. He was right. She did look less pinched and worried. 'She had a right face on her the other day.'

'She's got a lot on her mind,' I said.

Mark and Jed glanced at one another.

'It's a tough business,' Mark said. 'Hard to make a living.'

'It really is.'

'Constant money worries, I reckon,' he went on.

'I wouldn't know,' I said vaguely. This was a strange chat to be having. I looked at Jed for help, but his attention was on the TV screen.

Behind me, Ewan appeared, holding three pints of lager and making me jump.

'Who's got money worries?' he said. 'TV work not pay well?'

Gah, that stupid fib I'd told was going to stay with me all summer. I forced a smile. 'I've taken a bit of time off actually,' I said. 'Fancied a change.'

Ewan looked at me, seeming slightly amused. 'If you need a job, come and see me,' he said.

'Oh I think I'll have enough to keep me busy here actually.'

'I was telling . . .' Mark trailed off.

'Phoebe,' Jed said, his eyes still on the football. I looked down at the glasses I was holding and smiled to myself.

'I was telling Phoebe that it's a tough business,' Mark went on.

'So tough,' said Ewan, sitting down and pushing the drinks across the table to Mark and Jed. 'Lots of people pack it in because they just can't make ends meet.'

He looked over to where Liv was standing behind the bar. 'Is Olivia struggling?'

'She's fine,' I said firmly. Why on earth were they so interested in Liv's money, I wondered. The odd way the conversation had gone made me feel unsettled. But I pushed my suspicions aside and tried to concentrate on something else.

'Did you know the family that lived here before?' I asked. 'You said you worked with them. Do you know why they left?'

Jed looked at me sharply but he didn't speak, just turned his gaze back to the screen, even though the football was finished now and most of the other drinkers were leaving. Ewan leaned back in his chair. 'Why do you want to know?'

I shrugged. 'Just because we've got some of their stuff and I wanted to send it on,' I said. 'No biggie.'

Ewan smiled at me. 'That's nice of you,' he said, though somehow he sounded as though it was anything but nice. 'But no, sorry, I don't know where they've gone.'

'Maybe it was the ghosts,' Mark said. 'Maybe they got spooked.'

'What ghosts?' I made a face. 'Is the pub meant to be haunted?'

'Do you want to hear the story?' Mark looked gleeful and I felt a flicker of interest in what he had to say.

'Go on then,' I said. 'But hang on two secs.' I looked up and beckoned to Liv. 'Come and hear this.'

She came over. 'What?'

'Ghost story,' Mark said.

'Ooh yes please.' Liv loved a spooky tale. She pulled up another chair for me and one for herself and we both settled down. Even Jed turned his attention away from the television and on to his friend.

'I've lived round here my whole life,' said Mark. 'I grew up with these stories and you might think they're all rubbish but I reckon there's some truth in them. I've seen things myself that can't be explained.'

'Like what?' said Liv as another group of drinkers left the pub. 'Goodnight. Take care out there, it's started raining again.'

'I've heard things, cries and wailing.'

'In the pub?' I said doubtfully. 'Really?'

'No, outside on the cliffs,' said Mark. 'And I've seen strange lights and shadows.'

'Probably just the local kids having a laugh,' said Liv.

But Jed shook his head. 'No one goes on the cliffs. They're not safe.'

'I saw people up there this morning.' There was a footpath that went along behind the pub where I'd seen some walkers earlier, and remarked to Liv that we could do packed lunches for them to make some extra money.

'And there's literally a bus route that goes along the top.'

'The road's fine and the path's fine, but the grass nearer the edge isn't totally stable. You should go no further than the path,' said Jed quite sternly. I rather liked it. He held my gaze for a second too long and, flustered, I took a mouthful of lager.

'That's mine,' said Mark.

'God, sorry.'

He grinned. 'Have it.'

Ewan pushed his untouched drink towards Liv. 'Want one?'

87

She took it, smiling at him. 'Thanks.'

'Get on with the story,' Jed said crossly. He seemed to be in a funny mood this evening, I thought. Or perhaps that's just how he was. It wasn't as though I knew him.

'There are two stories,' Mark said. 'Both about doomed lovers and tragic endings. The first is the tale of Theodora and Diggory.'

'Theodora and Diggory?' scoffed Liv.

I giggled. 'Sound like the kids in my nephew's class in West London.'

Mark glared at me. 'This was hundreds of years ago,' he said. 'They're good old-fashioned Cornish names.'

'Sorry.'

'Theodora and Diggory were deeply in love,' Mark said. 'But they had to meet in secret because her father didn't approve. And one night, they plunged to their deaths from the clifftops, just outside. Apparently you can still see the lights from their lanterns as they search for each other on dark nights.'

I shivered, enjoying the spooky story.

'Years after Diggory and Theodora died, a young woman went missing. The story goes that she had heard the tale of Diggory and Theodora and went exploring on the clifftops to see if she could find any evidence of the doomed lovers. But instead, she too plummeted to her death. At least, that's what everyone thought, but her body was never found. It's said that on the nights when the moon is bright, you can see the girl, standing on the cliff. And if the wind's in the right direction, you can hear her crying.'

A sudden gust of wind threw rain against the windowpane and all of us jumped and then laughed at how creeped out we were.

'Do you want to know her name?' Mark said. He was clearly loving every second of this.

Liv and I nodded in unison and he grinned. 'Her name was Emily Moon.'

Liv got it straightaway. 'The Moon Girl,' she said in delight. 'She's the Moon Girl.'

'She's who the pub is named after,' said Mark triumphantly.

'Not after Phoebe then,' joked Liv.

The men all looked at me.

'Is your name Moon?' Jed said, interested.

I shook my head. 'Phoebe means Moon,' I told him. I pulled my necklace out with my thumb and showed him the little crescent. 'It's why I wear this.'

Liv wanted to know more about the other Moon Girl. 'What happened to her?' she asked. 'What happened to Emily Moon?'

'No one knows for sure,' Mark said.

I shivered, thinking of Ciara. 'How old was she?' I said in a small voice.

He shrugged. 'Fifteen? Sixteen?'

I looked down into my drink. Poor Emily Moon.

'It was a long time ago,' Mark added.

'So she just vanished?' Liv asked.

'The current's strong here,' Mark said. 'Anything that goes in the water at Kirrinporth ends up at Barnmouth. When we were kids we would chuck messages in bottles into the sea and they always washed up two miles down the coast. It's because of the way the coast is at this part of Cornwall. The current moves east but the way the land juts out . . .'

'David Attenborough will be turning in his grave,' interrupted Ewan, rolling his eyes.

'David Attenborough's not dead,' Liv pointed out. 'And he's more about the animals isn't he? I think you need that Scottish fella with the hair. He talks about coastlines. What's his name?'

But I just wanted to hear more about Emily Moon. 'So everything that goes in here, washes up there?' I said, trying to get the conversation back on track.

Mark nodded. 'Anything. Driftwood, fishing nets . . .' He glanced at Ewan defiantly. 'Messages in bottles. Bodies.'

'But Emily Moon never washed up?'

'Never.'

'So perhaps she didn't die?'

'If she didn't die, then whose ghost walks along the clifftop?' said Mark.

There was a second as we all stared at each other and then Ewan let out a bark of laughter that made me jump.

'We'll never bloody know, will we?' he said. 'Come on, let's leave these ladies to it.'

Obediently, Jed and Mark drained their pints and stood up and they all walked to the door. I was a bit disappointed but it was getting late and we needed to clear up. Liv followed the men. 'I'll lock up behind you,' she said.

I gathered the empty glasses from our table as Liv let them out. I noticed that Ewan said something to her and she nodded. They all called goodnight and Liv shouted back and then it was quiet. She went to push the door shut and as she did so, a deep keening moan sounded across the clifftop.

Liv and I both froze and she slammed the door, locking it firmly, then turned to me, half laughing, half scared.

'Wind,' she said.

'Wind.'

But I couldn't help shivering as we went upstairs to bed.

Chapter 14

Emily

1799

There was nothing on the cliffs. Of course there wasn't. It was broad daylight for a start and the path was busy with people going from Kirrinporth to the market at Barnmouth.

Arthur grinned at me in something that looked rather like triumph, tinged with the tiniest bit of disappointment. 'There's nothing here.'

I looked out over the sea, where the sunlight sparkled on the waves. 'It's daytime,' I pointed out.

He shrugged. 'We could come up here any night and not come across Theodora and Diggory.'

'I know,' I said, nodding. I sat down on one of the big boulders that lined the way across the cliffs.

'Mr Trewin made up that story,' Arthur said. 'But at least we have seen it for ourselves.'

He took my hand and squeezed my fingers. 'So now we have two mysteries to solve. We have the mystery of what Morgan wants with your mother, and we have the mystery of why Mr Trewin told us his ghost story.'

'Mischief,' I suggested. Mr Trewin struck me as the type of man who would enjoy scaring someone.

'I thought the same,' Arthur said. 'And what about Morgan?'

I watched a boat, far out on the horizon, and I swallowed, readying myself to speak. 'I'm going to keep watch on him,' I said. 'Find out what he's up to.'

Arthur squeezed my fingers again, and with his thumb he gently rubbed the back of my hand. It was a curious sensation that made my whole body feel like it frothed like the waves breaking on the shore. I liked it.

'Just be very careful, Emily,' he said. 'You are too precious to risk being harmed.'

I felt a strange fluttering in my stomach. We looked at each other for a moment and then across the grass came the sound of the church bell clanging the hour. Arthur stood up, letting go of my hand, much to my disappointment.

'I must go,' he said. 'Come and find me when you have news about Morgan.'

'I will.'

I watched him bound along the path with his long-legged stride and smiled to myself. I was lucky to have Arthur as a friend.

The rest of that day passed uneventfully, and the next. We had no visits from Morgan and the inn was quiet. I mostly stayed upstairs, trying to draw Arthur's face from memory. Eventually, the next day, I was so bored I went downstairs to find my mother. I found her sitting listlessly at a table in the inn, staring out of the window at the sea.

I touched her on the shoulder and she turned to look at me. Her eyes were pink and puffy and I thought I saw tear smudges on her cheeks, but she smiled at me.

'What's new, Emily Moon?' she said and I knew she had been crying from her words. That was what my father used to say to me when he came home after being out, even if he'd only been into Kirrinporth to buy cheese. She'd been thinking about him and it made her sad. Feeling a sudden rush of affection for her, I put my arm round her shoulders and pulled her close. She relaxed into my embrace for a second, then pulled away. I mimed eating and pointed to the inn's door and she nodded.

'We could do with some cheese and see if you can get some meat. And there's no flour so if you want bread you'll need to get that too.' She dug in her skirt and pulled out some coins. I thought it was Morgan's money and I didn't want it but I took it anyway because I was hungry.

I gave her a small wave and she went back to staring out of the window.

I did not like going shopping. I didn't like the people and the noise, but I knew if we wanted to eat, I had to go. So I trudged into Kirrinporth in the rain, pulling my cloak around me and trying to stop it trailing in the mud. My father had often tried to teach me how to ride, but I didn't like horses much either because I found them unpredictable. I preferred to walk.

As I went, I kept my gaze lowered so I didn't have to make eye contact with anyone, and as I approached the shops, I kept close to the buildings. I had found if I walked nearer the centre of the street I would forever be bumping into people, or jumping out of the way of horses. It was easier to be at the edge.

I would do the chores, and then go by the church and see if I could find Arthur, I thought. Though the rain was getting heavier and really I should get home as fast as I could. A carriage went by me, too fast for the small village street, and I ducked into a doorway to avoid being splattered with mud as it went. As I huddled there, out of sight from the road, I caught a glimpse of Morgan. He was striding through the puddles in his boots, nodding greetings to people he passed. Everyone got out of his way, I noticed. He didn't divert his path at all but people simply melted away. Like the parting of the Red Sea.

He walked across the street, behind the carriage that had

gone by in a flurry of mud, past where I was standing, hidden by the bay window of the shop, and down an alleyway just ahead of me.

Where was he going? I wondered. That alley led to a little courtyard, I knew, where people tied up horses. It was secluded and the sort of place a young woman like me would never go alone. I hesitated for a second and then followed him down the little narrow opening. At the end, I paused, not wanting to be seen. I could hear voices – Morgan's and someone else's. Next to me were some long, wide planks of wood, propped up against the wall, and before I knew it I'd crouched down and crept into the tiny space they made. I could see through the gaps between planks so I could watch Morgan and the other man and I could hear everything they were saying.

'Everything's ready to go,' the other man said. He sounded annoyed. 'You said it would be tonight. It's the new moon.'

'Storm's coming,' said Morgan.

'It's fine. There's no storm.'

'Storm's coming,' Morgan said again. 'The tide's wrong. We can't risk it.'

'But . . .'

'Not tonight.'

He spun around on his heels and went to leave, clearly thinking he'd had the last word, but the other man wasn't finished yet. He was taller than Morgan but lanky where Morgan was broad and muscular. He shot his long arm out, gripped the collar of Morgan's coat and yanked him backwards. I put my hand over my mouth to stop myself gasping out loud.

'Tonight,' the lanky man said. 'Or not at all.'

Morgan stood stock still, the man still gripping his collar behind him. Then, quick as a flash – so fast I didn't see how he managed it – he whirled round and suddenly he was behind the lanky man, pulling his arm up behind his back and pressing his face into the dripping wet wall of the courtyard.

'Tomorrow,' he said. 'Storm will have passed and the clouds will still be thick.'

'Tomorrow,' the lanky man squeaked.

'Sure?'

The lanky man tried to nod, but it obviously wasn't easy with Morgan's big hand on the back of his neck.

'If you don't want the job, then there's plenty who will help,' Morgan said with a growl. 'And we won't ask again.'

'I want the job,' the man managed to say. 'Tomorrow is fine.'

He said something else, something I couldn't hear, and I strained to listen. Morgan had clearly understood though, because he chuckled. 'You leave Janey Moon to me.'

I stiffened. What did my mother have to do with any of this?

Morgan gave the man another shove and pushed him into the wall a bit harder, then he let go and the man staggered. 'Don't be late,' Morgan said. The man shook his head and hurried off down the alley back to the street. Morgan let out a bark of laughter and followed him, more calmly.

I stayed in my little wooden hidey-hole for a while to be sure Morgan had gone, then I inched my way out and brushed down my dress. I walked back the way I'd come, slowly, so I could check no one was watching me emerge, and then I headed towards the butcher. My mind was whirling as I pointed to what I wanted from the butcher and paid for our meat. I tucked the package under my arm and walked as fast as I could towards the church.

What was Morgan planning to do tomorrow night that needed the darkness of a new moon and thick clouds? Why was he talking about my mother? What part did she play in it all? It was obviously something bad. I needed to speak to Arthur and see what he thought about it all. And, I thought, opening the gate to the churchyard, I was going to follow Morgan tomorrow night if I could. I was going to find out what he was up to and somehow I was going to make him pay for all the terrible things he'd done.

Chapter 15

Phoebe

2019

I was going to Kirrinporth. In the rain. Again.

I hadn't wanted to come. I'd actually been wondering if I could somehow avoid the little town completely for the rest of the time that I was here in Cornwall. I was still totally and excruciatingly embarrassed about what had happened with the little girl. But Liv, damn her, had other ideas.

'Can you go to the bank for me?' she'd asked.

I made a face. 'Can't you do it? Or leave it for now? How much money is there?'

She jangled a bulging bag of cash in my face. 'We did quite well last night and it seems people in Cornwall don't like to use contactless.'

I groaned. 'I'd rather you did it.'

'I've got stuff on.'

'Really?' I narrowed my eyes at her. 'What stuff?'

'Important pub manager stuff. You have to go.'

'But I don't want to.'

She grinned. 'That's why you have to.'

Liv's important pub manager stuff involved a trip to Barnmouth to see a wine supplier. She was using her car, so because it was raining, I decided to get the bus to Kirrinporth.

There was a stop just near to the pub and I didn't have to wait long before the little single decker rattled its way along the clifftop to pick me up.

When the bus pulled into the main square in the town, I got off along with the few other passengers and ducked into a shabby branch of Boots to buy an umbrella. It was still raining but I also wanted something that could hide my face if I happened to come across the mum and the little girl again. Or the man who'd called the police. Or the policeman.

I went to the bank first and paid in Liv's takings, then I wandered around for a while. It was quiet on the streets today, not surprisingly because the weather wasn't exactly welcoming. I wasn't sorry – it meant I was far less likely to come across anyone who'd remember my embarrassment. There were a handful of restaurants and coffee shops that were bustling with people and much to my delight, on my wanderings I went down a little alleyway and found a covered courtyard with a café on one side with chairs outside, and a bookshop on the other.

I spent a happy half hour browsing the books and in a section marked Local History, discovered a book called *Cornwall's Ghosts*. I flipped to the index and was thrilled to find Emily Moon mentioned. I felt drawn to her story. Perhaps because we were both Moon Girls, or perhaps because of Ciara James. But whatever it was, I wanted to find out more about the mystery surrounding her disappearance. On a whim, I bought the book and then went to the café across the courtyard to treat myself to a coffee while I read. I found a seat tucked away in the corner and opened my book.

Disappointingly there wasn't much information about missing Emily; just what Mark had said about how she had gone up on the cliff and plunged to her death. Then there was some over-written spooky nonsense about the wailing at night, which made me tut because it seemed ridiculous, and how Emily had been seen standing on the clifftop, looking for her lost love, who was a chap called Arthur Pascoe, which made me roll my eyes.

But it did say that there was a memorial for Emily in St Neot's church in Kirrinporth, so I drained my surprisingly good flat white, and asked the waitress for directions. Then I tucked the book under my arm, and went to find the church.

It wasn't hard to find, standing squarely at the edge of the town, but the memorial on the other hand proved more elusive. I walked round the churchyard twice and then, as the rain was still coming down on my new umbrella, I went inside to see if it was in the church instead.

Inside was dark and cool. I shook off the rain in the porch and put the umbrella in a stand – they were clearly used to the Kirrinporth weather – just inside the door by the large stone font. It took a second for my eyes to adjust to the gloom but when they did, I saw it was a church like any other. Sturdy, solid, with dark wooden pews and a glorious stained-glass window over the altar. And the walls were lined with memorial stones. Surely one of those would be Emily's?

Starting to my right, I walked slowly along, reading the names on the stones, pausing when I saw a memorial to the Diggory family and their baby daughter Theodora. I smiled wryly. Was that where the legend of doomed Diggory and Theodora came from? I reckoned so. At the front of the church, sitting on the first pew, was a man wearing a dog collar. He smiled at me and said hello.

'I didn't mean to disturb you,' I said, feeling awkward.

'Not at all,' he said. He stood up. He was in his forties, I guessed, with dark-rimmed glasses and hair that needed a cut. Exactly how a vicar should look, I thought. 'Are you looking for someone in particular?'

Oh no, did he think I was looking for him? I gazed at him

blankly, unsure of what to say. But he nodded towards the wall. 'The memorials?' he said. 'Are you looking for a particular one?'

I laughed in relief. 'Oh yes, I am,' I said. 'I'm looking for Emily Moon.'

'Then follow me.'

It was only tiny. A small grey plaque, about the size of the side edge of a brick with the names etched out of the stone. *Emily Moon 1783–1799* it said simply. *Requiescat in Pace.*

'Not what you were expecting?' said the vicar, obviously noticing my disappointed face.

I shrugged. 'I'm not sure what I was expecting really,' I admitted. 'Something with a bit more oomph I think. It's sad. She was so young.'

The vicar gestured for me to sit down and I slid on to the nearest pew. He followed.

'I'm Reverend Frost,' he said. 'But call me Simon.'

I shook his outstretched hand. 'I'm Phoebe Bellingham,' I told him.

'So what's your connection to Emily Moon?'

'I don't have one really,' I said. 'Except I'm staying at the pub – The Moon Girl – for the summer and I wanted to know a bit more about her.'

'You've heard the stories I suppose?' he said with a grin. 'The spooky tales of how she walks the clifftops?'

Slightly shamefaced I pulled my book out of my bag and showed him. 'It's all in here.'

'Oh lovely, can I see?'

I found the page and passed it to him. 'Do you know much more about it?' I asked.

He shook his head. 'Not really. I do know that Arthur Pascoe was the son of the vicar at this church. It was the vicar who put in the memorial stone, I've been told.'

'I've heard there were rumours that she hadn't really died?'

'Well, apparently they never found a body.'

'Someone told me everything that goes in the sea at Kirrinporth washes up at Barnmouth.'

'That's true enough. We used to throw messages in bottles when we were kids and get replies from lads we played football with.'

I smiled, wondering if he knew Mark and Jed. Then frowned as I thought about Emily disappearing. 'But if Emily wasn't dead then where did she go?'

'Perhaps she and Arthur just ran away like young lovers often do in stories,' Simon suggested.

'Perhaps.'

'You like mysteries?'

'I do,' I said. 'I'm a . . .' I stopped before I told him I was in the police. I didn't want to get into explanations of why I wasn't working at the moment. 'I'm a true-crime buff,' I said truthfully. Then I smiled. 'And I'm a bit bored, to be honest. My friend Liv is running the pub and it's not very busy so there's not much for me to do. I'm wondering if finding out more about Emily Moon would keep me occupied.'

'Sounds like an excellent idea,' said Simon. He leaned back against the pew. 'I don't know much about Emily Moon herself but I do know about the ghost stories.'

'You do?' I was surprised that a vicar was interested in spooks.

'There were no ghosts.'

I made a mock shocked face. 'No?'

'This coastline was rife with smugglers in the eighteenth century,' he said, settling down in the pew like he was telling me a bedtime story.

'What did they smuggle?'

'Drink mostly, I think. Whisky and rum. Tobacco. It was a vicious, brutal, lawless trade and while many people in the town were involved, and some turned a blind eye, there were others who didn't approve.'

'Sounds like crime nowadays,' I said.

Simon looked at me. 'You're right,' he said. 'Except now we

have a proper police force. This was back in the days when there were just volunteer village constables in every parish, who more often than not were in the pockets of the smugglers themselves.'

'No customs officers or border controls back then?'

'Not like we know it now, but there were customs officers. Revenue men they were known as. Lots of former soldiers were recruited, and they patrolled the coastline. There were riding officers on horseback and fast ships called cutters, sailing along the shore watching for smugglers landing goods.'

'Sounds dangerous.' I wasn't sure what all this had to do with the ghosts but I was quite enjoying the story.

'Very dangerous.' Simon nodded vigorously and his glasses slipped down his nose. 'The smugglers weren't beyond murdering anyone who got in their way. But to make sure people stayed away when they were doing their dastardly deeds, they told ghost stories.'

I was delighted. 'Really?'

'Really.' He pushed his glasses back into position. 'I've heard some of them would even paint children in phosphorescent paint and walk them up and down the cliffs.'

'That's amazing,' I said. 'Very innovative.'

'It did the trick. Everyone stayed away and the smugglers could do what they needed to do.'

'I heard about a couple of ghosts called Theodora and Diggory but then I saw those names on a memorial over there,' I said, pointing to the spot on the church wall. 'Perhaps that story was one the smugglers told?'

'Undoubtedly.'

I frowned. 'But Emily Moon was a real person,' I said. 'She's not a made-up ghost story told to scare people away. What does she have to do with smugglers?'

Simon shrugged. 'Pubs were used by smugglers as far as I know. They were good places to hide their contraband.'

'Big cellars,' I said. 'Lots of customers. Good distribution networks.'

Simon gave me a slightly odd look. 'Indeed,' he said. 'So there's a link between Emily Moon and the smugglers there straightaway, plus I think the story is that she disappeared around the time a big smuggling gang was caught by the customs men,' he said. 'There have been theories over the years that she was involved with the gang – some people even say she was the mastermind behind it all and that she ran off with the booty.'

I was pleased with all the intrigue. Digging into Emily Moon's disappearance would definitely give me something to do while Liv looked after the pub. And, I thought, it was a good way to dip my toe back into police work of a kind. Get back on my bike, as it were.

I grinned at Simon. 'I'm going to find out more.'

'I suppose it would be difficult to find out the truth after all this time.'

'Difficult,' I said, feeling my heart pound a bit harder with the thrill of it all. 'But not impossible.'

Chapter 16

Emily

1799

'And he definitely said Janey Moon,' said Arthur, frowning.

'Definitely.'

We were sitting in the churchyard. Well, Arthur was sitting; I was pacing up and down, desperate to get home to the inn and make sure my mother was all right. When I'd arrived at the vicarage, Arthur had been finishing up with his tutor, so I'd had to wait for him to put away his books before I could fill him in. And then it took me a frustratingly long time to get my words out. So now I was twitchy and anxious as he processed what I'd told him.

'You couldn't have misheard?'

'No.' I shook my head. 'He said "Janey Moon".'

'But whatever could your mother have to do with what they're planning?'

I took a breath. 'The inn,' I said. I'd had a lot of time to think about it all while I was waiting for Arthur to finish his schoolwork. 'It's why he wants to use the inn.'

'But does he want to do?'

'I don't know.' I was frustrated with how slow he was being, which was very unfair considering how patient he always was with me. 'I must warn Mam.'

Arthur made a face, and I felt a rush of anger. Morgan had killed my father, and now he'd got my mother messed up in whatever awful thing he was doing and I was the only one who could help her. As close to mute and helpless as I was, I had to try. I clenched my fists, showing Arthur I was ready for a fight and he nodded, resigned.

'Do you think it's smuggling?' he said.

I looked at him and nodded. 'Must be.' I sighed. I really wished it wasn't, because since the authorities had clamped down on free trade, the stakes had got much higher. The penalties were imprisonment or death, and that meant the goods that were smuggled had to be worth the risk. But what else could it be?

Arthur looked round to where one of the churchwardens – not Mr Trewin, but another stout, red-faced gentleman who I knew by sight – was walking up the path. 'We shouldn't talk here,' he said. 'Shall we go to the inn?'

I nodded.

'Come on,' he said. Arthur took my package of meat, which had been out in the warmth for too long already, and together we set off towards the inn as fast as we could.

Inside, the inn was quiet. Mam was leaning against the wall, talking to Petroc, who was sitting at a table, a tankard of beer in front of him. Much to my surprise, he wasn't the only customer – there were two other men, sitting by the window. I eyed them with suspicion. Morgan had said he could bring the drinkers back to The Ship, but I hadn't believed him. It seemed he had a lot of clout.

Mam's glazed eyes told me she'd already had a drink and she blinked at me as I walked by to put the meat into the cold pantry.

'Where you been?'

I showed her the parcel and she nodded.

'She's a good girl, my Emily,' I heard her say. I didn't know if she was talking to Petroc, or Arthur, or herself.

When I came back into the bar, after putting the meat away, I gave Mam's sleeve a tug and nodded my head towards the back of the inn.

'What?' she said, struggling to focus on me.

I tugged her again.

'I can't leave the customers,' she said.

I raised an eyebrow. There were only four customers, including Petroc and Arthur.

Arthur got to his feet. 'I'll keep an eye on things, Mrs Moon.'

Mam looked annoyed and I supposed I couldn't blame her. She didn't want to be leaving the only drinkers we'd had for months. But with what seemed to be enormous effort, she slowly straightened up. 'Come on then.'

We went upstairs, me in front and Mam behind, and into her bedroom. She sat on the bed and looked at me. 'What?'

I took a deep breath, willing my voice to work. 'Morgan,' I began. Mam sighed in an over-exaggerated fashion.

'What about him?'

'He's bad . . .' I said. My throat was clenching and my tongue sticking to the roof of my mouth, but I was determined to carry on.

Mam tutted. 'I know what he is,' she said. 'I know. But what choice do I have Emily Moon?'

'Da,' I managed to say. 'Da wouldn't want this.'

'Well he should have thought of that before he went off to God knows where with God knows who,' Mam said. She went to get up and, despairing, I pushed her back down on to the bed, gathered all my breath into my lungs and spoke.

'Da is dead,' I said.

Mam looked at me, her expression stricken.

'What?'

105

'Dead,' I said again. My throat was closing up and even my breathing was shallower.

'How do you know?'

I opened my mouth but nothing came out.

'How do you know?' Mam said again. She was crying now. 'How do you know?' She gripped my shoulders and shook me hard but I still couldn't speak. 'How do you know?'

Her aggression spent she slumped on to the bed.

'He's dead,' she whimpered.

I sat down next to her and stroked her hair as she cried.

'Are you sure?' she said.

I nodded, but I still couldn't speak.

Mam cried for a little while and then she sat up and wiped away her tears.

'He didn't take the dog,' she said. 'I knew he would have taken the dog.'

I nodded again. 'M . . .' I began but the word wouldn't come out. 'M . . .'

'Morgan?' said Mam. She looked different somehow. Her eyes were focusing and she looked more upright. More like her old self, I thought.

I took her hand. 'M . . .'

'I'll tell Morgan not to come again,' Mam said. 'We'll be right. Just you and me, Emily Moon. There's drinkers downstairs today and where one comes, others will follow. Maybe I'll speak to that farmer down the way, get us another pup. What do you think?'

I smiled, relieved that she'd listened to my worries, and she put her arm round me and kissed the top of my head. I forced myself to let her embrace me, trying not to wriggle away for once.

'Come on, let's see what that Arthur's doing downstairs,' she said.

Together we went downstairs. Arthur looked at me expectantly and I gave him a broad smile. It was all fine, I thought. We were going to be all right.

'Another ale for you, Petroc?' Mam said. Petroc grinned and held out his tankard and Mam swirled off to fetch it for him. I sat down in my favourite spot by the window and Arthur came to join me and we chatted quietly about nothing.

Gripping his tankard like a prize, Petroc wandered over to look out of the window, near where Arthur and I sat.

'Looks like rain,' Arthur said. 'Again.'

'It's going to be a wild night. I've heard.' Petroc looked at Arthur with a half-grin. 'I'd get home as soon as you can and stay there.'

Arthur pulled his shoulders back and I felt a flush of pride in him as he looked Petroc in the eye. 'I'm staying here for now,' he said. 'With Emily.'

'You look out for her,' Petroc said urgently. 'Make sure you look after her.'

'Of course,' Arthur said. He looked at Petroc carefully. 'You work for Morgan, do you?'

'Aye,' the man said. 'Morgan and Mr Kirrin.'

I rolled my eyes. Everyone worked for Mr Kirrin.

'What do you do? Something important no doubt?'

Oh Arthur was clever. He was using Petroc to find out what Morgan wanted with Mam. But surely Petroc wouldn't fall for his flattery?

It seemed I was wrong because Petroc sat down on one of the tables near us, ignoring Mam's tuts from the other side of the inn, and put his boots up on the chair. 'Bit of this, bit of that,' he said in a low tone. 'Morgan's a busy man and he'd struggle without me.'

'I don't doubt it,' said Arthur, looking impressed. He glanced at me, signalling with his eyes that he was at a loss about what else to ask. I tilted my head towards the cliffs outside the inn window, trying to remind him of the conversation I'd overheard the lean man have with Morgan, and he gave me a tiny nod.

'Emily and I were thinking of going for a walk on the cliffs. But if the weather's turned perhaps we'll have to go tomorrow instead,' he said. He grinned at Petroc, who was looking nervous suddenly.

The man shook his head fervently. 'You most certainly should not,' he said. 'Not tomorrow, not ever. Not after dark.'

Arthur scoffed. 'Why not?'

'Because of the ghosts,' the man said.

A chill went down my spine and I shivered. Petroc saw and turned to me. 'You're right to shiver, Emily Moon,' he said. 'Because the spirits are lively and they are lonely and they want company.'

There was a pause and Arthur and I looked at each other. I knew this man was talking rubbish, but just as with Mr Trewin in the church, it was hard to be rational when the inn was gloomy and the rain was lashing at the windows. I pulled my shawl tighter around my shoulders.

Arthur sat down on the table next to the man. 'Tell me, Petroc. I've heard stories too. Of doomed lovers called . . .'

Petroc's eyes widened. 'Diggory and Theodora,' he said in a hushed tone. I was almost impressed at his dramatics. Almost.

'They walk the cliffs at night, looking for others to share their pain,' he said. 'You can see the lights from their lanterns.'

'Emily's seen them,' Arthur said and I nodded. 'She's seen them and she was so afraid.'

'She is right to be afraid,' said Petroc. He reached out and gripped the top of Arthur's arm. I could see his long fingers digging into Arthur's coat. 'Stay away from the cliffs, young man.'

Arthur nodded gravely. 'You're absolutely right, sir,' he said. 'We most certainly will stay away. Won't we, Emily?'

I nodded too.

With a sudden smile, Petroc slid off the table and went to give his empty tankard to my mother. I watched as they chatted for a minute or so and then turned my attention back to Arthur. He was telling me about an apple tree he was growing in the garden of the vicarage. He'd attached a piece from one tree on to the root of another. It was very complicated and I was barely following his explanation but I liked seeing him so excited, and I was just happy to be there in the inn, with Mam chatting to Petroc and laughing – actually laughing – like old times.

And then Morgan arrived. He strode into the inn like he owned it, hanging his hat on the peg and nodding to Petroc.

'Ale, Janey,' he said.

In the corner, Arthur and I stiffened. Arthur fell silent, all apple trees forgotten. As one we both stood and went round to where Morgan stood looking at Mam. The way they were both bristling made me think of the farm cats I'd seen, hissing and arching their backs at each other.

'Ale,' Morgan said again.

'Not today, Morgan,' Mam said quietly. 'Not today.'

Morgan took a step towards Mam and I thought suddenly and too late that he was not a man who liked to be told what to do. Why hadn't I warned Mam how dangerous he was? Why hadn't I told her to go somewhere else when he arrived? Not face up to him like this.

'What did you say?'

'I said, not today. I'll be seeing you.' Mam nodded at him politely and turned away. A foolish move. Morgan reached out and grabbed her hair, pulling her towards him.

'What did you say?'

Mam gasped in shock. So did I. Arthur took a step forward and I pulled his arm to stop him.

'Ale,' Morgan said. He let go of Mam's hair and she righted herself and went to the barrel to pour him a drink. He drained it in just a few mouthfuls, wiped his lips with the back of his hand and then nodded at Mam again.

'Come,' he said.

Mam glanced at me. 'Not today,' she said again.

'Mam . . .' I croaked. But I couldn't get the words out, couldn't tell her that while of course I didn't want this for her – while I wanted her to have nothing to do with this brutish, brutal man – I didn't want her to stop it like this.

Morgan put his thick hand out and squeezed Mam's arm. His meaty fingers dug into her flesh. 'Come.'

Mam winced. Morgan squeezed harder. Petroc stood up. 'Morgan,' he said. 'Don't be this way . . .'

Before he could carry on, Morgan brought up his booted foot and landed it firmly in between poor Petroc's legs. The smaller man reeled away, clutching himself, tears in his eyes. Beside me, Arthur winced in sympathy. Without speaking, the other drinkers both left their drinks on the table and hurried outside, keeping their faces turned away from Morgan, and making sure he knew they'd not seen a thing. *Cowards*, I thought bitterly.

Mam pulled away from Morgan but he hung on and then, as she turned to look at Petroc, he hit her across the face with the back of his other hand. Her head jerked back and I cried out in fear.

'Come,' he said again.

With her nose bleeding, Mam looked at me. 'What choice do I have?' she said.

She let Morgan lead her out of the room and upstairs, and I started to cry. Arthur went to Petroc, who stumbled to his feet.

'Sorry,' he mumbled. He slumped on to a chair.

Arthur and I stayed still, huddled in our corner, until we finally heard Morgan's heavy tread coming down the stairs.

He plucked his hat from the peg and then turned to Arthur.

'So you're Arthur Pascoe?' he said, looking him up and down. Arthur shifted from one foot to the other, clearly uncomfortable, and gave me a questioning glance. I gave him a tiny shrug. I had no idea how Morgan knew who he was, or who his father was.

'I know your da,' Morgan said. He put his hat on his head and walked over to where Arthur and I sat. His boots left footprints on the clean floor. 'I like him. He's very obliging.'

'I think you're mistaken,' Arthur said. I liked the way his voice

110

was clear and strong, even though I could tell he was scared. 'You must be mixing my father up with someone else.'

Morgan looked at me. 'He thinks I'm getting mixed up,' he said, flashing a smile. 'Silly boy.'

Arthur had stood up and now Morgan slapped him on the back amiably but so hard that Arthur almost fell over. 'Of course I know your da. Reverend Pascoe is a good friend of mine. We help each other out all the time.'

'He's a fine man,' Arthur said firmly and Morgan hooted with laughter. The sound made me wince.

'They always are, Arthur. They always are.'

He spun round on his heel, smearing more dirt into the floor. 'If the daughter's anything like the mother, you're a lucky man,' he said to Arthur. He grinned at me, with a gleam in his eye that made me shiver. 'Very lucky.' He blew me a kiss and headed outside.

I stayed stony still, my face on fire with shame. Arthur shuffled his feet. Then Petroc – who I'd forgotten all about – gave a small cough and carefully, painfully stood up.

'Goodbye then,' he said. 'Stay away from the cliffs.'

He went out the way Morgan had gone. We heard his horse whinny and then the sound of hooves. Arthur came to me and wrapped his arms around me. It was the first time we'd ever been that close, but it felt so natural that I relaxed into his embrace. 'Morgan is a bad brute,' he said. 'They are making up the ghost stories so everyone stays away and doesn't bother them. And I think tomorrow night, we should hide on the clifftop and watch.'

'Really?' I whispered, scared about what we might find.

'Really.'

I nodded. 'We will find out what he is doing,' I said. I winced as a muffled moan came from upstairs. 'But first, I must look after my mother.'

Chapter 17

Phoebe

2019

'Are you opening for lunch today?' I asked Liv in the kitchen the next morning. She shook her head.

'No point,' she said. 'But I'm pleased with how the evenings have been going. We're not out of the woods – not by a long way – but it's promising. So I reckon I'll just open at teatime again and see what happens.'

'Sounds like a plan.' I switched on the kettle. 'What are you going to do until then?'

'I've got some stuff to do round the pub. Admin and whatnot,' said Liv. 'And then I'm meeting that Ewan Logan.'

'Really?' I wasn't sure why that made me feel unsettled, but it did. I put my hands on the worktop and felt the coolness of the surface on my fingers, and swallowed down my concern.

'Are you okay?'

I smiled at Liv brightly. At least I hoped it was brightly. 'Fine,' I said. 'So what are you meeting Ewan about?'

'I just want to see what he's got to offer.'

I thought of the strange blank business card he'd handed over and frowned. 'What does he even do? Is he a supplier?'

Liv shrugged. 'He's kind of a fixer. I've seen it before in places like this – where everyone's a bit mistrustful of strangers. He can put me in touch with suppliers, sort out events, find people like DJs or singers if we need entertainment. He just knows everyone and he can put me in touch with the people I need to run the pub successfully.'

'For a fee, I suppose?'

'A small one.'

'Right,' I said. 'A fixer.'

Liv looked at me, her head to one side. 'Phoebe,' she said, a warning tone in her voice. 'It's fine. Honestly. It's totally legit. Happens all the time.'

'Can't your head office help with this sort of stuff?'

She shrugged. 'Up to a point, but it's always good to have people on the ground. In normal circumstances I could talk with the last manager – find out which suppliers he used and whatnot. But I've got nothing to go on and Ewan could be the person to fill me in. I could do with him giving me a hand, to be honest, Phoebe. You know how badly I need this to work and at the moment it's not looking good.'

I nodded. I did understand her money worries and I knew it was better she made use of anything she could instead of turning to payday loans. Plus rationally I knew I was being overcautious.

'Ewan said he worked with the last licensee?' I said, thoughtfully. 'So as you can't get in touch with him, could you maybe ring that regional manager fella and ask him what he thinks of Ewan?'

'Actually that's not a terrible idea,' Liv said. 'I'll give Des a ring and see what he has to say about Ewan Logan. Just to be on the safe side.'

Feeling more reassured, I made tea for us both as she found her phone and called the regional manager. She took the call in the lounge but I could hear her laughing and when she came back into the kitchen she was all smiles.

'He knows Ewan vaguely,' she told me. 'Not well, he said, but he's met him a few times. And he says he's a great asset, especially in these strange circumstances.'

'That sounds good then.' I tried to smile but it was harder than I'd thought it would be. 'Hope he can help.'

Liv nodded. 'It is good. Listen, I know everything's a bit odd here, and you're being protective,' she said. She picked up her mug of tea and held it in two hands at her chest, like a shield. 'But remember, just because some people are bad, that doesn't mean everyone's bad.'

'I know,' I muttered. 'It's fine. I'm fine.'

'I'm not going into partnership with him. He's just helping us out. It's okay.'

'You're right,' I said.

'It's nice that you worry,' she said. 'And it was a good idea to call Des. Even in ideal circumstances it wouldn't always be the best idea to meet a strange man without doing some gathering of information first.'

'Ah, I have taught you well,' I joked. 'Shall we stalk him on Facebook too?'

Liv rolled her eyes. 'No, we can clean the loos.'

'Fine,' I said. But I made a mental note to google Ewan Logan later. I spent the morning helping her clean, chatting about the history of the pub and filling her in on everything Simon the vicar had said. Her eyes lit up when I mentioned going to the church.

'Was he hot?'

'Like Fleabag hot?'

'Was he?'

'No,' I giggled. 'Nice enough but kind of dishevelled and churchy. And married.'

'Ah well,' said Liv. 'Plenty more fish in the sea.'

A picture of Jed sitting in the pub popped into my head and I felt my cheeks redden.

Liv looked at me curiously but she didn't ask if I had any particular fish in mind. Much to my relief.

'So anyway, Simon the vicar said it was all to do with smuggling,' I went on.

Liv looked startled. 'Smuggling?'

'Yes, in the eighteenth century.'

'Like *Jamaica Inn*?'

'Exactly.' I explained what Simon had said about the ghost stories and Emily's disappearance.

'Was Emily Moon a smuggler?' Liv wiped down one of the beer pumps carefully.

'Maybe,' I said with a certain amount of glee. 'Perhaps she was a smuggler and ran off with the treasure, or perhaps she just ran away with her boyfriend.'

'Phoebe, you've got a gleam in your eye,' Liv said. 'Are you planning to investigate the case of the missing Moon Girl?'

'Do you know? I think I am.'

'I think that's a fabulous idea. There's so little going on here that I was worried you would be bored. And it might reawaken your mojo.'

I groaned. 'I hope so,' I admitted. 'Because I will need to get back to work at some point.'

With the pub shining like a new pin, Liv went to get changed for her meeting with Ewan and I caught up on *Homes Under the Hammer*. As I heard the bedroom door close, I pulled my phone out and typed Ewan Logan into the search bar. There were several hits but mostly from Ewan Logans in Ireland and Scotland – none of them were our man. I clicked on LinkedIn and read the bio of a Ewan Logan who was CEO of a soap company in County Antrim and then shoved my phone under my leg as Liv came back into the lounge, having ditched her scruffy shorts and vest top for a pretty maxi dress.

'You can sit in on the meeting, if you want to,' she said. I smiled. That was really sweet of her – understanding that I felt uncomfortable and wanting to make me feel better. I felt for my phone and slid it into my back pocket, then I stood up.

'No, it's fine,' I said. All my instincts were telling me to say yes. To join Liv and see what Ewan Logan had to offer. But I also knew Liv was right: the fact that bad people existed didn't mean that everyone was bad. I had to trust her. And Ewan Logan. Whoever he was. 'I'll leave you to it.'

'What are you going to do instead?'

'Actually I might go for a walk,' I said. 'Because check out the weather.' Sure enough, the rain had finally – finally – stopped and the sun was streaming in through the rather grubby windows.

'OMG, what's that yellow thing in the sky?' Liv said. 'I'd better put out the tables in the garden if this is going to last.'

'Do you want me to stay and help move furniture?'

'Nah, go for your walk. I'll get Ewan to help.'

'If you're sure?'

'Definitely. I'll put him to work – get him to make himself useful.'

I hovered uncertainly.

'Go,' she said.

I patted my back pocket to check my phone hadn't disappeared in the thirty seconds since I'd put it there, then I put my purse in my bag and looped it over my shoulder. 'Text me if you need me to come back,' I said. 'I'll just be in Kirrinporth.'

'I'll be fine.'

She would be fine, I told myself as I went downstairs. She was more than capable of having a business meeting. I knew what was happening. Des the regional manager knew what was happening. It was all fine. I let myself out of the pub and as I crossed the car park, Ewan drove in. He raised a hand to me in greeting and I waved back more jauntily than I felt. He was on his own, I noted with a strange sense of relief. No Jed or Mark. Liv wouldn't be outnumbered then.

I stopped for a moment at the top of the slope up to the road, taking a couple of deep breaths and thinking of the exercise the counsellor had told me to do when I felt panicky. *What can you see?* Sandra would ask. I looked at my feet in my flip-flops, taking in my unpainted toenails. I would buy some nail varnish, I thought. Or better yet, go for a pedicure. What could I smell? I breathed in. I could smell the sea and – I licked my lips – taste the salt. That was nice, actually. It was lovely being near the water. Calming.

Feeling more in control, I went on my way. I should call Sandra, I thought. Maybe she could give me some counselling over the phone and help me untangle my thoughts a bit. But for now, I was going to walk into Kirrinporth and see if I could find a library. Perhaps there would be some information on Emily Moon that would distract me from Ewan Logan.

Enjoying the sun on my face and the warmth on my shoulders, I strolled into the town.

Chapter 18

Emily

1799

Nervous about what I might find upstairs, I climbed the steps slowly and pushed open my mother's bedroom door. She was lying on the bed, facing away from me. Her hair was dishevelled and her dress was torn across one shoulder. A small money bag lay on the bed beside her.

I went round to the other side of the bed and sat next to her and gasped as she looked up at me. Her nose was swollen and blood was smeared across her face. Her eye was puffy and a purple bruise was beginning to bloom around the swelling eyelid. Her bare shoulder showed more bruises and where her dress was rucked up under her, I could see more marks on her legs.

'Emily,' she said quietly. 'I'm sorry.'

I shook my head, wishing I could speak to her, comfort her. But my voice wouldn't come. Instead I gently pulled her skirt down, covering the marks that Morgan's thick fingers had made.

'Stay,' I managed to say.

I ran downstairs to where Arthur was just walking away back

into town. I wanted so badly to call him back, but I knew Mam wouldn't thank me for involving him, so instead I went to the well and drew some fresh water. Then I took it in a bowl, and some clean rags, and went upstairs to my mother. She had managed to sit up and was leaning against the wall. The bag of money, I noticed, had gone. She must have tucked it away somewhere. The thought of us surviving on money my mother had earned in this way made me want to cry. But I could not cry. I had to help her.

Carefully I sat down next to her, dipped a rag into the water and gently dabbed it against her split lip and swollen nose, wiping away the blood. She let me do it, compliant as a child, just wincing occasionally. It took a while to get rid of all the dried-on smears but eventually she looked more like herself, though the bruise around her eye was still vivid and her nose and lips were still swollen.

Mam hadn't spoken the whole time I was tending to her wounds, but now she gave me a sad half-smile.

'Thank you, my girl.'

I nodded. What else would I have done? I picked up her comb from the table by the window, and gestured for Mam to sit forward. Again, obedient as a little girl, she did as I wanted and I combed through her hair, brushing out all the tangles and tugs. Then I gently twisted it up and fastened it with a pin.

Finally, I went to her wardrobe and found another dress and clean undergarments. Slowly she got up from the bed and, only flinching a bit, she took off the skirt and blouse she was wearing and pulled on the dress. I averted my eyes from the blue bruises on her inner thighs.

'Thank you,' Mam said again. She looked at herself in the reflection in the window – it was getting dark now and we could see ourselves in the candlelight from a lantern I'd lit. 'Oh what a mess I am.'

I shook my head. She was still beautiful. I took a deep breath. 'Sorry,' I said.

She smiled at me in the reflection as we stood side by side, and took my hand. 'This was Morgan's doing,' she said. 'Not yours.'

'My fault.'

'No,' she said firmly.

But I was right. If I'd done things differently, or explained everything better – not even better, explained things at all, earlier, or spoken more clearly – then perhaps she'd have understood how dangerous he was. I had to tell her the truth.

'Morgan . . .' I began.

Mam took a breath. 'I have to do what he wants, Emily,' she said. 'He's made that very clear.'

'He is dangerous,' I croaked.

Mam snorted. 'I know that.'

'He killed Da.'

Mam turned away from the window and stared at me. 'What?'

'Da.'

'Do not lie to me, Emily Moon,' Mam said furiously. 'As if things aren't bad enough with this.' She gestured wildly to her face. 'Do not lie.'

I tried to tell her that it was the truth but her face was red with anger. I felt awful for her. She'd lost her husband, she was doing what she had to do to put food in our bellies and – I knew – to protect me and here I was telling her awful things. Truthful things, but they were awful just the same. I couldn't speak. Mam stared at me as I opened and closed my mouth, desperately trying to get my voice to work.

'Talk to me,' she said, venom in her voice. 'Talk to me.'

Helplessly, I shook my head. I couldn't speak. I couldn't tell her what I'd seen on that awful night. And then I had an idea.

I squeezed her hand and tried not to mind that she flinched away from my touch. Then I darted out of her bedroom and into my own. I picked up my sheaf of papers and leafed through them until I found the ones I'd drawn that night. The sketches of Morgan's face, the distinctive white flash in his hair glowing in the moonlight, and my father's lifeless expression as his blood pumped on to the cobbles.

I tried not to look at the pictures too closely, but I gathered them up and took them back into Mam's room.

'Look,' I said, pushing them at her.

She turned away but I pushed harder. 'Look.'

Reluctantly she took the pages and leafed through them. Her expression went from angry to sad and then to furious again. Her cheeks were red as she turned on me. 'What is this?'

'Da . . .' I began.

'You are ill in your head, Emily,' she said. Tears were coursing down her cheeks. 'You are ill in your head and you have made up these awful stories to torment me. Why would you draw such awful horrible things?'

I shook my head wildly, trying to show her that I hadn't made this up but she gripped my arm and pulled me.

'Stop it,' she screeched. Her hair, which I'd so neatly tied up, was coming loose and she looked like a madwoman as she screamed in my face, her expression twisted with hate.

'I am doing what I can,' she cried. 'I have no money and no husband and the only way I can survive is to do what Morgan wants me to do.'

'No,' I sobbed. 'No.'

'And then you come along with your tales of your father's death and your evil imagination. Making things worse. So much worse.'

She was still holding the pictures, the one of Da on top, gripping them in her fist so tightly that her knuckles were white. She looked down at them in disbelief. 'How could you draw this, Emily? How could you draw such an awful thing?'

I opened my mouth but no sound came out, just a cry of frustration and despair.

Mam hit me round the head with the papers. It didn't hurt but the gesture broke my heart.

'How could you?' she said. She looked round and saw the

bowl I'd used to bathe her wounds. In one stride she was there, picking up the bowl and throwing the dirty water on to the floor. Then she crumpled up the pages and forced them into the bowl.

I tried to pull her arm, to get her to stop, but she was determined and strong and there was nothing I could do as she picked up the lantern, took out the candle inside and dropped it into the bowl.

The papers caught straightaway, the flame licking the edges. I watched, devastated, as the only tiny proof I had of Morgan's wrongdoing was eaten up by the orange fire. The smoke filled my throat and made me cough. Mam's eyes were watering but she didn't move, holding the bowl out in her two hands like an offering at church.

'Stop,' I begged. 'Stop.'

'You stop.' Mam's voice was rough with the smoke. 'Stop and listen to me. We have no choice, Emily. No choice at all. Morgan has shown us that. But if I do as he asks, then we will have money in our pockets and food in our bellies. And if I don't, then he will take what he wants and give us nothing.'

She looked at me over the top of the burning bowl. The fire shone on her face and gave her a demonic appearance that made me shudder. 'Do you understand?' she said.

I didn't speak or move.

'Do you understand?'

Suddenly, all my fight was gone, I nodded. Mam looked at me for a long moment, and then – still holding the bowl, which was just smouldering now, my pictures reduced to cinders – she turned and walked out of the bedroom.

I slumped down on to the bed. My tears were falling quickly now. What could I do? It seemed my efforts to protect my mother had all gone wrong. I had no proof of Morgan's bad deeds and no way to show anyone that he was a killer and a criminal.

Unless.

I sat up again and wiped away my tears.

Arthur had agreed to come with me and watch from the cliffs that very evening. We knew that Morgan was going to do something – that man I'd spied on down the opening had said as much. And Petroc had been so adamant when he told us to keep away that it was clear something was going on. Perhaps I could take my sketchbook with me while we watched, do some more drawings and show them to . . . who? The magistrate? The parish constable? I thought of Mr Trewin and winced. Perhaps not. But at least it would be proof of some wrongdoing at least.

Mind made up, I got off the bed. We would watch Morgan this evening and find out once and for all what he was doing.

Chapter 19

Phoebe

2019

I quite enjoyed my walk into Kirrinporth. It was definitely much nicer in the sunshine. I strolled along, concentrating on my surroundings and feeling the warmth on my face, and trying not to worry about Liv. I knew that despite her determination to look on the bright side, she was still worrying about money. I couldn't help with the cash – I was hard up enough given that I wasn't earning my usual wage – but I thought I might sit her down later and see if we could come up with some ideas to encourage more customers to come to the pub.

We'd not heard anything about where the former landlord had gone either and though I'd boxed up the family's belongings it still felt very much like we were living in their house and they could return any second. I'd get her to chase that Des, the regional manager, I thought. See if we could return some of the stuff to the family at least. Maybe if she felt more settled, she could concentrate on getting more customers. *And not have to rely on Ewan Logan,* a little voice inside my head said. I ignored it. At least I tried to.

Kirrinporth library was easy to find – just along from Simon's church. It was a small stone building that smelled like my old primary school. It had a children's section where two mothers perched on tiny chairs and tried to interest their toddlers in picture books, and a larger fiction section. I asked the librarian for the local history section and she pointed me right to the back, where some rickety stairs led up to a small mezzanine level.

It was quiet up there, with no other library-goers venturing up the creaky steps. I put my bag down on a chair and set about finding every book about smugglers that I could. I thought if I could find out more about the criminals who were arrested when Emily Moon went missing, I could perhaps work out if she was involved in some way. I loved the idea of her being the brains behind the smuggling gang. Or perhaps she was the person who'd blown the whistle on them. I was intrigued, that was for sure.

There were no shortage of books. I piled them all up on the table and leafed through them, looking for mentions of Kirrinporth, and I wasn't disappointed. It turned out, this sleepy little Cornish town was a hotbed of organised crime in the nineteenth century.

Gripped, I read about how the local lord of the manor, a man called Denzel Kirrin employed former soldiers to oversee the day-to-day business of smuggling, and didn't get his hands dirty himself. Instead he got rich on the proceeds of the crime, bringing in whisky, rum and tobacco and selling it on, like an old-world mob boss. He even had the local magistrates in his pocket, bribing them to turn a blind eye to his dodgy dealings. 'Probably all played golf together,' I muttered, thinking of how things worked these days.

I read for more than an hour, jotting down notes and marking pages with strips of paper torn from my notebook.

A group of very loud babies and toddlers arrived for rhyme time and I decided it was time for me to go. I picked three books with the most information about smuggling in Kirrinporth and wrote down the titles. I'd come back again. Tomorrow even. I was really enjoying finding out about the history of this odd little town.

Feeling happier than I'd felt since we'd arrived really, I set off towards the bakery where I'd had coffee yesterday to get some cakes for Liv. And there, coming out of the little alleyway that led to the covered courtyard as I was going in, was Jed.

'Phoebe,' he said, sounding thrillingly pleased to see me. 'How are you?'

'Good,' I said, trying to ignore the flips in my stomach that his presence gave me. 'Great. I was just going to buy some cakes for Liv and maybe grab a drink.'

'That sounds like an excellent idea,' he said. He glanced at his watch. 'I've got nowhere I need to be for now. Fancy a coffee?'

I thought about saying no, and heading back to The Moon Girl to check Liv was okay. But instead, I just pulled out my phone, saw there were no messages and grinned. 'Yes please.'

Jed led the way into the courtyard and I followed. Getting to know him better would hopefully put my mind at rest about Ewan Logan. After all, didn't they say judge a man by the company he keeps? And while I had that little niggle about Mr Logan, the only feelings I had for Jed were much more interesting. He really was very handsome.

We chose a table inside and Jed went to the counter to order while I went for a wee. I looked at my face in the mirror as I washed my hands. I wasn't wearing any make-up and my hair was a bit windswept from my walk. I rubbed my face to remove the library dust, combed my mop through with my fingers and much to my delight found some tinted lip balm in the bottom of my bag, so I slicked some on and hoped it would make me look fractionally more presentable, though I doubted it.

'What have you been up to?' Jed said as I sat down.

I grinned. 'Researching Emily Moon at the library.'

He looked interested. 'How come?'

I thought about how to explain my interest. 'There was a girl, near where I live in London,' I said, deliberately not giving too much away. I didn't want him googling. 'She went missing and it was big news locally. I got quite into it. Turns out I like true crime stuff.'

Jed gave me a look I couldn't read, and I wondered if he'd think I was a weirdo. The type who has theories about Jack the Ripper and writes to serial killers in jail. But then he returned my smile. 'Me too,' he admitted. 'I love unsolved mysteries. There are loads of podcasts I listen to.'

'Which ones do you like?'

We swapped recommendations for a few minutes. But I was more interested in Jed.

'Not working today?' I said.

He shook his head. 'I have odd days off.'

'What do you do?'

'Delivery driver.' He flashed me a bright smile. 'I'm one of those who leaves your parcels in wheelie bins and chucks them over garden walls.'

'A national treasure,' I said and he laughed. I liked making him laugh.

'Do you enjoy it?'

He shrugged. 'It's fine. I like driving round the area. I like meeting people.'

'Much nicer driving round here than through city traffic I imagine,' I said.

He nodded. 'So what did you discover about poor doomed Emily?' he asked, clearly having had enough of talking about himself. I was slightly disappointed with the subject change because I wanted to know more about Jed, but I went with it.

'Not much yet,' I admitted. 'But apparently there are rumours that she was involved with a smuggling gang, so I'm looking into that.'

'Involved as in she was one of the smugglers?'

I shrugged. 'Not sure yet. Possibly.'

'Were there female smugglers?'

'No idea,' I said cheerfully. 'The other rumour is that she grassed them up.'

'Brave girl.'

'Or a criminal mastermind.'

'Or a bit of both.'

We grinned at each other.

'There's a bigger library in Falmouth,' Jed said. 'It's got a big local history section, which might be helpful. And there is a chap who lives down towards Penzance who's an expert on local pubs. He's written some books that might be helpful. I can't remember his name but I think my dad's got a couple so I could ask him, and you could reserve them from the library if you like?'

I did like. 'Is your dad local?'

'Cornwall, but not this bit,' Jed said vaguely. 'I'll see him in a few days though so I'll ask him. If you give me your number, I'll message when I've found out more.'

'That would be great.'

Jed unlocked his phone and handed it to me. His fingers touched mine and sent a jolt through me. It had been so long since a man had this effect on me, I wasn't completely sure how to handle it. I covered my discomfort by focusing on his phone. His home-screen picture was a view over Kirrinporth harbour, which told me disappointingly little about what sort of man he was, though I was pleased it wasn't a photo of a woman or even kids. *Stop it, Phoebe*, I thought to myself as I typed my number in and pressed the green button to call my phone. 'Now I've got your number too.'

'I'd like to help with your research if I can,' Jed said, taking his phone back and typing in my name. 'Like I said, I'm really interested in this sort of stuff. So if you've got any questions, just let me know.'

'I've got one already,' I said, thinking of Liv back at the pub.

'Yeah?'

'It's not about Emily Moon.'

Jed frowned. 'What's it about?'

'The people who lived at the pub before we did.'

'Oh yeah, you mentioned them before. What about them?' Jed shifted in his chair, looking slightly uncomfortable. Or perhaps it was just because the chairs were hard.

'It's weird, they obviously left in a hurry because we have a lot of their stuff in the pub. I wondered if you knew them or why they went? Your mate Ewan said he did some work with the landlord.'

'Mike,' said Jed. 'Mike Watson.'

'That's it. Did you know him? Where's he gone?'

Jed shook his head. 'Just by sight really,' he said.

'So you don't know why they left in such a hurry?'

Jed looked out of the café window and then back to me. 'Family emergency, I heard,' he said. 'Some relative was ill.'

'Bit odd. Why would the whole family have to go?'

'No idea.' He shrugged. 'Could be anything really, couldn't it?'

He was right, but I was still disappointed he didn't know more. Jed picked up his phone but fumbled and it dropped on the floor. As he leaned over to get it, his jacket fell open and I thought I caught a glimpse of another phone in his inside pocket. But before I could properly look, he straightened up again, leaving me unsure if it had been a phone or something else. I closed my eyes briefly. I had to stop being suspicious of everyone I met. Even if Jed did have two phones, where was the harm in that? Lots of people did. My own dad, in fact. And that was simply so he could keep his work and home life separate.

'I have to go,' Jed said. 'It was nice seeing you. I'll let you know about those books.'

He gave me a wide smile that seemed more than a little forced, and headed out of the café door. I watched him walk past the window, hunched down in his jacket, hoping he'd glance in my direction and I could wave. But he didn't look up.

Chapter 20

Emily

1799

Arthur didn't come the next day. I waited impatiently for him as the evening grew closer but he didn't arrive.

Bored and listless, I dragged myself downstairs. My mother was short with me, and wouldn't look me in the eye. I couldn't blame her really. Everything was broken and I didn't know how to mend it. I just knew that the only way to stop this was to find out what Morgan was doing – and, if he really was smuggling, somehow alert the revenue men and bring him to justice. I felt helpless as I listened to Mam chatter to the few customers in the inn. She didn't seem as edgy as she normally was. In fact, she seemed lighter this evening, and I noticed she'd not had as much to drink. Was that because there were drinkers to serve? Or was it because she knew Morgan wouldn't be coming tonight? Perhaps she knew he was going to be busy elsewhere and that had brightened her mood.

Sitting in my usual spot by the window, I went over my plan in my head. I would wait for Arthur to arrive, I thought, which wouldn't be long because it was already getting dark. Then together we would go up on to the cliffs and see what we could find. We would hide behind one of the large rocks and wait for as long as we had to. Morgan was bound to show up sooner or later. After all, we knew he'd mentioned the inn to the man in the courtyard, and we knew their arrangements were for tonight – it all made sense.

Eventually, a group of three men came into the inn and ordered ale. My mother livened up more at the sight of customers, and I felt a flash of sympathy for her. She was a born hostess, living to make people happy and entertain and without customers she was like a duck out of water. Awkward and out of place. The two older men went to where Mam stood serving the drinks, while the other, a young chap not much older than me, sat himself down at a table and beckoned me over. I glowered at him, because I did not like engaging with customers, but he beckoned me again. So, with a great deal of effort I forced myself to get up off my chair and went over to where the young man sat.

'Emily?' he said in a low tone.

Surprised, I nodded.

'I have a message from Arthur.'

I blinked at him. He must be one of Arthur's friends. He knew everyone, Arthur did. He was that sort of boy. Able to chat to anyone from Mr Kirrin in the big house, to beggars on the street.

'Arthur says his father needs him and he can't get away this evening. And he says to tell you not to go alone. He said to be firm about that. Don't go alone.'

I didn't speak.

'He said you were quiet.' The young man looked amused. 'You've understood though?'

I nodded again.

'That's good,' he said. He glanced over at my mother who was laughing with the other two men at the counter. 'She's a fine woman, your mam.'

131

I followed his gaze and watched Mam present one of the men with a brimming tankard of ale as though he'd won a prize. This was how she was supposed to be. Light-hearted and friendly, and Morgan had taken all that away from her.

Giving Arthur's friend a small, tight-lipped smile, I turned away. What was I to do now? Arthur wasn't coming, but the fact remained that Morgan was going ahead with whatever he had planned for tonight and it might be the best chance I had to find out what he was up to.

It took just seconds for me to make my decision. It didn't matter what Arthur had said. I would go out to the cliffs alone and see if I could track Morgan down, just as we'd planned.

I waited until the sun had gone down completely and then gestured to my mother that I was going upstairs to sleep. She nodded, still focused on the few customers who were at the inn. Instead of putting on my nightdress, though, I swapped my pale dress for a dark grey one that I thought would help me blend into the shadows. Then I wrapped myself in my cloak and pulled the hood up over my fair hair and quietly slipped out of the back door.

I knew the clifftops like the back of my hand, because I'd grown up in Kirrinporth and those cliffs had been my playground as a child, but it still took me a moment to get my bearings in the darkness. My breath was coming in short, shallow pants and I had to stop for a moment to calm myself. I wasn't going to plunge into the sea like Theodora and Diggory, I told myself sternly. Theodora and Diggory weren't real and I knew where I was going. The night was chilly and the wind had a bite to it that made me glad of my cloak. I tightened it round my neck and crouched down behind one of the large boulders to wait.

It had been cloudy all day, and the clouds remained, but it seemed Morgan knew what he was talking about when it came to the weather because as I sat there, behind the rock, the wind rose up, blowing away the clouds, and the moon came out.

As the gloomy darkness lifted and the moon's silvery sheen

crept over the clifftops, I shrank down into my cloak. There was no one around as far as I could tell, but I didn't want to risk being spotted. And that's when I heard the mournful moaning I'd heard from the inn. This time though it was right beside me, louder than ever, and so unearthly it sent a shiver down my spine. I squeezed my eyes tightly shut, and pinched my lips together to stop myself screaming in fear. Was this Theodora and Diggory? Were they coming to find me and push me off the clifftop to my doom?

I stayed still, frozen in fright, for a few minutes, but nothing happened. There was no push. No icy cold spectral hands on my back, to shove me from my safe hiding place. Nothing, except the wailing sound and the wind whipping the hood of my cape round my neck.

Slowly, I forced myself to open my eyes, convinced I would see Diggory's spirit waiting there. But to my enormous relief, there was nothing. No one – living or dead – anywhere in sight. But my heart was still thumping. This was a big mistake, I thought. I should go home before I scared myself further, and come back when Arthur was around. But then I thought again of Mam's lightness when Morgan wasn't around and changed my mind, as the hooting, melancholy moaning started up again, right beside me. The wind blew across my face at the same time and I shivered. And then I had a thought. Carefully, I stood up, holding my cloak with both hands. Even on my feet, the boulder I'd been hiding behind was a little taller than me. It was smooth, cold grey rock with holes worn by years of rain and sea gales, and it was to one of those holes I now put my ear. There again was the wailing sound. A hollow, hooting, sad moan coming directly from the hole in the rock.

I let out my breath in a gasp and leaned against the boulder for support. It was the wind through the holes that made the sounds, I thought. Not ghosts. Not Theodora or Diggory. Just the wind. What a fool I was to let myself get so frightened. My father would laugh at me if he were here.

A shout from below made me jump again. I was easily scared this evening, it seemed. I looked out over the cove and there in the moonlight, I could see the outline of a large ship on the horizon. And then there was the slapping of oars on water. Blinking, I gazed across the see. And finally I spotted a rowing boat with two men – or was it three? – on board. The boat was laden with cargo, I could tell by how low it sat in the water. So it was indeed smuggling, I thought. Just as we'd suspected. I wondered what their booty was. Bottles of drink, perhaps? Tobacco? Who knew. The little boat was making good progress, carried with the tide as it headed into land. I gasped again. This wasn't Kirrinporth cove, where boats could land safely. Our little bay was rocky and the currents unpredictable; it was no place to bring in a boat. And yet, the rowers came closer and closer, calling to someone on the beach.

Intrigued, I lay down on my stomach and inched towards the cliff edge so I could look down on to the sand. And there, as I'd expected, was Morgan. He was wearing his tricorn hat; it hid his face and though the moon was bright it was too dark to see him clearly, but I could tell it was him from his stance. He stood staring out to sea, another man – who I thought was Petroc from his shape – at his side. When the rowing boat drew closer, they both waded into the waves and helped guide it up the beach.

I had another start of recognition as one of the men who'd been in the boat straightened up; it was the man Morgan had been talking to in the courtyard. Together, Morgan, Petroc and the men from the boat began unloading the cargo quickly and efficiently. They'd obviously done this before as they fell easily into a system with Morgan directing the proceedings and the others forming a line to pass whatever they were unloading up the beach. It was quite impressive to watch, so swift were they.

I couldn't see right to the top of the beach, where the sand met the bottom of the cliff I was on. I tried wriggling forward a bit more but it felt too precarious and the beach was too dim for my eyes to see exactly what the men were doing.

I would wait, I thought, until they came up the path on to the clifftop. I didn't envy them that trip. It was a difficult enough walk in the bright light of daytime and even without having your hands full. It always left me panting for breath, with legs that wobbled from the exertion, and I could never look back as I was clambering up. I'd done that once when I was much smaller and been stuck where I was, convinced if I moved a muscle I'd tumble down on to the rocks below. Eventually my father had climbed down to get me, and I'd sworn never to make that mistake again. How the men would make it with their arms full of . . . whatever it was . . . I couldn't imagine.

I hunched down again, covering myself in my cloak and waited for them to emerge at the top of the cliff. I waited. And waited. And yet they didn't appear. What was going on? I strained my ears for voices, but the only sound was the waves crashing on the rocks as the tide came in.

Confused, I stood up, looking back out to sea. But the ship was gone. Dropping to my knees, I peered over the edge again. To my utter astonishment the beach was empty. There was no sign of the men, no evidence of their cargo, and even the rowing boat had vanished. I rubbed my eyes. What on earth was happening? Had I fallen asleep and dreamed the whole thing?

Gathering my cloak around me, I walked back to the inn, still bewildered. I would draw everything I saw to help me remember, I thought. Inside, I darted upstairs and sketched as fast as I could, wanting to make sure I remembered every detail. My charcoal covered the pages as I captured the men on the beach, carrying their haul of goods from the boat. I paid special attention to the flash of white in Morgan's hair. When I'd finished, I paused, thinking for a moment. I normally kept my pictures tied together on a shelf at the end of my bed. But this was too important. I didn't want to risk Mam finding them and burning them as she had done with my drawings of Da's death.

I slid off my bed, and went to the window. The wide ledge,

where I'd sat that terrible night, had a shallow hidden compartment where I'd stored my treasures as a little girl – feathers and shells from the beach. I wasn't sure if it would still open. But I felt along the edge carefully, pushing down, and heard with satisfaction the catch release. I slid the pictures inside and pushed it shut again. No one would find that unless they were looking for it. They'd be safe there.

Satisfied, I began getting ready for bed. I would and go and find Arthur as soon as I woke in the morning. I would tell him what I saw and perhaps he could make sense of this.

Chapter 21

Phoebe

2019

I caught the bus back to The Moon Girl because – predictably – it had started raining. On the way I thought about where Emily Moon had gone and whether she really had died all those hundreds of years earlier. I wasn't stupid; I know I was interested in her story because of what had happened at work with Ciara James. I'd failed Ciara but perhaps I could somehow find out the truth about Emily Moon instead. Obviously it wouldn't bring Ciara back or ease her mother's suffering, but it would give me something to focus on and perhaps make me feel the tiniest bit like I wasn't completely useless. A way to make amends, almost.

And I thought about Jed. I'd been single for a while and since my troubles at work, I'd not thought about romance, but Jed was making me feel things I'd not felt in a long time. I liked how interested he was in everything I had to say, and how much he loved Cornwall. And his broad shoulders and strong arms were a definite plus. I smiled to myself as the bus rumbled along towards the pub. Maybe the summer was about to get more interesting.

When I got back to the pub, Liv was sitting at the end of the bar with her laptop open. She looked up as I bounced into the pub and gave me an alarmed look.

'What's happened? Are you okay?'

'Absolutely fine,' I sang, giving her a hug.

'Weirdo,' she muttered but she hugged me back.

I let her go – eventually – and she grinned at me. 'How was your walk?'

'I've been all over,' I said.

She snapped her laptop shut. 'Fancy a coffee?'

I shook my head. 'Just had one. With Jed.'

Liv looked thrilled. 'Tell me everything.'

She slid off her stool and took herself behind the bar. 'Sure you don't want anything?'

'Go on then. I'll have a cappuccino.'

She made the coffee and as she handed me my cup it rattled in the saucer and I noticed her hand was slightly shaky. I wondered if she'd been going over the accounts again. But before I could ask if she was okay, she nudged me.

'So what happened?'

'I bumped into him in Kirrinporth and we went for coffee,' I said. 'He's going to help me investigate Emily Moon.'

'Investigate Emily Moon, eh?' Liv said, making the words sound absolutely filthy.

I giggled. 'He's really nice.'

'And also extremely hot.'

'That too.'

'When are you seeing him again?'

I shrugged. 'No plans. Maybe he'll come in tonight?' I'd have to put some make-up on, I thought.

'How did you get on with Ewan?' I said, suddenly remembering what Liv had been doing while I'd been hanging out with Jed. 'Is he going to help? What did he say?'

A shadow crossed Liv's face but then she smiled. 'He was quite helpful actually. He's got a few ideas.'

'Like what?'

'Oh nothing worth boring you with.'

'I'd like to know.'

'Honestly, Phoebe, it's all just crappy pub stuff.'

Was I imagining it, or was her smile beginning to look a bit forced?

A draught from the door made me look round to where two couples had just come in. Liv straightened up and gave them her best barmaid grin before they could clock how quiet the pub was and change their minds. 'What can I get you?'

As the customers decided what to order, she turned back to me. 'Why don't you chill out upstairs. Have a bath. Read your ghost stories. Put your feet up.'

'Really?' I said.

'Go on, I'll be fine here. I've got some bits to do anyway. You can help out later. Hopefully it'll be busier then.'

Feeling slightly like I'd been dismissed, I got down from my bar stool. 'Give me a shout if you need me.'

Liv was right: the pub was busier again that evening. There was more football on, which helped. According to Liv anyway.

'Cheap beer and bar snacks,' she said, as the first customers arrived. 'Not what I was expecting from Cornwall, but it's good enough.'

'It's a world away from the surfers and posh families we were hoping for, isn't it?' I said sympathetically.

She shrugged. 'Beggars can't be choosers, Phoebe. As long as that till's going, I'm not complaining.'

I looked at her curiously. 'Is it good enough, though?' I glanced round the bar, where a few men and the occasional woman were gathered. It didn't strike me as the money spinner Liv needed it to be.

'It's a start.'

'So you said Ewan was fairly helpful? Did he come up with any bright ideas?'

Liv nodded. 'A couple,' she said. 'Do you mind collecting some glasses?'

I looked over to where she was gesturing. One lonely empty sat on a table. 'That one?'

'Yes please.' She turned her attention to a man who'd come up to the bar. 'What can I get you?'

Obediently, I slid off my stool and went to fetch the dirty glass. When I came back, Liv was in conversation with a couple who were sitting at the bar.

'You need to speak to Phoebe,' she said as I handed her the pint glass. 'She's been reading up about the history of the pub.'

'What's that?'

'These people are on holiday and they were wondering why the pub's called The Moon Girl. I thought you could tell them. Phoebe's doing some investigating,' she told the couple. 'She's in the . . .'

I jumped in. 'I'm interested in history,' I said, interrupting Liv before she could say I was a police officer. I didn't want to talk about my "real life". 'The pub's named after a girl called Emily Moon. She lived here – her mother ran the pub – and she disappeared without a trace, one night.'

The woman was wide-eyed. 'Was this recent?'

I laughed. 'God, no. Right at the end of the eighteenth century. More than two hundred years ago.'

'Oh that's a shame.' She was disappointed. 'I thought it was going to be like one of those true-crime mysteries.'

'It is true,' I pointed out. 'No one knows what happened to Emily Moon.'

'It's hard to care when it all happened so long ago, though,' the man said. 'It's not like Madeleine McCann or 9/11.'

'9/11 isn't a mystery,' his wife said.

'Isn't it?'

Inwardly rolling my eyes and feeling weirdly affronted at their dismissal of poor Emily, I spoke up. 'It's said that Emily's ghost walks the cliffs on moonlit nights, crying for her lost love.'

The man snorted.

'I thought exactly the same as you,' I said. 'Until I heard her.'

'You heard her?' the woman breathed. 'We both did. Me and Liv.'

Liv nodded. 'Wailing.'

'You should do ghost tours,' said the man. 'We did one in Bath. It was great.'

'It's not safe on the cliffs, unfortunately,' said Liv. 'But do you know, it's not a bad idea to play on the whole haunted pub thing. I might do that.'

The couple beamed at her as she offered them drinks on the house to thank them for their idea. When they went off to find a table, she turned to me. 'What was that about?'

'Ghosts?' I said.

'No, I mean why did you interrupt me when I was about to tell them you're in the police?'

I made a face. 'Not sure. I've not told anyone here. It feels a bit raw. I don't want to talk about what I do, and maybe have them remember what happened to Ciara. She was big news for a while – people could easily put two and two together. I'm not ready to chat about it.'

Liv looked thoughtful. 'That's understandable.'

'I told Ewan I worked in TV.'

'Ohhh,' she said, realisation on her face. 'I wondered what he was banging on about when he mentioned locations. That was you?'

'Afraid so.'

She grinned. 'Fair enough. If you want to keep it quiet, I'm happy to go along with it.' She bit her lip. 'It's probably for the best, and anyway, you're not officially in the police down here are you?'

'Exactly,' I said. Though I was actually. I may have been an officer with the Met but police were police in the UK.

'It's not a bad idea, though,' Liv was saying. 'The whole ghost thing. We can big it up. Get some spook hunters down here.'

'You're amazing,' I said. 'You see a business opportunity everywhere you go.'

'Maybe we can become one of those true-crime internet stories if we include the case of the missing Watson family,' Liv said, clearly enjoying herself. She put on a film trailer voice. 'What made Mike Watson and his family vanish without a trace one summer's night, leaving their possessions behind?'

'That reminds me – did you find out any more about them? Get an address or anything?'

Liv looked briefly disappointed that I wasn't running with her true-crime fun, but then she nodded. 'I didn't get an address but I did find out more. Des the regional manager said Mike's mother was in a car accident, so they had to go and be with her. They thought she was going to die, so that's why they all went in such a hurry. But she's fine now, though she's going to be out of action for a while. So they decided to stay.'

I made a face. 'Weird.'

'That's what he said.' Liv screwed her nose up. 'Who knows what goes on in families, eh?'

'Who knows?'

'Look lively,' Liv said, her attention taken by the pub door opening. 'Your mate's here.'

'My mate?' But already I felt my face growing hot as Jed appeared, looking handsome as ever. I was quite pleased to see he was on his own, not trailing after Ewan or with Mark by his side, but then – obviously – the door opened again and in they came. Jed nodded to me and I nodded back, trying to look casual. Ewan raised a hand to wave at Liv and she gave him a smile – a slightly odd smile, I noticed. It didn't quite reach her eyes. He pointed to a table by the window that overlooked the beach, and he and Jed went to sit there while Mark came to the bar. Within seconds, Jed and Ewan were deep in conversation. Jed was clearly explaining something to Ewan, with the help of beer mats and his phone.

I felt ridiculously and foolishly disappointed that Jed hadn't come to talk to me. God it was like being back at school with me getting myself in a tizz over a boy. But suddenly, the pub felt claustrophobic. I couldn't sit there with Jed over in the corner, paying me no attention. I had to look like I wasn't bothered.

I glanced out of the window and, pleased to see it was still light and it wasn't raining, I told Liv I was going for a walk and headed outside. With no destination in mind, I headed out on to the clifftop path and sat down on the grass, looking out over the sea. The sun was setting now and the sky had gone a deep blue while the water was a soft grey. I could see fishing boats heading out from Kirrinporth, and the lights going on along the coastline.

It was lovely, sitting out there. It was warmer than it had been for ages and the breeze felt smooth on my bare arms. I had to get outside more, I thought. It was good for me and my mental health. Sandra had often stressed how important it was for me to be out in the fresh air and had encouraged me to go running. I should dig out my trainers. It would be so invigorating to run along these clifftops with the sea crashing down below and the wind in my hair.

'Looking for Emily?' The voice made me jump and then, as I realised it was Jed, made my heart beat a little bit quicker.

'Just looking generally,' I said, turning to smile at him as he walked up beside me. My mood had been lifted by the scenery, and I found I was absurdly pleased to see him. 'Fancy joining me in my looking?'

He sat down next to me. I could feel the warmth of his thigh through my light summer dress and I liked it. 'What have you seen?'

'Fishing boats,' I said. 'That's about it. But it's nice out here.'

'It is,' he agreed. 'I find it very calming to be near the water.'

'It's funny to think that this is the same view that Emily would have seen from up here, all those years ago.'

Jed looked at me. 'You're really into this Emily thing, aren't you?'

I shrugged. 'I've got to be honest, if I didn't have her to distract me, I think I'd be bored stiff. This isn't how I imagined the summer in Cornwall was going to be.'

'You thought it was all blond surfers?'

'Blond surfers, posh students, nice middle-class families taking a house for the summer . . .'

'Yeah, that's the north coast,' Jed said with a grin. 'Rock, Padstow, Newquay.'

I rolled my eyes. 'And *Poldark*'s too far away too?'

'Not that far. But not quite near enough.'

I snorted. 'Well, *Poldark* or not, Liv doesn't need me as much as I thought she would. But I'm not ready to go back to London. Emily's keeping me interested.'

Jed glanced at me. 'I'm glad.'

I smiled, keeping my eyes fixed on the horizon. 'Me too.'

'I like when people visit the real Cornwall,' he said, sounding like a travel documentary. 'There's a lot more here than surfers.'

'I like surfers,' I said sulkily, annoyed that I'd misinterpreted his gladness as being about me rather than his beloved Cornwall. I didn't look at him but I got the impression he was smiling. And that made me prickly too.

'I should go back inside,' I said.

This time Jed did look at me. 'Or you could stay.'

I turned my head so I was looking at him too. Our faces were quite close together. 'Why?'

There was a glint in Jed's eye. 'Because it's nice sitting here with you,' he said.

I melted, all prickliness gone. 'Fine, I'll stay a bit longer.'

He grinned at me. 'I asked around about the Watsons leaving so suddenly.'

'You did? That was quick.' I was impressed with his keenness.

'Yes, apparently there was a problem with one of the kids. They had to move to be near a special school. Or a hospital. Something like that.'

Well, that wasn't what the regional manager had told Liv. How strange. I looked at Jed, but he didn't seem like he was telling a deliberate untruth. Instead he was gazing out to sea, his face calm in the twilight.

'Did you know there's a beach down there?' I said. 'Liv and I saw it from the pub. It's a tiny cove, tucked away underneath the cliffs. Did you know about it?'

'I did,' he said, smiling at me.

'I want to go down there.'

But he shook his head. 'You can't,' he said. 'It's not possible. There used to be a path down the side of the cliff, many years ago. But the wind and the rain and erosion have washed it away. You can only get to it by boat now.'

'Oh that's such a shame,' I said, genuinely disappointed.

'It is,' he said. 'Maybe one day I'll hire a boat and we can take a trip.'

'I'd like that.' Was I imagining it or were we closer to each other now? We were both almost lying down, leaning on our elbows with our legs outstretched.

I turned my head so I was looking at him. Our faces were very close to each other, but I didn't move away and nor did he.

'Me too,' he said and my pulse quickened. His expression was hard to read because it was getting darker now, but I could feel his breath on my face. He was going to kiss me. My stomach twisted just at the thought. He was going to kiss me and I wanted him to so badly it almost hurt.

Very gently, Jed leaned forward and our lips brushed.

'Phoebe,' he said quietly. I moved a tiny bit closer and we kissed properly this time. My head was spinning. I could smell the faint scent of Jed's aftershave and feel his stubble on my skin. It was perfect.

And then a lorry rumbled past on the road and made us both jump, and the moment was broken. Jed sat up.

'I'm so sorry, I have to go,' he said. He pulled his phone out of his inside pocket and I noticed that his screensaver was different from earlier. It was just a standard blue wavy pattern – not the photo I'd noticed in the café. 'Work.'

'Now?' I sat up too, trying and failing to hide my disappointment.

'I'm afraid so.'

He stood up and held his hand out to me to help me up. I got to my feet and brushed the grass from my behind. 'I was enjoying that,' I said.

He looked at me and I thought he was going to say something but then he stopped. Instead he kissed me again and then groaned. 'I really have to go.' He turned and walked back towards the pub, his long legs meaning he moved fast.

Slightly confused by everything that had just happened, but still floating on air after the kiss, I hugged myself. This summer had just got a whole lot more interesting, I thought with a grin. I was very glad we'd come.

Chapter 22

The euphoria of my kiss with Jed lasted a whole twelve hours before it all went wrong.

Liv had been closing up when I got back to the empty pub after the clifftop kiss. She looked at me with a gleam in her eye. 'Did Jed follow you?'

I flopped into a chair and sighed happily. 'He did.'

'And?'

I tried to look nonchalant. 'What do you mean?'

Liv threw a bar towel at me. 'Spill,' she said.

'He kissed me,' I said. 'Or maybe I kissed him. I'm not sure. But we kissed.'

'How was it?'

'Amazing,' I said. 'Dreamy.'

She grinned. 'Drink while you tell me all the details?'

'Glass of wine, please.'

Liv poured us both a glass and came over to sit with me, checking first that the pub door was locked firmly.

'Still a bit jumpy?' I asked.

She looked sheepish. 'I can't help it. It's so remote here, isn't it? And that wind doesn't help. And the ghost stories creep me out, even though I know they're ridiculous. And . . .' She trailed off.

'And?'

'Nothing.'

'You said and.'

'Did I?' She gave me a broad smile. 'I'm losing my marbles. I can't remember what I was going to say.' She slurped her wine. 'So tell me everything that happened with Jed. He's blooming gorgeous.'

'Isn't he?' I groaned. 'We had a good chat, and we were kind of lying on the grass, watching the sea and it just happened.'

'Did you . . .'

'No,' I shrieked. 'We were in plain view of the road.'

Liv gave a Sid-James-style guffaw. 'So what happened after that?'

I groaned. 'Then a massive truck roared past and made us both jump, and he remembered he had to be at work.'

'Ah that's annoying.'

'I know, just when it was all going well he ups and disappears.'

'Like Emily Moon,' said Liv in a spooky voice.

I glared at her and she stuck her tongue out at me.

'What job does he do?' she asked. 'Why did he have to go to work at this time of night?'

My stomach plummeted into my flip-flops. 'He's a delivery driver,' I said in a small voice.

Liv blinked. She didn't say anything but I could tell what she was thinking because I was thinking it too. Delivery drivers, unlike pub managers and police officers, generally didn't work into the night.

'Maybe he's doing some distribution stuff,' Liv said vaguely. 'Getting things where they need to be overnight.'

'Maybe he's married?'

Don't be so dramatic,' Liv said. 'Of course he's not married. There are loads of reasons for him to go to work at this time. He doesn't wear a wedding ring, does he?'

I thought of Jed's large, strong hands and shook my head. 'No ring.'

148

'Message him.'

'Now? He's only just left. I don't want to look like I'm too keen.'

Liv snorted. 'Tomorrow then.'

'Maybe.'

'Ewan was here when he went outside tonight. I made some comment about there being no prizes for guessing where he'd gone and Ewan laughed. Surely he'd have said then if Jed had a wife hidden away at home?'

'They all bloody stick together though, don't they? Men.'

Liv laughed. 'Do you want me to ask him? Ask Ewan if Jed's married?'

'Yes,' I said. 'No.'

'Which?'

'Yes. But subtly. Not in a "my mate fancies your mate" way.'

'Oh I'm brilliant at subtle,' Liv said. She leaned back in her chair, looking happier than she had when I first came back from my romantic clifftop encounter. 'I am the queen of subtle.'

'You're anything but,' I teased. 'Remember when I fancied Justin Blake at school? And you wrote it on the whiteboard, so everyone saw it?'

'That wasn't me,' Liv protested. 'Was it? Anyway, didn't you snog him at the Christmas disco when you were dressed as an elf?'

'I did.'

'So it had a happy ending.'

I laughed. 'I suppose so.'

'I'll find out more,' she said. 'Leave it with me.'

'So you're seeing Ewan again soon are you?' I said, ultra-casually.

'Not like that!' Liv looked horrified.

'I didn't mean in a romantic way,' I said. 'I meant for business. Do you really think he can help increase the pub's takings.'

She frowned. 'I'm not sure.'

'Do you think he's dodgy?'

Liv sighed. 'No, I don't, Phoebe. You're doing it again.'

149

'You just sounded like you had doubts.'

'I don't have doubts.'

'Are you sure?'

'Phoebe, I've been running pubs for a long time. I know what I'm doing.'

'So why do you need Ewan?'

'Because I don't know Cornwall and he's offering to help.'

'And he doesn't want anything in return?'

'Give it a rest,' she said. 'I told you, he's a fixer. He gets stuff done and obviously he gets stuff in return – he'll take a commission or I'll pay him for his time. But it's fine. It's above board. I checked with Des, remember?'

I nodded. 'Sorry,' I said.

The next morning I woke up early, before Liv, which was unusual. I lay in bed, listening to her regular breathing and thinking about Jed. That kiss had been amazing. But the more I thought about him running off, the more I thought how strange it was. Maybe he was married or had a girlfriend. Maybe he just wasn't that into me. It was hard to tell because I didn't trust my own judgement about anything any more. I'd made a mistake with Ciara James and she'd lost her life. I'd missed the little puddle-jumping girl's mother keeping a close eye on her. Who's to say I'd not misjudged Jed too?

I rolled on to my side and felt for my phone on the bedside table. Then I spent at least twenty minutes composing and deleting a message to Jed.

After discarding 'Thanks for last night!' (too perky) and 'I had a good time last night' (not perky enough) in the end I simply wrote: 'What are you up to today?'

I went for a shower and when I got back, Liv was awake. I showed her the message and she nodded approvingly.

'Perfect,' she said. 'I reckon he'll reply any second.'

But he didn't. He didn't reply all morning. I moped around

the pub looking sorry for myself until Liv took my phone off me and sent me outside to clean the tables in the garden.

'Do your thing,' she said. 'Anchor yourself.'

'I don't want to anchor myself in this moment,' I grumbled. 'I should have done that last night.'

She laughed, then frowned as her own phone beeped and she glanced at the screen.

'What's that?'

'What?' Liv's focus was on her phone.

'What's the message?'

She looked up at me, seeming mildly surprised as though she'd forgotten I was there.

'Oh just spam,' she said. 'Nothing important.'

'I'll clean those tables then.'

'Yes please.'

'Can I take my phone?'

'No.' She shoved it in her pocket and then looked at her own phone again, in her other hand, and did the same with that. 'Go,' she said. 'Go on.'

I cleaned all the tables and chairs. I dragged a patio heater out of the shed because, let's face it, it wasn't always warm. I stood for a little while gazing out over the sea, watching the waves, which today had little white tips, and thinking about Jed. And finally, when all that was done, I went back inside and begged Liv for my phone.

'Has he replied?' I said as she handed it over. But no. He hadn't.

'See if he's read it,' Liv said. 'He might be sleeping if he was working last night. Perhaps he's not seen your message yet.'

A tiny bit of hope flickered and then died as I saw that the message had been delivered and read just after I sent it.

Liv made a face. 'Maybe you should watch some *Homes Under the Hammer*,' she said gently. 'Might take your mind off things.'

But even that wasn't appealing. I shook my head.

'Go out for a walk then. Blow away the cobwebs.'

'Actually maybe I'll go running,' I said. 'I've not done any exercise since we've been here and I need to keep my fitness up or I'll be in a whole world of pain when I go back to work.'

Liv looked relieved. 'That's a great idea.'

'Want to come?'

She thought about it for approximately ten seconds. 'Nope,' she said. 'Busy.'

'Doing what?'

She shrugged. 'Bit of this, bit of that.'

'Fair enough. I'll see you later then.'

'Later,' she said.

Chapter 23

Emily

1799

I slept fitfully that night, tossing and turning as I thought about Morgan and his henchmen, not to mention their boat and all its cargo, vanishing into thin air. I hoped my sketches would be good enough to help me explain what had happened on the beach, when I spoke to Arthur.

Mam was in a foul temper the next day. She kept me busy all day with chores and cooking and cleaning and I didn't get a moment to myself to go and see Arthur. There was no sign of Morgan though, which I was thankful for.

Sadly my mother's mood was no better the following day. I helped her sweep the floors though she still barely acknowledged me. She was more gloomy today than angry, though her temper was short so I was very glad indeed when she finally said I could go. I gathered my drawings and headed out to find my friend. I didn't need to go far. He was on the road from Kirrinporth, walking towards the inn.

'Arthur,' I said, waving. I was very pleased to see him.

I rushed over to him and he gave me his usual crooked smile.

'That's a nice greeting.' He squeezed my arm and I flushed at his touch.

'I need to tell you,' I said. I took a deep breath. 'Morgan . . . the boat and the beach . . .'

'Hold on,' Arthur said with a frown. 'Slow down. Take your time. What happened?'

'I went on to the cliffs,' I began, thinking carefully about each word.

'Oh, Emily.' He looked disappointed briefly and then resigned. 'I thought you would.'

I shrugged. 'I had to know.'

'And? What did you find?'

I looked around me. The road was quiet but back towards Kirrinporth I could see the dust that suggested someone was riding towards us, so I pulled Arthur away from the thoroughfare, up the bank at the side, and found a fallen tree trunk for us to sit on.

'I watched,' I told him. 'I was so frightened because of the noises. The wailing noises. I thought it was Diggory and Theodora.'

'Really? There was noise?'

'It was the wind blowing through the holes in the rocks.'

'Of course it is,' Arthur said in triumph. 'Like when you blow across the top of a bottle. I can't believe I didn't work that out.'

'Then I saw the men,' I said. 'On the beach – Morgan, and others. I think Petroc was there.' I squinted my eyes and shrugged, to show it had been hard to see for sure. 'It was dark.'

'They were on the beach?'

I pulled out my sketches and handed them to him.

'Look,' I said. I tapped my finger on the paper. 'Rowing boat.' I moved my finger over to where I'd drawn the shadowy larger ship out at sea. 'Cargo,' I said.

'And the rowing boat came into the cove?' Arthur said, looking at the drawings. 'The cove below the inn? It's not safe for boats, is it?'

I shrugged. I'd thought the same as him but the men had obviously known what they were doing because they got there without damaging the boat.

A thought struck me and I found the picture of the man I'd recognised from the courtyard. I showed Arthur.

'This man was on the boat. I saw him the other day,' I said.

Arthur nodded, understanding. 'Ah, so Morgan clearly needed him for his seafaring skills?'

'Yes.'

'But what were they doing on the boat?'

I mimed moving something from one place to another.

'Bringing something ashore from the bigger ship?' Arthur said. 'Smuggling?'

I bit my lip. 'I think so.'

'What do you think they were bringing? Bottles? Or packages of tobacco?'

'I don't know,' I said, frowning.

'Did you wait for them to come up?'

This was the important bit. I had to make Arthur understand what had happened. I took a breath. 'I waited for them to come up from the cove, on to the clifftop, so I could have a proper look,' I said, painfully slowly. 'But they didn't.'

'They didn't what?' Arthur leafed through the scraps of paper, puckering his brow as he squinted at the pictures I'd drawn.

'Come up,' I said. 'They didn't come up the cliff and they didn't go back out to sea.' I opened my hands to show nothing. 'Gone.'

'That makes no sense.'

I made the gesture again. Arthur frowned.

'Could you have fallen asleep?' he asked.

I shook my head. 'No.'

Arthur looked up as the horseman I'd seen approaching drew nearer. 'That's Morgan,' he said. 'I recognise his horse. Come.'

He pulled my arm and we both ducked down behind the tree trunk we'd been sitting on. I wasn't sure why we hid but it felt like the right thing to do. Morgan thundered past on his horse, its hooves churning up the dirt. He was heading for the inn. I felt sick, thinking of my mam waiting there for him.

We waited for a few minutes until Morgan was out of sight and then Arthur stood up and brushed the dust from his britches.

'Shall we go down on to the beach and see what we can find?'

'Morgan?'

Arthur looked sheepish. 'I'm assuming Morgan will be . . . occupied . . . for a while.'

I closed my eyes briefly, hating the thought, but then I nodded. 'Yes,' I said. We should go while we had the chance.

'Do you know the way down the path?' Arthur looked a little worried. 'I'm not always confident with heights.'

I gave a small laugh. 'Da used to take me . . .'

As we walked back towards the sea, I told him as best I could, about how Da and I would clamber over the rocks to the water when I was little. And Da would show me the sea urchins and starfish that we could find in the pools that gathered when the tide went out.

'I always liked looking for crabs,' said Arthur.

'I am scared of crabs,' I admitted, pinching my thumbs and forefingers together. 'Pincers.'

Arthur looked at me. 'Scared of crabs, but not of the man who murdered your father and beat your mother?'

'I am scared,' I said. 'But . . .' I paused, thinking about the words to say. 'I want him to pay.'

We'd reached the top of the cliff. Arthur paused, looking down at the beach below. 'I'm scared too,' he admitted. 'But we can face this together.'

He held out his hand to me and I took it.

'Please don't let me go,' he said. 'I'm really not looking forward to going down there.'

I smiled. 'Come.'

I led the way down the winding path. Arthur had to drop my hand because we needed to balance and at parts where the way was especially steep, or the ground sandy and gave way beneath our feet, he dropped on to his backside and slid down like a child learning to walk. But we made it down the cliff safely and stood on the beach on wobbly legs. It was a very small cove, a tiny dent in the coastline. It was narrower at the top than where it met the sea, and the beach was dotted with boulders similar to the ones up on top where I'd hidden the night before, but smaller. The cliffs rose up on either side of us like walls in a prison cell, blocking out the weak sun and making me shiver. The tide was on its way out now and the waves were loud as they were sucked away from the rocks.

'Talk me through what happened,' Arthur said. 'Let's re-create it.'

I closed my eyes, trying to picture it.

'Morgan was here,' I said, walking over to where I'd seen him standing. 'And Petroc.'

Arthur came and stood next to me. 'Do you have the drawings?'

I found them in my bag and handed them over, still thinking.

'The boat came,' I said stretching my hands out as though I was pulling the boat myself. 'They guided it in.' I thought a bit more. 'Deep,' I said. I touched the side of my hand to my chest to show where the water would reach. 'Deep.'

'Past those rocks there?' Arthur pointed to where the receding tide was revealing a bank of jagged stones large enough to tear a hole in the hull of a much bigger boat.

'Yes.' I turned and looked up the beach. 'They pulled the boat up.' I started acting out what I'd seen the men do. 'Unloading.'

I position Arthur next to me and pretended to pass him a box, then went to the other side of him and took it, hoping he'd get what I meant.

'A line?' he said and I nodded, pleased how well he understood.

Arthur walked up the beach a little way, past where the high-water mark could be seen as a line of shells and seaweed. He looked carefully at the sand as he went and then paused. 'Here,' he said. 'You didn't dream it.'

I went over to him and there, on the sand, were lines showing that something heavy had been dragged up the beach. 'Most of the marks have been kicked over with sand,' Arthur said. 'They're hidden. But they must have missed this bit. Looks like they pulled the boat right up here.'

'So far?' I said, looking round me in confusion. 'Why?' I followed a path with my eyes, from the water, where I'd seen Morgan and Petroc grab the boat, up the beach to the marks by where we stood, and then towards the back of the cove where the sand met the sheer blank face of the cliff. There was nothing. Slowly, I walked towards the back of the cove, looking at the sand as I went, but I couldn't see any more drag marks. I simply couldn't understand where they had gone.

'Maybe they're the ghosts,' I said carefully. 'Not Theodora and Diggory.'

'There is no such thing as ghosts,' he said. 'So there must be an explanation.'

I turned and with my back to the sea and my hands on my hips, stared up at the cliff. An explanation, I thought. The cliffs weren't smooth as they dropped down towards the beach. Their surface was uneven and jagged, with little outcrops and bunches of long rough seagrass growing on them. I gazed at them, wondering how a group of men, a load of smuggled goods and a rowing boat, could simply vanish into the stone. And that's when I saw it. Below one rocky overhang, draped with grass, was an opening in the cliff.

'Arthur,' I said. 'Look.'

Together, we ran up the beach to the crack in the stone. It was wide – wider than it had looked from where I was standing – and taller than either me or Arthur. I pointed to the gap. Could they have gone in there?

Arthur, bless him, glanced round and found a piece of drift-wood on the beach and some dried-out grass. He handed the wood to me. 'Hold this,' he said as he gathered the brown grass into a bundle. Looking round again, he found two sharp pieces of flint near the bottom of the cliff and began striking them together, sending sparks into the air around him.

'Dammit,' he muttered as the sparks failed to land where he

needed them to. He tried again, and this time the pile of grass began to smoulder. Gently he blew on it, turning the smoulder into a flame. 'Now hold the wood in the fire,' he said. I did as he said and watched as the wood caught alight at one end. 'We have a torch,' said Arthur triumphantly.

'Well done,' I said, admiringly. I gave it to him, not wanting the flame to scorch my hair.

'Now we can see where we're going,' he said.

Arthur and his makeshift torch went first, through the narrow gap in the rock. For a little way it was narrow – about as wide as my outstretched arms – and dim and then suddenly the passageway opened out into a much wider tunnel.

'Oh,' I breathed, looking around me in wonder. It wasn't huge, but it was wide enough for Arthur and I to stand side by side with space to spare. The floor was dry and sandy, and the walls were cool. 'Did someone make this?'

Arthur looked impressed. 'I rather think they did. Or at least, they've improved on what nature has provided.'

He moved the torch gently from one side to another, and in the flickering light of the flame we both looked around us. At one side of the tunnel, propped up on its edge and leaning against the wall, was the rowing boat. Its oars were neatly stacked on top.

'There,' I said, pointing. My shadow was enormous on the wall of the tunnel, looming over the boat like a sea monster.

Arthur nodded. 'But no cargo,' he said. 'Shall we keep going?'

'Look. Lantern.'

There were lanterns carefully placed in small hollows carved out of the stone. Arthur lit the candle inside with his makeshift torch and then stamped out the flame he'd been carrying and threw the stick out of the cave door.

I was trembling with fear, feeling the weight of the cliffs pressing down from above us, but I nodded. 'Let's carry on.' My hand felt for Arthur's in the dark and I was relieved when my fingers found his and we gripped each other tight.

On and on we went, deeper into the cliffs. And up, I thought. We were going up. We couldn't hear the waves any more. Just the sound of our breathing and my own heart pounding. And then, after a good five minutes that seemed much longer, we came to two roughly made stone steps and a wooden door. We stopped. Arthur's face looked pale in the orange light from the lantern.

'Shall we open it?' he whispered.

I nodded first then shook my head. 'No,' I said, clutching him. 'Listen first.'

He put his ear to the wood and listened for a second or two. Then he shook his head. 'I can't hear anything.'

I took a deep breath. It was either go through this door or back through the tunnel and I had to admit, neither seemed an attractive prospect right at this second. 'Let's open it,' I said.

There was no lock on the door, just a latch. With a slightly shaky hand, I reached out and opened it, pulling the door towards me.

'I'll go first,' Arthur said. He stepped over the threshold and I followed. It was a room. A proper room, with distempered walls and a table. There were barrels stacked at one end, a broom leaning against one wall, and on the table were bottles of drink – I wasn't sure what – and packages.

'Cargo,' said Arthur. 'That must be the cargo you saw them unloading.'

I nodded, but I couldn't speak. Suddenly everything was clear to me.

'What's the matter?' Arthur turned to me, his eyes concerned. 'What's happened?'

I took a deep, shuddery breath. 'I know where we are.'

'Where?' He looked around himself but he didn't recognise the room we stood in. Why would he? He'd never been here before. But I had.

'We're in the inn,' I said, concentrating on every word. This was important. 'This is the cellar. I'm home.'

Chapter 24

Phoebe

2019

My running stuff was at the bottom of my drawer. I pulled it out, and put it on. I glanced out of the window to check the weather and then found a hoodie too, which I tied round my waist. Just in case.

Liv was nowhere to be seen when I went back downstairs. I'd left my phone on the bar to stop me checking it but now I picked it up and looked at the screen. Nothing. Gah.

I put in my earbuds, turned my music up loud, and headed outside.

I glanced back at the pub as I went. The sign swayed gently in the wind, showing the figure of a young girl, bathed in an ethereal glow, perched on the edge of a cliff. I'd not paid much attention to it when we arrived but now I could see that the scenery in the picture was obviously based on the cliffs where I stood. I felt a little flutter of sadness for poor Emily Moon. For what had happened to her.

I didn't really want to run along the clifftop because it just reminded me of kissing Jed, but it was better than going along the side of the road to Kirrinporth. So I took a breath, concentrated on the sound of my trainers hitting the ground, and the music in my ears, and started to run.

The footpath ran alongside the road for a short while, then snaked off across the clifftop. It was easy to follow because the long grass was flattened by ramblers' feet, and there were occasional signposts telling me I was on the Great Cornwall Way. The cliff edge was about the length of a football pitch away, marked with fairly inadequate wooden posts. There was no one else around and in between songs I could hear the waves crashing down below and the seagulls screeching.

Running had been a good decision, I thought. I could feel the endorphins doing their job and my mood lifting as I went. Maybe Jed was just busy. It had only been a few hours. It was fine. I had absolutely no reason to worry.

I would distract myself with more Emily Moon research. I still had no idea what had happened to her and seeing her picture on the pub sign had made me realise I was desperate to find out.

I ran for about half an hour until I reached a stile and the path turned inland towards another small village that I could see in the distance. Somewhere to explore another day, I thought. The wind had got up, and the sky over the sea was darkening – it looked like more rain was heading our way – so I pulled on the hoodie I'd had tied round my waist and turned back the way I'd come.

I ran more slowly on the way back, thinking about Emily Moon and the gang of smugglers. I could see how easy it would be to plunge from the clifftop in the dark and I wondered why she'd been up there in the first place – if she had been up there of course. Perhaps she was acting as lookout for the smugglers. Or spying on them.

With Jed's warnings about the cliffs not being safe ringing in my ears, as I got closer to the pub, I left the path, and walked carefully towards the edge. It was rockier at this point, with large boulders scattered here and there. Wanting to concentrate properly, I turned off my music and put my earbuds into my pocket, listening to the waves far down below.

Gingerly, I crept along, watching where I was standing. But the ground beneath my feet seemed firm and I grew in confidence a bit. Maybe it was nothing to do with smugglers at all. Perhaps Emily Moon had just heard the ghost stories and wanted to see for herself. I imagined her coming up here to see where Theodora and Diggory had died. And then I pictured her ghost standing on the cliff edge, crying. Poor girl. I pulled up my hood and hunched down inside my fleece as the wind blew and I shivered, nearly jumping out of my skin as I heard an unearthly cry coming from right beside me.

Heart thumping, I froze to the spot. The cry came again, a kind of hollow keening wail.

'Jesus,' I whispered, feeling mildly foolish at how scared I was. It wasn't even night-time, for goodness' sake. Were there daytime ghosts?

Screwing my courage up, I forced myself to turn around to where the noise was coming from, genuinely expecting to come face to face with the spirit of Emily Moon. But to my great relief, there was no one there. Obviously.

'Get a bloody grip, Phoebe,' I told myself. And then the noise came again, just as the wind whipped my hood from head. But again there was no one there. There was nothing except the boulders scattered around.

'Ah ha,' I said out loud. The boulder next to where I stood was a particularly big one, its grey surface pocked with hollows and holes. I went to it and touched it. It was cold under my fingers. The wind blew again and as it did, the air rushed through one of the holes in the rock and made the unearthly noise.

'Oh thank goodness,' I said, laughing with relief and slight embarrassment at my own silliness. The sound of the wind blowing through the rocks must be where the ghost stories came from. Emily Moon didn't stand on the cliff edge calling to her lost love. Of course she didn't. She was long-dead and the cries were just the wind.

But knowing the truth now didn't stop my legs from trembling or my heart from thumping. Needing a minute to get myself together I sank down on to the grass and sat with my back resting on the boulder, looking out over the sea.

I breathed in deeply, going over my calming techniques. Though I was pretty sure Sandra hadn't meant for me to use them when I'd been spooked by a ghost.

It took a few minutes to feel calmer but the deep breathing helped. Once I was back to normal, I went to stand up when I heard a shout from below. This time, thankfully, it was very definitely earthly. But Jed had said the beach was inaccessible. So now, hearing the shouts, I wondered if someone was in trouble. Perhaps a boat had washed up in the tiny cove and couldn't get out again. Or maybe – my blood ran cold – someone had fallen. I had to see what was happening.

Very slowly and carefully, I got on to my belly, wriggled right to the edge of the cliff and peered over feeling my head spin as I stared down at the churning waves. To my extreme relief, I couldn't see any boat. Or anyone clinging to the cliff.

The shout came again and a laugh this time. That definitely didn't sound like someone in trouble. I turned my head, trying to ignore the queasiness I was feeling from hanging over the edge of the cliff, and looked. To my astonishment, I saw two men down below in the little cove. One was standing close to the water and the other was sitting on another of the large boulders, smoking a cigarette. They were shouting to each other and laughing. And as I watched them, my heart began thumping again because I recognised them. Both of them. It was Jed and Mark. What on earth were they doing down there?

Whatever Mark and Jed had been doing, they were finished. Mark stood up from where he sat on the big boulder and threw his cigarette end into the sea. Jed obviously thought that was a bad idea, which despite myself I couldn't help thinking was quite sweet, so he fished it out again. Then he shoved it down the back of Mark's T-shirt and the pair of them tussled for a minute like schoolboys.

Eventually they stopped wrestling, both laughing, and stood looking out to sea. Jed pointed at something and Mark nodded, then they both looked behind them, at the back of the tiny cove. It was a tiny horseshoe bay, the size of a city cul-de-sac. There was a small amount of beach but the sand was grey and coarse, not soft and golden. And most of the cove was scattered with more cement-coloured rocks that had fallen from the cliffs or washed up over the years. From where I lay on top of the cliff, I could see the roof of The Moon Girl, and down to Kirrinporth itself with its houses tumbling down the hill towards the sea. But where Jed and Mark stood was sheltered by the sheer cliffs. A bit further along the path either way and you'd not see them down there. That was interesting.

The hairs on the back of my neck were prickling. Why had Jed lied to me about the beach being inaccessible? He'd clearly not got there by boat because there was no sign of so much as a rubber dinghy on the tiny patch of sand. What was he doing down there with Mark?

The wind blew through the rocks again, making the unearthly sound. Smugglers, I thought. Emily Moon was linked with smuggling. What if there was still smuggling going on in Kirrinporth?

I wriggled backwards, away from the cliff edge and sat up, feeling my head spin again. What was I thinking? Jed was a nice man. He wasn't a bloody smuggler.

But, the voice in my head said he'd lied about the beach being out of bounds. And Mark told the ghost story, just like the one Simon said was told to keep people away from the cliffs when the smugglers were doing their thing. And I'd had an uneasy feeling about Ewan since the start.

I put my head in my hands. What was wrong with me? First there was the drama with the little girl in the town, and now I thought Jed, Ewan and Mark were modern-day smugglers? Honestly. I didn't seem to be getting better at all. I was suspicious of everyone, making snap judgements and not thinking things through. I'd never be allowed back to work at this rate.

I strained my neck to see Jed and Mark again. They weren't doing anything wrong, I told myself. So what if they were down on the beach by the pub? Perhaps they were birdwatching. Or fishing. Or anything really. Why did I even care? It wasn't private property. Maybe me talking about the beach last night had made Jed want to investigate. Perhaps he'd just been interested to see if he could get down there because I'd asked him.

I watched for a second as Jed's dark hair, and Mark's gleaming bald head began what was clearly a tricky ascent up an overgrown path to the side of the cliffs. I followed the route they would take with my eyes and realised there was a marker, covered in long grass but easy enough to spot if you knew it was there, just a few feet along from where I sat. That must be where the path came out on to the clifftop. I jumped to my feet, brushing the sandy dirt from my front and behind. For reasons I couldn't quite understand, I didn't want to be there when Jed and Mark got to the top.

I bounced on my toes and took off, running as fast as I could back towards the pub. As I reached the car park, breathing heavily, I looked back at the cliffs and saw Mark and Jed emerge on to the path by the marker. I'd go down there myself, I thought. Go down to the beach and see what was there.

Chapter 25

Emily

1799

Arthur was looking at me, bewildered. 'What? What are you saying, Emily?'

I threw my arms out, gesturing to take in the room with its white walls, barrels and bottles of drink. 'This is the inn,' I said. 'We came through the cliff and into the pub.'

Arthur looked round, realisation dawning on his face. 'The cellar . . .' he breathed. 'How can this be?'

I made a slope with my arm and walked my fingers up it. Arthur understood.

'That's why the path was sloping upwards,' he said. 'We were going up through the cliff. This is astonishing.' He was shaking his head as though he couldn't quite believe it. 'Astonishing work.' He put his hand to the wall. 'It must have taken several men and months of digging to create this. Astonishing.'

But I wasn't interested in the work needed to build a tunnel. What was important to me was why there was a tunnel leading from the rocky cove below to my home. And, with a sinking feeling, I understood exactly what was going on.

'This is it,' I said slowly. 'Why Da died.'

'I don't understand.'

I didn't know who had dug the tunnel. Like Arthur had said, nature probably had a hand in it. And perhaps someone stumbled on it one day and realised they could make use of it. 'This tunnel is old,' I began.

'I believe there were tunnels used during the Civil War,' Arthur agreed.

'It's a path from the sea to the inn.'

'And from the inn, out to Kirrinporth and beyond.'

'Smugglers,' I said, grim-faced.

'I think this is the proof we were looking for, don't you?' said Arthur, and I nodded

I thought about that awful night, watching my father and Morgan arguing outside the pub and winced. 'Da said no.' I stumbled over the words, wanting to make sure Arthur really understood. 'Morgan asked and Da said no.'

Arthur nodded, encouraging me to continue.

'He killed him. And now Mam is desperate.' I rubbed my stomach, showing I meant hungry. 'He did that. And now she will do what he asks.'

There was a pause, as Arthur took it all in. 'He's evil,' Arthur said. 'I really believe that.'

I thought back to the night Da had died. How he had told Morgan it was too risky, because now he had a wife and a daughter and he didn't want to do it and I frowned. 'Da used to help,' I said, convinced I was right. Morgan had said he never used to worry about the risk so perhaps Da was in on it for a while. Was this all his fault?

But Arthur shook his head. 'Everyone was doing it, Emily. You remember what it used to be like? Before they clamped down on it. We all got bits and pieces from free traders. Everyone did it.'

'Everyone?'

Arthur shrugged. 'It doesn't matter, Em. It doesn't. Not now.'

But I was angry, suddenly. 'It does,' I said. Da had adamant that night. He said there was nothing Morgan could do to change his mind. What if he had agreed to help? Things could have been so different. 'He was too honest,' I said.

'Good for him.'

'No,' I almost shouted. 'Everyone did it. Why not him? He would still be alive.'

'Not now they don't. Ten years ago, maybe. But things are different now, Emily, and he was right, your da. It is risky. The penalties are too great. Why do you think they sneak around, and tell ghost stories to make sure people keep away if it wasn't risky? If the revenue men find them, they'll be hanged. And if your father had got involved, he'd have hanged too. He was right to say no. Even though it cost him his life.'

'I miss him,' I said. 'I miss Da.' I started to cry and Arthur took me in his arms and smoothed my hair and wiped my tears and held me close until my sobs stopped.

'Better?' he said.

I nodded. I was a little embarrassed about showing him my emotions, but I'd enjoyed how he'd held me and now he'd let me go I felt cold. 'Thank you,' I whispered.

Arthur patted my arm. 'I will always look after you, Emily Moon,' he said. 'You mean the world to me.'

I looked up at him, my Arthur, who I'd known since I was a little girl and who I loved more than anything else on this earth. There was a look in his eye that I'd not seen before and it both scared and thrilled me. 'Arthur,' I began but before I could carry on, he'd gathered me into his arms again and he kissed me. His lips were soft and dry and the kiss was light at first and then deeper as I leaned into him, my heart thumping.

When we finally broke apart, he grinned at me. 'I think that means you're my girl now.'

I laughed, a little bubble of joy that burst out of me. 'I've always been your girl.'

Arthur laced his fingers through mine. 'I am going to marry you one day. You'll be Emily Pascoe.'

'Emily Moon,' I said firmly.

He laughed. 'Call yourself whatever you want. You'll be my wife one day. You'll see.'

I didn't argue. I very much hoped he was right. I couldn't imagine anything nicer than being Arthur's wife. But talk of weddings seemed a world away from where we were right now – in the cellar, surrounded by illegal goods, with my father dead and my mother drunk and in the pay of criminals. I had no idea what to do about it.

'What now?' I said to Arthur, looking round at the piles of contraband liquor and what I suspected would be tobacco. 'Take some? Go to the revenue men?'

'But what if Morgan and his crew realise it's missing?'

I bit my lip. If Morgan knew we'd found his smuggled goods, then we'd be in danger; there was no doubt about it.

'He'd move it,' I said.

'And he'd work out it was us, I'm sure of it,' said Arthur, alarmed. 'So should we get the revenue men to come to the pub? Search the cellar?'

'They won't listen,' I said despairingly, thinking of Mam and I throwing ourselves on Mr Trewin's mercy, and being ignored. 'And Mam . . .'

'Your mother would be the one in trouble, because she's the one with the contraband in her cellar.'

'She would hang.'

Arthur shuddered. 'So we need to wait, until the next time they're bringing something in,' he said thinking carefully. 'And get the customs men to see it with their own eyes.'

'Maybe Mam knows?' I asked, remembering how a few days earlier, she had moved some barrels out of the cellar. She'd said she didn't want them in the cellar because of damp. But now I wondered if she just didn't want to have a reason to go down there. She didn't want to see what was in it. 'Turning a blind eye,' I said.

'Wise woman, given the circumstances,' Arthur said.

'Is that enough?' I said. Would pretending to be ignorant be enough to stop her going to the gallows? I felt my heart beat faster at the thought.

'Perhaps,' said Arthur. 'Maybe your mother could speak out against Morgan and his gang. Help the revenue men to catch them? Then perhaps she'd face a lesser punishment.'

I put my hands on my head in anguish. I didn't know what to do for the best.

Arthur put his arms around me again and leaned my head on his chest.

'My father would help her,' he said. 'I'm sure of it. He could speak to the magistrate on her behalf. Talk of how she was left destitute when your father was killed – by Morgan.'

'Would he?'

'I'm certain. He admires your mother. He's said it before. Always says she is full of life and determination.'

'She was,' I said. 'No longer.'

'I remember when your father died, he was most concerned and said he was even considering visiting the inn himself. Wouldn't that be a sight to see? A vicar visiting an inn.'

He laughed, but my mind was still troubled. 'Could we talk to your father?' I said. I thought we should see if he would support us and Mam, before we went to the revenue men.

I trailed off because Arthur had stiffened in my arms. 'What?'

He unravelled himself from my embrace and went over to where the bottles of spirit were neatly laid out on the table top.

'This is what you saw them unloading?'

'Yes,' I said, not really understanding what he was doing. I pointed out the barrels and the big tea chests, then the bottles, and the larger packages, that had been inside. Under the table were the chests I'd seen. Their tops were open and inside were more of the same bottles and several similar-sized packages. I assumed they had opened a few to check it was all there.

'These bottles?' Arthur picked one up.

'Yes,' I was confused. 'These bottles.'

'This is brandy.'

'What's the matter?'

'I've seen this brandy before.'

'In the trunks?' I pointed to the chests on the floor but Arthur shook his head impatiently, looking upset.

'No, Emily. I've seen it at home. On my father's table.'

'When?' Surely this was a coincidence. Surely?'

'Last night,' Arthur said, grim-faced. 'I saw it last night. He said a friend had given it to him. He had a drink with Mr Trewin.'

I gasped. 'Mr Trewin?'

'The very same.'

I thought hard. 'Did Mr Trewin give your father the brandy?'

Arthur looked like he would cry. I wanted to go to him, to comfort him as he'd comforted me, but something in his expression told me to let him speak.

'On the night you spied on Morgan, my father said he needed me to help him prepare the eucharist for a woman in Kirrinporth who was very ill. Not likely to last the night. He needed to go and say prayers with her.'

I nodded. It seemed a worthy way to spend an evening.

'I helped him get ready, but in the end he didn't go. He said she was much improved and the doctor no longer thought she would die.'

I shrugged. 'Good news.'

But Arthur sighed. 'He knew I was planning to go for a walk with you. I told him. I think he made up the story about the dying woman to stop me going near the cliffs.'

'Really?'

'I don't know. Perhaps.' Arthur looked wretched. 'And then last night, he went out around eight o'clock – after dinner. When he came home, he had the bottle of brandy with him. He said it was a gift. And then Mr Trewin arrived and he took him into his study. I heard them making a toast to benevolent friends.'

172

'Oh, Arthur,' I breathed. 'Can this be possible?'

'I thought Mr Trewin may be involved when he spun us that tale,' Arthur said. He started pacing across the cellar floor. 'And I thought about telling my father I wasn't sure he was trustworthy. But I thought better of it, because Mr Trewin is a churchwarden, for goodness' sake. He is man of God, just like my father. How could a man of God be involved in smuggling, I thought.' He snorted. 'Well, it seems I got that very wrong, didn't I?'

I was staring at him. 'Not just a churchwarden,' I said slowly.

Arthur looked despairing. 'No,' he said. 'Mr Trewin is the parish constable. And he is appointed by the magistrate.'

I felt completely helpless. If Morgan was smuggling, and Mr Trewin knew all about it, it seemed there was nowhere for us to turn.

'I do not know what we should do,' Arthur said. He was deathly white, his freckles standing out on his pale skin. 'We have no options left. Everyone is playing their part in this crime. My father included.'

This time I did go to him. I caught him in my arms and held him to my chest. We didn't know anything for sure yet.

Arthur's eyes burned with shame and fear. 'I know that my father is in this up to his neck. I just don't know what we should do about it.'

Chapter 26

My head was spinning. It seemed we were trapped. There was nothing we could do to stop Morgan. If we went to the revenue men, they might not take us seriously. Especially if such important men were involved. And if the revenue men did listen to us, then we could be sending my mother and Arthur's father to the gallows. But even knowing all this was true, I felt we had to act.

'We have to tell,' I said into Arthur's neck. I knew we had to report what we had found.

Arthur pulled away from me. 'No.'

'Arthur,' I said, struggling to find the right words to convince him. 'He killed Da.' I knew only too well how brutal these men could be. How could we stand aside and let them continue?

'Reporting them means a death sentence for my father,' said Arthur. His eyes were wild.

'No,' I said. I hoped they would never send a minister of the church to the gallows, though I didn't know that for sure.

'They will do whatever they have to do to protect each other,' Arthur hissed. 'The magistrate isn't going to take the blame, is he? Or Mr Trewin? It will be my father who hangs, not them.'

We weren't wrapped around each other any more. In fact there was a space between us that seemed to be growing.

'My father, and your mother,' Arthur went on. 'If we report it, and your mam is hanged for it, how will you feel?'

I felt sick. 'I don't know what to do.'

'Nothing,' he said. 'We do nothing. That's what your father wanted. That's why he told you to stay quiet.'

My chest felt tight at the memory. My throat narrowed and I gulped for air. 'That's not fair,' I gasped.

'None of this is fair,' Arthur said. His face twisted and again I thought he might cry. 'Not one bit of this is fair. It's not fair that your father died. It's not fair that Morgan thought your mother could be of use. It's not fair that my father, my good, kind, godly father is somehow involved in the distribution of illegal goods. And it's definitely not fair that we're here, witnessing it all.'

He looked at me, his angry face softening slightly. 'I don't know what to do either.'

Looking worn out, he sat down on the floor, leaning against the wall of the cellar. I sat down next to him, gathering my skirt around my knees. We stayed like that for a while, neither of us speaking. I was imagining different scenarios in my head. Arthur, I knew, gave me some credibility. There was very little chance of the revenue men believing me if he wasn't with me when we went to see them. Not when everyone in Kirrinporth believed me to be a simpleton without a voice. I needed him – not least for his voice. But he was right. Reporting this smuggling meant reporting my mother for giving Morgan a hiding place, and his father for doing whatever he was doing to help them. How could I live with myself if our interference meant the death of our parents?

'We could warn them,' I said suddenly.

Arthur looked at me, hope flaring in his eyes. 'Warn your mam? And my father?'

I nodded.

He looked thoughtful. 'We could go to your mother and my father and tell them what we know. And we tell them we're going to the revenue men because we want Morgan punished.'

I stood up, and mimed moving the bottles and crates, looking at Arthur. He nodded. 'If they know the revenue men are coming, they can do whatever they need to do, to make it look as though they aren't involved. Hide the cargo. Get their stories straight. And Morgan will still be caught.'

'Yes,' I said. Could this work?

But Arthur's expression was serious. 'What if they tell Morgan?'

'What? Why?'

'I don't know, Emily. But they might. They're obviously both in his pocket. Your mam's desperate. A woman on her own? What options does she have if the inn's not making money? Morgan is the only thing keeping her from the gutter. It's in her interest to tell Morgan. If we warn her what is happening, then chances are, she'll go straight to Morgan and tell him.'

'She wouldn't.'

'Can you trust her?'

'Yes.'

He raised his eyebrows at me. 'Sure?'

I leaned my head back against the wall of the cellar, thinking about the demonic look in Mam's eyes when she burned my pictures. 'No.'

'Me neither. This morning I would have trusted my father with anything. Not now.'

'We do nothing?' I said, feeling anger bubbling up inside again. Did he really mean that? For us to do nothing and for me to watch Morgan coming to my mother's inn. To her bed. For me to stay quiet and let him do what he wanted to do with her and with the inn. And never to tell anyone that he was the reason my mother was such a mess. That he was the one who killed my father, whom I loved and missed every day. I swallowed a sob. 'He gets away with it?'

Arthur turned his head to look straight at me. 'I'm afraid so.'

'No,' I said. I was not going to let this happen. I scrambled to my feet.

'What are you doing?' Arthur looked alarmed.

'Customs men,' I said. I was going to tell them what I knew.

'You can't.' He got up, springing to his feet like a cat.

'I can.' I felt like I was seeing things clearly at last. If Arthur wouldn't come with me, I would go alone. I didn't care if they laughed at me, or called me simple, or if I couldn't speak. I would make them hear me somehow.

Arthur grabbed my arm. 'What about my father?'

'Your father is a man,' I said. I couldn't say anything else but from the resigned expression on Arthur's face, he understood what I meant. That his father had choices where my mother had none. That he had money where my mother had none. And that he had made his choice to get involved with Morgan and I believed it was time for him to face the consequences. I shook Arthur's hand from my arm. 'Let me go,' I said.

'Emily,' Arthur began. 'Please don't do this.'

I felt my throat clench. I tried to reply but no sound came out. I'd never been mute with Arthur before. Never. Not even in the worst days after Da's death.

He reached for me again but again I shook him off, feeling along the door mantel for the key – my mother always left keys on top of doorframes because she hated the jangle of a keyring. To my relief, I found it, unlocked the door and put the key back on top. Then with a look of disdain at Arthur over my shoulder, I opened the door and slipped out into the inn hallway.

My heart pounding and my blood rushing in my ears, I went into the main part of the inn where Mam was staring into a drink.

'Kkkk.' I tried to tell her I was going to Kirrinporth but my throat had tightened too much and I couldn't speak. She barely looked up at me, just nodded her head.

A man I recognised as one of the inn's customers from before Da's death, and who'd returned since more drinkers had come back, glanced at me. 'I'm going back that way, Emily love. Want to hop in?'

177

I nodded eagerly, trying to show him speed was of the essence here. I wanted to be gone before Arthur either made his way out of the cave and up the cliff path, or came out through the door to the inn. The man clearly understood I was in a hurry for he drained the last dregs from his tankard and then followed me out of the inn to where his horse and cart stood. Infuriatingly slowly he checked the horse's harness. I watched the top of the cliff, expecting to see Arthur's red hair emerge any second. But it didn't and I climbed in to the trap, and off we went.

The man – his name was Mr Regis I remembered now – chatted to me the whole way and didn't seem to mind that I wasn't answering. My occasional nods were enough to keep him going.

He set me down in the marketplace, with a cheerful tip of his hat. I put my hand to my heart, to show I was grateful and then set off again. I hitched up my skirt and ran through the crowds of people in the square, and down towards the sea wall, which skirted the beach, and reached out into the water. At the end of the wall was a small, squat square building, like a tiny castle. The customs house. I knew the revenue men had an office there, but I had no idea if they would be there or out on their horses patrolling the shoreline, or even off in the cutters, sailing along the coast and looking for smugglers. But it didn't matter. I was here now and I had to try. I burst through the door, and it was only when the two men inside looked up, I realised I had not prepared what to say – if in fact I could say anything at all.

'Hello,' said one of the men. He was younger than I'd expected the revenue men to be. He was wearing a shirt and britches and his red jacket was draped on the chair where he sat. 'Are you lost?'

I shook my head, still short of breath. My throat felt so narrow I feared I might faint if I couldn't get some air.

'Are you all right, miss?' the other man said. He was older, with a greying beard. 'Sit down.'

He pulled out a chair for me and I fell into it. My breathing was slowing down now. I held out a hand to show him I was fine and I was about to speak. The men both looked at me expectantly. But my throat was clenched, and though I tried, I couldn't make a sound.

'I know you,' the older man said. 'You're the Moon girl. From the inn on the cliff?'

I nodded, trying desperately to speak.

'She doesn't talk,' the older man said to his colleague. 'She's not right in the head. Bit simple.'

I shook my head, and dug into my bag for my sketches of Morgan bringing the cargo ashore, thrusting them at the men. The younger one took them and glanced at the top one, which showed the lanky man ankle-deep in the waves.

'You do drawing do you?' he said in a tone like fathers used with their small children. 'That's nice.'

He held the bundle back out to me and in frustration I batted them away. The papers scattered across the floor and the younger man tutted. 'No need for that.'

I threw my hands out in despair, begging them to understand, to see that I wasn't simple, but they both looked at me blankly as tears sprang into my eyes. This was hopeless. I buried my face in my hands. All was now lost. I couldn't protect my mother or avenge my father.

The older man put his hand on my shoulder gently. 'I'll take you home,' he said. 'Come on now.'

What choice did I have? I nodded and watched as the younger man gathered up the drawings that showed what sort of wrong-doings Morgan was up to, and put them carefully into my bag.

'You keep those,' he said kindly. 'They're obviously precious to you.'

With slumped shoulders, holding my bag close to my chest, I followed the older man out of the customs house and up to the stables near the shore.

As I stood waiting for him to get the horse, I felt the weight of eyes on my back. I turned, thinking it would be Arthur, and felt cold fear drip down my spine when I saw Morgan. He was standing a little way from the stables, watching me with interest. Had he seen me with the revenue man? I made to walk away and pretend I was doing chores for my mother, but before I stepped on to the path, Morgan raised his hat to me and with an expression that suggested amusement, much to my confusion, he went on his way.

In relief and frustration, I leaned against the wall, watching the kind revenue man. He was speaking to a stable hand in a low voice and I clenched my fists as they both sent sympathetic glances in my direction. I wasn't some poor girl who needed pity. I needed them to act. But unless I could tell them that, how would they ever know? I supposed that was the reason for Morgan's amusement. He knew there was nothing I could do to stop him.

With tears silently rolling down my cheeks, I climbed into the trap with the bearded customs man. It was over.

Chapter 27

Phoebe

2019

It had been raining for days. It was too wet to go running and it was too miserable for walkers on the cliff path, so the few passing customers we'd had at first dwindled to nothing. I had time on my hands but the weather meant it would have been foolhardy to try to get on to the beach to see what Jed and Mark had been doing.

Jed himself was another misery. He'd not replied to my message. He'd read it, and ignored it. I felt stupid and annoyed and unhappy all at once, but I still hoped he might turn up at the pub with Ewan and Mark in tow. He didn't though. There had been no sign of them at all.

All of that would have mattered less if Liv had been her usual self. We could have holed up in the pub, watching romcoms on Netflix and eating pasta, and having a laugh to pull me out of my gloom. But she was equally miserable and whatever I suggested, she turned down. 'I'm just not in the mood, Phoebe,' she kept saying. She opened the pub each evening, but by the third evening, when no one had come in, she looked so fed up I was despairing.

I was sitting on the sofa by the window, looking out over the grey, swirling sea, and Liv was standing in the middle of the pub, flicking through the channels on the TV trying to find something to watch that wasn't football, when we heard an engine outside.

Liv straightened up. 'What's that? It sounds like a bus.' She darted to the booth that overlooked the car park steps and peered outside into the gloomy evening light. 'It's a bus,' she said in delight. 'It must be a coach tour.'

I was delighted. 'Are they coming in?'

'They are.' Liv clapped her hands. 'Best smiles, Phoebe.'

We both plastered grins to our faces as the door opened and in came a group of about twelve or fifteen people. All in their seventies, all wearing cagoules.

'Oh thank goodness,' said the woman in front as they entered. 'We were worried you'd be closed and we're all desperate for a wee.'

'Welcome,' Liv said. 'What an awful evening to be out on a trip.'

'We've been down to the Lizard, but the roads are so terrible because of the rain, it's taking longer to get back than we expected. Neil's doing a great job, though. I wouldn't want to be driving in this rain.'

There was a murmur of assent and one of the men, who I assumed was Neil, nodded modestly.

'What can I get you?' said Liv, clearly wanting more from this group than just chat.

'Teas and coffees?' said the woman.

'Oh for heaven's sake, Barbara,' said another woman. She put her very nice, bright blue handbag on to the bar, and peeled off her cagoule, holding it at arm's length as though it disgusted her. 'I'll have a red wine, please.'

'It's only five o'clock, Jan,' said Barbara.

'Sun's over the yardarm somewhere.'

I decided I rather liked Jan.

I helped Liv keep track of all the orders while the day trippers went backwards and forwards to the toilets and settled themselves in seats. The whole atmosphere in the pub had lifted, thanks to their arrival. Liv was beaming and doing her usual brilliant job at keeping everyone happy. It was so nice to hear the buzz of conversation and laughter for once.

'This is more like it,' said Liv out of the corner of her mouth as she passed me with two more coffees. 'If only we could get coach trips like this every day.'

'You'll have to get them to spread the word,' I said.

She nodded. I watched her go over to Barbara and Neil – who were clearly the organisers of the trip – and put the coffees in front of them, pausing to chat.

And then my eye was caught by one of the men. I'd not really noticed him before – hadn't even see him come in with the others. He was a bit younger than the rest of them, and while they were all in walking gear, he was wearing jeans and trainers. He was standing by one of the tables and he was holding Jan's distinctive bright blue bag. I watched in horror as he slid open the zip, put his hand inside and then pulled out her purse.

'Stop!' I shouted. Without pausing to think, I was across the pub in two strides. I saw a glimpse of the man's alarmed face as I grabbed his wrist and pulled it up behind his back. 'Put. That. Down,' I hissed into his ear.

He dropped the purse straightaway. The pub had gone silent as soon as I shouted. Everyone was stock still, watching me. I went to pick up the purse but I was still holding the man's wrist and it was awkward and before I could reach it, a hand reached out and took it. Jan. Slowly, she stood up, holding her purse and looking at me in disbelief.

'What on earth are you doing?'

'This man was stealing your purse,' I said, breathlessly. 'I am making an arrest.' Everyone gawped at me and I corrected myself. 'A citizen's arrest.'

Jan sighed. 'Let him go,' she said.

'He took your purse out of your bag,' I said.

'Because I asked him to.'

I blinked at her.

'He's my husband,' she said. 'He was going to get us more drinks while I went to the loo.'

I dropped his wrist as though it was hot and stared at him.

'Your husband,' I repeated. 'I thought . . .'

Jan glared at me and I regretted my earlier admiring thoughts about her. 'You were wrong.'

Everyone stayed silent for a second. I could feel their eyes boring into me, then Liv – bless her – spoke up. 'More drinks, was it? Another red wine for you?'

Jan shook her head. 'I think we're done here.'

Around me, the other customers were spurred into action, finishing drinks, pulling on their cagoules.

'I'm sorry,' I said helplessly. Jan and her husband ignored me.

One by one the customers trooped out of the pub into the wild, rainy evening that was – it seemed – preferable to spending one more minute in close proximity to me. Only Barbara turned back as they were leaving to say a quick 'thank you' to Liv.

As the door banged shut, Liv glared at me.

'What the fuck, Phoebe?' she said.

I felt awful. I'd been so sure the man was up to no good, and then so wrong. Again.

'I'm sorry, I just saw him with her bag and acted out of instinct.'

'But your instincts are whack. What's wrong with you? First that woman with the little girl in Kirrinporth, now this?'

I sat down in the chair where Jan had sat just five minutes earlier and buried my face in my hands. 'I'm not sure what to say, Liv,' I said eventually, lifting my head up and looking at her. 'I'm so sorry. I was doing much better, and then the rain and Jed . . .'

Liv's face softened. 'I know.'

'But I still chased away the best customers we'd had for days.'

'I know that too.'

'Listen, why don't we brainstorm some ideas,' I said, desperate to make it up to her. 'We could do that ghost evening or something. Get some more customers in?'

She looked at me and for a second I thought she'd say no. But then she gave a tiny smile. 'Yeah, okay. You get a pen and paper and I'll go to the loo.' She gave me a sly look. 'Make sure no one nicks anything while I'm gone.'

I stuck my middle finger up at her, relieved – and slightly surprised – that she was being so chilled about it all. I went behind the bar to find the notebook I knew Liv kept there, and then settled myself on a stool to wait for her. As I sat down, the phone next to me lit up with a message. I glanced at it, thinking it was mine, and read the first part of the message on the screen. The sender was BTG Bank and it said: 'We have received your payment of £5000. This will show on your credit card account within . . .'

What? How could Liv have paid £5000 off her credit card debt? I must have read it wrong. But before I could be tempted to touch the screen and light up the message again, she came back into the bar.

'What have you got?' she said. She picked up her phone and I saw her read the message and give a tiny, odd smile. Then she put the phone into her pocket and grinned at me. 'Wow me with your thoughts.'

Slightly unsettled, I held up the blank page to show her.

'It's a team effort,' I said.

We took a bottle of wine, and sat in the bar, scribbling down ideas, while the wind blew a gale outside and rattled the windows. Our ideas were all fairly silly and I wasn't sure any of them would increase business, but at least we were doing something. Because, I told myself, I must have got it wrong about that £5000. Liv still needed the pub to be successful.

'What about murder mystery nights?' I suggested.

'It's not 1988,' she said. 'Do people still do those?'

I whacked her with the notepad on her arm. 'They're very popular.'

'Is that what you do with your police mates?' she teased. 'Solving pretend murders for fun?'

I chuckled. 'No,' I said. Then I smiled. 'Well, I've been to a couple.'

Liv whooped in triumph. 'I knew it!' She grinned at me. 'How's your investigation into Emily Moon going, by the way?'

I shrugged. I'd been half-heartedly googling the history of Cornwall while the weather had been bad, but the Wi-Fi was so slow it made it hard work. I'd also been reading the ghost story book, but I'd not found anything else of interest. Instead, I'd been thinking about Jed and trying to resist messaging him, and wondering why he'd lied about the beach being inaccessible. 'Not well,' I told Liv. 'I've not found out anything about poor Emily Moon and her ghostly wailing. Unless you count the fact that the ghostly wailing isn't her.'

'I do count that,' Liv said, straight-faced. 'Because I was worried.' Then she frowned. 'But how did you find that out?'

I'd not told Liv about my run along the clifftop, other than that I'd been. I'd not mentioned the wind blowing through the boulders, nor Jed and Mark on the beach. I didn't want to worry her, or make myself sound any more "whack" as she called it, than I already did.

'Up on the cliffs there are these huge grey stones,' I said.

She nodded. 'I've seen them.'

'And they have holes in them that the wind blows through. And when it catches at a certain angle, it makes a weird crying sound.'

'That's amazing,' Liv said in wonder. 'So that's where the stories come from?'

'Must be. I think I was just lucky to be on the cliff at the right time. I messaged my vicar friend about it and he said he's lived here his whole life and never heard it.'

'Well, if we want to make some money out of ghost hunters, keep quiet about it,' Liv said. Just then, as though to warn us that we shouldn't joke about spooks, there was a loud thump from

186

outside the pub and another. We both leapt into the air and clutched each other. 'What was that?' I said. 'Is someone there?'

Thump! There it was again. Liv and I froze, listening carefully, and then as understanding dawned on Liv's face, she started to laugh once more.

'It's the shutter,' she said. 'Outside the window. It must have come loose and it's banging in the wind. I'll sort it.'

She stood up but as she did, she knocked the table and our half-drunk bottle of wine fell on to the pub's stone floor and smashed. 'Bollocks.'

'You sort the glass; I'll do the shutter,' I said. Without much enthusiasm, we both trailed over to the cupboard where I grabbed my rain jacket and Liv found the dustpan and brush. I pulled my waterproof on and, bracing myself, headed outside into the wild night. It was supposed to have cleared up by now, I thought, as the rain splattered my face. The forecast yesterday said tonight would be fair. 'Fairly awful, more like,' I mumbled. I found the loose shutter and fixed it back against the wall, bending over the little metal hook to make sure it stayed in place.

As I turned to go back inside, though, my eye was caught by a light up on the cliff. It was a steady beam – not flashing or flickering – so it definitely looked electric rather than ethereal, to my relief. It wasn't moving, so it wasn't someone with a torch, and strangely enough, it was blue. A deep blue light shining out across the sea.

I squinted at it, half expecting the light to start flashing and reveal itself to be a police car or an ambulance. But no, it was still and steady. A small bit of me wanted to walk up to the cliff and see what it was, but a much larger part of me wanted to get inside, out of the rain, and not risk plummeting on to the rocks in the dark windy evening. So I turned my back on the light, and went to find Liv.

Chapter 28

The storm went on all night and kept me awake for hours. Every bang and thud made me jump, and sent my heart pounding. I felt unsettled and on edge and I kept going over everything in my head.

What were Jed and Mark doing on the beach? It was ridiculous to be suspicious because it was, after all, a pretty little cove and this was a seaside town in summer. But he had definitely told me you couldn't get down there. Why had he lied? And, he'd said something different about the Watson family leaving The Moon Girl. Though that could easily be a misunderstanding, I told myself. Couldn't it?

Then there was Liv's text message from the credit card company. Where had she got £5000 from and why hadn't she told me about it? It was the not telling me that made me particularly uneasy, because we didn't have secrets. Not really. And that made me wonder if she'd done something wrong. But then wondering if she'd done something wrong made me feel guilty. Was it me being unnecessarily suspicious again? After all, Liv had always had a very strong moral code and she'd always been proud of me for being in the police. But then again, she was in such a weird mood.

I turned over in bed and thumped the pillow to get it in a better position. This was silly. I was seeing things that weren't there because of what had happened with Ciara James. First, I'd seen the little girl in Kirrinporth all alone when her mother was close behind, then I'd branded Jan's husband as a thief. Now I was suspecting Liv of doing goodness knows what to get her hands on five grand. It was crazy. I had to get a grip. So what if Jed lied, and Liv was acting strange, and the last family to live here disappeared, and I had niggling doubts about how trustworthy Ewan Logan was . . .

I sat up in bed. It was still darkish and Liv was asleep, but I couldn't stay here tossing and turning and imagining all sorts. I was going to send myself spiralling right back into the gloom I'd felt after Ciara had died if I wasn't careful.

Quietly, so I didn't wake Liv, I slipped out of bed, picked up my Cornwall ghost book and my phone, and pulled on my dressing gown. Then I went downstairs and made myself a coffee on the fancy machine that I was finally getting the hang of, and went outside into the little pub garden.

The Moon Girl's outdoor space wasn't fancy but it had the most incredible view across the cliffs and along to Kirrinporth harbour. The sun was coming up and the grey morning light shone on the flat sea. I felt my mood lift, just a tiny bit, and tried not to notice that the beach – the little cove where I'd seen Jed – wasn't visible from here.

Obviously it was raining. Not heavily, just a light drizzle. But I sat under the porch and watched the sun rise, scrolling through my sluggish social media feeds and leafing through the ghost book. I just wanted to distract myself from my intrusive thoughts and calm my racing brain.

Eventually, when the sun was properly up and the rain had almost stopped, and I'd read all the showbiz news on the Mail online, even the bits about random American reality TV stars that I'd never heard of, I thought I should probably get dressed. And I was starting to get hungry. Liv would be up by now and maybe we could have breakfast together.

Back inside, I put my coffee cup on the bar. The shutters were open so Liv was clearly around but I couldn't hear her moving around and she was nowhere to be seen.

'Liv?' I called. Nothing.

Tying the belt on my dressing gown more securely, I wandered through the pub, out into the hallway behind the bar, and jumped about a foot in the air as Liv appeared through a door I'd barely noticed before.

'Oh God,' I gasped, dropping my ghost book on the floor with a thud. 'Shit, Liv.'

She looked as startled as I was. 'Phoebe.'

'What's in there?'

She glanced behind her guiltily, as though I'd caught her robbing a bank. 'Nothing,' she said. 'Just the cellar.'

'God, of course. I'm so stupid. Sorry, Liv.'

She relaxed, leaning against the door. 'You just gave me a fright that's all. I wasn't expecting to see you. I thought you'd gone running.'

'I wasn't expecting to see you, either. I thought you were still in bed.'

'I wish,' she said.

We stood there in the hallway, weirdly awkward for two best friends, for a second. Then Liv's phone rang making us both jump again. She yanked it out of her pocket and I saw Ewan Logan on the screen. 'Hi,' she said, answering the call. She turned away from me a bit and I recognised my cue to leave.

'I'll get dressed,' I said.

She looked over her shoulder at me and nodded. 'It's all sorted,' she said into the phone. 'Everything's fine.'

I went upstairs feeling my mind starting to race again. Liv was being so weird and I didn't understand why, just that it was definitely something to do with Ewan Logan.

As I stood under the shower, I went over everything in my head. Liv's unexplained windfall and her odd behaviour. Jed and

Mark on the beach. The Watson family leaving the pub in the way they had. Nothing made any sense. I needed to do something. Perhaps it was just me seeing problems everywhere. Perhaps it was all part of the way I'd reacted to Ciara's death and my excessively suspicious nature. But I couldn't just ignore it.

I wrapped a towel round my hair, pulled on my dressing gown and went out on to the landing to see where Liv was. Her mug of coffee had been drunk and I could hear her downstairs in the pub, so I quietly went back into the bedroom, shut the door and pulled out my phone. Then I called Stacey from my team at work.

She was so pleased to hear from me, I felt a tiny pang about missing work – the first I'd had since I was signed off. We chatted for a few minutes and then I paused. 'I need a bit of a favour,' I said.

'What are you up to?'

'Nothing dodgy, I promise,' I said, crossing my fingers as I spoke. 'We can't track down the old landlord from this place. Liv's asked head office and they don't seem to have a forwarding address for him. We've found some of his belongings that we need to return. Wondered if you could check it out?'

'Okay.' Stacey sounded doubtful. 'What's his name and last known address?'

I told her what I knew.

'And he's in Cornwall now?'

'No idea.'

'Mike Watson isn't exactly an unusual name so there will probably be a few of them.'

'I know. Just give me whatever you can find.'

Stacey sighed. 'Promise it's nothing dodgy?'

'It's me, Stacey.'

'Might take a few days.'

'That's fine.'

She paused. 'Fine,' she said eventually. 'I'll give you a ring when I've got something.'

'Actually, Stacey,' I said. 'Could you check someone else for me too?'

'Go on then.'

'Ewan Logan.'

'Address?'

'Don't have it. Cornwall somewhere.'

'I'll do my best, but I can't promise anything.'

'Thanks, Stacey. I owe you.'

We said our goodbyes and I ended the call, feeling slightly as though I'd just betrayed Liv's confidence.

It was another quiet day at The Moon Girl. Few customers, no sign of Ewan, and no message from Jed. Liv was distracted and uncommunicative all day and eventually I gave up and went to bed early, feeling more than a little miserable.

Fortunately, I woke the next morning to glorious sunshine. It was nothing if not inconsistent, this Cornwall weather. But just the sight of the brightness peeking round the curtains raised my spirits. Liv was already out of bed, and I was in no hurry to see her, so I grabbed my running stuff from the clothes horse in the bathroom and headed outside to make the most of the day before the rain started again. I did the same route as before, along the cliff path, telling myself I was just going for exercise. I just wanted to get some endorphins. That was all. There was nothing else to it.

But, as I came back to near the pub, I slowed down, just a bit, and crossed over from the clifftop path, which ran along beside the road, to the edge of the cliff, where I'd seen Jed and Mark come up from the beach.

I stopped, doing a couple of half-hearted stretches in case anyone was watching me. There was a small stone marker hidden in the long grass that told me I was in the right place, and a sandy, gravelly break in the vegetation that had to be the top of the path down to the cove. I peered down. It looked steep. Very steep. And not particularly stable. But I knew Jed and Mark had climbed it, so I knew it was possible.

Was I really going to do this? Really? What if I ended up like Emily Moon? Another Moon Girl spirit doomed to walk the clifftops for eternity? I snorted at my own ridiculousness. And, with a deep breath, I put one foot on to the path and set off.

It wasn't easy going. There were a few times when my foot sent a stone skittering down to the beach below and made my heart thump. I found if I concentrated on looking at my trainers I got on better than if I looked at where I was heading, which still seemed a long way down. There was one bit that was so steep I gave up trying to walk and sat on my bottom instead, scooching down the hill like a toddler going down stairs.

It felt like a very long time but eventually I stood on the beach with my legs wobbling uncontrollably and my heart pounding. I turned and looked back where I'd come from. It was very high. I did not look forward to climbing back up there.

'Brilliant, Phoebe,' I said to myself. 'Well bloody done.'

Well, I was here now. With my legs still trembling slightly, I wandered round, trying to see what the men had been looking at. But I was none the wiser. There was the sea, there were a lot of rocks making the waves crash and froth, there was a shingly-sandy beach and there were the cliffs looming up from where I stood.

'Come on, Sarge. You're a detective. Do some detecting,' I told myself sternly.

I walked down to where the sea met the sand and slowly paced from one side of the tiny cove to the other, looking at the ground, the rocks, the view . . .

And then, finally, just as I was about to admit defeat and start the long, steep climb back to the top, I saw it. I was scanning the very bottom of the cliff, where the rocks met the beach when I noticed there was a crack. A big crack. A crack that looked like it could be big enough for a person to fit through. I walked over to the sheer face of the cliff to check it out more and realised that up close it was even bigger than I'd thought. Could I go inside?

Intrigued, and slightly scared, I took my phone from my

leggings pocket and turned on the torch, shining it into the hole. It went back further than I could see. I sighed. Now I had to go in. Of course I did. How could I not?

Carefully, I went through the crack in the rock. It was more than big enough for me to get through and it quickly widened out into a dry, sandy-floored tunnel. My torch lit up the way as I wandered deeper into the cliff. This was incredible. I remembered going on a school trip to some caves near where we lived, where people had stayed during the war because they were the perfect air-raid shelter. This felt similar to that and I wondered if someone had dug them out, or if they were natural. I walked on, quite comfortably, expecting to find my way blocked by a rock fall, or have the tunnel come to an end any second, but it didn't happen.

I was walking uphill, I realised as my legs started complaining and my breathing became more uneven. Quite steeply uphill. Was this another way up the cliff? I hoped so. It would be a much nicer way to the beach than that awful steep path. I was actually quite enjoying this. It was exciting and I couldn't wait to tell Liv what I'd found. Might cheer her up, I thought.

And then I came to three rough stone steps and a door. The frame around it was old, dark wood. But the door itself was modern. Like the sort of door you'd get in a bedroom or a living room. It looked really out of place just standing there, in the stone wall of the cave. I felt as though I was in a weird version of Narnia or some other children's adventure story. Should I open the door? Hell, yes.

I thought it might be locked but the handle turned easily and the door opened. I stepped through into a large room. It was cool, thanks to its stone walls – the same as the walls of the tunnel – and the two air-conditioning units to one side. Opposite where I stood was a row of metal barrels fixed up to some complicated-looking pipes and cables. There were some branded boxes of wine, bottles of spirits and some other barrels stacked neatly in one corner, and a few boxes of crisps next to them. Confused and disorientated I stared around me. What was this? Where on earth was I?

The ringing of a phone made me jump. I looked at my own silent mobile, bewildered. I heard running footsteps and then Liv's voice as she answered: 'Oh hi, Mum, I was just going to call you . . .'

And suddenly it all became clear. I was in the cellar of the pub. Somehow, the tunnel led from the beach to The Moon Girl.

I sat down on the stone floor, still feeling like I didn't quite understand what was happening. Was this tunnel what Jed and Mark had been checking out when they were here the other day? Was it what Liv had meant when she came out of the cellar and told Ewan it was sorted? What on earth was going on? I didn't have the faintest idea, but it seemed to me to be very clear that something dodgy was happening here.

Chapter 29

Emily

1799

Frank – the bearded customs man – was sweet to me on the ride home. He pointed out some animals in the fields, and told me a funny story about his dog. I tried to smile but it wasn't easy to concentrate on what he was saying when my mind was busy trying and failing to make sense of what I'd just seen. When Frank pulled up the cart at the inn, he asked me kindly if I wanted him to come in with me. I shook my head, not wanting to have to listen to my mother's questions about why I'd arrived home with a revenue man.

'I'll see you inside, miss,' he said. He helped me jump down and, true to his word, waited until I was inside the door before he tugged on the horse's reins and set off.

Inside it was quiet and dim. I leaned against the wall, trying to breathe normally. My argument with Arthur, my race into Kirrinporth and seeing Morgan watching me had all made me feel weak. I took a deep breath and then another. That was better. My heart was slowing finally, but I needed to lie down. I would go upstairs and sleep for a while and perhaps I would come up with a new way to deal with this problem.

I went through the lounge bar, towards the stairs, and there, his large frame filling the doorway, was Morgan. His face was red from the wind and his trousers were speckled with mud. He must have ridden like the wind, cross-country, to get here so fast.

'Hello, Emily,' he said.

I ducked my head and made to dodge by him, but he was quick. He shot out an arm and grabbed my wrist. I squealed and tried to twist away but he held on fast.

'Come with me.'

I tried to resist but he was so much bigger than me, and so strong that there was nothing I could do. He half dragged me out of the inn doorway and up the sloped path to the clifftop. I looked round desperately, wondering where my mother was. Would she come to my rescue? Even if she knew what was happening I wasn't sure she would help. I wanted to cry out but no sound came from my mouth and my mother didn't appear. I was on my own.

At the cliff, Morgan let go of my wrist and pushed me away from him. I stumbled on the uneven ground and fell, hurting my arm, and he laughed.

'What are you thinking, Emily Moon?'

I tried to get up, scrambling on the grass to get a grip with trembling hands. Morgan put his muddy boot to my chest and pushed and I fell back down. I was crying now, silent gasping sobs that hurt my throat. Would he throw me from the cliff? I knew first-hand how brutal he was, how little he thought of taking a life. He could easily lift me up and throw me down on to the rocks. I looked up to where he loomed over me, blocking the sun.

'You are interfering with things you don't understand,' he spat. 'This is bigger than you, little girl. You need to back off before you ruin everything.'

I opened my mouth to tell him he was evil. That he'd killed my father and raped my mother and he would pay. But my traitorous, weak, stupid throat clenched and once again no sound came.

'Did you think to report me?' Morgan said quietly. He reached down and pulled me to my feet. My legs were weak and gave way under me but he held me upright. 'You can't win. And so help me, if I ever see you poking your nose where it doesn't belong, I will throw you from this cliff and you will never be seen again.' He laughed. A horrible mocking laugh that made me cry harder. 'You were going to report me, Emily Moon? You? A simpleton who can't string a sentence together? No one would believe you.'

'No,' a voice said behind him. 'But they would believe me.'

Morgan turned, taking me with him, and there was Arthur, looking for all the world like the king he was named for, riding to the rescue on his large, black and white horse. We'd not heard the hooves over the wind on the clifftop. My legs went weak again, but this time it was in relief.

'You're a boy,' Morgan said with scorn.

'I'm almost grown. And I'm the son of the Reverend. Respectable. Educated. I know everyone in Kirrinporth and they know me.'

Morgan's grip loosened slightly and I knew Arthur's words had hit home. 'You're a child. I could throw her from this cliff now and my problems would be over. And there would be nothing you could do to stop me.' He made as though to push me over the edge and I let out a croaky shriek.

Up on his horse, Arthur nodded. I had no idea how he was keeping so calm. I was shaking and sobbing, but he was in control. 'That is true,' he said. 'But I am on a horse and can be in Kirrinporth before you.'

'And where would you go?' Morgan was mocking now. 'To the parish constable, Mr Trewin? To my good friend Mr Trewin?'

On his horse, Arthur pulled himself up straighter. 'I have friends too,' he said. 'My father is a good friend of George Winston, the magistrate.'

I gasped. Bringing the magistrate into this was risky. After all, we'd already talked about how he could be involved too. But Arthur was carrying on regardless.

'Mr Winston would have no difficulty in hearing what I had to tell him,' he said confidently. 'You would be hanging from the gallows by tomorrow.'

As far as I knew, Arthur had never spoken to Mr Winston. I'd never seen him at church or in the company of Arthur's father. In fact, I wasn't even sure what he looked like because he lived in Barnmouth, where the court house was. But Morgan obviously didn't know that – thank goodness.

Morgan threw me roughly on to the grass again and spat at me. I rolled to the side to avoid the spittle and then lay still, weeping.

'If any revenue men come to call on me, I shall kill you both,' he said to Arthur. 'I will kill you and I will enjoy it.'

Arthur didn't move. He stayed where he was, his horse's hooves planted firmly on the ground. Morgan snorted. He pulled his hat down over his eyes and strode off towards the pub. We heard his horse whinny and saw the dust fly up as he rode back towards the village. And only when we were sure he had gone, did Arthur slide from his own horse's back, tied him to a nearby post, and come to me where I lay on the grass.

He gathered me into his arms and I clung to him, shaking and sobbing and trying to explain what had happened.

'Slow down,' he said. 'Slow down and breathe and tell me all.'

We sat on the grass together, Arthur's arms still around me, and I tried to get the words out.

'I went to the customs house,' I said eventually. 'I took the pictures, but I couldn't speak. I tried so hard.'

'Right . . .'

'One man . . . he was kind. He brought me home. But Morgan saw me.'

'At the customs house?'

'Outside.'

'Watching you?'

'Apparently.'

'He's a nasty piece of work,' Arthur said. 'He is playing us all for fools.'

I thought for a moment. 'Smuggling is not new,' I said.

'Not new at all,' Arthur agreed. 'I know my own father often turned a blind eye and everyone in Kirrinporth bought the goods that were sold by the free traders.'

I nodded. I remembered the same happening when I was a little girl, Mam coming home with wool or tobacco for Da. And now I thought about it, I was sure Da had bought drink for the inn on occasion.

'Maybe they used the tunnel?' I said.

Arthur nodded. 'Maybe. I can't say I agree, but I know how it is.'

'How it was,' I said, deliberately. I'd been thinking of nothing else since I left the customs house.

'What do you mean?'

Very slowly, I explained what I thought. 'Morgan is making this work for his own good,' I said. 'Forcing the folk of Kirrinporth to smuggle goods and taking the money.'

Understanding was growing on Arthur's handsome face. 'So everyone's doing what they did before, but instead of them selling the goods and making money from the deal – money they need for food or clothes or fuel for their fire – Morgan's taking the profits?'

I nodded, thankful he'd realised what I was trying to say.

'He's getting rich while others suffer,' Arthur said. Then he paused. 'Is it Morgan who is getting rich or is it someone else?'

I raised my eyebrows, questioning what he meant.

'Morgan knows everyone,' Arthur pointed out. 'He's friendly with my father and with Mr Trewin . . .'

With a start I suddenly realised that it had been no coincidence that Morgan turned up at the inn just after we had been to ask Mr Trewin for help. No doubt he had revealed how desperate my mother was, and Morgan had decided it was the right time to arrive. I stared at Arthur, feeling sick at the thought of how deep the evil ran in Kirrinporth. Who knew who else was involved in this?

'He's probably friendly with the revenue men too,' Arthur said, his horrified face mirroring mine.

I nodded, thinking of him tipping his hat to Frank, the revenue man who brought me home.

'This is awful. What will we do?'

'I've an idea,' I said. Arthur looked at me with what could only be described as pride on his face.

'Go on?'

I swallowed. 'Catch him.'

Arthur screwed his face up. 'How will we do that?'

I knew there was no hope of me explaining my plan so I took my pictures from my bag again, and found a piece of charcoal. In a few strokes I drew Arthur and me, standing on the clifftop, where we were sitting now. Then I pointed to my eyes, and out to sea.

'We'll watch him,' Arthur said. I nodded. 'To see when the smuggling begins?'

I nodded again. 'Every night,' I said. I knew we couldn't risk missing them bringing in the next load of cargo.

'Then what?'

I turned to the page again. This time I drew Arthur on his horse, riding away from the clifftop. I added some dust flying up from the horse's hooves, showing he was travelling as fast as he could.

'So when the smuggling is underway, I jump on my horse, ride into Kirrinporth and go . . . where?' Arthur said. 'To alert the customs men?'

'Yes,' I said. 'Catch him red-handed.'

Arthur was looking hopeful. 'And then he won't be able to wriggle out of it,' he said. 'Even if he has one or two allies among them, he can't have all the customs men in his pocket, surely?'

I shrugged.

'My only worry is I ride to the customs house, and they don't believe me.'

'We must try,' I said. I lifted my eyes from the paper and looked at Arthur. 'He is a bad person and we are good.'

Arthur sighed. 'You are speaking sense,' he said. 'I know that. It's our duty to make this right. I know you were speaking sense when you said the same thing in the caves. I'm sorry I resisted. I was wrong.' He squeezed me closer. 'Can you forgive me?'

I smiled up at him. 'Of course.'

'If we are united, then we can take on Morgan – we can take on the world,' Arthur declared.

I chuckled. 'Not the world. Just Morgan,' I said.

We smiled at each other for a second, but then he frowned, a shadow crossing his face. I gave him a questioning look. What was wrong?

'I have been thinking about my father,' Arthur said. 'I believe he provides Morgan with transport. On several occasions I've seen the gate to our stables open when I've been going to bed. Once I went downstairs and locked it, thinking the stable hand had left it open accidentally. And then, I woke in the night – which is unusual for me as I generally sleep like the dead – and when I looked out the gate was open again. At the time I thought I was dreaming, but now I'm piecing it together in my head. I believe my father lets Morgan use his carriage and horses to move the goods. His is a recognisable carriage and no one would ever suspect it was carrying contraband.'

I stared at Arthur. What he was saying made perfect sense, but that didn't mean it didn't shock me. Reverend Pascoe, part of the smuggling trade.

Arthur smiled at my expression. 'I think he's been doing it for years. Not often, but occasionally and if he was asked,' he said. 'But doing it to help those in need is one thing. Doing it to line the pockets of those like Morgan, or Mr Trewin, or goodness knows who else, is another.'

Arthur took a breath. 'If we're going to tell the customs officers, I'd like to warn my father. Tell him what we're planning so if

202

Morgan is caught and speaks of all the others who are involved, my father can be asleep in bed, and there would be no evidence of his wrongdoing.'

I nodded.

Arthur took my hand. 'I think you were right about your father too. I think that's why Morgan killed him. He asked to use the tunnel, and the inn to store his goods, and your da said no.'

Tears filled my eyes. 'Brave,' I said. I wasn't angry with Da any more. He'd stood up for what he thought was right.

'Undoubtedly. Your father was brave, but he was murdered for his courage. And now your mother is all mixed up in it too.'

I screwed up my face. 'Warn her, too?'

Arthur didn't hesitate. 'Of course, she's your mother.'

'But . . .' I began, thinking of how Arthur had pointed out that she was part of it all. That Morgan was paying her and that she was desperate.

'She is scared of him,' I said.

'That's true.'

Suddenly our plan to bring down Morgan seemed far too hard. Too dangerous. Too risky. I shuddered. How could we stop him when we were barely grown, I couldn't speak when I had to, and our families were tangled up in it all?

I threw my head back in despair. 'We are no match for Morgan,' I croaked.

'We can stop him together,' Arthur said. 'I love you, Emily, and you love me, and together we can stop him.'

He kissed me and I kissed him back firmly. I hoped he was right because it seemed like we were taking on an enormous fight that I wasn't sure we could win.

Chapter 30

Phoebe

2019

The cellar door was slightly ajar, so I could hear Liv's conversation with her mum clearly. Luckily, she was a walker and talker – she always wandered around while she chatted – so I lurked behind the door until I heard her voice fade away and then I slid round and into the hall of the pub and shut the door behind me. My head was spinning and all I knew was that I wanted to speak to Liv, tell her what I'd found and what I suspected. I sat down on the stairs and waited for her to finish her phone call.

When she wandered back out into the hall, she jumped to see me there. 'God, Phoebe. Where did you come from?'

I looked at her wondering how to explain everything. 'I've been for a run,' I said.

'I can see that.' She leaned on the bannister and examined me carefully. 'You were gone ages. Are you okay?'

'I'm fine. Liv, I need to speak to you . . .'

'Fancy a coffee?' she said. 'A nice one from the proper machine in the bar?'

I nodded mutely, still trying to work out what to say. How did you tell your best friend she may have inadvertently – or even, I winced thinking of her credit card bill, deliberately – got mixed up with something criminal?

Liv's phone rang loudly, making us both jump. She glanced at the screen. 'Regional manager,' she groaned. 'Probably wants sales figures. Might take a while. Jump in the shower and I'll put the machine on.'

I nodded and she answered the call. 'Des, I thought you might call today.'

Slowly I got to my feet and went upstairs to shower. I took my time washing my hair, thinking about everything that had happened and trying to piece it all together. And the thing I kept coming back to – ridiculous and far-fetched as it sounded – was Emily Moon and the smugglers. It just all seemed to fit – tunnels and ghost stories and all that. What if this was the same thing? But a twenty-first-century version. Modern-day smugglers – an organised crime gang, bringing in something illegal from abroad.

I rubbed shampoo into my hair and thought about what they could be smuggling. Drugs was the obvious choice, but perhaps it was firearms? Or even people. I shivered even though the water was warm. Could they be people traffickers? Fleecing desperate refugees out of their life savings in return for dangerous passage to a remote part of the UK? Urgh. This was awful. I felt my heart rate rising and tried to breathe evenly and concentrate on the smell of the shampoo and the feeling of the water on my skin.

I had no reason to think anything like this, I told myself sternly. Liv was right: just because there were bad people in the world, didn't mean everyone was bad. But try as I might to be rational, I kept coming back to smuggling. I knew I had to speak to Liv, because it seemed like she was involved somehow – though I was convinced she would never have agreed to anything illegal. I knew her. She was mouthy and streetwise but she was a good person. She'd never done anything dodgy; I was sure of that.

I turned the water off and dried myself, wondering what she would say if I presented her with my suspicions. She wouldn't be overly impressed, I thought, remembering how she'd reacted when I'd tried to arrest Jan's purse-borrowing husband. And if she was involved somehow, I would have to make sure I didn't point fingers. Liv was inclined to be defensive if she thought she'd got something wrong. I would say I'd found the tunnel and perhaps someone was using it for something dodgy. Perhaps I could suggest going to the local police. Give her a way out. That would work.

I pulled on jeans and a T-shirt, and dragged a brush through my damp hair, then wandered back downstairs to find Liv. She was behind the bar, fiddling with the coffee machine.

'Cappuccino?'

'Yes please.'

I perched on a stool and leaned on my hands. 'How was Des?'

'Not as annoyed as I'd expected.' She made a face. 'He said he knows it's a tough location and to hang in there.'

'Well, that's positive.'

'Yes,' said Liv. But she didn't sound very sure. 'Chocolate?'

I nodded and she sprinkled some cocoa on top of my cappuccino with a flourish, then pushed it across the bar towards me. 'What did you want to talk about?'

'You're going to think it sounds crazy,' I said.

'Go on.'

'I found a . . .'

Liv turned the handle on the coffee machine to steam the milk and my words were lost in the hissing and bubbling.

'Sorry,' she said, turning it off again. 'Say that again. You found a . . .?'

'Tunnel. On the beach.'

Liv raised an eyebrow. 'You went on the beach?'

'There's a path down from the cliff. It's really steep, though, and a bit hairy in places. But I was down there, and I found a tunnel. It goes from the beach, up through the cliff to the pub cellar.'

'I know,' Liv said.

I stared at her over the top of my coffee froth. 'You know?'

'Of course I know. Well, I know there's a door in the cellar, so it had to go somewhere. But I assumed it wasn't used. The door looks like it hasn't been opened in years.'

'I literally just came through it.'

'Really?' She looked alarmed. 'I should check that, because having an unlocked door will get me in trouble with the insurance.'

I couldn't believe how blasé she was being about all this.

'Liv,' I said. 'Aren't you worried?'

'About what?'

'About the tunnel?'

She made a face. 'No. Should I be?'

'I think so.'

'Why?'

'Because of the smugglers.'

'Phoebe, my love, you're sounding a big unhinged. What smugglers? What are you talking about?'

'I think that back in Emily Moon's time, the smugglers used the tunnel to bring contraband in through the pub.'

'Right.'

'What if it's still happening?'

'Smugglers?'

'Yes.'

'Like pirates with barrels of beer on their shoulders and those three-cornered hats?'

'No,' I was sounding unhinged to my own ears now too. 'Present-day smugglers.'

'Smuggling what?'

'I don't know for sure and I've never worked in major crimes. Drugs? People?'

'I hope they are smuggling people – maybe they'll stay for a drink,' Liv said. She started clearing away our coffee cups, obviously fed up with the conversation.

'I think we should go to the police,' I said desperately.

Liv stared at me. 'What?'

'I think we should go and say we found the tunnel and someone's clearly using it for dodgy reasons and they should investigate.'

'Phoebe . . .' Liv began, then she stopped.

'I know it sounds crazy,' I said. 'I know that. But I really believe something bad's happening here. What about the Watsons disappearing like that?'

'They had a family emergency.'

'And now the tunnel.'

'It's, like, a thousand years old.'

'But it's obviously been used recently.'

'Probably just kids,' Liv said. 'Think about how much we'd have loved somewhere cool like that to hang out when we were teenagers. Somewhere to stash our fags and the booze we sneaked out of our parents' house.'

I nodded. That was true. Maybe Liv had a point. But I couldn't rest.

'You said yourself it was weird that the pub's still open,' I said. 'You said you didn't understand it.'

'It's scheduled for redevelopment.' Liv started stacking the cups in the glasswasher at the end of the bar. 'They want to keep it open until the work starts so people don't forget about it. It's going to be a gastropub, I think. A destination venue.'

'Really?'

'Really. It's all happening, Des said the plans have gone in to the council.'

I felt unsettled and odd, as though the ground was shifting below my feet. Because everything Liv said made perfect sense. All of it. Except I knew Ewan had phoned Liv and she'd been in the cellar and had told him it was sorted. And I knew that I'd seen Jed and Mark on the beach. It was like pieces of a jigsaw all slotting into place. I opened my mouth to tell Liv what I'd seen and then shut it again. For some reason, I didn't want her to know that I'd watched them down below the cliffs. Liv was looking at me, worry in her eyes. 'Phoebe, are you okay? You're acting so weird.'

'I'm fine,' I snapped. 'It's not me who's weird.'

She raised an eyebrow. 'Who?'

'Ewan.'

'Phoebe, he's not some local crime lord. He's a bloke who knows people, that's all.'

'I just have a feeling . . .'

'Like you had a feeling about that kid in Kirrinporth?' Liv said. I winced at the memory of the child's mother yelling at me. 'Or the bloke who was stealing a purse in the pub?' I flinched again and Liv's face softened. 'You're still not right, Phoebe,' she said softly. 'That business at work. And that's fine. It was a horrible thing to happen and I think once you're back on your feet and back at work you'll be a better police officer than you were before. But for now you're wobbly and you're crazy suspicious about people who aren't doing anything wrong. You're just jumping to conclusions and spending too much time researching Emily Moon.'

I bit my lip. Maybe she was right. I knew that I'd made mistakes. And yet I was really sure about this. 'I just think we should tell the police,' I said.

Liv nodded. 'I know, love,' she said. 'But you'll go in to the police station, and you'll speak to someone and you'll tell them your name and they'll check you out and they'll find out you're a police officer who's off sick with what I think might be some sort of PTSD, and . . .'

She trailed off but I understood what she was saying. In fact, with a flash of insight I saw myself as she was seeing me. Fragile and suspicious and getting everything wrong. Perhaps Mark and Jed had just been exploring the beach. Perhaps they knew about the tunnel and just wanted to see it for themselves. There was an explanation for everything. I nodded. 'Sorry,' I whispered.

Liv smiled. 'It's not your fault,' she said. 'Just take some time out, relax, and let me get on with running the pub, eh?'

'Okay.' I got down from the bar stool where I'd been sitting. 'I think I might go and watch some *Homes Under the Hammer*.'

Liv grabbed me as I went past and pulled me into a hug. 'You'll be all right soon,' she said. 'You'll be better again.'

I felt close to tears suddenly. I wriggled out of her embrace and blew her a kiss. 'Got to get on,' I said. 'I think they're doing a country cottage today. Might get some ideas for the pub refurb.'

Slowly, I climbed the stairs to the living room, feeling sad and confused. An hour or so on the sofa watching people rip up manky carpets and pull out avocado bathroom suites would make me feel better.

I curled up on the couch and turned on the TV. Outside, the sky was darkening – again – over the sea but it felt cosy in the lounge, hearing the sound of Liv bustling about downstairs. I must have fallen asleep because I woke later on to see *Homes Under the Hammer* had finished and been replaced with the lunchtime news. There were voices coming from the bar, which meant there were customers – good news for once. I would wash my face and head down to give Liv a hand, I decided.

I plodded out on to the landing and stopped as I heard Liv say my name. Peering over the bannister to reply, I saw she wasn't calling to me as I'd thought, but instead she had her back to the stairs and was talking to someone I couldn't see, about me.

'Phoebe's seeing things that aren't there,' she was saying. I frowned. Why was she discussing me with a customer? 'She's fine.'

I leaned over a bit further to see who Phoebe was talking to, and wasn't remotely surprised to see Ewan Logan, leaning against the wall.

'Just make sure she's not going to bother us,' he said. He spoke in a way that sounded casual but there was an edge to his voice that made the hairs on the back of my neck stick up. 'It's up to you to stop her.'

'She's fine,' Liv said again, but she sounded less sure this time. I drew myself back, away from the bannister so I could still hear, but not be seen. Liv, though, was finished. 'I need to get on, Ewan,' she said.

'Just do it.'

'I will.'

I heard the door to the bar open and close as they both went back to the pub and I stayed where I was for a moment, taking some deep breaths. What was happening here? Suddenly I wanted to get out of there. Away from The Moon Girl and the cliffs and Ewan bloody Logan and all my worries about what they were doing. I needed a distraction. I would go to the library and find out some more about Emily Moon, I thought. I would take my laptop and use their Wi-Fi and do some proper research.

Feeling marginally calmer, I went into the bedroom to get my stuff. It was only as I was stuffing my laptop into a bag that I noticed that Liv's belongings had all gone. Curious, I picked up my bag and went across the hall into the master bedroom. We'd packed up all the Watsons' bits and pieces but it still felt like someone else's room. That clearly didn't bother Liv, though. Her suitcase was on the end of the bed, her trainers were on the floor, and her dressing gown was hanging on the back of the door. She'd moved bedrooms.

It didn't matter in the slightest, of course. And in fact it made perfect sense. Two women in their thirties were really past the stage of sharing a bedroom. But I couldn't help wondering why she'd done it and if our conversation earlier had anything to do with it.

I turned to go, and noticed on her bedside table was her bracelet. The one with the dove on it, which I'd bought her for her twenty-first birthday. It was curled on the top of the table like a little silver snake. I reached out and touched it gently. She never took it off. Never. Just like I never took off my moon necklace. It was a symbol of our friendship, and our loyalty to each other. But here it was. I felt tears prickle my eyes. What was happening here?

Chapter 31

Still upset about the bracelet, I thought about shouting to Liv to tell her I was going into Kirrinporth and then changed my mind. I didn't want to see her or Ewan Logan. So I put on my shoes, grabbed my waterproof jacket, slung my bag on to my shoulder, then I ran down the stairs and out of the side door.

Outside, the drizzle clung to my face, but I didn't mind. I felt like it was waking me up. I walked at a good pace, all the way into the village. I was thinking about anything but what was going on with Liv and Ewan Logan and how badly I'd misjudged Jed. I just wanted to distract myself for a while and I thought reading some more history might do the trick.

But as I got into the village, my eye was caught by the tiny police station on the main road. It was just a shopfront really; a small neighbourhood office where tourists could report lost phones, or local people could ask for advice on home security.

I stopped walking, looking at the posters in the window for Crimestoppers. How many times had I despaired that people hadn't reported something suspicious? How many times had I thought *why didn't you tell someone?* Well now it was me who was suspicious and me who had to tell someone.

Quickly, before I had time to change my mind, I crossed the

road and pushed open the door. Inside it was dim and quiet. There was a counter with a long Perspex window like in the post office, to stop anyone leaping over I assumed, and racks of leaflets about window locks, or bike registration. To one side was a bell with a sign saying *please ring for attention*.

I would just say that I'd seen some suspicious activity on the beach, I thought. I'd not mention the pub, or name any names. Just suggest they should have a look down on the sand. With my approach worked out, I pressed the bell.

It took a second for anyone to answer then I heard a door open and a man appeared behind the window. As he emerged into the gap in the window, my heart sank. It was the police officer who'd been there when I had the incident with the little girl. I closed my eyes briefly, hoping he wouldn't recognise me, but he was already smiling.

'Hello there,' he said. 'Come to report another crime have you?'

I opened my mouth to speak but he'd not finished. 'So we've done the child kidnapped by her mother. What about the dog being dognapped by its owner?' He chuckled, pleased with his own joke.

'I made a mistake,' I said, not laughing.

'Lighten up,' he said. 'It's just banter.'

Glaring at him, I said: 'There is something . . .'

'You're staying at the pub, aren't you?' he said suddenly. 'The Moon Girl?'

I nodded and he grinned again. 'I heard someone made a citizen's arrest on a fella for nicking his wife's purse.'

I forced myself not to react. 'Really? I didn't hear that.'

He looked at me carefully. 'No?'

'No.'

There was a pause.

'So what did you want to say?'

I couldn't tell him anything now, could I? I couldn't blurt out some vague suspicions about dodgy dealings on the beach, without sounding like I'd had one too many drinks. Unless I told him I was in the police. But like Liv said, as soon as he looked me up, he'd see what had happened and realise I was signed off sick. It wouldn't take long for him to realise it was my mental health that was an issue, as I was quite clearly fine physically and he was already questioning the way I'd reacted to things. He could even, I thought, take it on himself to report any concerns about me. And that could possibly harm my return to work.

'What do you want?' He spoke slowly, as though I was hard of hearing.

I made my decision on the spot. 'Thought I'd lost my phone,' I said. 'But I was wrong. Sorry.'

Feeling his amused eyes on my back, I spun on my heel and walked quickly out of the police station. I emerged into the sunshine, and blinked as my eyes got used to the light. I took a deep breath, and thought again about the techniques Sandra the counsellor had taught me to stop a panic attack in its tracks. 'Think of one thing you can feel, one thing you can hear, one you can see, one you can taste and one you can smell,' she'd said. I breathed in again. I could hear a van's diesel engine, making me think of black cabs in London. I could smell the fumes from its exhaust. I could see . . . I looked round and, there, across the street, I thought I saw Jed, leaning against a wall, watching the police station, his tall frame standing out among the people who drifted past.

My stomach lurched. I blinked again and when I looked up, there was no one there. I shook my head. This technique wasn't working; it was making me see things that weren't there. Things – people – I wanted to see or ones I didn't? I wasn't sure. I shook my head and checked the spot across the road once more – it was deserted. Then longing for calm, I headed to the library.

Inside, the library was quiet and the Wi-Fi signal was strong. Thankfully, I sank down into one of the squishy chairs with my laptop on my knee and browsed social media for a while, marvelling at how quickly it loaded compared to the clunkiness of the feeds on my phone, had a nosy at what everyone from work was doing by logging into my emails and soon logging off again when it seemed there was nothing very interesting happening, and browsed through some summer dresses on ASOS knowing that with the weather the way it was, I'd never get to wear them.

And then I thought about poor Emily Moon. The other Moon Girl, who'd vanished and whose mystery I still hadn't solved. So I googled smuggling in Cornwall, chose a nice site with lots of pictures and started to read. It was pretty interesting but there was nothing specific to Kirrinporth, nor Emily herself, and I couldn't concentrate. Everything I read made me think of Ewan, Jed and Mark. Smugglers moving their contraband through tunnels and hiding it in pub cellars? Bingo. Telling ghost stories to make people stay away? So far, so familiar.

Casually, as if I was pretending to myself that I wasn't doing it, I pulled up the work crime system. I wasn't sure it would work on public Wi-Fi, and sure enough it wouldn't load. So instead, I linked my laptop to my phone, and bingo. Then, knowing I shouldn't really be doing what I was doing, and feeling mildly guilty, I put in my password. I wasn't sure if it would work given that I was off sick, but it did. I couldn't access everything but there was enough there to give me more info. I wasn't expecting to find loads of information on smuggling in the Met's records but I typed in smuggling and pressed return and my screen filled with links to reports. I took a deep breath, clicked on the first one and started to read.

I spent an hour or more reading every detail I could about organised-crime gangs and how they trafficked drugs, firearms and even people. I did neighbourhood policing really and my part of London was all about the street crime. We spent a lot of time trying to stop local kids getting involved in county lines operations. I'd never really thought about where the drugs came from in the first place – that was a job for my colleagues in serious and organised crime. But this was gripping. And, more importantly, it all added up. I read about how they often used small boats or yachts to bring goods – or people – ashore. How they had contacts in various places to help smooth the way – I remembered Liv's regional manager who seemed oddly relaxed about the pub making no money.

A thought occurred to me and I opened a new window and typed in Cornwall council planning department. Once I'd found the right page I went to put in the pub's postcode and paused. I didn't know it. I sent a message to Liv asking her, and wondering if she'd be suspicious about why I needed to know, and she replied straightaway. 'What are you buying?' she asked and I breathed a sigh of relief. 'Just checking out ASOS,' I wrote. She sent back a smiley face and I typed the postcode into the search bar.

There was nothing. I searched for Kirrinporth and found planning applications for extensions and conversions and refurbishments and all sorts going back several years but nothing for The Moon Girl. No plans had been submitted. But perhaps Liv had just misunderstood what the regional manager told her. I shut the council webpage and looked again at the trafficking reports on my screen, deciding which one to read next.

'You look engrossed,' a voice said. I looked up to see the librarian smiling at me.

'I'm reading about local history,' I told her and she looked pleased.

'Then you'll like this.' She held up a large book. 'Are you Phoebe?'

I was surprised. 'Yes?'

'Someone just rang the library and asked us to give you this book when you came in. My colleague Sue recognised you from the description.'

'Who?' I said, feeling like I was on some sort of weird reality TV show. 'Who phoned?'

She shrugged. 'It was a man. He didn't leave his name, just said to tell you this was the book he mentioned.'

'And he knew I was here?'

'Apparently.'

Jed. It had to be. Perhaps I had seen him by the police station after all. But why would he leave a book for me? Was it some kind of weird code?

'Do you want it?' The librarian was waiting for me to respond.

'What?'

'The book.'

'I guess so.'

She handed me a battered A4-sized hardback with a shiny cover showing a painting of a pub perched above a harbour wall.

'Thank you,' I said uncertainly. She grinned at me and wandered off.

I studied the cover. The book was called *Historic Pubs of Cornwall* and I assumed it was one of the ones Jed had mentioned that his dad had read. Feeling faintly ridiculous, I looked around me, half expecting to see him standing there. But he was nowhere to be seen. This was very strange. I supposed it was sweet of him to make sure I had the right book to help with my research, but I would have preferred him to just send me a message.

Still, I had it now. I opened the book, hearing the spine crackle as though no one had read it for a long time, and I turned to the index. There was a reference to Emily Moon. I smiled to myself. Jed may have been ghosting me after our kiss, but this was a nice thing to do. So, getting myself comfy, I sat and read the story of Emily Moon and her sad, untimely death.

Emily Moon, the book said, had been a bit of an odd one. The writer said she'd been called simple because she couldn't speak. People called her the Moon Girl and felt sorry for her. So she really was another Moon Girl, I thought, playing with my necklace. Emily lived in the pub, which had been called The Ship Inn back then, and drew pictures. On the page was a reproduction of a sketch of a dark-haired woman with amused eyes. The caption told me it was Emily's mother, Janey Moon, drawn by her daughter. The sketch was in the museum at Barnmouth, it said. Maybe I should visit? I looked at Janey's face and wondered if Emily had looked like her mother and what had happened to the other pictures she drew. Had anyone had kept them safe over the years?

Emily, the book went on, had plummeted to her death from the cliffs. At least, that's what all the evidence suggested, though her body was never found. Her sweetheart, Arthur Pascoe, left Kirrinporth shortly after her death. Perhaps he was heartbroken, I thought. I turned the page, hoping for more, but the book moved on to a story about a shipwreck near a pub in Barnmouth. That was all there was to say about poor Emily Moon.

So I was still none the wiser about what had happened to her, and I had a knot in my stomach that was making me feel unsettled. Perhaps Emily had been murdered by the smugglers I thought. The stories I'd read about what they did back then had told me they were pretty brutal and wouldn't think twice about killing anyone who got in their way. And that made me think about Liv and what she might have got mixed up in.

My heart was thumping, partly through sadness for Emily, but mostly because I suddenly realised that if my suspicions were correct, if Ewan and his crew were involved in organised crime, then this was really, really dangerous.

With shaky hands, I shoved my computer and the book into my bag. I needed to go. Without looking back, I hurried out of the library.

Chapter 32

Emily

1799

I tossed and turned all night, falling into a fitful sleep full of night-mares about Morgan just as the sun came up. When I eventually woke, with an aching head, I got dressed quickly and gathered together all my drawings. I took the ones of Morgan on the beach, and my sketches of Arthur and me in my dream world, travelling across the wilderness on our cart to build a life together. I found some pictures I'd drawn of Da before he died, and Mam, and added them, too. Then with some difficulty because I hadn't written anything since Da died, I wrote along the top of the pages. On the smuggling drawing I wrote Cal Morgan, and on the one of Da I wrote Amos Moon. And at the bottom of each one I wrote EM.

Then, leaving out two sketches of Da and two of Mam, I care-fully put the drawings into my hiding place on the window seat. I had an uneasy feeling that I wouldn't be coming back here and I wanted to leave evidence of what had happened.

I put the pictures of my parents into my bag, and went to find my mother. I'd been fretting about her going to the gallows with

219

Morgan and I knew I couldn't rest until I'd warned her that – if everything went to plan – his time was up.

I found her in the cellar, counting barrels of ale. I averted my eyes from the contraband, though I couldn't help noticing there was much less there than there had been. Clearly most of it had been sold or moved on.

'You've surfaced, have you?' Mam said, not looking up. 'Can you take two bottles of brandy upstairs for me?' Her annoyance with me had eased as her bruises had faded. She heaved one of the barrels across a bit and groaned. 'This is a man's work.'

I gave her a small smile. Mam had never complained about heavy lifting when my father was alive. She wasn't tall but she was wiry and strong with arms that felt as hard as rock when she tensed her muscles.

She smiled back, reading my mind. 'I know,' she said, almost to herself. 'I can do it. Would be nice to have someone around to help though.'

That was the perfect opening for me to bring up Morgan. But after everything that had happened the last time I'd tried to speak to her, could I speak? I hoped desperately that my throat wouldn't tighten and concentrated on my breathing as I held my hands out for the two bottles.

Mam handed them over, looking at me with mild concern. 'Are you feeling unwell?'

I shook my head, breathing in and out, in and out. 'Mam . . .' I managed. She looked at me in surprise and I tried again. 'Mam?'

'What?'

In and out, in and out. 'Morgan.'

Mam let out an exasperated gasp of breath but before she could start on me, I held my hand out, trying to calm her. To my relief, she sat down on the table, her skirt billowing around her, and crossed her legs. 'Go on then,' she said defiantly. 'What about him?'

I breathed in again, and out, planning my words carefully. 'Morgan is smuggling.'

Mam leaned back on her elbows and looked at me. I met her stare, trying to communicate with more than words.

'I know,' she said.

There was a pause as I tried again, but Mam jumped off the table and wiped her hands together to get rid of the dust.

'Is that it?'

I put down the bottles of brandy, thinking that I could use my hands to show her what I wanted to say, instead of speaking.

'Morgan,' I said again. I mimed a rope being slung round my neck and pulled up sharply with my hand to indicate being hanged, tipping my head to one side and closing my eyes as if I was dead.

'Morgan's not in trouble,' Mam said.

I shook my head vigorously and pointed at my mother instead. 'You,' I said. 'You.' I made the same action again, pulling the invisible rope around my neck.

Mam's expression softened.

'Oh, Emily,' she said. She came to me and put her arm round my shoulders. 'You worry too much.'

'Da,' I began, but she was still talking.

'I know,' she said. 'I miss him too.'

She sat down on the table again and this time gestured for me to sit with her. I moved the bottles aside and perched beside her and she took my hand.

'I loved your father,' she said. 'And when he went, I thought I should die because it was just too hard.'

I felt a wave of sorrow at the thought of how my mother had missed Da as much as me. More, perhaps.

'I thought my heart was breaking. And the inn was empty. All I had was you. My daughter, who didn't say much before and who said nothing now.'

My eyes filled with tears. I'd never meant to make things worse for her. If I could have made myself more like other people, I would have.

'Sorry,' I whispered, but Mam patted my hand as if to say it didn't matter.

She carried on talking. 'We had no money, Emily. None at all. Your father was good at many things, but he spent every penny he ever earned. And when he was gone, there was nothing left in the pot.'

She took my chin in her fingers and turned my face this way and that, examining me. 'You are skin and bone, my girl. Skin and bone. And that's on me. It's my fault.' She sighed. 'I have been no mother to you since your da went.' I noticed she was still avoiding saying that Da was dead. I thought she had decided to ignore everything I had told her and I couldn't blame her. How else would she get through the days?

'I know I have been drinking too much,' Mam went on. 'I know things aren't perfect, still, but they are getting better. We have food on the table, and a fire burning in the hearth. And do you know why, Emily Moon?'

I shook my head, even though I knew what she was going to say.

'It's because of Morgan.'

'No,' I said miserably but Mam shushed me. 'He is the reason we had mutton yesterday, Emily. He is the reason I have this new dress and there is bread upstairs waiting for you to eat. He is the reason the drinkers have come back to the inn and the reason your cheeks are getting plumper.'

He was also the reason for the bruises on her face, and the marks on her legs, the tears she cried at night when she thought I was asleep, and the dullness in her eyes, but I couldn't say that.

'I know he's involved in free trade,' Mam went on. 'And there's some that don't approve. But he's the only reason we still have a roof over her heads.'

I looked at her. Her face was close to mine and I could see the remains of the bruises around her eye and hear the tremor in her voice.

'You will hang,' I said, slowly and carefully, but more loudly than I'd managed to speak for months.

Mam took my hands and I let her. 'No, I won't,' she said. 'Trust me.' She looked straight at me, but I couldn't read her odd expression. 'Trust me,' she said again. Her voice sounded urgent. I nodded and, impulsively, I threw my arms around her and pulled her to me. She relaxed into my embrace for a second, then she pulled away.

'Leave it, Emily,' she said. 'Just leave it.'

I wasn't sure if she meant the show of affection or my feelings about Morgan, but either way it seemed the conversation was over. Mam slid from the table again and turned her attention to the barrels once more.

'There's bread for you upstairs,' she said.

I watched her back for a second, hoping she might turn around and carry on talking, but she didn't.

Later that evening, I sat by the window of the inn, watching the moon rise up over the sea. It wasn't full – that was still a few nights away – so I was fairly sure Morgan wouldn't be planning to bring any goods in yet. In fact, he was here with his friend, sitting at a table and grabbing my mother whenever she passed by. Claiming ownership, I thought. He was calling out to customers as they entered, greeting them and saying his Janey would get a drink for them. It made me feel sick. I glowered at him, but he gave me no more attention than he'd give a worm in the mud. Mam had shot me a warning glance once or twice, telling me to stay quiet. She seemed different since our chat in the cellar. Stronger, I thought. I half wondered if she had something planned but then dismissed the idea. She'd have told me, I thought.

I went back to gazing out over the sea and only looked up as a shadow fell over me. It was Arthur.

Pleased to see him, I smiled and he gave my arm a small, affectionate squeeze. I liked the way his touch made me feel.

'Shall we go for a walk?'

I nodded.

'There's a chill in the air this evening,' he said. 'Take your cloak. I'll meet you on the cliff.'

He went out the front door of the inn, while I went into the hall to find my shawl and then out of the back door and round the stables. When I got to the clifftop, Arthur was standing with his hands in his pockets, staring at the moon.

'Three more nights, I think?' he said. 'We should watch from tomorrow, just in case.'

I nodded. He was right. We didn't want to miss it.

He put his arms round me and kissed me. I shivered with pleasure.

'Your father?' I asked when we broke apart. Arthur's face clouded over.

'I did. I was right about it all.'

I widened my eyes in surprise. Even though the evidence had all pointed to Reverend Pascoe being involved, I'd never really believed it. Was Morgan really using his coach?

'He denied it at first,' Arthur went on. 'He claimed he had no idea what I meant. But there on the shelf was the same type of bottle we saw in the cellar.'

I rolled my eyes, though it was getting properly dark and I knew Arthur couldn't see.

'I told him some of what we know.' Arthur ran his fingers through his hair in exasperation. 'He is weak, Emily. So weak. He is clearly scared of Morgan . . .'

I squeezed Arthur's arm, nodding to show that his father was right to be scared. 'He is a murderer,' I said.

'Indeed. But I believe my father should fear the gallows more.' He sighed. 'I just worry that he will tell Morgan everything if he so much as frowns in my father's direction. He'll be so scared that he'll just let everything slip.'

I pulled my shawl more tightly around my shoulders, listening intently.

'What did you say?' I asked carefully.

'I didn't tell him what we were planning,' Arthur said. 'I don't want him warning Morgan off. Instead, I said I'd heard rumours from the customs men that they were looking for those helping smugglers and that he should be careful. I said quite forcefully that he should keep all the gates and doors locked. And to make sure they stay that way all night.'

I breathed out in relief.

'I've done all I can.' Arthur pulled me close to him. 'At least, I hope so.'

I hoped Reverend Pascoe would heed Arthur's warnings. He was a nice man, I thought. Kind and caring. I didn't want to see him hang because of Morgan's misdeeds.

'And your mam?'

I shrugged, clasping my hands together at my chest, showing that I hoped it was going to be all right. Arthur nodded.

'So we will watch the beach tomorrow evening then?' he said.

I nodded. The moon wasn't full yet but we did not want to miss our chance to prove Morgan's guilt. He was clever when it came to predicting the weather and if there was a storm on its way he could decide to land the goods sooner.

Arthur nodded, looking out over the sea. 'I believe you're right. We should start watching tomorrow in case they bring the cargo early.'

I followed his gaze to the horizon.

'Where do the goods come from, I wonder?' he said thoughtfully. 'France? Holland?'

Carefully, I repeated the names of the countries he was listing. The words felt unfamiliar and magical on my tongue. 'Where else?'

'Spain,' Arthur said.

I repeated the name, hissing the S like a snake. I liked how it sounded.

'Maybe one day I will take you to these places.'

But I shook my head. 'Not there,' I said.

I felt in my pocket for a scrap of paper, and a stub of charcoal.

And then I drew, in just a few lines, a wide, open space and a tiny horse and cart with us on board.

'Da told me stories about a place where there are no people,' I said, taking my time over each word. Arthur's eyes widened and I smiled.

'He said it was just space and sky.' I sighed happily. 'Just space and sky.'

Arthur was looking at me, a curious expression on his face.

'And that's what you want, is it? Somewhere where there is nothing?'

'Space and sky,' I said again. I screwed up my face. 'It's just a dream.'

'Maybe we can find somewhere like that one day,' Arthur said. 'Somewhere to start from the beginning.'

I nodded. That was it exactly. Starting from the beginning. I found people to be difficult. They said the wrong things and they didn't always act as they should. I didn't understand the rules that other people just seemed to know. No, not rules. What was the word? Conventions, that was it. How people were supposed to be. Maybe in a new land it would be easier. Maybe the conventions would make more sense if I was there at the beginning. I smiled to myself. It was just a silly dream, but it made me happy.

'My father wants me to follow him into the church,' said Arthur suddenly.

'I know,' I said.

'I could not imagine anything worse.'

I nodded again. I knew that, too. Arthur loved growing things. He loved being outside and feeling the earth in his fingers. Spending his days in a dim, airless church would finish him.

'In all this space do you think there would be enough for some fruit bushes? Perhaps an orchard? Maybe some vegetables?'

'Yes,' I said, grinning. 'Yes.'

Arthur nodded, as though I'd just confirmed what he'd been

thinking. 'Then it sounds very much like your dream land would suit me, too.' He grinned at me. 'Shall we go there together one day?'

I was thrilled at the very thought. 'Yes please,' I said. I snuggled into him, pretending – for a few moments at least – that it wasn't just a dream and that maybe we could escape together one day.

Chapter 33

Phoebe

2019

'Shit,' I said to myself as I walked back to the pub. 'Shit, shit, shit.' I was totally rattled by everything that had happened – the police officer's amused "banter" about my crime reporting, Jed leaving the book for me at the library and, it seemed, hanging around outside the police station and the library to watch me. That was borderline creepy, not romantic in the slightest. And I'd messaged him asking if he'd left the book and he'd not replied to that one either.

I walked so fast out of the village that I was sweating and out of breath by the time I'd got halfway back to The Moon Girl. I was worried about what was going on at the pub, scared Liv was involved, and suspicious as to why Jed had been following me. But what could I do about any of it? There had to be a bigger police station in Truro. I could go there, but as soon as they contacted the officer in Kirrinporth they'd be told that I was flaky and not to be trusted.

At a loss, and worn out, I wandered away from the road up on to the grass verge where there was a little viewing spot. I sat down on the bench with a sigh and looked out over the sea. I could just glimpse the roof of the pub from here and I wondered what Liv was doing.

I pulled my phone from my pocket and rang Stacey at work, hoping she'd be at her desk. I was in luck – she answered almost straightaway.

'Good timing,' she said when I'd said hello. 'I've just got an email with all the info. I'll forward it.'

'What does it say?' I was too eager to wait for the email. 'Can you give me the basics?'

'Right, the man, Ewan Logan?'

'Yes?'

'Fake name. There was a Ewan Logan born at around the right time – early 1970s – but he died as a baby.'

'Oldest trick in the book,' I said. Taking the name of someone who'd died was an easy way to get a birth certificate and become legit.

'You sound pleased?' Stacey said.

'Not pleased really, just that I knew he wasn't what he seemed,' I said. I was relieved more than anything. Perhaps my instincts weren't all whack after all, despite what Liv said. 'What else have you got?'

'Okay, so the family – the Watsons?'

'Yes.'

'Nothing. No record of anyone of that name.'

'What?'

'Nothing.'

I leaned back against the wooden struts of the bench. 'Nothing?'

'I'm forwarding the email now, so you can see for yourself.'

'The whole family? Nothing from the pub?'

'Nope. Nothing.'

'What about the kid? He went to Barnmouth Primary School. I've seen a photo of him with the school logo on his jumper.'

'Even the kid.' Stacey sounded slightly exasperated, but she always sounded a bit like that so I pushed on.

229

'Does that mean what I think?'

'It's possible,' she said.

'Witness protection?'

'That's the only thing that makes sense to me. But there's no way to know for sure, of course.'

'Christ,' I breathed. It made sense, with the vanishing act and the lack of a forwarding address. And, frankly, it was better than the alternative I'd been imagining of a mafia-style hit on the whole family.

'Phoebe, are you okay?' Stacey said. 'This sounds pretty serious stuff.'

'I'm fine,' I lied. I held my hand out in front of me, noticing with dismay, that I was shaking. 'Honestly. It's nothing.'

'Witness protection and fake names doesn't sound like nothing to me.'

I took a second, trying to decide what to tell her. 'It's not nothing, exactly, but honestly, you don't need to worry.'

'Just be careful.'

'Actually, Stacey,' I said, sensing she was ending the conversation. 'Can I get you to check one more thing?'

'Go on.' She sounded less than enthusiastic. 'What do you want?'

I couldn't believe I was about to say the words, but I had to know for sure. Because perhaps my instincts hadn't been whack about Ewan Logan but they definitely were when it came to Jed. 'Can you just run the name Jed Saunders?'

'Who's Jed Saunders?'

'Someone who's been hanging round the pub. I wanted to see if he's trustworthy. Can you check if he's got a record?'

'Want me to do it now while you're on the phone or later and email?'

'Now.'

'Fine, hang on.' I heard her typing and then she breathed out. 'Shit, Phoebe. What is this?'

'What?' My heart was pounding. 'Is he dodgy?'

'It's just flagged up to contact DCI Richardson at Devon and Cornwall Police.'

'Really? That's weird.'

'He's obviously a person of interest in a case,' Stacey said.

'Wouldn't it say that though?'

'Maybe they do stuff differently down there. So will you?'

'Will I what?'

'Contact this DCI Richardson?'

I thought for a second and then shook my head, even though Stacey couldn't see me. 'Nah,' I said lightly. 'It's not important. Just a whim. I'll just make sure Liv doesn't leave him alone with the takings.'

'You're sure you're okay?'

'I'm sure.'

Stacey and I said our goodbyes and I ended the call. I sat on the bench for a second and thought. I was really shaken by the whole thing and I felt sick and trembly. This had suddenly gone from being a puzzle to an enormous, and probably very dangerous, mess. What had we stumbled into here? It was like being in an episode of *Line of Duty* and I had a really bad feeling about it all. Liv was clearly involved in some way, and I'd been snogging one of the baddies.

'Oh God,' I moaned, putting my head in my hands. Even though I'd known Jed was hanging round with Ewan, I'd trusted him. He was just so . . . nice. What an idiot I'd been. I gave a snort at my own stupidity. There I'd been suspecting all the innocent people like Jan's poor husband of being up to no good, and ignoring the bloody criminal on my doorstep, just because he was a good kisser. What if DI Blair found out about all this? I could lose my job. The thought made me feel even sicker than I already did.

I took a deep breath, trying to slow down my racing heart. I should probably just let everything be. Keep my head down and let whatever was happening, happen. Clearly the local police were on to it. It was being dealt with. At least, I hoped it was. But then again. How could I when my best friend was involved? I thought about Liv taking off her bracelet and pushed the memory away. She was my oldest, most loyal friend and I knew that if she was involved in something illegal, it was accidentally. I needed to find out more.

For the first time since I'd spoken to Stacey I started to feel a bit better, because alongside my conviction that Liv hadn't meant to get involved in this whole mucky business, I felt a little flicker of excitement and intrigue. A flutter of interest. A reminder of why I loved my job – or at least why I had loved it before the Ciara James tragedy. And, I told myself, this time I'd been right, hadn't I? I was right that something was up. With Ewan at least. I'd got it very wrong about Jed. *And possibly about Liv*, a tiny voice in my head warned, but I ignored it.

Yes, I needed to find out what was going on and what it had to do with Liv. Maybe this was just what I needed to give my confidence a boost and get me back on the bike.

But perhaps I had to do it my way.

My phone rang in my hand and I glanced at the screen to see Stacey's number.

'What's up?' I said as I answered.

'Not sure.' She sounded flustered. 'I just had a call.'

'From?'

'From DCI Richardson at Devon and Cornwall Police.'

'No way.'

'Way.'

'What did DCI Richardson say?'

'She said she'd seen that I'd looked up Jed Saunders and was there a reason?'

'Shit,' I said. 'What did you say? Did you tell her it was for me?'

Stacey scoffed. 'No. I said it was a typo. That I'd meant to write Ted and accidentally put in Jed.'

I was relieved, though I didn't completely understand why. 'Nice one. Did she buy it?'

'Think so. There's no reason for me to be searching some Cornish criminal from Lewisham, is there?'

'Guess not.'

Stacey was quiet for a second then she spoke. 'Phoebe, you're not involved in anything dodgy are you? I'm not going to get into trouble for this?'

'No, honestly I promise. There have just been a few odd things going on round here and I wanted to check some names.' I didn't like lying to her, but I wasn't sure what else to do.

'Sounds like you need to go and speak to the local police,' Stacey suggested.

'That sounds like a good idea,' I said, knowing that I had absolutely no intention of doing what she'd said.

I ended the call. This was confusing and frightening and, yes I had to admit, exhilarating. What I needed was to write everything down, like I would at work. I wanted to make clear notes about everything I knew and what I needed to know, and then I could make a plan about how to deal with it all. Because it seemed to me I was about to start an investigation into Ewan, Mark and Jed, and – I had a horrible feeling – into Liv, too.

Slowly I stood up from the bench, and started to walk back to the pub, thinking it all through. Liv was in the bar when I got back, pulling a pint. I was pleased to see there were a few more drinkers in than there had been recently.

'Need a hand?' I said as I walked past, fairly half-heartedly I had to admit.

She barely looked up at me. 'All good.'

I was glad. I bounded up the stairs to what was now my bedroom – not ours – and shut the door. Then I found a notepad and pen, sat on the bed, and began scribbling down everything I knew about the men.

Which turned out to be a lot and also not enough.

I looked in dismay at my notes.

"Ewan Logan," I'd written. "False identity." Then: "Jed Saunders, under investigation?" And finally: "Mark?" I didn't even know his surname.

Underneath I jotted down: "On beach." That proved nothing. But there was the tunnel. And Liv being jumpy about the cellar. Liv generally, I thought. I added some vague scribbles about her credit card bill being paid off and the conversation I'd overheard her have with Ewan.

The biggest thing was the Watsons possibly being in witness protection. But it was also the thing I had no hope of proving. This was desperate. I put the notebook to one side and lay down on top of the duvet with a sigh. I was putting two and two together and making five. Maybe my instincts were whack, after all.

I lay there for a while, and then I sat up again and pulled the library books I brought home with me out of my bag. I put the one Jed had reserved for me to one side. I didn't want to read about pubs and I didn't want to think about why he'd been watching me. Instead I turned to another book I'd borrowed, about Cornish smugglers. Maybe reading about old-time criminals would give me some clarity on the modern-day types.

I read about taxes and ships coming from abroad and customs houses, and then I sat up suddenly as I reached a section on the goods being landed.

The smugglers would shine a light out across the sea to signal to the ships when it was safe to come into shore, I read. A light. Like the blue light I'd seen shining the other night. Was that a signal to someone out at sea?

There it was again, that flicker of excitement. What if I watched each evening to see if there was a light? To see if there was a pattern to it, or it changed? Then I might be able to work out when the next shipment of goods or – urgh – people was due and catch them in the act. If I took photos or video, then I'd have something concrete to take to the local police. I smiled at the thought of that smug Kirrinporth PC's face if I presented him with evidence of a local organised crime gang.

Watch the lights, I thought. That's what I would do.

Chapter 34

Emily

1799

Arthur and I spent two long, cold evenings on the clifftop watching in vain for any sign of Morgan and his crew's illicit activities. It was uncomfortable and tense, but I didn't mind really. I quite liked being out under the stars with Arthur. Just us two and the great expanse of ocean. We passed the time imagining my dream world. Our dream world now.

'Where will we go?' I said, nestling in the crook of Arthur's arm. We were sitting on the grass, leaning against one of the big rocks that scattered across the top of the cliff.

'We will get ourselves a horse and cart,' he said. 'We'll load it up with everything we need for a new life. And then we'll head across the land where no one has been before.'

'And . . .?'

He chuckled. 'When we find a good spot, we'll build a farm. And we'll grow wheat. Maybe I'll take cuttings and seeds with me from my garden. We'll build a house for us all to live in.'

'All?'

'Me, you, the babies we'll have.'

I'd flushed with pleasure at the thought of growing a family with Arthur. Far, far away from the people in Cornwall, and the rules I didn't understand, and the noise and hustle and bustle. I wished it was a real place, and not somewhere that only existed in our imaginations.

I looked up at the sky where the moon was just beginning to rise. It would be full tonight, I thought. I wondered if tonight would be the night Morgan's goods came ashore. It depended on the tide, I supposed, and the wind. All manner of things.

Arthur looked up as I did. 'And the moon will come up when the sun goes down, just as it does here. And the rain will fall and water the crops. It's the same as here. But bigger and emptier.'

'Can we . . .' I began. Suddenly a figure rose up out of the shadows in front of us and my words became a gasp of fear. Arthur gripped my arm.

'What's this?' said a voice. The figure came closer and I could see it was Morgan's right-hand man, my father's old friend Petroc. His stocky shape was silhouetted against the moonlit sea. Arthur and I scrambled to our feet, still clutching each other's hands. I wanted to kick myself for being so stupid. We'd assumed the men would be down on the beach, and hadn't bothered keeping quiet or taking care to listen for footsteps. And now we were discovered and our plan was ruined.

'What are you doing?' Petroc hissed. I saw the flash of a blade in his hand and felt my legs go weak.

'Emily and I came outside for a walk,' said Arthur. His voice was shaky.

Petroc stepped closer. He was a head shorter than Arthur, but twice as wide and I had no doubt at all that he could hurt or even kill us both if he wanted. In his hand he held an unlit lantern. I feared he could cosh either one of us round the head and we'd be dead before we knew it.

'I seen you watching Morgan,' Petroc said. 'You watching him, and me watching you.'

'That's not true,' Arthur stammered.

Carefully, as though he was taking real pride in his actions, Petroc put the point of his knife into Arthur's neck. Arthur squeaked and I felt helpless rage that these bad men were causing so much everywhere they went.

'Why were you watching Morgan?'

'We weren't . . .' Arthur began again. Petroc pushed his knife a bit harder and I saw a drop of dark red blood trickle down Arthur's neck and on to his shirt.

'Why were you watching Morgan?' Petroc said again.

He made to push the knife once more and I gasped: 'Stop!'

Petroc kept the knife at Arthur's throat, but he turned to me, giving me a frightening smile that showed the gaps in his blackened teeth. 'Oh, she speaks,' he said. 'So, Miss Emily. Why were you watching Morgan?'

But I could say no more. My throat clenched and though I opened my mouth, nothing happened. I tugged on Arthur's sleeve. Surely he could see that this couldn't be any worse. We may as well confess to Petroc; we were as good as dead anyway.

'We want to prove he's smuggling,' Arthur said slowly. 'We want to tell the revenue men when he is bringing contraband ashore and we want to see him hang.'

'What do you care if he's smuggling?'

'He killed Emily's father.'

Petroc looked from me to Arthur and back again. He nodded his head. 'I was sorry about that. I liked Amos.'

I stared at him, unwilling to accept his apology, if that's what it was.

'You want to see him hang?' Petroc said.

Arthur and I both nodded.

'So do I,' said Petroc. He took the knife from Arthur's throat and tucked it in his belt. 'The man's a brute.'

Not totally understanding, I clung to Arthur, still staring at Petroc. 'What?' Arthur said. 'What are you saying?'

Petroc sighed. 'I'm in. I'll help you.'

'We don't need help.'

Petroc smiled his ugly smile again. 'I think you do,' he said. 'If Morgan finds you as I found you, he will kill you. I can help.'

'Why would you do that?'

'I can't lie, I've made a good living from free trade over the years,' Petroc said. It was like we were chatting over a drink in the inn, not trembling on a cliff edge. 'But when Morgan got involved it was all different. The risks are too great. The rewards too few.'

Arthur looked at Petroc curiously. 'And that's all, is it?'

The older man met his stare for a second, then dropped his gaze to his feet. 'I know what he's been doing to your mam,' he mumbled. 'I can't bear to see how he treats Janey.'

Petroc had been drinking in the inn since I was a little girl. He would often help Da with odd repairs to the roof or the stable doors and Mam would always reward him with a drink.

'I've always been fond of your mam,' he said. 'She's a good woman, is Janey Moon.'

Arthur nodded. 'She is.'

'It ain't right.'

'It's not.'

Petroc sat down and arranged himself comfortably at the bottom of the rock. 'Sorry about the knife,' he said. 'I knew you wouldn't tell me 'less you were scared.' He took the knife out of his belt and laid it on top of the lantern and another tin he'd been carrying. 'So, what's the plan?'

Arthur and I exchanged a look. Then we both sat down too.

'We simply thought to watch from up here to see when Morgan's contraband was landed. Then I would ride for the revenue men and they would catch him in the act,' said Arthur shrugging.

My eyes fell on Petroc's lantern and I felt a sudden rush of fear. 'Tonight?' I croaked. Would Morgan be smuggling his goods soon?

Petroc shook his head. 'Twas supposed to be but the tide's too high and the waves too rough. The boat will be dashed on the rocks' he said. 'I've come up to light the lantern. We've got red glass we put in when it's not right. They see the red light and stay out at sea.'

Arthur stretched his leg out and tapped the tin with the toe of his boot. 'What's that?'

'Ooh that's good, is that,' said Petroc. 'Phosphorus.'

Arthur looked interested. I had no idea what he was talking about.

'It glows in the moonlight.' Petroc looked delighted. 'Like a ghost.'

Now I understood. The strange ethereal light I'd seen wasn't a spirit – it was Petroc's paint.

'I just paint the outline of a figure on the rocks,' said Petroc proudly. 'Keeps people away.'

'This is clever,' said Arthur. 'Very clever.'

'I heard that in Devon, they painted a horse and carriage,' said Petroc, showing his gap-toothed grin again. 'Whole thing. Wheels, doors, horse, all of it. Except the horse's head. And then they sent it galloping through the town at midnight looking for all the world like a headless horse.'

'Inspired,' breathed Arthur.

'Morgan won't go for that fancy stuff, though,' said Petroc. He seemed disappointed. 'So I just slop it on the rocks, light the lantern, and go.'

'Which rocks?' Arthur asked. But I'd had enough of this chatter and wanted to know if Petroc really was going to help us. I tugged Arthur's sleeve and he nodded, understanding.

'Will you help us?'

'I can keep him on the beach for longer,' Petroc said. 'Give you time to get the customs men down here.'

'That's good,' said Arthur. 'But what about you? You might be arrested too.'

Petroc shook his head. 'I'll take myself off in time, don't you worry about me.' Then he frowned. 'But it's not just Morgan you need to worry about you know?'

I felt another cold trickle of fear down my spine. What did he mean?

Petroc shrugged. 'They're all involved. Mr Trewin. Mr Kirrin . . .'

'Even Kirrin?' Arthur was shocked.

'Oh he don't get his hands dirty but he's the one pulling the strings.' Petroc leaned towards me and I tried not to flinch away from him when he was being so kind. 'And if any of them get a hint that you were involved, they won't be best pleased.'

Arthur and I both nodded. 'What should we do?' Arthur said.

'Keep quiet, stay out of trouble, it'll blow over,' said Petroc. 'Just be wary, that's all.'

I was shaking so violently and my teeth chattering so loudly that I wasn't sure if it was with fear or because of the cold night air.

'Will they hurt us?' I said slowly with a great deal of effort.

Petroc shrugged. 'Probably not. But it's not a chance I'd want to take.'

Suddenly, he threw his hand out across my body and Arthur's, warning us to be quiet.

'What's that?' he said in a low voice. 'I heard hooves.'

I strained my ears and there, through the darkness, a whinny echoed.

'Someone's coming,' Arthur said.

We all got to our feet hurriedly. Petroc crept round the side of the rock and I followed, heart thumping. Up ahead, coming down the path I could see a dark figure and where the moon shone on his head I could see the bright streak of white in his hair.

'It's Morgan,' Petroc hissed.

'Was this you?' Arthur sounded furious. 'Did you know he was coming?'

But Petroc shook his head. He looked just as scared as we did.

'Petroc, you fool. What's going on?' Morgan shouted. 'Is

someone here with you? I heard voices. Is it you, Emily Moon? Janey said she'd gone out.'

We all looked at each other in terror. He knew we were here. He would kill us. A tiny sob escaped my lips. And then I had an idea. I pulled my cloak off and pushed it into Petroc's hands, gesturing over the cliff. To my huge relief, he and Arthur caught on immediately.

'Scream,' hissed Petroc. 'Scream.'

For once, my throat didn't betray me. I opened my mouth and let an ear-piercing shriek out. It split the night.

'Go,' said Petroc. 'Go.'

Arthur grabbed my hand and pulled me and we both ran as fast as our legs would carry us along the cliff edge in the shadows and up on to the grass verge. Then we hunched down in among the trees and watched as Morgan appeared in the moonlight.

'Petroc you're a blithering idiot, what have you done?'

Petroc was gripping my cloak like a shield. 'It was the Moon girl, sir,' he said. His breathing was ragged. 'I was just lighting the lantern and she came at me. She gave me such a turn. I thought it was a bloody spirit. Some unearthly beast come to torment me.'

Morgan snorted and Petroc carried on. 'I just panicked. I lashed out and she slipped. I tried to stop her but all I got was her cloak.' He peered over the edge of the cliff. 'She's gone. I'm sorry, sir. I'm sorry.'

There was a pause. I could see the gleam of Arthur's eyes in the darkness and hear our uneven breaths.

Then Morgan gave a bark of laughter. 'She went over, did she?'

'We should help her,' Petroc said. I was more than a little disturbed by how well he lied. Could we really trust him?

Morgan clapped the smaller man on the back, so hard the sound bounced round the clifftop. 'It's too late for that,' he said. He was jovial. 'Come, let's finish up here and then have a drink.'

'What about Janey?'

241

In the shadows, I stiffened at the mention of my mother. Arthur put a gentle hand on my arm, warning me to stay still and quiet.

'She's already had a drink. She won't notice her foolish daughter's gone until tomorrow,' Morgan said, sounding very much like he was pleased about it. 'It means we can bring in tomorrow's shipment unheeded. Come, let's get the lamp lit. You do the paint.'

Whistling, Morgan busied himself with the lamp while Petroc sloshed paint on to the rocks. Arthur and I stayed where we were, hunched down under the trees. I was still shivering and Arthur pulled me close and wrapped his own cloak around me to keep me warm.

Eventually, the red light shone out across the sea and Petroc put the lid back on the paint tin. Without glancing in our direction – he was worryingly good at this – he nodded to Morgan. 'Shall we?'

Morgan picked up my cloak, which was still lying on the ground. 'If we leave this here, someone on their way to market will come across it and eventually someone will realise the Moon girl took a tumble,' he said. 'Then we won't need to tell Janey anything – the news will reach her in another way.'

He balled up the cloak and threw it and it snagged on one of the rocks, hanging there like soiled laundry.

'Always finding someone else to do your dirty work,' Petroc said with admiration. He picked up his tin of paint. 'It's your turn to buy the ale.'

'It's always my turn,' Morgan complained without any real annoyance.

And joking with each other as they went, the men strolled away, towards the inn, leaving Arthur and me alone.

Chapter 35

Phoebe

2019

I lay in my bed, looking at the other side of the room, where Liv had slept until a few days earlier. It was raining again and the wind was strong. I assumed – though I was no expert – that meant it wasn't safe for boats to head into the little cove. I'd check the light tonight again. It had been blue for the past few nights, shining out over the sea, so I'd been pretty sure there hadn't been any smuggling going on, though I was knackered because I had been staying up late to watch in case the light changed.

There had been no sign of Ewan, or Jed and Mark. I was pleased, because I wasn't sure how I'd be able to act normally around them now I knew that Ewan was a fake name and Jed was in the sights of Devon and Cornwall police. At least this way I didn't have to pretend.

'Phoebe?' Liv was calling. With a fair amount of effort, I got myself up off the bed and plodded to the top of the stairs. She was frowning up at me. 'Have you just got up?'

'I was tired.'

She rubbed her forehead, looking worried. 'I need to go out. I was wondering if you could mind the bar for me? But if you're not up to it . . .'

'Where are you going?'

'To speak some local breweries about getting some craft ales put on.' She frowned again. 'Is that okay?' There was a sarcastic edge to her voice.

'It's fine.' My tone matched hers and I wondered how we'd got here after so many years of friendship. 'I'll be down in ten minutes, if you can wait?'

'Thanks.'

I showered quickly and threw on some clothes, then headed downstairs to the bar. Liv was hovering by the door, looking professional with a folder and papers. 'I'm hoping to get us some guest ales,' she said. 'We can promote them and hopefully they'll make people want to come here.'

I didn't really care about guest ales, but she seemed nervous and I did care about that, so I smiled. 'I bet you can charm their socks off.'

'I hope so.'

She gave me a small wave. 'Open the door at eleven, or thereabouts. Any problems, just give me a call. I'll be back by the end of lunchtime.'

She headed out of the door and I was left alone in the bar. I checked my watch – I still had almost an hour before I had to open up. I could watch some *Homes Under the Hammer* on iPlayer, I thought. Or, I could go and have a look in the cellar. I thought about it for thirty seconds, then casually sauntered to the door of the pub, and stuck my head out to check Liv's car had gone. It had. The weather was looking clearer too. The wind had obviously blown the rain away and it was brightening up. Satisfied that Liv was out of the way, I locked the pub door again and headed for the cellar.

Quietly, I went down the steps and felt for the light switch. It was just as it had been the other day. Barrels of beer, boxes of wine and spirits. A pile of boxes of crisps. Nothing untoward. Nothing that would suggest anyone was planning to hide drugs, or firearms or illegal immigrants anywhere. I was almost disappointed.

I checked my watch again. I still had a while before opening time. So I started at one side of the cellar and began to search. I wasn't sure what I was looking for, really. Just something that shouldn't be there. I opened boxes, moved barrels and shifted bottles but found nothing. Until, I opened a box of cheese and onion Walkers and there, on top of the crisps, was a brown A4 envelope.

I took it out, thinking it was just a mistake. Perhaps Liv had put her post in there accidentally. But there was no name on the front and it was heavier and thicker than a letter would be. With slightly shaky hands, I very carefully peeled open the flap, making sure I didn't tear the paper, then peered inside.

It was money. Cash. A stack of £20 notes and a few tenners. I pulled it out of the envelope and looked at it. Was it fake? I held one of the notes up to the light, but it seemed legit. Liv was hiding cash in a box of crisps and I could only think of one reason why – she was being paid for doing something dodgy. For letting Ewan use the tunnel and the cellar, presumably. Perhaps for helping him in other ways. I had no idea. But the cash and the text message I'd seen from Liv's credit card company proved to me that my best friend was involved in this – whatever it was.

'Bloody hell, Liv,' I said out loud. 'Bloody hell.' I was scared for her and what she'd got tangled up in. I even felt guilty that I'd somehow allowed her to get into this mess without noticing. But mostly I was angry. Furious, in fact. What on earth was she thinking? She wasn't stupid. Considering I'd been friends with her for most of my life, I suddenly felt like I didn't really know her at all. This wasn't just her life she was messing with; her actions were putting my whole career in peril. How could she? How dare she?

Seething, I pulled my phone out and took a photograph of

the money, and the envelope. Then I carefully put the cash back and sealed the flap again, hoping no one would see it had been opened. I laid it on top of the crisps, took another photograph, then shut the box. I wanted to make sure I had evidence, if I needed it.

Still angry, I went upstairs and sat on the window seat in my bedroom, staring out over the sea. My mind was racing and I wanted to scream. How had things got so bad for Liv that she'd get mixed up with a bunch of criminals? Maybe she didn't have a choice, a voice in my head warned. Maybe they'd threatened her and she had no choice. But why didn't she tell me? I wondered. Why didn't she come to me, her oldest and best friend, and ask for help? I could have sorted it. I was sure of that. Why didn't she trust me to help her? Clearly we didn't have the friendship I thought we'd had.

Slowly, and sadly, I reached up and unclasped my moon necklace, letting it drop into my hand. That was that, then. Twenty-five years of friendship done and dusted. With a sudden rush of fury, I kicked out with my leg, slamming my trainer into the end of the window seat. Everything had fallen apart, and I didn't know what to do about it.

Listlessly, I stood up and as I did so, I noticed that a panel at the end of the window seat was sticking up. I'd obviously dislodged it with my kick. Just what I needed, another thing to feel guilty about. Perhaps I could put it back, without damaging it more? I dropped my necklace into my pocket, and turned my attention to the window. Gently, I pushed the panel downwards and as it clicked into place I realised it was held with a catch. It was supposed to open – I hadn't broken it at all.

Intrigued, I pushed again and the panel sprang open. It was a little hidden compartment. How exciting. I peered inside, wondering if there was anything in it and hoping for the glimmer of gold or the sparkle of jewels. But no, all that was inside was a roll of cobwebby paper.

Gingerly, I reached in and pulled out the pages, then I sat down on the window seat and unrolled them, sneezing as the dust tickled my nose.

It was lots of little sketches, of people's faces, and boats on the sea, and a horse and cart travelling across a wide-open expanse of countryside.

'Sweet,' I said out loud. They looked very old, but I had no idea when they'd been drawn. My heart, though, was thumping with a flicker of excitement. Emily Moon drew pictures, I remembered. She'd drawn the picture of her mother that I'd seen in the book about Cornish pubs Jed had reserved for me in the library. Had she drawn these? With shaking hands, I leafed through the pictures until I found one that had EM in the corner.

'Emily Moon,' I said in delight. 'Emily bloody Moon.'

And then my phone beeped with a reminder that it was time to open the pub.

'Shit,' I muttered. I wanted to have a proper look at these drawings; I didn't want to serve customers. But I'd promised Liv, and I didn't want to make things worse between us than they already were. So I tucked the pictures inside the Cornish pubs book, and took it downstairs to the bar.

Chapter 36

Emily

1799

I woke up, stiff as a board and freezing cold in a tumbledown shed we'd found at the edge of the woods. It must have been used by a shepherd, Arthur said, or one of the men who worked in the forest. Either way, it was dry and warmer than being outside all night. I'd urged Arthur to go home, but he'd refused to leave me. Instead he'd pulled my cloak down from the rock where Morgan had left it, and when we'd found the shed, and lain down to sleep, he'd tucked me in like a child.

He was next to me now snoring gently. I watched him for a moment, marvelling at how young he looked, bundled up in his cloak. My heart swelled with love for him. He was so brave and clever.

Obviously feeling my gaze on him, Arthur stirred and opened his eyes.

'Good morning,' I whispered.

He sat up. 'Are you all right?'

I nodded. 'Are you?'

'Nervous, cold . . .' He rubbed his back. 'And stiff.'

I giggled, mimicking his gesture to show that I was suffering in the same way. Curled on a hard floor had not been the most comfortable place to sleep.

Arthur looked at me, biting his lip. 'I've done a lot of thinking overnight,' he said.

If felt nervous. What was he going to say? Had he changed his mind about helping bring Morgan to justice?

'Remember when we were small and the soldiers returned from fighting in America?' he said.

I blinked at him. This wasn't what I'd expected him to say.

'Remember?'

I thought carefully, shaking my head. I'd only been a baby when that war had ended.

'I don't remember them coming home either,' Arthur said. 'But I remember the stories they told afterwards.'

I sat up straighter. Now that I did remember. Probably better than Arthur, truth be told. I'd sat in the corner of the inn when the men came to drink, slapping each other on the back, and telling tales of guns and battles and sinking ships. They'd told Da and Mam all about their adventures and the losses they'd suffered. I'd seen injuries compared and heard stories of terrible wounds. I nodded.

'When you were telling me of your dream world, it reminded me of the stories some of those men told.'

I frowned. What did he mean? My dream world was still and silent, not full of angry soldiers with rifles. But Arthur went on. 'Not the tales of the fighting, but the stories about the country.'

'America,' I said slowly.

'It's enormous.' Arthur looked excited. 'It's bigger than we could ever imagine. And there is so much there to discover.'

I was trying to make sense of what he was saying.

'I have heard of people there, packing up their belongings and travelling into the unknown,' he said. 'They travel and they find somewhere they like the look of, and they build their lives there.'

I breathed out, in astonishment. That sounded exactly as I

had imagined it. I wondered if Da's stories had not been from his imagination after all, but instead him passing on to me what he'd heard. Perhaps as a little girl, I'd thought this new world sounded so perfect that it had to be imaginary.

'Space and sky,' I said slowly.

'Exactly.' Arthur clutched my hands. 'I think we should go.'

Now I was really astonished. Go to America? Across the sea? 'It's far,' I stuttered. 'So far.'

'We could never return,' Arthur said. 'We would have to say farewell to my father, and your mother. We would never see Cornwall again.'

I thought about Mam all alone in the inn and how I would feel to leave her there. But then I thought about staying. I thought about living in the inn and hiding from customers when they got too rowdy. I thought about Arthur being guided into the church by his father instead of spending his days growing fruit and vegetables as he wanted. I thought about everyone calling me the Moon Girl and talking about me as if I wasn't there, or laughing at me behind my back. And I smiled.

'America,' I said. 'We can go to America.'

Arthur stood up, like he was giving a sermon in his father's church.

'At first I thought we had to wait. I thought we would work hard and save enough money for our passage.'

'On a ship?' I asked. I'd seen large sailing ships from the shore, of course, but I couldn't imagine how someone like me would find their way aboard one.

'They sell tickets in Plymouth,' Arthur said. 'But I must warn you, the journey is said to be hard and long.'

I shrugged. I couldn't begin to imagine what it would be like, and so the idea of a long journey on board a ship held no fear for me.

Arthur continued. 'I thought you could find a position as a housemaid or kitchen girl – anything that didn't need much talking. I would finish at school and get taken on as an apprentice to one of the farmers to learn all I could about growing and tending crops. And then we would get married and travel across the ocean to America.'

My heart was thumping. I wanted this so badly I could taste it. I pictured a huge, empty landscape, with our little cart crossing it. Just us. No one else. But while I could see us in America, the bit that stopped my imagination running away with me was Arthur's plan to find the money. Would anyone in Kirrinporth employ the strange, silent Moon Girl? I doubted it. And would Arthur's father let him become a farmer's apprentice instead of a reverend? It seemed unlikely.

Arthur was shaking his head, too.

'But we must go now,' he said. 'We can't stay.' He sat down next to me again and turned to face me, his boyish face looking serious and determined in the dim light of the cabin. 'This will be the one and only night we will spend here,' he said. He shuffled over on his backside so he was closer to me and took me in his arms. 'We shall leave Kirrinporth tomorrow.'

'Tomorrow?' I gasped.

Arthur bit his lip. 'Remember how Petroc said everyone is involved in this? Mr Trewin? Mr Kirrin?'

Of course I remembered. I nodded.

'They won't be happy if Morgan goes to the gallows. I fear they will come after us. Seek revenge.'

I widened my eyes in shock. I knew Morgan was dangerous, of course I did, I'd experienced his violent nature first-hand. But Mr Trewin? Mr Kirrin? Was this true?

Arthur sighed. 'I just think we should leave while we can.'

I pulled my cloak up, showing him the dust from where Morgan had thrown it on to the boulder. If everyone thought I was dead, then surely there would be no danger?

'People think you have fallen from the cliff, you are right. Your cloak may not be there for them to see but I don't think Morgan will keep quiet about it for long. We should just let everyone believe that.'

251

'Mam?' I mumbled. Would she be grieving for me, even now?

'Perhaps it's for the best. Just for the time being.'

I bit my lip. I couldn't bear to think of my mother weeping for me when she was still grieving for Da. But maybe Arthur was right.

'Your da?'

'I will tell him that I am seeking my fortune elsewhere. Once we're settled we can write to them and let them know we are safe. My father can tell your mother.'

'Money?' I asked. How would we pay for this?

'I will ask my father,' Arthur said. 'And if he cannot help, I will sell my belongings. I have some jewellery that was my mother's, I have my horse.'

'For me?' I said softly. I couldn't believe he was willing to sacrifice so much.

'For us,' he said.

We kissed and I felt lighter than I had since Da had been killed. Suddenly I had a future, something to look forward to. Something to work for.

My stomach grumbled loudly, breaking the mood. Arthur and I both laughed. 'I'm hungry too,' he said. He got to his feet. 'We have a long wait until nightfall. You stay here. Don't go anywhere because we don't know if Morgan or his men will be roaming around the clifftop. I will go home and find some food.'

I didn't want him to go, but I knew he was right.

'I'll ask a few people if they've seen you,' he said. 'Start to spread the word that you're missing.'

I nodded, trying not to cry. I didn't want him to leave me here alone. What if Morgan came? What if something happened to Arthur and he didn't come back? I felt an urge to gather him to me and keep him with me, to keep him safe. I didn't want him going back to Kirrinporth where Morgan and Mr Trewin and Mr Kirrin and goodness knows who else were free as birds to snatch him and hurt him.

He saw the fear in my eyes and bent down to kiss me softly.

'Stay quiet,' he said. 'No one will know you're here, if you don't make a sound.'

I gave him a withering look. I was hardly about to start chattering now, was I? He chuckled and, with a certain reluctance, I gave a small smile, too.

'Stay safe,' he said. 'I will return in an hour.'

But he didn't.

Chapter 37

Phoebe

2019

The lunchtime rush at The Moon Girl was an older couple who'd been out for a walk and clearly only came in to use the loo but felt obliged to order a coffee, and two geeky-looking students wearing hiking boots and waterproofs, and with university-branded ruck-sacks on their backs, who had pints of lager and chatted loudly and enthusiastically about rock formations. That was it. Two coffees and two pints of lager. Wherever that money in the cellar had come from, it most certainly wasn't from the takings at the pub.

I stayed behind the bar, glancing at the book and wondering if I could get the pictures out while there were customers here. I didn't want to risk them getting beer spilled on them so I left them where they were, and spent my time worrying about Liv instead. More than once I took my phone out to call her and tell her I'd found the money, but then put it away again. What would be gained by confronting her?

Just as I was losing the will to live with the students' chatter, the door opened and in came Simon the vicar. I greeted him like a long-lost friend. He ordered a Guinness and when I looked alarmed at the prospect of pulling his pint, he came round to my side of the bar and did it for me.

I was impressed and told him so.

He grinned. 'I worked in pubs when I was younger.'

'Well I wouldn't have expected that.'

'We're just normal people, you know. We men of the cloth.'

'Apparently so.'

Simon held his pint up so I could admire it. 'Still got it.' He took a sip and smacked his lips. 'Now, delicious as this is, I didn't just come in for a drink. I brought you something.'

He put down the glass and want back round to where he'd left his bag. Looking triumphant, he pulled out a sheaf of yellowing pages, tied together with a cord.

'This,' he said, putting it down on the bar, 'is the memoir of Reverend Horace Pascoe, vicar of this parish in the 1790s.'

'Oh my goodness,' I breathed. 'Arthur's father? Have I got that right?'

I pulled the papers towards me. It was typewritten and I looked at Simon questioningly.

'Some eager parishioner typed it up in the 1970s, I think,' he said. 'It's genuine though. I've also got this . . .'

He dug in his bag again and this time produced a small leather-bound notebook, in a ziplock sandwich bag. 'This is the original,' he said. 'It's really delicate so I've been keeping it in this bag to protect it. I've cross-referenced it with the typewritten version and it all seems accurate.'

'So Arthur's father kept a diary?'

'He did.'

'Does it mention Emily?'

Simon made a face. 'No,' he said.

'Oh.' I was absurdly disappointed.

'But, it does mention Arthur. May I?'

I pushed the bundle of papers towards Simon and he untied

them and started leafing through until he found a page, about two-thirds of the way in, marked with a Post-it Note.

'Here,' he said.

I leaned over the bar to see where he was pointing. 'It was around this time that I lost my only son, Arthur,' I read aloud. 'I had hoped he would follow me into the church, but he was determined to follow his own path. I never saw him again.' I paused, feeling sad for this man who long ago said goodbye to his son forever.

'What does that mean?' I said, bewildered. 'Lost him how?'

Simon shrugged. 'I don't know. It reads almost as though he died, but then the bit about him following his own path sounds as though he just did something other than becoming a vicar.'

I frowned 'So why do you think this is related to Emily?'

'Well, because it happened at the same time,' Simon said. 'Reverend Pascoe is writing about 1799 here, and that's the date on Emily's memorial stone.'

'If Arthur died, surely he would have a memorial stone too?' I said thoughtfully. 'Or a grave?'

'Perhaps he did – somewhere else in the church maybe, and it's been lost over the years. Some of the stones in the churchyard are so old that the writing has been worn away.'

'Would there be a record of a death?'

Simon shrugged. 'Parish records are patchy when you go back so far.'

'Maybe he did die when Emily did.' I said. 'Perhaps they both fell off the cliff, like the fictional Theodora and Diggory.'

'A tragedy,' said Simon, looking genuinely sad for the long-ago teenage lovers.

'I found pictures,' I said. 'I've not looked at them all properly yet, but I think Emily drew them.'

'Oh my days.' Simon's expression brightened. 'Show me.'

I went to get the book and took out the pictures. Then Simon and I sat at a table and spread them all out in front of us. There were a couple of the woman – Janey Moon – whose picture was in the book. We compared the sketches to the reproduction on the page and nodded at each other. They'd definitely been drawn by Emily. There were some of a man, one of which had Amos Moon written in childlike writing along the top. Then there were some of another man, with a white streak in his hair and rugged good looks that made me think of Ewan Logan and shudder. His picture had Cal Morgan written on it.

'Look at this one,' Simon said. It was a sketch of the beach below the pub. On the horizon was a large ship, and a smaller boat was on the shore. A line of men – I could see one of them was Cal Morgan because of his distinctive hair – were unloading cargo.

'Smugglers,' I breathed. 'She drew the smugglers.'

'This is astonishing,' Simon said.

I was scanning the other pictures. 'But did she draw them to show someone what they were doing?' I wondered aloud. 'Her version of taking a photograph with her phone? Or was it just for fun – all from her imagination?'

'What about these ones?' Simon held up the pictures showing a little covered wagon, heading out into the wilderness. 'This landscape doesn't look very Cornish.'

'It reminds me of something,' I said. 'But I can't think what.'

'Don't think about it, and it might come to you.'

I nodded. 'Thank you for bringing the diary to show me,' I said. 'You've taken my mind off things and cheered me up.'

'Were you miserable?' Simon gave me a steady look that made me think anyone could tell him anything and he wouldn't be shocked.

'Not miserable, just worried about my friend Liv.'

'Is she miserable?'

I shook my head. 'We had a bit of a falling-out,' I admitted. 'She's doing something I don't think is the right thing to do.'

'That's tricky,' Simon said.

'It's really tricky. I'm just worried she's going to get into terrible trouble.'

He screwed his nose up. 'You can't stop her if she's set on it,' he pointed out. 'And nor should you try really. People have to make their own mistakes.'

'You're right.' I knew he was speaking sense. But I didn't like it.

Simon started putting the papers back into his bag. 'I have to go,' he said. 'But I'm glad this was helpful.'

'It was great, thank you.'

'Don't worry about your friend.'

'I'll try not to.'

But that was easier said than done. Simon and I said goodbye and I sat in the empty pub, staring at my phone aimlessly, only putting it away when Liv came into the pub.

I tried to be normal with her, even though I wanted to grab her shoulders and scream at her about the money I'd found. 'How was your meeting?'

She gave me a forced-looking smile. 'Yeah, great. I've put in some orders. Let's hope it pays off, eh? Any customers?'

'A couple,' I said. 'Very quiet.'

She rubbed her eyes, looking exhausted. 'Thanks anyway.' She jumped as her phone vibrated in her hand, and she glanced at the screen and sighed.

'Problem?' I said.

She didn't answer, still looking at the message.

'Liv, are you okay?'

She blinked at me. 'Sorry,' she said. 'I was just . . . erm. Just work.'

'You'd tell me if anything wasn't okay, wouldn't you?' I said.

'Definitely.'

But I knew she was lying.

'I need to make a phone call,' she said. 'I'll be upstairs.'

I heard her slowly walk up to the flat, her steps heavy and sluggish. I had no way of knowing for sure, obviously, but I was certain her message was from Ewan and it was him she was calling now. And that made me think that things were happening tonight. The storm had cleared and the sun had even come out. It was looking like being a calm night.

Suddenly I made up my mind. Liv was in trouble and I needed to act. Maybe she'd taken off her bracelet. Maybe she hadn't come to me for help. But she was my best and oldest friend and I was damned if I was going to let something bad happen to her. The way I saw it, I had to catch Ewan and his cronies – yes, even Jed – in the act. If I could stop them somehow, before they got as far as stashing their goods or – I felt dizzy for a second – people – in the pub cellar, then Liv's involvement would be irrelevant. She might need to give evidence later, but I was fairly sure she'd get away with a rap on the knuckles.

Decision made, I felt marginally better. Now I just had to come up with a plan.

Chapter 38

Emily

1799

Arthur was gone ages. Hours and hours. I bit down my rising panic, tried to ignore my hunger and thirst and paced around the tiny hut. One, two steps one way, then the same the other way.

I scratched drawings on the dusty floor of the shed, a few lines to show the little wagon in my imagination. To remind me what we were aiming for.

My hunger grew. And my thirst. I was used to being hungry of course, I knew how to ignore an empty belly. But my lips were dry and my tongue was sticking to the roof of my mouth. I felt weak and shaky. What if Arthur didn't come back?

After the afternoon slipped into early evening, I made a decision. I had to go and find him. I had to know he was all right. And perhaps that meant we wouldn't catch Morgan in the act, but so be it.

I pulled my cloak around myself and crept out into the twilight. The birds in the woods were noisily settling down for the evening, chirruping and tweeting in the branches above. I strained my ears, listening carefully for any sound that could be approaching footsteps.

As I drew close to the path that led out of the woods and towards Kirrinporth, I heard a twig snap. With my heart beating faster, I drew back into the shadows behind a tree.

But to my relief, it was Arthur who came into view, scurrying carefully through the dim light.

I reached out as he passed me and touched his arm and he jumped in fear, stifling a shout as he saw it was me.

'Emily,' he gasped. 'Oh my goodness, I thought you were Morgan.'

I wrapped my arms round him, feeling his heart thumping wildly. 'Sorry,' I said quietly. 'I was scared.'

Arthur glanced around us fearfully, then he took my hand and in silence we hurried back to the shed.

Once we were inside, I shut the door and checked it was secure, then I turned to Arthur, throwing my hands out fiercely, showing him I was angry that he'd been away so long.

'Sorry, sorry, sorry,' he said. 'I was getting things together. We need to be prepared.'

He grinned at me and threw me some bread wrapped in cloth, and a flask of water. I drank the water first, then tucked into the bread greedily.

'I packed a bag,' he said. 'I thought we should be ready. Just in case. I took some cuttings from the garden. And some seeds.'

I rolled my eyes. He'd said the journey was long and hard. Could seeds and cuttings even survive?

Arthur smiled at my disbelieving expression. 'I know,' he said. 'But they just might grow. These seeds could be the first things we grow in America.' He looked very pleased with himself. 'And I brought you this.'

He showed me a roll of paper and some sticks of charcoal, as well as a bottle of ink and a pen. 'You can draw the plants,' he said. 'Keep a record of everything.'

I was thrilled. I liked the idea of drawing plants much better than drawing murderers.

'I have all the money I could find. It's not much,' he warned.

'And some of my mother's jewellery. I thought if we go to Plymouth we can ask around, find out how much we need to get passage on a ship. If we need to, we can find work in Plymouth. Something we can do together. We are a team. And I truly believe if we stay together, we will make a success of this.'

I felt a flutter of fear. I hoped he was right, but while I was as enthusiastic about travelling to America as he was, I was terrified about what the night might bring. We had to make it through to morning before we made plans.

'Morgan?' I asked.

Arthur shook his head. 'No sign of him. But I spoke to my father.'

'And?'

'I said nothing of our plans. I just reminded him to lock the gates.'

I bit my lip. This all seemed too real now. What if Reverend Pascoe forgot? Or warned Morgan?

'And I saw Mr Trewin,' Arthur said.

I gasped. Had he been suspicious that we knew what the smugglers were up to?

But Arthur grinned. 'I doffed my hat to him, and asked if he'd seen you on his travels.'

I widened my eyes, startled by Arthur's boldness.

'He said he hadn't seen you, but then he asked was I worried about you.'

'Ohh,' I breathed. Why would Mr Trewin think Arthur was worried about me, unless . . .

'I think, perhaps, Morgan has started spreading the word about your tragic accident already.'

I closed my eyes, wondering if word had got to my mother yet. But I knew this was the only way. Because these were dangerous men we were dealing with and I didn't want Mam to be at risk if there were any reprisals.

A thought struck me. 'Where is your horse?' I asked Arthur.

'At the inn. I put her in the stables round the back, though. That way no one should really notice she's there.'

'Good.' I sighed. Now we just had to wait for nightfall. And hope everything goes as we planned.

Time passed so slowly I thought I would die of boredom and nerves. Arthur and I talked about Plymouth. I'd never been but he had. He told me what it was like, warning me it was busy and noisy. I felt sick at the thought of being among so many people, but I calmed myself by imagining our new life in America.

Eventually it got dark and we crept outside of our hut, through the trees and out on to the grass at the top of the cliff. We were both silent, both scared, both gripping each other's hands tightly.

We found a spot, behind the rock that Petroc had painted, which was beginning to glow in the darkness, and crouched down to watch the beach. I pulled my cloak around me and Arthur gasped. 'Look,' he said, tugging on one side. 'You're glowing.'

I twisted round and sure enough, my cloak was shining like the rocks. It must have been from when Morgan threw it against the wet paint. I started to take it off but Arthur stopped me.

'You'll be cold without it. It's fine – it's like a disguise.'

I breathed out slowly. 'I look like one of Petroc's ghosts.'

'You could be Theodora and I am Diggory,' Arthur joked.

We chuckled for a moment, and I felt my nerves release just a bit, and then movement along the moonlit clifftop caught my eye. 'Arthur,' I said quietly, pointing.

'It's them,' he said.

Four figures were making their way down the path to the beach. I recognised Morgan and Petroc – the white streak in Morgan's hair gleamed in the moonlight, like my cloak. We watched them slowly navigate the steep path.

'I think they'll take the little boat from the cave and row out to the ship,' I told Arthur.

'Will they go now? How long before the ship comes?' Arthur said.

I shrugged. 'I can't see anything yet, can you?'

Arthur squinted into the horizon. 'Nothing.'

Suddenly it all seemed very real, and very dangerous. I thought of Mam all alone in the inn, waiting for Morgan's cargo, but instead finding the revenue men in the cellar. And possibly facing awkward questions and suspicion herself. Arthur had promised his father would speak up for her – but would he really? Arthur himself always said his father was weak. What if he was too scared to stand up for Mam? I looked at the men, making their way down the path and made a sudden decision.

I stood up quickly. 'Stay here,' I said carefully and quietly.

Arthur turned to me in confusion as I pulled my cloak off and gave it to him. I didn't want to be seen.

'What are you doing, Emily? Where are you going?' Arthur looked bewildered.

'Mam,' I said.

He grabbed my hand but I shook him off. This was too important and I had to be fast. I had to make sure everything at the inn was arranged to look as though Mam had no knowledge of what Morgan was doing.

I hitched up my skirt and ran as fast as I could across the grass, keeping to the shadows at the edge of the trees. I raced past the stables and round the back of the inn. The building was in darkness and I stood for a second, letting my eyes adjust. It was very late now, and I assumed Mam was in bed with enough drink inside her that she wouldn't hear me.

Quietly, I felt along the doorframe for the key, grateful for Mam's habit of leaving the key for anyone to find but also disappointed that she was still so trusting. I opened the door to the inn. I crept inside and into the lounge area, where I hoped the fire would still be smouldering. It was, so I lit a lantern, turned the wick down low and then went back out into the hallway. I paused for a moment at the foot of the steps, listening for any noise from Mam but everything was silent.

Feeling more confident that she was out cold and unlikely to wake, I made my way to the cellar door and went down the stone stairs, turning my lantern up so it lit the space more brightly. There was the door that I knew now led to the tunnel. There was nothing in front of it, giving it space to open. Mam had rearranged the cellar to give Morgan easy access to the inn. But with everything made so easy for him, it was obvious that my mother was involved. That was what I had to change.

I put the lantern down and checked the tunnel door. It was unlocked, so I felt along the frame for the key, locked it firmly and put the key back on top of the door. Then I dragged some barrels around the cellar, stacking them in front of the entrance to the tunnel so it was blocked. I kicked away the marks in the dust on the floor that showed they'd only just been moved. I didn't want there to be any chance of Mam getting into trouble. This way it looked as though she'd had no knowledge of what was going on down on the beach.

And, I thought with a certain amount satisfaction, now I'd locked the door to the tunnel and blocked it with barrels, there was no escape for Morgan. If he tried to run from the customs men, he'd be trapped on the beach.

Confident I'd done all I could, I slipped back out of the cellar and locked that door too.

I went towards the door, then changed my mind. Quietly, I crept up the stairs to Mam's bedroom. She was lying on her bed, snoring gently. I delved into my pocket and found the small sketches I'd made of her and Da. The ones I'd not hidden in my window seat. I tucked one of her and one of Da under her pillow and kissed her forehead. Then I ran downstairs again, put the lantern out, locked the back door of the inn behind me, replaced the key and took a breath. Time to go.

I ran all the way back to the clifftop, back to Arthur. I'd not been away long – my breathlessness showed how swiftly I'd moved – but I knew he would be worried.

I found him crouched behind the rock, watching the beach intently. He jumped when I put my hand on his shoulder.

'Oh thank goodness it's you,' he whispered. 'Did you go to the inn?'

I nodded. I couldn't catch enough breath to try to speak, so I mimed turning a key.

'You locked the door to the tunnel?' He looked impressed. 'Good thinking.' He handed me my cloak and I pulled it on, grateful for its warmth because the night was growing cold. 'Morgan and Petroc are on the beach. The other two men went out in the boat, but they're not back yet. I can't see anything.'

I gestured to show that we should go nearer and he nodded. Slowly we both got on to our bellies, and like worms we wiggled our way to the edge of the cliff. We could see more clearly now. Morgan was sitting on a rock, his gaze fixed out to sea. Petroc was pacing along the shore. Clearly he was getting on Morgan's nerves, because the taller man kept speaking sharply to him, causing Petroc to stop walking for a moment and then start his pacing again.

And then the ship appeared, far out to sea. I clutched Arthur's arm and pointed.

'That must be it,' he said, squinting through the gloom.

We watched for a while, both of us straining to see. 'I can hear something,' Arthur said. And sure enough, the rowing boat came into view, low in the water, thanks to her heavy cargo.

I hissed at Arthur, giving him a nudge. He had to go as fast as he could. He scrambled to his feet now, looking frightened and very young. 'I'll get them to send riding officers and a cutter, if they can.'

I nodded.

He gave me a quick, scared smile. 'I love you, Emily Moon,' he said.

I blew him a kiss and clasped my hands to my heart in response, telling him I loved him too.

Light on his feet, Arthur raced away towards the stables. I sent up a prayer that the customs men would be ready and willing to listen and act and then turned my gaze back to the beach.

If I'd thought time had gone slowly while we were waiting

for night to fall, I'd been wrong. Now the wait was unbearable. Each stroke of the oar was excruciating, each slap of the waves against the prow of the boat like torture. But eventually, the boat reached the beach and Petroc and Morgan waded into the water like I'd seen them do before.

It took them a while to unload the cargo because there was a lot of it. This time it was mostly packages. Tobacco, I guessed, though I didn't know for sure.

Unlike last time, tonight the men didn't form a chain to pass the packages up the beach to the cave. Instead Morgan and Petroc pushed the little boat back out to sea. With delight, I realised this meant there was more cargo to come, which meant they'd be there for a while yet.

Petroc fumbled a few times, dropping packets or taking a while to pass them on. He was stalling, I realised. Deliberately taking his time because he knew they had to stay on the beach long enough for the customs men to get there.

By the time the packets were inside the cave, the boat had reappeared and the whole process started again. This time I could see bottles and barrels. Heavy loads. Again the men formed their line and started taking the contraband into the tunnel. It was hard work, clearly. Their shouts echoed round the cove and once more Petroc was clumsy and unhelpful.

With tempers obviously fraying, Morgan shouted at his right-hand man. I couldn't hear what was said, the wind whipped the words from their mouths before they reached me, but the tone was sharp and angry. One of the other men tried to grip Morgan from behind, but the big man shook him off and rounded on Petroc. I was pleased things weren't going smoothly but I felt fearful for Petroc. I hoped Morgan wouldn't turn violent.

Out of the corner of my eye, I saw a shadow. I turned my head and there, snaking down the path, were three, four, five revenue men. I felt weak with relief. We'd done it.

But down on the beach, things were getting nasty. Morgan had clearly lost his temper completely and launched himself at Petroc. Ignoring the shouts from the other men, Morgan punched poor Petroc in the face and the smaller man fell to the ground like stone. I watched in horror as Morgan pulled out a knife, looming over Petroc. This was all so wrong. Terrified Morgan was going to kill my father's old friend, I struggled to my feet, my glowing cloak billowing around me.

I took a breath and, hoping my throat wouldn't tighten and betray me, I opened my mouth and shouted: 'Stop!'

I had no idea if they could hear what I cried, but they must have heard something because Morgan turned towards me. Realising his attacker was distracted, Petroc kicked out and Morgan's knife fell on to the sand. I watched as Petroc crawled away and melted into the shadows at the edge of the beach. Morgan and the other men were frozen, staring up at me on the clifftop. I could see their frightened faces.

'It's the Moon girl,' I heard Morgan shout, a quiver in his normally strident tones. 'Petroc, it's the Moon girl.'

Suddenly I realised what was happening: With the ethereal glow to my cloak, and the moonlight shining on my blonde hair I must have looked like a spirit standing there on the clifftop. I laughed. Finally Morgan would understand how it felt to be scared out of his wits.

As the smugglers on the beach stared up at me, the revenue men reached them. There were shouts and a scuffle. I crouched back down out of sight to watch, while one revenue man got a punch to the nose that splattered blood across his face and down his red coat. Morgan was shouting for Petroc but the smaller man had vanished. I was pleased he'd got himself away. He wasn't blameless, but I knew he wasn't a bad man; he'd just made some foolish choices.

More customs men arrived on horseback and charged down the cliff path to the beach. Out at sea, I could see the cutter bouncing over the waves towards the ship. It was over, I thought. Morgan had been caught red-handed, the smugglers were in chains, and Arthur and I were free.

Chapter 39

Phoebe

2019

When I thought more about my plan to wait on the clifftop and see what Ewan was up to, I realised it didn't make sense. There was little point in me in loitering up the top, just to see what was happening. I'd simply be in the same situation as I was now. No, I decided, I needed to be in the thick of the action. I needed to be on the beach where I could take photographs if I could. It was proof I needed.

I needed to time it carefully – too early and I'd be bored and uncomfortable, or worse, fall asleep and miss all the action. Too late and I risked being spotted. I had to get down that steep, precarious path before dark, but not so long before dark that Liv wondered where I'd gone and came to look for me.

I decided to head down to the cove at about eight o'clock. But it was only just gone five, now. I had hours to kill before I could go.

Needing a distraction, I went upstairs to my room and sat on the window seat. I imagined Emily sitting there herself, more than two hundred years ago, and smiled to myself. Now I had more information, I might be able to find out something else about the other Moon Girl.

I opened my laptop and the book on Cornish pubs, ignoring the memories of Jed that it brought back, and pulled out the pictures of the man with the white streak in his hair.

'Cal Morgan,' I said out loud. 'Who were you? Why did Emily draw you?'

I typed the name into the search bar, added Cornwall, and 1799, and hit return, and watched as the little wheel span round painfully slowly.

Eventually, the page of results crawled up the screen.

'Bingo,' I said. I clicked on the top one. It was a link to a page about notorious Cornish criminals and I felt a little shiver of excitement. Was this it?

Cal Morgan, I read, had been tried, convicted and hanged on charges of smuggling in 1799.

That was it. No mention of Emily, or Arthur, or The Ship Inn.

Disappointed, I searched again, adding smuggling this time. Different results appeared now. I scrolled down, and stopped on a site about criminals who escaped justice. Could this be it? Was Emily a smuggler who got away with the loot?

I scanned the page until I found what I was looking for, breathing out in excitement as I read the details.

Soldier Cal Morgan ran a smuggling ring out of Kirrinporth in the late eighteenth century, the page said. *He had fought in the American War of Independence and returned to Cornwall with a white streak in his hair, which rumours said was caused by the horrors he had experienced on the battlefield.*

I gave a little shiver of delight. This was good stuff.

Morgan was a large man with a certain charm and a great knowledge of the Cornwall coast, the tides and the weather. He enlisted various locals to work for him – whether through fear or favour it is not known – and was eventually hanged when customs officers chanced upon him and his gang bringing in the largest cargo of contraband ever landed in the county.

'Chanced upon,' I said out loud. Sounded like a tip-off to me.

Many people believed Cal Morgan was working for the wealthy landowner Denzel Kirrin, whose family had founded the town of Kirrinporth in the Middle Ages. Denzel left Kirrinporth with his family shortly after Morgan's trial.

'Like a mafia boss,' I muttered.

But here was the interesting bit. I read on. *Rumours at the time said a local teenager, Emily Moon, had disappeared the same night as Morgan was arrested. The story was that Morgan had killed the youngster's father several months earlier. Eager to see the murderer face justice, the bold teen had warned the customs men where to catch Morgan in the act of smuggling in his haul, and plunged to her death as she did so. Now stories are told about the young girl's ghost walking the cliffs above where Morgan was caught. The nearby pub, The Ship Inn, was renamed The Moon Girl in her memory.*

'Emily,' I breathed, feeling absurdly disappointed to have more confirmation that she had died that night. 'You brave, stupid girl.' I imagined her, a slight blonde waif of a thing if the pub sign was true to life, taking on a soldier. I picked up the sketch of Morgan's rugged face and broken nose and imagined him towering over Emily in a red coat, like the soldiers wore in *Pride and Prejudice*. She had to have been so bold to take on a man who'd seen enough horrors on the battlefields in America to turn his hair white.

'America,' I said thoughtfully. Why did that ring a bell? I frowned, trying to catch the thought, and leafing through the pictures as I did. And there it was. The sketch of the little wagon, travelling across an empty land. I pulled it out of the bundle and held it up. '*Little House on the Prairie*,' I said in delight. The wagon looked like the one the Ingalls family travelled in. Had Emily gone all the way across the ocean to start a new life in America? It seemed unlikely, but the thought was enough to give me hope. I so wanted to know that clever, strong, brave Emily Moon hadn't died that night.

I googled Emily Moon and America and sighed in disappointment as nothing useful appeared.

But, what about Arthur? I thought. Emily's sweetheart, who followed his own path? What was his surname, again? I thought for a second and then typed in Arthur Pascoe and America and waited for an age for the connection. Eventually it brought up reams of results. The top one was a fruit and vegetable business in Massachusetts. I snorted. That wasn't my Arthur Pascoe. I tried again, this time adding Emily's name.

Once more, after a painfully long time, the first result was the same link to Pascoe's Fruit and Vegetables. Mostly out of boredom, I clicked on the name and read through the "About Us" section that came up with growing disbelief.

We were founded by English settler Arthur Pascoe and his wife Emily in 1825, the copy read. *The company has grown and we now supply fruit and vegetables to hospitality businesses throughout the Eastern Seaboard, as well as packing, preserving and exporting fruit and vegetables across the world. The Pascoe family are still involved in the business and our current chairman, Phil Pascoe, is Arthur's six-times great grandson. Arthur's book,* Apple Farms of Massachusetts, *illustrated by his wife, Emily, is available to buy in our farm shop.*

'Oh. My. God,' I said in absolute delight. 'Emily escaped.'

I wanted to cheer, because I was so thrilled. She'd got away. She'd got the baddies locked up and then she and her sweetheart had sailed away across the ocean and started a new life growing fruit and vegetables and drawing pictures of apples. She deserved more than a tiny memorial plaque in the church.

Absolutely thrilled to bits, I took screenshots of the info to show Simon, and then paused. The only other person I could think of who would be as excited as I was about Emily's miraculous escape, was Jed. Urgh.

Thinking of Jed made me realise I had to get moving. I had to find a hiding place on the beach and get into position before it got dark. It wasn't going to be easy.

I shut my laptop, feeling content that Emily had triumphed, and I tucked the pictures away inside the book. Then I put on my running gear, choosing black leggings and a dark grey hoodie that would help me hide in the shadows. My trainers were bright luminous yellow, so I sneaked into Liv's room and took her black pair, hoping she wouldn't notice. I grabbed a bottle of water and a couple of cereal bars from the kitchen, and then, after a moment's hesitation, I went back into my room and slipped my warrant card into my pocket. I wasn't intending to arrest anyone, but it was good to be prepared.

As Liv was being snappy and barely talking to me, I didn't feel I needed to tell her where I was going. Instead, I jogged away from the pub along the cliff, thinking that if she happened to look out she would simply see me heading out for a run. Then I doubled back to where the path down the sheer rock began. I wasn't hugely keen on going down that way again but it seemed more sensible than going through the tunnel. I wondered if Emily had done the same thing when she'd caught Cal Morgan in the act and I hoped some of her bravery would rub off on me.

It took me ages to get down, because my legs were really wobbly, but eventually I found myself on the sand. I sat for a minute on a rock to catch my breath and look at my surroundings, hoping a suitable hiding place would present itself. Nothing was obvious but neither had the tunnel been obvious, so I decided to do what I'd done before and walk carefully around the cove, checking every nook and cranny.

Slowly I wandered round the beach, the whole time feeling horribly aware that it would be getting dark soon and I was running out of time. And then, to my relief, I realised there was a space behind one of the bigger rocks at one side of the cove. The rock was taller than me and jagged, like a piece of cliff had sheared off and landed on the sand. It was triangular and at an angle to the cliff behind it, reminding me of the Flatiron Building in New York. It wasn't large, but I could fit in between the rock and the cliff face that hugged the beach and be hidden.

I put my water bottle down on the sand behind the rock and went back out into the middle of the beach to check if I could see it. No, it was shielded, thank goodness. That was my spot then. It was chilly but dry and sheltered. I tucked myself in and shimmied along until I was at the narrow end where the rock was almost touching the cliff. From there I had a clear view of the beach and could see where any boat would come ashore. I was all set.

It was a long wait. I had my phone but I resisted the temptation to browse, if I even had a signal. I didn't want to risk draining my battery. The evening got darker and darker and I amused myself by trying to remember the names of all the girls in my class at school, the ingredients for my favourite recipes, the words to old favourite pop songs and thinking about Emily and the way she'd brought Cal Morgan to justice.

I wasn't sure I was doing the right thing by waiting on the beach. Not remotely sure. But I knew I had to do something and knowing Emily had done the same – without the police training and experience I had – made me feel better. I tapped the reassuring lump of my warrant card in my pocket and took a breath. It was going to be fine.

Up above me, I saw a gleam of blue. The light was on and signalling out to sea. I tipped my head back and watched, hoping it was going to be different and sure enough, instead of the steady beam I'd seen over the last few evenings, this time it was flashing. The irony of it looking like a police car wasn't lost on me. I wondered if they'd done it deliberately – partly as a sort of disguise because no one paid much attention to blue lights – and partly to stick two fingers up at the people who might try to stop them. Whatever the reason, it was proof that I was in the right place at the right time. Now I just had to wait and see what happened.

The time dragged. Every minute felt like an eternity. It was so dark, I could barely see in front of my face. I'd never be able to take any photos at this rate. But then, thankfully, the clouds began to clear and the moon shone down on the sand, giving everything a kind of cold, bluish glow. I was amazed. I'd never really seen moonlight like this before – in London everything was just tinged yellow from the streetlamps. The sea was shimmering white, and I could see right across the cove. It was perfect for my stakeout, and also pretty spooky. The noise of the waves was constant but I could hear the occasional hoot – an owl I assumed – that made me jump every time.

I froze as I heard the sound of a stone skittering down the cliff. Had it been dislodged by an animal or the wind? Or was someone coming? Was this it? With every one of my senses on high alert – Sandra would be pleased that I was so present in the moment, I thought wryly – I stayed absolutely still, peering out at the beach. I could feel the wind in my hair and taste the salt on my lips and feel the thumping of my heart in my chest. I concentrated on breathing slowly and evenly and waited to see if someone appeared on the beach. I couldn't see the bottom of the path from my hiding spot, so instead I trained my eyes on the middle of the sand, where I'd seen Jed and Mark when I'd first had my suspicions. No one was there.

Everything was silent, except for my steady breaths. And then, suddenly, someone was behind me, one hand over my mouth to stop me screaming and a thick arm around my middle.

Terrified I kicked out, squirming to get free but my attacker gripped tighter.

'Stop wriggling,' he said in a low, horribly familiar voice right in my ear. My stomach lurched in fear, disappointment, upset – because it was Jed.

I turned my head desperately trying to see him and there he was, a black beanie hat pulled down over his eyebrows and dark clothes like my own.

I squirmed some more, trying to get to my warrant card in my pocket, and he gripped tighter.

'I'm going to let you go,' he said. His breath tickled my ear. 'But you can't make a sound because you'll ruin everything.'

I nodded. There was no point in screaming anyway – no one would hear me. Cautiously, Jed released me and I stood, staring at him, in the tiny hiding space between the rocks that was really too small for two people. My leg muscles were tightening, ready to run, but Jed was very close to me, blocking any escape route, and I was wedged into the space so I couldn't reach my pocket. Sweat beaded on my lip. What could I do? Could I talk my way out of this one?

'I need you to stay calm,' Jed said. He didn't sound calm. His whispers were ragged and broken and his eyes were wild. 'What on earth are you doing here, Phoebe? Why are you here?'

He took a step back and I saw my chance. I shifted on the sand and now I had more space, I felt in my pocket and pulled out my warrant card.

'I'm here to arrest you,' I hissed, showing him my card. Jed's eyes widened in shock. 'Jed Saunders, I'm arresting you on suspicion . . .'

I trailed off as Jed reached for his pocket. Did he have a knife? A gun? Shit, I was in too deep here. I should have bloody patted him down.

'Stop,' I said. Quick as a flash, I grabbed his wrist – just as I'd done with the handbag "thief" in the pub – and pushed him against the rocky wall, trying not to show my fear.

Jed groaned as his back hit the stone. 'You don't need to be so rough.'

'Do you have a weapon?'

'I don't have a weapon,' Jed said. He sounded like he was trying and failing to control his annoyance. 'I just need you to get something out of my jeans pocket. Can you do that?'

Still gripping his wrist, I nodded. 'It's not a syringe or anything dangerous?'

'I promise. It's my left pocket. I'll keep my hands where you can see them.'

He raised his arms above my head. Keeping my eyes on him in case he did anything, gingerly, I reached down, trying not to notice how strong and well-muscled his torso was as it pressed against me, or how snug his jeans were. I tried to keep my breathing regular as I put my fingers into his front pocket and slid them down until I felt a small, hard rectangular shape. A familiar shape. With my heart in my trainers – Liv's trainers – I eased it out and gave him what I'd found. He flipped it open and lifted it up so I could see it but I already knew what it was. It was a warrant card. Jed was a police officer and I was in trouble.

'DS Jeremy Stanton,' he said in a furious whisper. 'And you've just walked into an active undercover investigation.'

'DS Phoebe Bellingham,' I said, equally furious. 'And why the bloody hell didn't you tell me who you were?'

Jed – or Jeremy, whatever his name was – snorted. 'Because I'm undercover,' he said, his voice dripping with disdain. 'And telling a barmaid who I really was would have ruined that.'

'I am not a barmaid. I'm in the Met.'

He shrugged. 'Then you should know better than to interfere with an investigation.'

'I didn't know it was an investigation,' I said. Our voices were getting louder.

'What were you planning to do?' Jed said. 'Jump out and arrest Ewan all by yourself?'

It was so exactly what I had been planning to do that I flushed. 'No. Just take some photos. Get proof.' I looked at him. 'What were you planning to do? Arrest him all by yourself?'

'Border Force are standing by out at sea, and my back-up team are on the cliff.' He checked his watch. 'Well, they will be. It's a bit early yet.'

Well, that told me. Suddenly all my anger left me and I felt really stupid. I leaned against the rock.

'I'm sorry,' I whispered. 'I've had . . . a bit of a hard time recently. Something happened at work and it messed with me a bit.'

Jed's expression softened, the tiniest amount. 'That's not unusual.'

'And then some things happened here . . .'

Jed's mouth twitched. 'I heard.'

'You did?'

'The handbag thief? Everyone heard.'

I rubbed my forehead. 'I thought if I went to the police abut Ewan, they'd laugh at me.'

'They would have told you it was being dealt with.'

'Well I know that now,' I said. I was embarrassed and miserable and I just wanted to be anywhere other than there. 'Anyway, I'm sorry to get in your way. I'll go. Leave you to it.'

'Probably for the best. Will you be all right getting up the cliff in the dark?'

'No.'

Jed looked worried. 'You could go through the tunnel. Just be quick. Ewan's not due for another hour or so, but we don't want to take any chances.'

A thought occurred to me. 'Does Liv know?'

'About tonight? No.'

'Is she in trouble?'

'Possibly.'

'That's not fair, Jed.'

'Jeremy.'

I scowled at him. 'I'm going to go,' I said. My mind was racing. I could get back to the pub through the tunnel, lock the door behind me and move some stuff in the cellar so it was in front of the door. Make it look like Liv wasn't involved. It wasn't perfect and it wasn't entirely ethical but Liv was a tiny cog in a very big wheel; she didn't deserve to be in trouble for this.

'Go quickly but carefully,' Jed said. 'Get back to the pub and go to bed.'

He was beginning to annoy me now. 'I'm not stupid,' I said.

He looked like he was going to argue about that then changed his mind. 'Just go.'

He stood aside to let me out of our tiny hiding place, and I took a few steps on to the beach then froze as I saw someone coming down the path. Jed saw it too. He grabbed my shoulder and pulled me back into the gap between the rock and the cliff. We stood there, staring at each other.

'It's Ewan,' I breathed as he came into view on the beach.

'He told me 2 a.m.,' Jed whispered. 'It's not even one yet. The bastard.'

'Do you think he's got wind of who you are?'

'No, I think he wants to avoid sharing the profits.'

'What are you going to do?'

Jed looked worried. 'Nothing,' he said after a moment. 'Border Force aren't going to be here for an hour, and my back-up officers won't be in position yet.' He groaned. 'All this work and it's going to pot because I don't have back-up.'

I looked at Ewan who was standing in the middle of the beach, smoking a cigarette and looking out to sea at the ship, which was coming closer. And then I looked at Jed. 'You've got back-up,' I said.

Chapter 40

'Oh no,' Jed said. 'No.'

'What choice do you have? Either you let me help or all your hard work undercover goes to waste.'

'It's really irresponsible to do anything when there's only two of us.'

I shrugged. 'There's only one of him.'

Jed looked at me. 'We could arrest him now,' he said. 'Keep him up the back of the beach, out of sight, and I'll go back undercover and meet the people bringing in the goods.'

'What are they bringing in?'

'Drugs.'

I relaxed a tiny bit. I could deal with drugs. I was just relieved it wasn't guns, or a load of terrified people.

'Call for back-up now,' I said. 'We'll sort Ewan out and hopefully the back-up will be here by the time the boat gets here.'

Jed peered out at the sea. 'They're coming now. There's a smaller boat on its way.'

'Then we don't have time to waste.'

My heart was thumping but I was loving this. I felt like I'd been re-energised. Switched on, somehow. Everything was in sharper focus. I could hear the sound of the waves and the hum of the boat's engine on the sea, and Jed's breathing. I gripped his hand. 'We can do this, Jed.'

He nodded. 'Sure?'

'Sure. Get your back-up team ready.'

Decision made, he pulled out his phone, crouching down so the light couldn't be seen by Ewan, who was still looking out to sea, watching the boat come closer.

I thought about Liv who would be waiting at the pub, nervously waiting for Ewan to appear in the cellar with a load of drugs. Turning away from Jed slightly, I pulled my own phone out and paused for a second. 'Working late,' I typed. 'Won't be back. Go to bed and lock all the doors.' I added an emoji of a policewoman and hoped that would be enough to let her know what I meant. I knew I was playing with fire but I also wanted to protect my friend, and though I was fairly sure no one would check our phones, if they did, I wanted to be sure that our messages could be innocent.

I watched the little dots bouncing around, telling me Liv was replying and then she replied. 'Off to bed. Be careful.'

I had no idea if she understood but I'd done what I could.

Jed nodded at me. 'On their way, but we need to act now if we're going to get Ewan sorted before the boat arrives.'

'I'm ready. What do you need me to do?'

Quickly, Jed outlined his plan, speaking quietly into my ear. Him being so close to me made it difficult to concentrate but I forced myself to pay attention.

'Okay?'

'Okay.'

I stayed where I was, while Jed crept along the shadows on the back of the beach. I watched him, my heart in my mouth, praying Ewan wouldn't turn around. Eventually, Jed reached the bottom of the path, crept up a few steps and then jumped down on to the sand. 'Oi oi,' he called.

Ewan jumped and turned around. 'Christ, Jed,' he said. 'You gave me a heart attack. What are you doing here?'

'Could say the same about you,' Jed said, said, sauntering across the sand with his hands in his pockets. 'Thought we were meeting at two?'

'Got a message that they were coming earlier,' Ewan said so smoothly that I wondered if he was telling the truth. If he was lying, he was very good at it. 'I tried ringing you and Mark but couldn't get hold of you.'

'Signal's patchy,' Jed said. He looked out across the sea. 'So what's the plan, then? Is that them?'

Understanding what Jed was doing, I carefully took my phone out again and turned it to video, recording what was happening. The picture was dark but the moon was bright enough that Jed and Ewan were both recognisable.

'That's them,' Ewan said. 'They'll be here shortly.'

'And how much have they got?'

Ewan grinned at Jed, his eyes shining in the darkness. 'A lot,' he said. 'We're quids in, mate. Once we get it shifted.'

'Through the tunnel,' Jed said.

'Yes, through the tunnel.' Ewan was snappy and I hoped Jed would sense his tone. He did. He sat down on one of the rocks and sighed happily. 'I'm going to buy a new car,' he said. Ewan laughed. 'I've got a mate who can find you something.'

'I don't want one of your dodgy mates' knock-offs,' Jed said. I was impressed by how well he shifted from being an undercover cop with me, to one of Ewan's team. His body language, the way he walked, even his voice, were all slightly different. 'Will there be enough for something really flash?'

'We'll see you right,' Ewan said. 'We've got some debts to pay first.'

'Who?'

I winced. *Please don't say Liv*, I thought to myself.

'Des Lincoln mostly,' Ewan said. 'We'd have been stuffed after that bloody Watson family legged it if it wasn't for him.'

In my hiding place, I was open-mouthed with shock. Des Lincoln was Liv's regional manager. It seemed everyone was involved.

Jed stood up and I knew he was about to make a move. I balanced my phone on the rock, so I'd have my hands free to help if I was needed.

'Just going for a wazz,' Jed said. He walked up towards the back of the beach and then shouted: 'Shit! Ewan!'

Ewan turned round. 'What is it?'

Jed stayed silent. Ewan called again and when there was no answer, he hurried up the beach. I heard a thud and an exhalation of breath and then Jed called out. 'Phoebe?'

I emerged from behind the rock. Jed had Ewan face down on the ground, his hands cuffed behind his back. Ewan was swearing aggressively and trying to stand up, but Jed had his knee in the small of his back so he couldn't get up.

'He had a gun,' Jed said. 'It's over there somewhere. Can you find it?'

I hated guns but I did as he asked, scanning the sand for the weapon. I found it and then holding it like it was hot, gave it to Jed. Deftly, he took out the bullets and tucked the gun into his waistband.

'I'm going to meet the boat,' Jed said. 'Can you keep an eye on this one and update the back-up?'

'Course,' I said.

I eyed Ewan suspiciously. 'The boat's nearly here. No shouting out to warn anyone.'

'Fuck off.'

'That's rude,' I said mildly. 'Give me your phone then, Jed. And shall I take him into the tunnel? Get him out of the way?'

'Not a bad idea,' Jed said, throwing me his phone, which I caught – thank goodness. 'Go on then.' He grinned at me. 'It's Jeremy.'

I grinned back. This was scary and it felt like the stakes were very high but I was running on adrenaline and I felt brilliant.

I pulled Ewan to his feet. He struggled a bit but he let me lead him into the tunnel. I guessed he was thinking he could try to make a break for it, through the pub when the time was right. He stumbled on the uneven ground and sat down with a thump.

'Stay there,' I told him. I left Ewan in the tunnel, hoping that Liv had locked the door to the pub, took Jed's phone out of my pocket and opened it. There was only one number stored, and one conversation in the messages folder. I tapped it and added my own message.

'Immediate back-up urgently required,' I typed.

'Standing by,' the reply came.

I took a few steps backwards and looked up at the clifftop. I couldn't see anything. I supposed I had to trust they were in the right place.

Down by the sea, the boat was in the cove and approaching Jed where he stood right by the edge of the waves. The engine cut out, and the boat coasted quietly into shore. Jed waded out to help pull it up and out of the way. I stayed in the shadows by the entrance to the tunnel, hoping Ewan wouldn't shout out. Carefully I glanced round the rocky doorway but he was nowhere to be seen. As I'd suspected, he'd made a run for it. I snorted. He wouldn't get far if Liv had locked the cellar door. And if she hadn't . . . I pulled out the phone again and added: 'Please cover The Moon Girl pub. Suspect in handcuffs and exit blocked but stand by.'

The boat was on the sand now. There were three men inside, all dressed like Jed, in dark clothes. I could hear them talking softly but not what they were saying. They began unloading packages from the boat and I took a breath. This was it. 'Go,' I typed on the phone with trembling fingers.

There was a second when I thought the message hadn't gone through, and we'd be there all alone with the gang, and then suddenly the cove was flooded with light, and figures ran from behind me towards the boat. I'd not even seen them coming down the path, but they must have been creeping towards the cove the whole time. There were shouts and without very much trouble at all, the three men were all restrained. Still blinking in the bright lights – which now I realised were coming from police cars up above – I went into the cave and found Ewan sitting a little way up the tunnel looking furious.

'She locked the fucking door,' he told me.

'Is that right?'

He kicked out at me and I swerved. 'Watch it.' I pulled him on to his feet again and yanked him out of the tunnel and across the sand, and handed him over to one of the back-up team. Jed was standing a little way away. He looked absolutely exhausted and my heart went out to him. It couldn't have been easy, living a double life for months.

'Well done,' I said, handing him his phone. 'You did it.'

'It was nearly a disaster.'

'Nearly, but it wasn't.'

'Thanks to you,' he said. He turned to me and gave me a tired smile. 'If you hadn't been here, I'd have had to give up and go home.'

'Rubbish,' I said, pleased with the praise.

Out at sea, a speed boat bounced across the waves and Jed rolled his eyes. 'Border force,' he said. 'Late as ever.'

He looked into my eyes, and I felt my legs go weak. Though it might just have been tiredness. 'Listen,' he began. 'I've got stuff to do here and you should probably go and introduce yourself to my team. The DCI is up the top – her name's . . .'

'Richardson,' I said, as everything fell into place. 'She's DCI Richardson.'

Jed raised an eyebrow. 'How did you know that?'

'I got a colleague to look you up,' I admitted. 'But it flagged up the search and DCI Richardson called her.'

'Oops,' said Jed chuckling. 'Did you look up Ewan as well?'

'Fake name,' I said. 'And the Watson family? Are they in witness protection?'

'They are. Today's arrests are the final piece of the jigsaw.'

I looked up at the clifftop, where I could see figures moving about.

'I should go.'

'Let's catch up tomorrow, shall we?' Jed reached out and put his hand on the top of my arm.

I put my hand on top of his and smiled at him. 'You did really well,' I said.

Jed – Jeremy – leaned towards me and kissed me on the cheek, lingering slightly longer than was necessary.

'I'll see you tomorrow,' I said.

Chapter 41

Emily

1799

We stayed in our little shed for another night, though we didn't get much sleep. Instead we made plans for our escape to Plymouth. Arthur was adamant we had to go the next day and I understood why. We knew Mr Trewin and Mr Kirrin were part of Morgan's smuggling operation, but we didn't know who else was involved. If George Winston, the magistrate, was on Morgan's side he could be free by nightfall. Even if Morgan swung for his crimes, we'd still be in danger.

I felt cold at the thought of going to America, suddenly. We may have got Morgan arrested but travelling halfway across the world seemed a very frightening idea.

Arthur saw my face. 'Have you changed your mind? We could stay in Plymouth . . .'

'No.' I was definite about that.

'London then?'

I thought of the people and the smells and shook my head. 'Space and sky,' I said carefully.

'Then America it is.'

I nodded. It was strange, I thought, because my whole life I had never imagined myself anywhere else but Kirrinporth, and now I couldn't imagine staying here a day longer.

Arthur frowned. 'There is one thing we should do before we leave, though.'

I raised an eyebrow in query.

He leaned over and kissed me and then stood up, full of purpose, and peered outside the little cabin. 'It's getting light,' he said. 'Come, let's go before anyone wakes.'

We rode together on his horse, back along the path to the village. I kept asking where we were going and he kept saying I would see when we got there. And then we were outside the church. I turned round and looked at him, questioningly.

'You'll see.'

He slid down and held his hand out for me to do the same, then he tied up the horse and together we walked into the church.

'Wait here,' he said.

I sat patiently in a pew, next to the Diggory family memorial, and wondered what he was up to. He'd said his goodbyes to his father, as far as I knew. What more was there to say? I felt a brief moment of resentment that Arthur had a proper farewell while my poor mother was left thinking I was dead. Morgan had stolen my father from her, and now her daughter as well. It didn't seem fair.

'Emily?' Arthur appeared at the side of the church, his father behind him looking bleary-eyed but cheerful. 'Will you marry me?'

I stood up and then sat down again as my legs went weak.

'I thought it didn't seem proper to ask you to travel across an ocean with me without us being officially man and wife,' Arthur said. 'My father said he shall marry us right now, if you're willing.'

He came round the pews and stood at the end of my row, then he reached out and took my hands in his. 'So will you? Marry me?'

I stood up properly now and threw myself into his arms, nodding vigorously. Of course I would marry him.

Reverend Pascoe looked over at us. 'Emily, you will need to speak to say the vows.' He frowned. 'Will you manage?'

I swallowed. 'I . . .' I began. My throat tightened and then, as I looked at Arthur, it relaxed again. 'I will try,' I said.

Arthur grasped my hand tightly. 'Then let's be wed.'

Reverend Pascoe glanced round at the empty church. 'This is not strictly legal,' he said in a low voice. 'We have not read the banns, and we have no witnesses.'

'And the bride is dead,' Arthur said, straight-faced. I giggled. I cared not one bit for legality and I thought God wouldn't either. I just wanted to know that Arthur was mine and I was his.

Reverend Pascoe nodded. 'Given the circumstances, I believe we can do away with the rules.'

'Thank you,' I whispered.

There was no posy of flowers, no hymn singing, but Reverend Pascoe read solemnly from his *Book of Common Prayer* and simply missed out the bits asking anyone to speak up if they knew of a reason why we shouldn't wed.

He turned to Arthur first. 'Wilt thou have this woman to thy wedded wife?' he asked.

Without hesitation, Arthur nodded. 'I will.'

'And now, Emily,' Reverend Pascoe said. 'Wilt thou have this man to thy wedded husband?'

I took a deep breath, feeling all my muscles clench. And then, thankfully, I spoke. 'I will.'

Arthur beamed at me.

To my astonishment, I didn't even stumble over the rest of our vows. I said them clearly and with genuine feeling. When Reverend Pascoe said we were man and wife, Arthur and I held each other close and my face ached from smiling so broadly. I felt like a weight had lifted from my chest and that I could breathe properly for the first time since my father had been killed.

Reverend Pascoe kissed me gently on the cheek. 'You are a brave woman, Emily Moon,' he said. 'I'm proud to call you my daughter.'

'Emily Pascoe now,' Arthur said.

I smiled at him. 'I think I'll always be Emily Moon inside.'

Hand in hand we went to the door of the church.

'We need to be swift,' Arthur said. 'It's early still, but people will be waking soon. We need to get on the road to Plymouth and away before anyone sees us.'

Reverend Pascoe slapped Arthur on the back and then, to my surprise, pulled him into a hug. 'God speed, my son,' he said. 'Write to me from America.'

'I will.'

'Emily, take my horse from the stables,' Reverend Pascoe said. 'I know you do not enjoy riding but you have bags to carry and it is a long way.'

'Thank you,' I said. I felt that riding held no fear for me now.

Arthur and I loaded up the horses and, riding side by side, we set off towards Plymouth. We had not long left the village behind, though, when I looked across towards the sea at the roof of the inn, which I could just see in the distance.

'I need to say goodbye,' I said. 'I need to see Mam.'

Arthur, bless him, nodded as though he had been expecting me to say this. And without a word to convince me otherwise, he tugged on his horse's reins and turned it around. I followed.

We tied the horses up in the stables and quietly headed into the inn. The door was open and inside to our great surprise, was Petroc. He jumped to his feet when he saw us.

'Good Lord,' he said. 'Good Lord. I thought you would be long gone.'

'We were on our way, but Emily wanted to say goodbye to her mother.'

Petroc patted my arm. 'You are a good girl, Emily Moon.'

'Emily P . . .' Arthur began but I shook my head at him to quiet him. There was no time for explanations now.

'Where is my mother?'

'Upstairs,' Petroc said. He gave me a wink. 'Everyone thinks you're dead and that your ghost is walking the cliffs.'

'I got some of your paint on my cloak,' I told him. 'Morgan saw me.'

Realisation dawned on Petroc's face. 'I heard him shouting and bawling,' he said. 'I thought he just wanted me to show myself to the revenue men.'

'No awkward questions?' Arthur said.

Petroc shrugged. 'Not so far,' he said. He shifted on his feet. 'Janey said she'd speak for me if the revenue men come calling.'

I looked at him, stern-faced. 'You take care of her.'

'I truly will.'

Satisfied, I left the bar area and climbed the stairs to my mother's bedroom. She was sitting on her bed, with her back to me, staring out of the window at the sea.

'Mam,' I said softly. She turned around and looked at me in disbelief.

'Emily?'

'It's me.'

Mam got up slowly and came round to where I stood. Her hair was wild and her eyes swollen with tears. She looked at me and then reached out her hand and touched my face and my shoulders and my waist. 'Emily,' she said again. 'They said you were dead. They said you'd fallen from the cliff and died.'

'Petroc said that, so Morgan didn't come for us,' I explained.

Mam gathered me into her arms and I felt her tears on my neck. 'Oh, my girl,' she said. 'My girl.'

Eventually I untangled myself from her embrace. 'We can't stay, Mam,' I said. 'It's too dangerous and we have a new life to live.'

She nodded. 'Where will you go?'

I took a deep breath. 'America.'

Mam's eyes widened. 'But that is so far.'

'A new life in a new world.'

'I always knew you would do great things, Emily,' she said.

'Not great. A farm perhaps? Some fruit trees. Maybe a baby. Ordinary.'

'Wonderful.'

'Will you be all right?'

'I believe I will,' Mam said. 'Petroc says people will drink in the inn again now Morgan is gone.'

'It wasn't your fault.'

Mam looked ashamed. 'Don't make it easier to live with.'

'Put it behind you,' I urged her, gripping her hands. I wanted her to realise that the best way of getting revenge was to make The Ship the best inn in Kirrinporth.

I kissed her and she hung on to me for a moment, then let me go.

'Wait there,' she said.

She dropped to her knees and I watched in surprise and bewilderment as she disappeared under the bed. There was a creak and she pulled up a floorboard. 'Here we go,' she muttered. 'Here it is.'

She backed out again and triumphantly held up a small bag made of sackcloth. She thrust it at me and wiped her hair away from her face, leaving a streak of dust on her cheek. 'It's for you.'

Not understanding, I took the bag and looked inside. It was money. A lot of money. More money than I'd ever seen in my life.

'What's this?'

'It's Morgan's,' Mam said. She looked defiant. 'He never told me about it, but I saw him hide it under there a couple of weeks ago. He thought I was stupid, but I'm not. I knew he was up to no good. I was planning to leave.'

I stared at her in surprise.

'When you told me you were worried I'd hang,' she said. 'I'd already planned to go. I thought we could leave the night Morgan brought in his cargo. Go to Devon, perhaps. Or further.'

'Mam,' I breathed, remembering how adamant she'd been that everything would be fine. I was filled with admiration.

'But then they said you were dead,' Mam went on. 'And I didn't have the energy to go. So I left the money where it was.' She grinned at me suddenly. 'He'd want you to have it,' she said.

I laughed out loud. I was fairly sure Morgan would want anything but. I looked at Mam, then I paused and opened the bag again, shaking out some of the coins and notes on to the bed. 'We'll share it,' I said.

Mam nodded and I tucked the pouch into my skirt for safekeeping.

'We need to go,' I said. I pointed to the bed. 'Check under your pillow.'

Mam grabbed me and kissed my face all over. 'Goodbye,' she said. 'Goodbye, Emily Moon.'

Without looking back, I turned and went back downstairs to find Arthur. 'Let's go,' I said. We waved to Petroc and headed outside to the horses.

'All right?' Arthur said.

I nodded. I pulled out the bag and showed him the money. 'Look.'

Arthur's eyes were like saucers. 'Where did your mother find that?'

'Morgan's,' I said in delight.

'Tainted money,' said Arthur.

But I shrugged. The way I saw it, it was better we had it than it stay hidden under the floorboards at the inn. Like I'd said to Mam, I believed that us living well and having a good life was the best revenge we could have. Morgan had tried to destroy everything we loved, but we had won.

'Morgan is gone,' I said. I shook the bag so the coins jangled. 'We won, Arthur.'

Arthur frowned for a second, then his face cleared. 'We're going to America,' he said. He picked me up and spun me round. 'We're going to America,' he said again.

Once more, we climbed on to our horses and headed towards the road to Plymouth and our new life. As we passed the inn, I looked back. Mam was in the window looking out, the pictures I'd left under her pillow clutched to her chest. She lifted her hand to wave and I waved in response. I put my fingers to my lips, reminding her to stay quiet and she nodded.

'Goodbye,' I whispered.

Chapter 42

Phoebe

2019

The pub was quiet and dark when I finally got home, hanging with tiredness but still buzzing with adrenaline. I crept upstairs and into my bedroom, where I switched on the light and jumped out of my skin to see Liv sitting up in the other single bed.

'Jesus,' I said.

She pushed back the duvet, came over to me and squeezed me tight.

'I've been so worried, Phoebe. What's going on?'

I peeled her off me and she got back into bed.

'Tell me,' she demanded.

'Ewan's part of some big organised crime ring,' I said, unzipping my hoodie and taking it off. 'Jed's in the police and he's been undercover, getting all the details, and now Ewan's been arrested.'

'Shit,' said Liv. 'Jed's in the police? What will happen now? Am I in trouble? Did you know about this? Are they my trainers?'

I grinned, feeling under my pillow for my pyjamas.

'Erm, yes Jed's in the police, he's called Jeremy really. I'm not sure what will happen now, I'm meeting Jed tomorrow. I will work hard to make sure you're not in trouble. I didn't know anything but I was suspicious. And yes, they're your trainers. Sorry.'

Liv shrugged. 'Doesn't matter. Can you tell me everything?' She patted her bed. 'Get in.'

So I got under the duvet with her and told her all my suspicions about Ewan and what he was up to, how I'd seen them on the beach and put two and two together, thanks to my research into Emily Moon.

'And you didn't know Jed was undercover?' she said.

'Not a clue. Not until I saw him on the beach.'

'Shit.'

'I could have blown the whole thing,' I said.

'But you didn't. You helped him.'

'I had to go and meet his DCI,' I told her with a shudder, remembering the hard stare DCI Richardson had given me at the top of the cliff.

'Was she angry?'

'Weirdly, no. She was nice, actually. She said thank you.'

'Do you think DI Blair will be angry?'

'I'm signed off,' I said. 'I'm really not supposed to be doing any sort of police work. I might get into trouble for that.'

'Will you have to go back?'

'Probably.' Having spent weeks feeling decidedly meh about rainy old Cornwall, the thought of going back to London suddenly didn't seem as appealing as it might have once done.

'I guess I'll come back with you,' Liv said.

'But you're here until the end of the year, aren't you? Can you break your contract?'

She snorted. 'I imagine I'll be fired.'

I took her hand. 'Tell me what happened.'

'Promise you won't hate me?'

'Of course.'

'Ewan came to see me. He said he'd heard money was tight and he could help with some extra work. He made it sound totally legit at first. I said I was interested, obviously. But then when it became obvious that it wasn't above board, I said no.'

'Why didn't you tell me?'

She paused, folding the duvet cover in between her fingers.

'I was scared. He put more and more pressure on me, and then he showed me printouts of my credit card bills, Phoebe. I was scared what he might do if he knew you were in the police.'

'Did Ewan pay your credit card bill?'

'You know about that? You should be a detective.'

I nudged her again, more forcefully this time. 'You shouldn't leave your phone lying around if you don't want people to read your messages.'

'I didn't ask him to pay it,' she said, biting her lip. 'He just did it. And then I owed him and there was nothing I could do to get out of it.'

'It's not your fault. He saw a weakness and he exploited it.'

'I've got no idea how he knew so much about me, but he knows everyone.'

'I was lucky he didn't pay me any attention,' I pointed out. 'Imagine if he'd found out who I really was.'

Liv shuddered. 'I bet he's mates with that PC in Kirrinporth who was rude to you. Honestly, he's got friends everywhere.'

'Des Lincoln,' I told her, remembering. 'He's one of them.'

'No way!'

'Apparently. And the Watson family are in witness protection. DCI Richardson said it was the wife who acted. The husband was going along with it, letting them use the tunnel and whatnot because they had something on him – like they had with you. She thought he was cheating on her, did some digging and found out the truth, and basically went and sat in the police station with the kids until they agreed to help.'

'Bloody hell.'

'I think you got off lightly,' I said.

Liv looked like she wanted to be sick. 'I was so ashamed, Phoebe. I even took off your bracelet because every time I looked at it, I felt like I'd let you down.'

'No,' I said firmly. 'You could never let me down.'

Liv looked at me. 'You took your necklace off too.'

'Because I saw your bracelet on your bedside table and I was cross with you.'

'Where is it?'

I put my hand in my pocket and pulled it out. 'It's right here.'

'Can I?'

I unfastened the clasp and put it round my neck and Liv did it up for me. Then I helped her with the bracelet.

'I'm so sorry,' she said.

I put my arm round her and hugged her. 'It's all going to be okay.'

'Do you think so?'

'You'll probably have to pay the money back,' I said. 'And be a witness. But none of this is your fault.'

Liv squeezed me tightly. 'I'm so pleased we're friends again.'

We both fell asleep like that, squeezed into the same single bed, like we used to spend sleepovers when we were kids. I was woken late the next day with the sun – actual sun – streaming in the window and my phone buzzing madly on the bedside table. I snatched it up before it woke Liv, though she was dead to the world, and I took it into the kitchen. I had a gazillion emails, from DI Blair and from colleagues in Lewisham. I made myself a cup of tea and scanned through them. Everyone was being really nice, saying that they'd heard what I'd done, and that I'd done a good job. DI Blair even said I was being considered for an award, which was exciting. But then he added: 'Unfortunately we can no longer support your sick leave. Please call me to discuss your return to work.'

I made a face at my phone. It was slightly disconcerting to realise that while I had missed police work, I'd not missed London at all. Doing something different had got me fired up and I couldn't imagine going back to Lewisham and investigating the same crimes I'd been investigating my whole career. I typed a reply asking to use all the annual leave I'd accrued while I was off, and sent it off just another email landed in my inbox, from DCI Richardson. I read it with a certain amount of surprise. It seemed I had a lot to think about.

My phone rang in my hand and I answered it straightaway. It was Jed.

'Did I wake you?'

'No,' I said. 'Been up for hours.'

'Really?'

'About ten minutes.'

He chuckled. 'Wondered if you fancied a walk?'

'Definitely.'

'I can be at the pub in half an hour, if that works for you?'

'Perfect.'

I ended the call and dashed into the shower and then spent ten minutes asking a bleary-eyed Liv her opinion on different outfits.

'This top?' I said, holding up a floaty blouse covered in little flowers. 'Or this one?'

'The first one,' she said, pointing to the second one.

I tutted. 'Which trousers? Jeans? Or shorts?'

She looked straight at me. 'Is this a date? Or is it work?'

'It's work,' I said. 'Definitely work. Sort of.'

'Do you want it to be a date?'

'No. Yes.'

She grinned and knelt up on the bed. 'That top, those denim shorts because your legs look great in them, and your Converse, because you might go for a walk and you don't want to be scuffing about in your flip-flops. What are you doing with your hair?'

I frowned. 'I've done it.'

'Nope,' she said. 'Put it in a messy bun so it looks like you're not trying, and also it makes your neck look all long and elegant and maybe he'll want to kiss it.'

'It's not a date,' I said, suddenly nervous.

'Just in case.'

Liv helped me do my make-up, because I found my hands were shaking and I couldn't put mascara on. She twisted my hair up for me and checked my outfit. Then she nodded approvingly. 'Good.'

Heart thumping, I blew her a kiss and went downstairs to wait for Jed. He was there almost instantly, looking handsome in jeans and a plain black T-shirt. I found that I couldn't stop smiling as I looked at him. And, much to my surprise and delight, he seemed to be the same, grinning broadly at me.

'How are you today?' he said. 'None the worse for the adventure?'

'Actually I feel really good,' I said. 'Back to my old self. My pluck has been restored.'

'I'm glad to hear it.'

'What's the latest on Ewan?' I asked. 'Fancy a coffee? Though I must warn you, I'm not so good with the fancy milk frothing.'

'Yes please. And just normal milk is fine,' he said. 'He's in magistrates' court later. I don't think he'll get bail.'

'I hope not.' I felt a tiny trickle of fear down my back, as I turned on the coffee machine and waited for it to warm up.

'We've raided lots of locations this morning,' Jed went on. 'We've got the beginning of the whole network.'

'That's amazing,' I said. I poured the coffees into takeaway cups. Jed picked up his cup and I took mine, and together we went out into the sunshine. Without discussing it, we walked towards the clifftop and sat down where we'd kissed that day.

'So it's all worked out,' I said. 'You've caught all the baddies.'

'Some of them. But now we've got those, we'll get more,' Jed said. 'It's like Jenga. If you pull one bit out – and this is an important bit because it's the supply bit – it all falls apart.'

'You've done an amazing job getting all the information,' I said. 'How long were you undercover for?'

'Almost a year.'

'Shit.'

He took my hand. 'I'm so sorry about what happened,' he said. 'I was such an idiot.'

I nodded. 'That's true enough.'

'I'd worked so hard getting Ewan's trust. Making myself useful. I even drove some delivery routes, you know. That was all true. And then you turned up and distracted me totally.'

I grinned. 'Sorry,' I said, not meaning it in the slightest.

'When we kissed that night I thought I'd totally blown it. I had no idea what to do. That's why I legged it. And why I was ignoring your messages. I thought if I could just get through the arrests I could tell you the truth. Little did I know you were conducting your own bloody investigation.'

I smiled out across the sea, enjoying the feeling of his hand in mine.

'It's going to be weird going back to normal,' he said.

'I can't get used to you being Jeremy and not Jed.'

'Actually, my family called me Jed when I was little, because my brother is Ed,' he told me with a smile. 'He used to say we were Ed and Jed and it stuck. So it was an obvious choice when I needed a name.'

'Can I keep using it then?'

'If you like.' He let go of my hand and looked down at the top of his coffee cup. 'Will we be speaking to each other much? You'll be back to London soon, I imagine.'

'I should be. I don't have much reason to be off sick now.'

'That's a shame.'

'I've got some annual leave to take, so I thought I'd do that for a couple of weeks while I sort myself out.'

Jed smiled at me again. 'I'm on leave too,' he said. 'So if you're at a loose end and you need some company . . .'

'I'd like that,' I said. 'Wait until I tell you what I've found out about Emily Moon.'

He grinned. 'You cracked that case too?'

'I did.'

'The Met are lucky to have you.'

I pulled at a piece of grass next to me and looked out over the sea. 'Thing is,' I said, ultra-casually. 'I'm not that keen on going back to London.'

'Really?'

'I got an email from your DCI Richardson this morning.'

Jed looked at me, one eyebrow raised.

'She said there was a chance of a sabbatical. Six months working for Devon and Cornwall Police, just in case I was interested.'

Jed shifted slightly on the grass, moving closer to me. He was leaning back on his elbows and I noticed now that his arm was behind me, so if I leaned back too, I'd be nestling against his broad chest. Suddenly it was hard to focus on anything else except him.

'What do you think?' he asked. 'About the sabbatical?'

I swallowed. 'I think it would be a really good idea for my career,' I said. 'Something different. A new challenge . . .'

And then I didn't say any more because his lips were on mine and we were kissing.

'So you're staying then?' Jed murmured eventually.

I grinned at him. 'I'm staying.'

Acknowledgments

When I planned this book, I wanted to write a story that combined *Jamaica Inn* and *Line of Duty*. So I should thank both Daphne du Maurier and Jed Mercurio for the inspiration. What I ended up with, I think, is more of a Famous Five book, so thanks also to Enid Blyton! My friends Chris Bailey-Green and Jo Minnis helped with my very important and hard-hitting queries about police work ("can you fit a warrant card in the front pocket of your jeans?") and Poldark on Netflix helped with the Cornish scenery when I was locked down in South London, far away from the sea and the cliffs.

Thanks to my fabulous agent Felicity, and my editor Abi, who are always supportive and creative in equal measure, and thank you to all my lovely readers. Hope you enjoy this one!

**Keep reading for an excerpt
from *The Secret Letter* . . .**

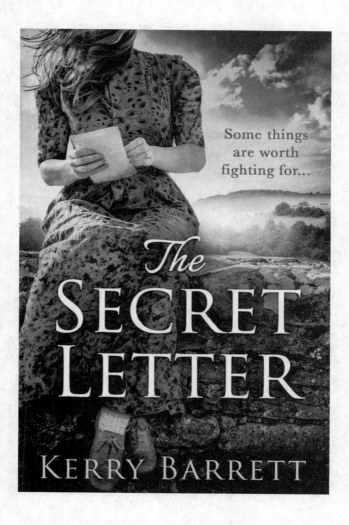

Some things
are worth
fighting for...

The
SECRET
LETTER

KERRY BARRETT

Prologue

Esther

December 1910

I picked up the letter I'd written and read it over to myself. I knew he'd never see it, but it made me feel better, just putting my feelings down on paper. Putting everything that had happened behind me.

'Sometimes the fight is part of the fun,' I'd written. I smiled sadly. That was exactly how I felt, and why everything had gone so wrong between us; there had just been no fight.

Picking up my pen again, I signed the letter with a flourish and then wafted the paper, waiting for the ink to dry. I wouldn't send it. There was no need. But I wanted to keep it somewhere safe, somewhere I could find it if I ever needed to remember why I'd done what I'd done.

I glanced round my small bedroom, looking for inspiration, and my eyes fell on my fabric bag, stuffed under the bed. I pulled it out and opened it and found inside the wooden photograph frame holding the only photograph I had of my former love. Perfect. But first I had to change something else. On my bedside table was my journal and tucked inside was a photograph of myself. It had been taken at a recent suffragette rally and vain as it sounded, I loved the way it made me look. I had my chin raised slightly and a flash of fire in my eyes. I looked like a woman to be reckoned with.

Smiling, I opened the back of the picture frame and took out the photograph that was in there. Should I throw it away? No, he was part of my past no matter how horribly things had ended. Instead I put it into the bag and pushed it back under the bed. Then I put the photograph of myself into the frame, folded up the letter and put it in an envelope, carefully tucked that behind the photo and fixed the back on securely. I proudly stood the photograph on my bedside table. I would keep that picture with me, wherever I ended up, and every time I looked at it I would remember that I had been made stronger by everything that had happened.

'The fight goes on, Esther,' I said to myself. 'The fight goes on.'

1

Lizzie

August 2019

I stared at the building where I would spend most of my time for the next year, or even two, with a mixture of hope, fear and resentment.

'Just a few months,' I whispered to myself. 'Just a few months, and then you can get back to normal.'

I pushed my sunglasses up on top of my head so I could see better and squinted in the brightness. It was an old-fashioned school building. The sort of building that in London would have been converted into luxury flats years ago. It had black iron railings, a paved area at the front with hopscotch markings and two entrances, over which in the stonework was carved "boys" and "girls". I knew that at the back was a more modern extension, but staring at the front I felt like I'd gone back in time.

My stomach lurched with nerves and I took a step backwards, lowering my sunglasses again like a shield.

'Chin up, Lizzie,' I told myself sternly. 'You've got this.'

But I wasn't sure I did have it.

It was mid-morning but it was quiet. No one was around and I was glad. School didn't start for another ten days though I'd come to Elm Heath early so I could move into my new house, get settled in, and generally find my feet a bit. It was very different here from my life in Clapham and I knew it was going to take some getting used to.

I took a deep, slightly shuddery breath as I thought about my ex-husband, Grant, who was – as far as I knew – still living in leafy South-West London. Predictably, he'd managed to emerge from the disaster of the last couple of years smelling of roses despite being asked to leave Broadway Common School before he was pushed. Never had the phrase "men fail up" seemed truer than when I'd discovered he'd walked into a fancy job in some think-tank, advising local councils on education policy and was earning more now than he'd ever done as a head teacher. Which was ironic considering one of the many, many things he'd done wrong was being creative with some of the school budgets.

Under my sunglasses, I felt a tear start to dribble down my nose and I reached up with one finger to wipe it away. I had to stay strong or I would fall apart. And yes, it wasn't fair that I'd been treated with suspicion too, even though an investigation had proved that I hadn't been involved in Grant's misdemeanours whatsoever. But it was harder to prove I didn't know anything about it, because while he was head of the huge junior school, I was in charge at the infants' school next door. And as I'd soon discovered, no one really believed that I was innocent, despite what the official reports said. I'd waited for Grant to clear my name – to speak out on my behalf. But I was still waiting. Because as it turned out, Grant telling everyone I knew nothing would have effectively meant admitting he'd done all the things he was accused of. So instead he stayed quiet.

With the trust gone in our marriage, I'd found myself moving back to my mum's house at the ripe old age of thirty-eight. And with the trust gone in my job, I'd resigned and applied for new posts all over the place – just to get away from London.

'And here I am,' I said out loud, still looking at Elm Heath Primary. Elm Heath was an ordinary school. It wasn't a super, high-performing school; it was just a normal, nice-enough village primary. And that made it the perfect school for me to prove myself.

There was no doubt everything that had happened had left me needing to show the teaching world that I still had it, and I thought Elm Heath would give me that opportunity. As far as I could see, it was just a bit old-fashioned. The last head teacher had been in her job for yonks, and she'd been quite resistant to change. I thought I could drag the school into the twenty-first century, revitalise it, get my mojo back and then go back to London and to normality. Albeit a Grant-free normality.

I forced a small smile. This was just a blip, I thought to myself. Just a small hump in the road of my career. And perhaps a slightly bigger hump in the road of my personal life because despite everything he'd done, I still missed Grant. I missed being part of a team. The Mansfields. Grant and Elizabeth. A double act. A "you two". Now it was just me.

Sighing, I picked up my bag. I'd moved into my tiny terraced house yesterday – my whole life reduced to a few boxes of books – but it was still chaotic and I had a lot to do to get sorted before term started. I really should get on with it.

As I turned to walk away from the school a voice shouted from the playground.

'Ms Armstrong? Yoo-hoo! Ms Armstrong!'

I ignored it for a split second and then looked back over my shoulder as it dawned on me that I was Ms Armstrong. I'd applied for this job in my maiden name – part of my plan to be "me" instead of Grant's other half.

Across the playground, a short woman – perhaps ten years older than me – came barrelling towards the gate.

'Wait!' she called. 'I'll let you in!'

I groaned as I recognised her from one of my interviews. It was Paula Paxton, the deputy head. Grant would have said she was the perfect mix of overenthusiastic and underachieving. Though she'd been very nice to me when I met her before, I just wasn't really in the mood for company.

'Ms Armstrong,' she panted as she unlocked the gate. 'I saw you from my office and thought you would want to come in rather than lurk outside. So I said to myself, I said "Paula, run downstairs and let her in – she doesn't want to be lurking outside," and I raced downstairs and then when I saw you pick your bag up, I thought I'd missed you.'

Faced with such jollity, I winced. Despite how nice Paula had seemed at my interview, I wasn't sure I could deal with her kindness today when I was feeling fragile. She saw my reaction and she paused while opening the iron gate.

'I'm babbling,' she said. 'I always babble when I meet new people. I'm sorry.'

I managed a weak smile. 'Don't be,' I said.

She reached out and took my bag from me.

'Coffee?'

I smiled more genuinely this time. 'Coffee would be great.'

I followed her through the echoey corridors of the school. Generally, I disliked schools out of hours. They needed the children to make them feel alive, I always thought. But today, I appreciated the quiet stillness of the building. It was cool inside, no fancy air-conditioning could compete with hundred-year-old thick stone walls.

I was wearing a vest top, cropped jeans and Havaianas that flipped and flopped loudly down the hall. Paula Paxton was dressed for work in a neat wrap dress with court shoes and – I thought – nude tights. It was thirty degrees outside, and it was the summer holidays, so I wondered if she dressed like that all the time. On the beach. At the gym.

'God, I'm so hot,' she said, over her shoulder. 'I've been to a funeral.'

Oops.

'Sorry,' I muttered, feeling horrible for having had nasty thoughts about her. Paula waved her hand at me.

'Nah, don't be. It was some client of my husband's firm. I only went so I could bring the car home afterwards because I need to go to the supermarket later, and I could have got the bus, but I'll have a lot of bags . . .'

I smiled and she stopped.

'Babbling again,' she said. 'Here are the offices.'

She opened a door on her left. It was an original, thick with paint and with a wobbly window on the top half.

Inside was a sort of reception area with seating and two desks for the secretaries I assumed. Beyond it were two more doors, similarly old-fashioned, one marked "head teacher" and one marked "deputy head teacher".

'I'm on the left,' she said. 'I teach as well, obviously, so I don't use my office much. But I have the coffee machine. Milk and sugar?'

After suffering in too many staffrooms where the only refreshments on offer were clumpy catering tins of instant, I was pleasantly surprised to hear there was a coffee machine. I smiled.

'Just milk, please. I'll just have a look at my own office if that's okay?'

'Hold on,' she said. She opened the top drawer of one of the desks and pulled out a key.

'This is yours.'

I wondered if there was any point in keeping a key just centimetres away from the door it unlocked but I didn't say anything. Instead I simply unlocked the door.

'I'll fire up the Nespresso,' Paula said. 'Well, it's not a real Nespresso, because they're so expensive. It's just the Marks and Sparks version, but I find it's just as good . . .'

She trailed off, much to my relief.

'Just come in when you're ready.'

I nodded and, taking a deep breath, I went into my new office.

It was pretty bare. There was a big desk by the window, a round table, and two empty bookcases. On one wall there was an old-fashioned black and white photograph of a young woman wearing what I thought was Edwardian dress, and a fierce expression.

'You're going to have to go,' I told her out loud. 'I can't have you looking down on me so disapprovingly.'

My voice bounced around the empty room.

Suddenly overwhelmed by everything, I sat down at my new desk and put my face in my hands. This was my last chance to save my career and start again but it just seemed like a huge task. Was this going to be a massive mistake?